The Coin Box

Volume 1

Calling of a Circuit Rider

Stephen Brooks

(1764-1855)

DOUG RADKE

ISBN: 13: 978-1974369690

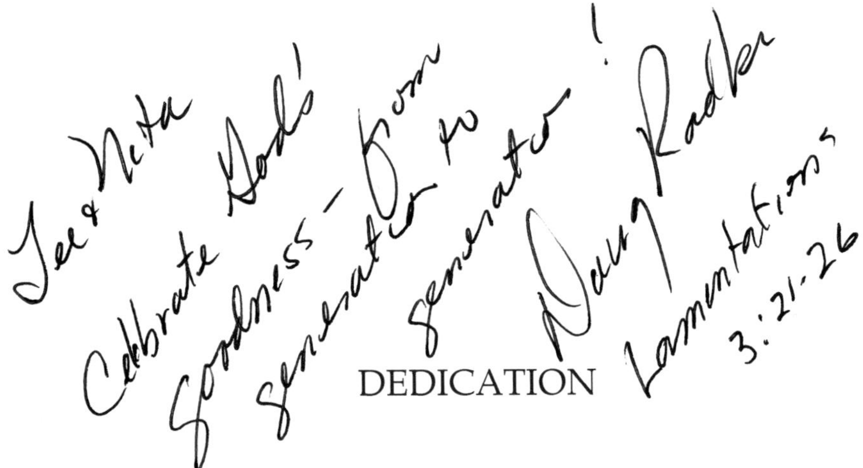

DEDICATION

"One generation shall praise your works to another, and shall declare your mighty acts." Psalm 145:4

In memory of generations past: Harry and Lydia (Brooks) Anderson, Merlin and Doris Radke, Dave and Gloria.

In gratitude for generations present: Betty Rae and Dan, Lisa, Trisa and Erin.

In celebration of the next generation: Wyatt, Weston, Eli, Zoe and Islee.

"For the LORD is good and his love endures forever; his faithfulness continues through all generations." Psalm 100:5

CONTENTS

ACKNOWLEDGMENTS

First and foremost I want to thank you, Betty Rae, for your rock solid support throughout this writing adventure beginning with seeds of inspiration gathered on our cross-country camper trip and ending with the final editing and last period. You have listened with patience to my reading of each paragraph as chapters and then finally a book took form. You provided thoughtful feedback and offered valuable creative suggestions along the way and you lovingly adjusted to my tendency to be far off somewhere in the 18th century these past many months. You even shed a few tears with me as the story unfolded. There is no question; you are my life's best chapter!

Linc DeBunce, you accompanied me on the journey physically as we traveled to explore historic sites in Nashville, Tennessee. More importantly, you went with me on the mental and emotional rollercoaster of birthing this novel. I treasure your friendship, true silver and gold as compared to the paltry coins that enter this narrative.

Kay Midgett Sheppard, we met online in the course of genealogical research focused on Hyde County, North Carolina, and you graciously responded to my questions with substantive documented bits and pieces of the Brooks family tree. Experiencing your warm Tennessee hospitality and the lively Bluegrass music added a vivid exclamation point to those interactions.

Chris Bryant, your encouragement during our coffee chats and your ideas about self-publishing kept me motivated to write.

Brian DeBunce, your formatting and editing wisdom and assistance have been invaluable.

Introduction

My story about Stephen Brooks begins when I was in ninth grade. It was fall quarter, seventh hour, Ms. Anderson's social studies class. There are two vivid memories of that term that I can recall as if they happened yesterday. One was a major news event. The other involved a challenging, but at the time seemingly insignificant, class assignment.

The event is etched in my mind as well as the social consciousness of my generation. When I arrived at class on that fateful day, Ms. Anderson was in tears. Now I had seen teachers in tears before but only as a result of our raucous adolescent shenanigans. This was different. Amid sobs she reported to us that our President, John F. Kennedy, had been shot in Dallas, Texas. Details were sketchy but it appeared he had not survived the assassination attempt. The full implications of this event would be revealed in the days to follow. I only recall at that moment that my parents had voted for the Republican candidate so I wasn't sure how to respond to the Democrat's horrific death. Over that Thanksgiving weekend I gradually came to understand, along with citizens of every political stripe, what this murder meant to our country.

The assignment also was presented that fall. We were to research our family roots and write a paper on our "tree" of relatives. Initially the task created some real discomfort for me. My maternal grandparents, who lived next door, bore the last name of Anderson. For some days I was deathly afraid that I might in some way be related to my Social Studies teacher. I did not welcome that possible revelation. So with some trepidation I prepared to interview my grandfather, Harry R. Anderson Sr.

Grandpa, with the help of his older sons, had built the family home on the banks of Swamp Creek, Kenmore, Washington, back in the 1920's. My mother, Doris May Anderson, had grown up there. In May of 1936 she married my father, Merlin Earl Radke. My parents obtained nearly an acre from the five acres my grandfather had purchased as "stump land." Oh the adventures I had growing up, but that's another story.

Grandpa was sitting in his favorite chair in the darkened living room. Macular degeneration had taken a toll on his eye sight but not his mind. Grandma was not so fortunate. Her short term memory was gone and she could hardly follow a conversation, repeating the same questions over and over. And so I asked the critical question regarding my Anderson heritage.

I was greatly relieved to learn that our family tree was made up of Scottish Andersons. Ms. Anderson, blond and blue eyed, had shared her Scandinavian roots when presenting the assignment so this was wonderful news indeed. I learned that my two time great grandfather, John Anderson, had immigrated with his family in 1849. My great grandfather, David Fairbairn Anderson, was born shortly after they arrived in the United States. He traveled the Oregon Trail in a covered wagon from Kansas to Rosalia, Washington before my grandfather was born.

Grandpa went on to say that there was a circuit riding minister in our family tree. At the time I assumed he was referring to the Scottish Presbyterian side of the family. I held on to that unchallenged assumption for the next forty-five years.

And so we pick up the story in 2017. Two interests have occupied a fair amount of my time in retirement. One is researching my family history; the other is collecting coins that match key dates in their lives. That is how I met that circuit rider my grandfather had mentioned so many years ago. His name was Rev. Stephen Brooks, my 4x great grandfather.

Grandma Anderson was born in Little Rock, Arkansas in 1885. Her maiden name was Nancy Brooks. Disliking the name Nancy, she changed her name to Lydia. She had been unable to contribute her story when I was researching that ninth grade assignment. Grandpa, however, had kindly included the critical piece regarding her heritage that had lodged in my memory…circuit rider.

I began to follow the trail from Little Rock to Greeneville, Tennessee to the Outer Banks of North Carolina. Stephen was born in 1764 at Cape Hatteras, North Carolina. He was laid to rest at Mt. Pisgah Cemetery, near Greeneville, Tennessee in 1855. What an amazing life span of over 91 years.

He was twelve when our nation began the fight for independence.

His first career was as captain of his own ship. But a restless heart led to a spiritual transformation.

Converted to Christ through the Methodist Episcopal Church, he followed Bishop Francis Asbury through the

Cumberland Gap to Kentucky in 1789/90. That is where he served his first circuit as a Methodist minister.

He eventually located near Greeneville where he both farmed and continued to serve as a local preacher.

He was a delegate at the convention that called for Tennessee statehood in 1796.

He was an active and devoted member of the Greeneville Mason's Lodge.

He spoke out against slavery and was a member of the Manumission Society formed in East Tennessee.

These "main facts" of his life story are agreed on by those who have researched the records. But I am intrigued by where my imagination takes me when I envision the rest of Stephen's story. What conversations did he engage in? What dangers and conflicts crossed his path? What hopes and fears nurtured his faith and shook his courage? What issues and events stirred his righteous indignation and moved him to action?

This is where my interest in numismatics (coin collecting) enters the picture. I have constructed my historical novel of Stephen's life around various coins that circulated during his lifetime and that he might have picked up, collected, or been given as mementos of his journeys. These various coins go into his "Coin Box." New coins are added while old coins are re-examined, triggering vivid and sometimes painful memories.

I have attempted to stay true to the outline of his life and times, allowing my imagination to fill in the blanks and expand the narrative. Significant Revolutionary War happenings have been woven into the story. Some of the characters are historical figures who lived through those trying times, others are created to add to the drama.

Stephen, you saw much, lived well and left a lasting legacy. I am proud to be your distant grandson and glad I can re-tell your story for future generations to enjoy and ponder.

Chapter 1

PIRATE TREASURE

Young Stephen opened his eyes and listened intently. The fierce cyclone must have passed in the night for Stephen could no longer hear rain pelting the tiny window pane and the rafters no longer creaked with the gusts of wind. It was early September, 1769. The major hurricane that had made landfall at New Bern, North Carolina, had moved north across Cape Hatteras and was now cutting a path of devastation through Virginia. Folks would talk about that great storm for many years to come.

Stephen was glad the storm had moved on, he was eager to break the confines of the small Brooks family home and explore the beaches near his home to see what the storm had left behind. It was still dark outside and his siblings were fast asleep. Peeking over the edge of the loft where he slept with his brothers and sisters, Stephen could see his mother reading her Bible by the light of the fireplace. His younger sister, Sally, was playing on the floor next to her mother.

Stephen carefully eased his way over his sleeping brothers, William and Jacob, and made his way down the ladder to the main living area. His mother spotted his movement and gestured for him to come to her. Sitting the Bible on the table next to her, she pulled young Stephen on to her lap and whispered in his ear.

"Did you sleep well my little one?"

"Yes, mother, I am glad the storm is over."

"Me too child; I pray your father and brother Isaac are safe with their ship and crew." Stephen's father had sailed out to sea to ride out the waves and wind. He might not be back at anchor near Brooks Point for a few days, depending on where the storm had driven them and if there had been damage to the vessel.

"I will pray for Father and Isaac too. What were you reading?" Stephen questioned, fidgeting with the sleeve on his mother's night robe.

"I was reading about your namesake in the Bible."

"What is a namesake, mother?"

"Your name is Stephen, the same as your father and your grandfather. But your name is also found in the Bible, in the Acts of the Apostles, chapter seven. See, my son, you bear the name of a very brave man who loved God more than anything else." Stephen, not yet six years of age, squinted at the words on the page.

"I want to be a brave man too" he said softly.

"And you shall be, my little Stephen" his mother whispered back. The rap on the door interrupted their conversation. "See who it is, Stephen." Stephen jumped from his mother's lap and scurried to the door. Lifting the latch he opened the door.

"Morning, Papa."

"And good morning to you, my little grandson," Jacob Farrow scooped up Stephen with his strong arms and held him high overhead. Stephen giggled. Placing Stephen back on the wood floor, Jacob turned and moved toward Mary.

"How did you fare the night, daughter?"

"I did not sleep well; I was worried for Stephen and Isaac. Has there been much damage in the village?"

"The Midyetts lost part of their roof. Hezekiah's shed is gone. Some of the homes are flooded from the storm surge. Franklin's sloop was pushed from its mooring and has sunk off shore. It will take some time and effort to clean up and make repairs. But, Praise God, there has been no loss of life. I believe Stephen was wise to take to sea with his ship. He should be fine."

"I hope he is home soon, father," Mary rose from the fireplace rocker and with worried look gazed out the window toward Pamlico Sound where the sunrise to the east was beginning to spread light across the watery landscape. Sally began to fuss for her mother's attention.

"Father, could you please take Stephen for a walk on the beach while I tend to Sally?"

"Certainly, I could use some fresh air myself. Stephen run and get dressed, but quietly so you don't wake your brothers and sisters."

"Yes, Papa." A walk on the beach was just the news that Stephen wanted to hear and in what seemed only seconds, he was back down from the loft, dressed and ready for the adventure.

Jacob and Stephen climbed the large sand dune that separated the village from the ocean to the east. Cape Hatteras, shifting sands and all, was constantly being refashioned by tides and winds and cyclones. With the storm passed, the seas were already quieting. Stephen ran as fast as his little legs would carry him near to the water's edge.

"Stephen, not too close, there may still be sleeper waves that could pull you to sea." Stephen turned back toward Jacob and shouted,

"I will be careful, Papa."

They walked for some time. Stephen would stop and examine broken shells and kick over pieces of drift wood, on the hunt for some priceless remnant from the storm. Jacob stayed close, admiring the curiosity and determination of his young grandson.

Stephen stopped suddenly, his attention focused on a small piece of metal partially buried in the sand. He picked up the object and stared intently at the marks on both sides. "Look what I found, Papa." Stephen rushed to Jacob's side and showed him his discovery. "What is it?"

Inspecting the irregularly shaped piece of copper, Jacob, brushed off the sand and rubbed away some surface corrosion until he could see the date 1624."Why, I believe you may have found a pirate coin, my lad."

Stephen jumped up and down with delight. On other walks he had found many interesting things on the beach but never a pirate coin. He clutched the coin in his hand, thinking about just the place where he would hide his new treasure.

"Stephen, let's sit and take a rest. Would you like to hear a pirate story?"

"Oh yes, papa." They found a driftwood log for a bench and Jacob began his tale.

"The most famous pirate in these parts was Edward Thatch. He had a thick dark beard so people called him

Blackbeard. He sailed these waters when I was a lad of only ten or so years. His pirate ship was called Queen Anne's Revenge and she was armed with forty cannons. He and his crew robbed many a ship of their valuables, including coins like the one in your hand."

"Papa, I play pirates with my brothers. Was Blackbeard a bad man?"

"It is wrong to steal what belongs to others, Stephen. While Blackbeard may not have been as mean and cruel as some stories make him out to be he did break laws and was eventually killed in battle just off Ocracoke Island south of here. That was long ago, years before your father was born."

Stephen fingered the coin and pictured Blackbeard fighting for his life with a flintlock pistol in one hand, a cutlass in the other. "Tell me more, Papa."

Jacob shifted his weight on the log and stretched his old tired muscles. Looking out to sea he continued, "there are some local yarns told that you had forbears in your family who sailed with Blackbeard." Jacob stopped, wondering if maybe he had shared more than he should with his young grandson. "But you best ask your father about those stories."

"Were you ever a pirate, Papa?"

"Hmm," Jacob mulled over how he might get himself out of this tight spot in the conversation without revealing too much or too little. "When I was growing up we lived off of what the sea brought us. Shipwrecks were quite common off these dangerous shoals and we took what came our way on the waves, from timbers to goods, to even coins. In some ways we were land pirates, I guess you could say."

"Did you have a cutlass or pistol?" Stephen asked, his eyes wide with wonder?

Jacob chuckled loudly at his grandson's query, as he recalled childhood memories of life on this sand spit called Cape Hatteras. "Our only weapon was a donkey or maybe a horse, lad."

"How is a donkey a weapon?" Stephen looked puzzled.

"We, oh I mean some of the men in the village, would take a donkey and hobble it by tying a rope around two legs. They would strap a lantern to the donkey at night and lead it wobbling along the shoreline. Sometimes distant ships would see the bobbing light and think there was a safe harbor here. Sailing closer to shore they would be shipwrecked on the shoals. To float free of the sand bars they would throw boxes of goods into the sea which we, I mean the men, would be eager to retrieve from the beaches." Jacob could see from Stephen's fidgeting that he had lost his listener somewhere out at sea. Clearly this was a bit too much for a 5 year old to understand. Getting up, Jacob took Stephen's hand. "Let's walk a bit further before we go home."

Stephen went back to his beachcombing. Jacob spotted a bit of timber that must have been washed ashore from an old wreck. He picked up the small block of wood, considered it from all angles and formulated a plan.

They arrived back at the Brooks home with quite an appetite. While Jacob was hungry for some breakfast, Stephen was proudly showing off his pirate coin to his siblings. At the moment, that was more important to him than eating.

It was midday when Stephen's father sailed back to anchorage at Brooks Point. Young Stephen was waiting on the sandy beach jutting out into the bay. Before the captain could step to shore his son was ready with his question. "Papa said we have pirates in our family. Will you tell me about them?" Stephen rushed to his father's side and looked up eagerly awaiting a response. It was not exactly the greeting that the tired captain was expecting.

"Stephen, my son, those are just old sailor's tales, there is no truth in them. We come from fine Connecticut stock. Now let's go home, enough about pirates." Captain Brooks could see the disappointment in his son's eyes, but he was too exhausted from fighting the cyclone the past few days to engage his son in any further conversation. He was much more eager to kiss his dear Mary and fall asleep in her embrace.

Later that evening, Stephen made his way up the ladder to the loft and his sleeping straw mat. He waited until his brothers and sisters had fallen off to sleep. Carefully he pulled the loose knot free from the floor board next to his bed and placed his pirate treasure in the hole. He put the knot piece back in place, securely hiding the coin from the sight of his brothers and sisters. With images of fierce pirates in his young mind, Stephen drifted off to sleep.

Chapter 2

CHRISTMAS 1770

"It's snowing," William shouted as he opened the door and burst into the room. Young Stephen rushed to the doorway and looked out as the huge white flakes fell from the stormy sky. Stephen had never seen snow before. Snowfalls were a rare occurrence on Cape Hatteras. He hurried outside without even stopping to put on a coat. Flakes landed and melted on his nose and cheeks as he looked up at the sky. Stephen danced a jig of glee as he spun about trying to catch the flakes.

"Stephen, you will catch your death of the cold, come put on your coat," his mother urged from the open doorway. Stephen ran to the doorway and fetched the coat from her hand. "Take your sister Charity with you so she can play in the snow, too."

Most of the flakes were melting as soon as they hit the ground, but as the quantity of flakes increased, a slushy gathering of the wet flakes began to accumulate. At that moment a white ball whizzed by his head. William was forming another snowball before his first had barely smashed against the wall of the house. Stephen and his brother Jacob joined in the fun, trying to hit their older brother with their own snowy creations. Their sisters, Easter and Charity were also now outside, helping their little sister Sally try and make a snowman. It was all over in minutes as the snow turned back to rain, washing away what little remained on the ground.

Stephen, Jacob and the girls headed back indoors while William returned to his chores outside. Hanging his coat on the peg by the door, the soon to be seven year old took in the holiday scene. It was Tuesday, December 25th. Wonderful scents wafted from the room. His mother had been cooking for what seemed like days in preparation for the evening party. She knelt by the fireplace, lifting the lid from the pot, she stirred the seafood muddle. The aroma of the simmering stew, comprised of sea mussels, clams, scallops, shrimp, flounder, squash, potatoes, leeks and various spices filled the lad's senses and stirred his appetite. It was his favorite dish. A venison roast was cooking on the spit above the coals and open flame, juices sizzling as they hit the fire. Breads and other baked goods cluttered the family table.

The Brooks family had a well-established path which they traversed leading up to the celebration of Christ's birth. They carefully followed the advent prayers and Bible readings in the Anglican Church's *Book of Common Prayer.* So for four weeks they had been preparing for this day. While this was to be a feast day, there had been more sober days of fasting and reflection as they contemplated their own sin and the coming of the Savior.

That morning the family had gathered and recited the nativity day prayer and had read the epistle selection from Hebrews and the Gospel portion from St. John chapter one.

The words and the ritual were confusing and meant little to Stephen, but he did his best to listen and imitate the actions of his siblings and parents. He was much more interested in the food being prepared and the possibility that there might be some small gifts given to him that Christmas day.

The brief outdoor excursion in the snow had taken Stephen away from this arithmetic figuring. His mother was trying to teach him how to add simple numbers.

"Son, one plus two is? Write your answer on the slate and bring it to me please." The lad was clearly having a hard time concentrating, "Stephen, did you hear me?"

"Yes, mother?" Stephen looked puzzled, he had been peeking out the small window, hoping that the rain had turned back to snow and had not heard the addition problem.

"Never mind, Stephen, I have much work to do for our dinner. Practice writing your numbers and letters while I prepare for our guests. Grandpa Brooks and Grandpa and Grandma Farrow will soon be here."

Stephen lifted his slate and began to carefully form the number 3 with a piece of chalk. But his attention again shifted to the sights and smells of the room. Papa Farrow had hinted that he might have a Christmas gift for him and the boy daydreamed about the possibilities. He was especially fond of his maternal grandfather. He had yet to meet his father's father, the eldest Stephen Brooks. Grandfather Brooks had recently moved to the Lake Mattamuskeet region across Pamlico Bay on the mainland. He had long been a widower and with his health now failing it had seemed wise to move closer to his sons Thomas and Stephen.

The irritating scratch of the chalk on the slate disturbed the quiet of the room. William, who had come in from his chores, rolled his eyes at his younger brother's noisy efforts. Jacob, Stephen's ten year old brother, moved to his defense.

"Here, hold the chalk like this," he offered.

The Farrows were the first to arrive. Grandma Amey greeted the children and quickly moved to the side of her daughter to assist in the food preparations. She had brought a large tureen full of squash soup as well as some pumpkin tarts.

In his typical fashion, Papa Farrow hoisted into the air his two youngest grandchildren. First, Sally, then Stephen was lifted high overhead. They, in turn, laughed aloud in delight. He hugged his granddaughters Easter and Charity. Handshakes were extended to the older boys, Isaac and William and Jacob.

"Merry Christmas dear children," he exclaimed.

"Merry Christmas, Papa," they all answered in unison.

A gust of wind moved through the room as the door opened and the two older Stephens entered. "Boys, come meet your Grandpa Brooks." They lined up in order by age and introduced themselves for the first time to their paternal grandfather. He stood acknowledging the older boys and their sister Easter, but knelt down to make eye contact with both Charity and Stephen.

"I have so longed to see you children. Oh how I wish your grandmother could be here and share in this happy family time. And where is your little sister, Sarah?" At mention of her name the four year old came running across the room and into her grandfather's embrace.

The adults continued to engage in their own greetings

as the children returned to their various activities. Stephen picked up his slate anew, determined to not make any sound as he touched the chalk to the slate. Grandpa Brooks, seeing him at work, crossed the room to see what he was up to. The number 3 was still etched on the slate. His grandfather carefully took the chalk from his little hand and marked a 1 in front of the 3.

"Now what is the number?" He asked.

"Thirteen, Grandpa," Stephen answered with confidence.

"Very good, do you know how many colonies there are?" the old man asked.

"Yes, the same number."

"Can you name them, my boy?"

"I will try. We live in North Carolina, then there are South Carolina and Georgia, Virginia, Connecticut, Rhode Island, Delaware, Pennsylvania, New York, Massachusetts Bay, New Hampshire, Maryland, and, and…New Jersey." Stephen proudly concluded.

"Excellent. You deserve a Christmas reward for your fine knowledge of numbers and geography." Grandpa Brooks reached into his trouser pocket and retrieved a small item.

"See the number 3 here?" Stephen looked closely at the coin in his grandfather's large weathered hand. "This, my son, is a three pence with King George III's likeness on the other side. Perhaps, someday, the colonies you named will have coins of their own. The next time your family travels to New Bern or Bath, you can use this coin to buy yourself a toy or book." He took the coin and admired it carefully.

"Oh thank you Papa." But He didn't tell him that he had

other plans for the coin.

It was time for the younger children to eat as they would not be permitted to stay up for the adult party. The children gathered around the table for the blessing and anticipated feast. Before they could fill their plates, Grandpa Brooks interrupted,

"Look under your plates for a Christmas gift." Twelve year old Easter and her brother Jacob admired their six pence coins. Charity smiled holding her own three pence. Sally gleefully fumbled to get hold of her shiny silver penny. Stephen, looked but found nothing under his plate, but soon remembered his treasure, the bright three pence and grinned with thanksgiving along with his siblings. Grandpa Brooks then gave the older boys, Isaac and William, a shilling each. Each one from oldest to youngest expressed their gratitude to their new grandfather.

The seafood muddle was even better than Stephen had remembered. He gulped down the chowder that he had helped create. Isaac had taken Stephen and Jacob out fishing in their father's small dory they used to travel from shore to the larger vessel anchored off shore. Fifty or so rods off Brooks Point they had caught the flounder which their mother had added to the savory stew.

The children were just finishing the pumpkin tarts when Papa and Grandma Farrow presented their own Christmas gifts to the children. There were whittling knives for the older boys. Jacob, named for his grandfather, received a small hatchet. Easter, Charity and Sally each received hand-made clothing items fashioned by Grandma Farrow. Stephen waited in keen anticipation as his granddad extended his gift which he had been hiding behind his back.

"Do you remember our walk on the beach last fall?" Jacob asked. "'twas the day you found your pirate coin and I retrieved a piece of boat timber."

Papa Farrow had crafted the driftwood into a small box which he now gave to his grandson. Stephen's eyes grew wide with wonder as he took the cover off the box. Inside was a pouch made of fine red cloth. "Your grandmother sewed the"-- Before Papa could finish his sentence, Stephen shot across the room, scurried up the ladder, pulled the knot piece from the floor next to his bed mat and retrieved his pirate treasure.

As quickly as he had gone up the ladder he was back down and beside his grandparents. Opening the tiny treasure chest he pulled the drawstrings to open the red pouch. He carefully placed his first pirate coin in the folds of the bright cloth. He then added two more pirate cobs, the term his father had used in describing the beach finds, into the pouch. Stephen, over the course of the previous winter, had found these cobs while on walks with his Papa. There was one more item to be deposited. Stephen took the three pence, Grandpa Brooks' gift, and added it to the Cape Hatteras shore discoveries. Closing the coin box he ran and hugged his grandparents.

"Thank you Papa, Thank you Grammy, Thank you Papa Brooks. This is my best Christmas ever." When Stephen had first learned to talk, Grandma Amey had become Grammy, the name had stuck and it was Stephen's special term of endearment for his grandmother.

Gift-giving complete, it was almost time for the younger children to retire to their lofty perch from which they would be able to watch the Christmas events unfold. Only the two oldest boys, Isaac and William, would stay up for the evening. Uncle Thomas had just arrived and the fiddle in his grasp foreshadowed the dancing and singing to follow. Other neighbors would soon be arriving.

Mary Brooks prepared to light the Christmas candle. She placed the tallow candle on the table, dreading the offending odor that the candle would emit, but it was the best she had. Her husband stopped her before she could touch the wick.

"Wait, my dear, use these instead." Stephen took three candles from a leather pouch. "I traded for these in Portsmouth. They are made of sperm whale oil. They are brighter in light and best of all will not produce that awful smell." Mary took the candles and embraced her husband. She placed the Christ candle in the center of the table and set the other two candles at opposite sides of the room. They would add a special light and joy to their holiday evening. The growing darkness of the home was softly transformed by the glow of the candles and the fire on the hearth.

"Children," their father spoke. "Hear the glad tidings of Christmas:

Joy to the World, the Lord is Come
Let earth receive her King.
Let every heart prepare Him room
And Heaven and Nature Sing."

While the children wished they could stay up they dutifully marched to the ladder and each scaled the steps to their bed mats. Maybe they couldn't stay on the main floor for the adult festivities, but they could easily peer below the railing and take in the joyous events below.

The adults first enjoyed the foods that had been so

carefully prepared for the evening. Toasts of rum-laden eggnog concluded the dinner and soon folks were singing and dancing to Thomas's efforts on the violin. The boys took in the unusual entertainment with glee. Eventually the music softened and the adults engaged in quieter conversation. Stephen turned his attention from the party to his Christmas coin box. In the dim light he examined the coins one at a time, then carefully returned them to the small red cloth sack, drew the string tight and placed them in the box. Safely closed, the tiny treasure chest went on the shelf next to his bed mat.

Drowsy and ready for sleep, Stephen closed his eyes, but sleep did not come. He really needed to use the chamber pot. His siblings had all fallen asleep and Stephen was unsuccessful in locating the familiar vessel in the darkness. No other option available, he would have to go outside and use the privy.

Stephen moved down the ladder as quietly as he could, hoping not to disturb the adults. His mother spotted his movement and correctly interpreting his need, she nodded toward the door. He slipped on his shoes and lifted the door bolt. On the porch he looked back through the small window pane. Only his mother had spied him and he was quite proud of his stealth.

The morning snow clouds had moved west and the stars and half-moon provided enough light for Stephen to negotiate his way across the yard to the privy. Relieved he turned back to the warm light of the home. He had only taken a step or two away from the privy when he was startled by the sharp barks of Tippy, the Gibb's large bulldog. He thought he heard talking on the village path and moved to the corner of the shed to take a look. Suddenly, a hand grasped his shoulder. The pungent waft of rum overwhelmed Stephen's senses as he looked up at the stranger, silhouetted in the moonlight. His crooked nose, missing teeth and bad breath added to the horror. He could see the man was not alone but accompanied by two others.

"Well, what have we here, mates? "He spoke in slurred speech.

"A cabin boy for sure," chimed in one of the others.

"Mighty young, but we could train him easy," added the third.

"Be ye up to sailing the high seas?" questioned the man who held him fast by the shoulder.

Stephen twisted with all his strength. Breaking free of the man's grasp, he ran as fast as he could to the house and hoped for safety. He crashed through the door and into the subdued party setting. Everyone turned from their conversations to look. Mary rushed to the side of her son. Before anyone could speak the three drunken sailors stumbled through the open doorway and into the light of the room.

"Will you look at this feast, mates," the ringleader of the three said as he reached for a turkey leg on the table. Mary stepped to block his way to the food.

"Move, wench," he muttered as he pushed her aside. Her husband and the other men rose in defensive posture.

"You are not welcome. Leave at once or we will,"--young Stephen's father shouted as he rushed to protect his wife.

"Or you will what?" The sailor finished Stephen's sentence. "We be British sailors come from our ship at

Ocracoke harbor. You must feed us and if need be shelter us. It is the quartering law." The man was in his face and the stench of alcohol was overwhelming. The sailor also had his hand on his pistol. Stephen and his guests were all unarmed. They could not win a fight under these circumstances and unfortunately the inebriated sailor was correct. The colonists had to quarter British forces if requested.

"Take what you wish and then be on your way. The shed out back has fresh straw if you must stay." Stephen hoped his appeal would satisfy the edgy men.

"Ah, that is a better response, old man. You know we could have the press gang visit your lovely family and friends here. The British navy is always looking for some new recruits. Why we might even find some of your fine lads would make excellent seamen or cabin boys."

The sailor's words sent chills through Stephen, Mary and all of their family and guests. Young Stephen's siblings in the loft were now awake and terrified as well by the actions and words of the men who had invaded the peaceful Christmas gathering. It was not an idle threat. Each knew of men, even boys, who had disappeared from families on the Cape. Tricked or forcibly taken by the recruiting gang, they had been "pressed" into naval service. Some had eventually made their way home, others had never been heard from again. This too was one of the King's oppressive laws that deeply stirred the antagonism of the colonists.

Fortunately the sailors seemed content with the abundant table delights. They moved around the table stuffing their pockets to the full with meats, breads and tarts. "We will be on our way. If we need lodging we will be back." The food-laden men shuffled toward the door. The spokesman of the group stopped above young Stephen and with a harsh smile gestured. "Best be on your guard lad, you never know when we might be back, I bet you won't be making any late night trips to the privy in the near future." All three men laughed as if on cue and then were gone into the darkness. The elder Stephen closed the door and slid the bolt tight.

"Bloody British," he swore. Stephen and his brothers and sisters were shocked to hear their father speak such a taboo and profane term.

"Back to bed, Stephen," his mother reassured him with a hug and he climbed back to his bed. The boys and girls heard more "bloodies" that night as the men reflected on the terror they had just experienced. Slowly each drifted off to sleep. The last words Stephen remembered were spoken by his grandfather Jacob Farrow, "We will not have peace until we are free of the tyranny of the King."

Chapter 3

A SAILING ADVENTURE

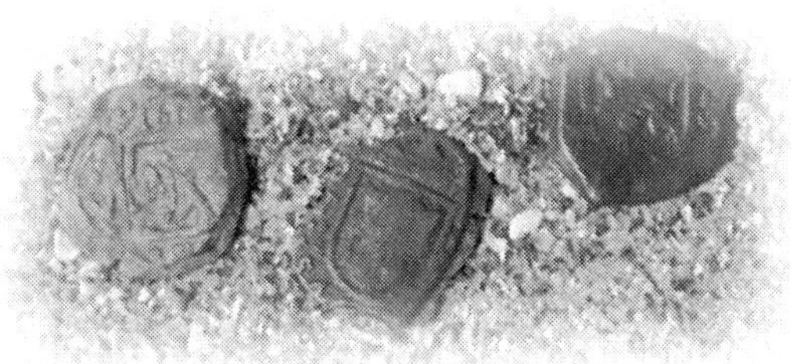

The traumatic events of Christmas day had left their mark on all of the Brooks' family members. Young Stephen made sure to visit the privy before dark or demanded that one of his older brothers accompany him. Isaac, who was old enough to be kidnapped by press gangs, spent more time looking over his shoulder when out about the village on his own. The children also picked up on cues from their parents that they were increasingly anxious about the welfare of the entire family. Sometimes it was a whispered conversation. At other times it was harshness in their tone of voice as they responded to the children's rambunctious behaviors. In addition to these new anxieties, everyone was experiencing a case of cabin fever as the short and sometimes stormy days of winter passed slowly.

Stephen loved to walk the beach with his Papa Farrow following these storms, always hoping to add to his small collection of coins. Not long after his February birthday, the seven year old discovered a small silver coin in the shifting sands of the weathered cape. His grandfather called it a Two Stuiver, a Dutch coin.

"It is said that the Dutch purchased Manhattan Island when settling their New Amsterdam with coins just like this. It was a bargain for the colonists, but robbery for the natives." Papa handed the coin back to his grandson, shaking his head as he ended his sentence.

Stephen later showed his new find to his father who added a bit more to the coin's story. "Look at that date, 1728, why that was my birth year." Stephen took the coin from his father's strong hand and focused on the lion and crown images. He turned it over and sounded out the letters.

"Hol…lan…dia."

"That is the country of Holland. It is Europe," his father added. "Dutch ships have passed this way and some have remained, come to rest on the bottom of the ocean off our dangerous Outer Banks coastline. I would guess that your treasure was washed ashore from such a wreck."

When he learned the significance of the coin's date, Stephen knew this Stuiver would not be spent but would be kept in the special box he had received for Christmas.

The big announcement came at family super in early March. "How would you all like to take a sailing adventure?" Father surprised them. They were all thrilled by the news. Almost all that is. Easter recalled their last trip and her stomach churned in anticipation of the rolling sea and heaving deck of the ship. "I have tar barrels to take to Portsmouth. We will sail there first, unload our cargo and take on goods which we will deliver to the town of Bath. We wish to be there for Resurrection Sunday, March 28th. We will leave at high tide this Wednesday."

Stephen could hardly wait. He loved the sea, from the

salt air to the porpoises swimming ahead of the ship to the flapping of the sails in the breeze. He had not been to Bath since his sister Sally's baptism three years earlier, a visit he was too young to remember. To break free of the confines of the house and narrow cape and enjoy the lengthening days of sunshine on the water would be an adventure indeed.

It took several trips to ferry, by dory, all of the family members to the *Hannah Marie*, anchored off Brooks Point. Papa Farrow and Grammy were also on board. Jacob and his son-in-law had been discussing the purchase of land near Mt. Pleasant across the wide bay on the mainland.

The *Hannah Marie* was named for Stephen's paternal grandmother who had died years earlier. The schooner, built in New Haven, Connecticut, was especially designed for the coastal trade Captain Brooks engaged in. With two masts and traditional gaff topsails she was easy to maneuver and her shallow draft was perfect for the thin dangerous waters of Pamlico Sound. She could also out race larger and heavier craft if the need arose.

Stephen's brother, Isaac, at sixteen years of age, now served aboard the ship and was fast becoming very adept at managing the rigging on the upper gaff sails. Mary looked on with some measure of concern as her son scampered around on the narrow rope ladders. A misstep at the mast heights could seriously maim or even kill her oldest son. Knowing that her son would not respond kindly to her anxious pleas she kept silent and sent a prayer heavenward for his safety.

All aboard and anchor weighed, the *Hannah Marie* moved on the high tide, her sails catching the wind they tacked south toward Portsmouth. Easter was already feeling the familiar twinges in her stomach and she positioned herself near the railing. Young Stephen moved freely about the vessel. This was a new liberty for the lad. Previously, on short excursions with his father, he had been secured by a rope about his waist to one of the ship cleats. But he was older now and there were also many eyes to track his activity. The risk of falling overboard undetected was unlikely.

Captain Brooks guided the ship with a steady hand on the wheel. His knowledge of deeper channels and hidden sandbars was the envy of seasoned sailors up and down the cape. As they passed by Ocracoke Island, Papa Farrow caught Stephen's attention and called him portside. "Son, we are near the spot where the Queen Anne's Revenge, Blackbeard's infamous ship, went aground. This is where he was killed and his crew captured."

The boy's mind flashed back to the pirate coins safely stored at home in his treasure box. As he looked toward the distant shore of Ocracoke he could imagine the cannons belching flame and smoke, rival crews clashing fiercely and finally the crafty pirate fighting bravely to the death. His daydream was interrupted by his brother William's shout.

"Look starboard, there she blows." Off to the right of the ship the humpback whale had just surfaced and was already headed back under the surface. Young Stephen had seen the whales from a high sand dune perch, spouting their misty breaths far off the shores of the cape, but he had never been so close to the mammoth creatures before. He watched in amazement as the giant breached clear of the waves and returned to the depths with a flap of her huge tail. He waited, hoping to spy the whale again. However, the next puff of spray was far off in the distance. The humpback was making better time than the *Hannah Marie*.

Portsmouth Island was also now visible on the starboard horizon. The crew began to take in sail as they came in sight of Portsmouth village and the harbor. Stephen looked on with pride as his father maneuvered the ship close to moorage. Isaac threw the heaving line to men positioned on the dock who in turn pulled the ship hawsers to dockside where the schooner was secured. Two larger ships were moored nearby. Isaac and William moved the gangplank in position and Easter was the first to cross, eager to set her feet on solid ground again.

The harbor area was abuzz with activity. Portsmouth village, the largest European settlement along the Outer Banks, was strategically located adjacent to the narrow channel leading from the Atlantic Ocean, past Ocracoke Island to the north, into Pamlico and Core Sounds and the few towns scattered inland along the coastal estuaries. It was a lightering port. Larger ocean-going ships would lighter or unload their cargo at Portsmouth, take on goods for export, and return to Europe. Smaller schooners, like the *Hannah Marie*, would then transport the imported goods to coastal communities.

Stephen stayed with his older brothers at dockside. He wandered down the length of the dock, spying a harbor seal as it bobbed beneath the surface. A huge leatherback turtle cruised not far away. The sight of the ancient looking reptile fascinated the lad. Papa Farrow had observed his grandson's stroll on the slippery dock and had followed at Mary's urging. Stephen reached up and grasped his papa's huge strong hand and together they turned back toward shore.

His father had rounded up some men to off load the tar barrels on the deck of the *Hannah Marie*. The North Carolina tar was destined for British naval yards and other European ports where it would be used in shipbuilding. The pine forests of North Carolina were a prime source for such tar, along with pitch and turpentine, two other common exports of the region.

Stephen couldn't take his eyes off of the men moving the barrels. He had seen one or two of these black-colored men on Cape Hatteras, but here the dark-skinned men outnumbered the few white men in charge. Seeing him stare and sensing his questions, Papa spoke. "They are from across the ocean, the land of Africa, brought here to do our hard work. They are called slaves, my son." Jacob struggled for words, wondering how to explain the social and commercial structure of slaves and slave owners to a seven year old. Fortunately the lad seemed satisfied with his brief description and was now more interested in chasing seagulls on the dock. The old man knew that the harsh realities of slavery would crash in on the childhood world of Stephen soon enough.

Jacob and Stephen soon caught up with Mary, Grammy, and the other children. They spent the afternoon visiting a few small shops in Portsmouth village. At one point, Stephen thought he spied one of the British sailors who had harassed him Christmas day. A closer peek from behind his mother's skirts, however, relieved his anxieties. Papa Farrow headed off to secure some food from the local tavern. He returned with some potted meat sandwiches which were quickly devoured by the children and adults.

The Brooks and Farrow families spent the night cramped into the small quarters of the *Hannah Marie*. In the morning the crew and the same black slaves Stephen had observed the day before loaded an assortment of imported goods onto the schooner. By mid-morning they were under sail. Captain Stephen informed his family and crew of a change in their travel plans. "We have some royal goods we must deliver to his majesty the Governor's Palace in New Bern."

The news of their detour was received differently by various family members. Some, especially Easter, sighed with resignation. But young Stephen was thrilled with the prospects of additional days on the water. He occupied his grandfather's time with near constant chatter and a barrage of questions. "Are we almost there? Is that an island? What is it called? Will we see more whales? I'm hungry." On it went. Jacob, with the patience of Job, tried to answer each of the lad's inquiries. He nodded and winked at his beloved Amey and she could tell he was really enjoying every minute of the voyage too.

They sailed by Cedar Island on their portside and up the Neuse River arm of Pamlico Sound. New Bern was situated at the confluence of the Neuse and Trent Rivers. Established by Swiss immigrants in 1710, it was the second oldest of European-American towns in North Carolina. Only Bath was older.

The five man crew moved quickly to complete the tasks involved in docking and securing the *Hannah Marie*. Captain Brooks gathered the men together and to their delight released them for shore liberty until the next morning. The Brooks extended family heard his final warning. "Be ready to sail in the morning, if you be drunk you will not leave New Bern nor sail with me again." With the crew set free, the Captain turned to his family and in-laws, "I believe it is time to visit the Palace."

The sights and sounds of the busy town had already filled the senses of the visitors. New Bern was not at all like their sleepy little village on Cape Hatteras,. It even dwarfed Portsmouth. The valued crate, a British-made chandelier, was loaded on a rented wagon and the younger children climbed aboard, each hoping to be the first to spy the Palace.

Their father pointed out how the founder of the town had laid out the two main streets in the form of the Christian cross. The home of the British administrator and Colonial Governor of North Carolina, William Tryon, soon came into view. The impressive brick mansion was indeed palatial and had just recently been completed after nearly three years of construction. The opulent style and extravagant costs at taxpayer expense had resulted in the colonists' derogatory nickname for the residence- Tryon Palace.

Mary, her mother Amey, and the younger children toured the lovely European gardens surrounding the mansion. Stephen had never seen such a landscape. Bright spring flowers were abloom. Bees and hummingbirds were busy gathering and spreading pollen. He also noticed, what Papa had called, 'slaves' at work grooming the shrubs and trees.

Meanwhile the older Stephen, his father-in-law Jacob, and oldest son Isaac delivered the crate to the carriage house in back. "Would you look at all this," Jacob voiced his disdain. "Our imperial governor lives here at our expense. First it was the awful stamp act, then excessive tax revenue to construct this monument to the old British goat." Stephen nodded in agreement and added his own commentary.

"Why even now Lord Tryon is off seeking to quell the voice of dissent raised by those radical Regulators in the west of the province. I am almost inclined to join them after seeing his Palace." Jacob weighed his son-in-law's words and before he responded looked around to make sure no one could hear his words.

"I believe the conflict with the Regulators is only a foreshadowing of a greater conflict to come, Stephen. While Tryon may be successful in silencing those western rebels, the rumbling going on in the colonies is intensifying. We may all have to make some hard choices regarding where our loyalties lie in the days ahead." Isaac had been listening intently to the men's conversation and finally interjected the question that was heavy on his mind.

"Will there be war with the British?"

"There may be my son," Stephen responded, placing his hand on Isaac's shoulder. "That is why I am considering a purchase of land from your grandfather on the mainland near Lake Mattamuskeet. I am afraid that if tensions increase, Cape Hatteras will be a dangerous place to live. Amid the coastal bays, islands, sloughs and marshes we may be better able to hide out from privateers and the British navy and keep our family safe."

"Enough talk for now," Jacob broke in, "Let's find the ladies and children and locate a fine tavern where we can enjoy an evening super."

"That is a fine idea indeed, Jacob."

The *Hannah Marie* sailed at high tide the next morning.

Stephen was again at the side rail as the schooner moved down the Trent River and into the wider Neuse River estuary toward Pamlico Sound beyond. On the shore he could see men logging fallen timber and posed yet another question for his dear grand papa. "What happened to all the trees?"

"Do you remember that fierce cyclone a year and a half ago? It was the morning we walked the beach after the devastation and you found your first pirate coin. This is where the storm first hit land. Thousands of trees were blown down by the strong winds. The men will use the trees to make lumber, tar and turpentine. Like the barrels we off loaded at Portsmouth."

"I feel sorry for the trees," Papa.

"Me, too, lad....me too."

The youngster thoroughly enjoyed the next few days on the water as the *Hannah Marie* sailed on toward Bath. At evening tide, his father would anchor the ship in protected bays and he would get to go fishing in the dory with his older brothers. At Bay River, he caught a large redfish, which his mother later prepared for their supper. His father went with the boys on their fishing trek up Goose Creek and later built a fire on the beach and made a shore lunch of the striped bass they had caught. It was all wonderful fun and Stephen would long cherish the memories of those special days on the water.

Chapter 4

BATH

The *Hannah Marie* responded to the steady hand of her captain and turned starboard, up Bath Creek to the town of Bath, located a few miles up the estuary. As they neared the docking area Papa Farrow beckoned to young Stephen.

"Lad, this was once the home of Edward Teach. Plum Point off to port was where he is said to have lived."

"Blackbeard the pirate, I remember, you told me about him on the beach. Are there still pirates here, Papa?"

"No, I don't believe so. It is a fine town, the oldest in all of North Carolina." Stephen was a bit disappointed to learn that he would not be seeing any pirate ruffians on their visit. But he did look forward to adventures ashore.

At dockside, the crew unloaded the goods they had taken on at Portsmouth. The Brooks and Farrows headed up Craven Street, eager to explore the village. It took a while to adjust to the solid ground. Little Stephen stopped and closed his eyes. He could still feel his body swaying to the rhythm of the waves. But after a short while his sea legs became land legs again. The families secured lodging at a fine tavern and settled in for a welcomed night's rest.

The next morning, after breakfast, Mary outlined the day's plan. "I must return a book to Father Stewart at St. Thomas church. I would like us all to visit the revered Father."

"Can William and I take a look around Bath while you go to the church?" Isaac questioned.

"I suppose so." Mary nodded.

"Amey and I have need to do some shopping. We will meet up with you later for supper later," Jacob added.

"Mary, I need to oversee the loading of goods we will be taking to Ocracoke on our return trip to the cape. Please convey my warmest greetings to Father Stewart."

Mary tried to hide her disappointment in response to the excuses of her older sons, father and husband. She well knew her religious sensitivities were not equally embraced by all in her family circle. With some resignation in her voice, a cue she hoped they would detect, but reasoned they would miss, she wished them a good day.

Father Stewart had come to Bath from Ireland in 1753. His first task had been to complete St. Thomas church which for some years had remained unfinished. Not long after his arrival his wife and young children died during an outbreak of yellow fever. While comforting other grief stricken townsfolk he had met his second wife, the widow Porter. To their union was born a daughter Rosa. The second Mrs. Stewart died not long after Rosa's birth and the minister was soon looking for a wife to help him raise his daughter. So the widow Johnston became his third wife. Following her untimely passing, the widower had found solace in the arms of his fourth wife, the recently widowed spouse of Michael

Coutanch, a wealthy merchant and civic leader of Bath. The couple now lived in the fine parish Glebe house that had been constructed under the watchful eye of Father Stewart. Mary and her young children now made their way to that residence on Adams Creek. One of the Anglican priest's slaves answered the door.

"We are here to see Father Stewart."

"I will see if he can see you now." Minutes later the Black woman returned and ushered them into the study where the priest was seated. He immediately recognized Mary and the children and signaled them to come near.

"Mrs. Brooks, it is so good to see you. A joyous Resurrection season to you and your family. I imagine your husband is dockside?"

"Yes, he sends his greetings and looks forward to seeing you on Sunday. Isaac and William are out exploring the sights along Water Street. We have come to return the book you lent me when we were last here." Mary reached out and handed him the volume which he took and placed on the end table.

"Thank you, Mary. Bring your dear ones here. I would rise to greet you but alas my legs are not strong. I suffered severe injuries during the fall cyclone of '69 and the pain is still with me. Let me see, this must be Esther, who, if memory serves me, goes by Easter. Next is Jacob, then sister Charity, young Stephen and little Sara. What a lovely family you have."

"We are heaven blessed, Father." Mary was impressed by his recall. He had baptized each of her children and rarely had seen them but for those special occasions yet he clearly remembered each one by name. As she looked at the seated priest she could hardly believe how he had aged since their last visit. She had heard news that he was sick and might not live long. She now believed the prediction might be sadly true. One at a time, she brought her children before the tired and weak man of God. Making the sign of the cross, he talked quietly with each one, blessed them and prayed for them.

When it was Stephen's turn, he pulled the seven year old up on his lap and softly questioned him. "And what do you like to do, lad?"

"I love to sail with father, I love to catch fish, I love to walk the shore with Papa and look for old coins," Stephen blurted out in a rush of words.

"What coins have you found?"

"I have three old Spanish pirate cobs, a Dutch Stuiver that carries the date of my father's birth, 1728. Then Papa Brooks also gave me a three pence last Christmas. I keep them in a special carved box that Papa made for me," Stephen proudly answered the aged priest.

"Today is Maundy Thursday, the day we remember our Lord Jesus Christ, and celebrate his Last Supper. Our King George III will give out many three pence Maundy coins today to the poor in London, England. When you look at your coin, you must remember Christ and his sacrifice for us and also remember to help those suffering poverty."

"I will try to remember." Stephen responded, making the sign of the cross in response to the priest's action and words.

Stephen's younger sister, Sara, then took her appointed turn and received the blessing in word and sign.

Sensing the strain and toll of their visit on the priest,

Mary gathered her children and spoke her farewell. "We must be going now. We will see you again this Sunday." Mary knelt before him, making her own sign of the cross blessing to the one who had meant so much to her own spiritual journey. She could see tears on his cheeks as he took and kissed her hand. Mary rose and turned to leave scurrying the children ahead of her. They were almost to his study doorway when he called out.

"Wait, Mary." The old man rose from his chair and hobbled to the large book shelf lining one wall of his study. He searched the library that had first come to Bath years before, a gift of one of his predecessors and found the book he was looking for. Pulling the book from the shelf he struggled to cross the room. Mary moved quickly toward him and took the book he was holding out to her.

"It is called *The Pilgrim's Progress*. It was written by John Bunyan and is a moving story of our faith journey here on earth. You do not need to return it. It is my gift to you and your family. Read it and may it provide light and strength for difficult days ahead as you make progress to your heavenly home."

"Thank you, Father Stewart. I will read it to the children as well." Mary could now feel the warmth of her own tears, in a sense mingling with those of the dear minister she loved.

"Oh, one more thing," the old man, now leaning on his desk to keep from falling, pulled out a drawer and picked up something. "Stephen, look at this." As he spoke, he almost fell into his chair, weakened by the trek across the room. Stephen came close and examined what he now realized was a coin in the Father's hand. "This is a coin from my native land of Scotland, minted in 1679, almost a hundred years ago. That was a time when Scotland still had coins of her own. Now you will only find British coins in circulation there. What do you see on this side of the coin, my lad?"

"It looks like some kind of flower?"

"It is the lowly thistle weed, yet come to be the symbol of my beloved Scotland. Let me tell you a story of why it is on the coin. Many, many years ago, Scotland was being invaded by fierce Vikings from the north. Scottish clans had gathered to defend their homeland. At night the Vikings landed their war craft on the beach and with stealth moved forward to attack the clans who were unsuspecting of the battle at hand. To aid in the quietness of their surprise attack the Vikings removed their boots and crept toward the camp. It is said that stepping on the thistles they cried in pain as the thorns touched their feet. Those cries saved the clans as they rushed to strike down the invaders who were now unable to maneuver amid the thistle patches they had encountered. It may all be the stuff of legend, but there is a deeper lesson here, my boy. God saved his people with the help of the lowly thistle. The miracle is that He can use the weakest and the smallest to save His people. I hope you will remember that truth, young Stephen as you grow to be a man."

"Thank you for showing me your coin."

"Ah, lad, it is no longer my coin, Take it son. Add it to your collection. Place it in your special treasure box and each time you hold it, remember my thistle story and know God loves you.

Stephen ran and hugged the priest who in turn pulled

him to his lap once more and kissed him on the cheek. In the years ahead, Mary would often recall the events of this meeting for her son, intensifying in his young memory the kindness of the gentle man and his story of the thistle. Stephen gave the Scottish Bawbee coin to his mother for safe keeping until their return to Cape Hatteras.

Much of the rest of the Easter weekend passed in a blur for Stephen. Good Friday was a day of fasting, something that was quite beyond the boy's understanding. The rituals of Resurrection Sunday also were difficult to grasp. He did perceive that the religious events of the weekend were significantly more important to his mother than his father or grandfather.

Monday found them back on the water. The *Hannah Marie* headed south down Bath Creek then turned east on Pamlico River to the open waters of the Sound. Passing Swan Bay on portside they headed north along the coast line until they came to Wisockin Bay. Near the mouth of Crooked Creek they anchored and Stephen's father and grandfather took the dory to shore to investigate some land holdings around Mt. Pleasant. Jacob Farrow had purchased land here some years before and his son-in-law was interested in possibly purchasing some of this land and relocating his family if tensions continued to escalate with Great Britain.

From there they crossed to Ocracoke Island for a final delivery then traveled north to Cape Hatteras village and home. Back in the safe confines of their house, Mary gave Stephen the Scottish Bawbee. The coin in turn was placed with care into the red pouch with his other treasures and stored in the little box. In future years, whenever Stephen looked at the token of Father Stewart's kindness, he would be transported in time back to the deck of the *Hannah Marie,* to the streets of Portsmouth, New Bern, and Bath and their spring sailing adventure of 1771.

Chapter 5

THE MOVE

Stephen carefully removed the Scottish coin from the red pouch and stared intently at the image of the thistle. At supper his father had shared the sad news. The kind and generous priest was dead. He had died just weeks after their visit to Bath. Stephen's father had just returned from the Hyde County courthouse in Woodstock where he had recorded the land deed for the property he had purchased from his Father-in-law, Jacob Farrow. While there, he had heard about the priest's untimely death.

But Stephen was troubled by more than the death of Father Stewart. His father had also told the family that they were moving to the mainland. Stephen fingered the coins he had collected along the beaches of Cape Hatteras and doubted that he would ever find any coins in the swamps and sloughs surrounding his new home. The lad placed the coins back in the pouch and returned the pouch to the coin box. Scurrying down the ladder he approached his father who was seated by the fireplace.

"Are you ready for your reading lesson, my son?" When he was not away at sea his evening ritual was to help each of his boys with their learning.

"I, I"…Stephen paused, stumbling to find words.

"Speak up, lad!"

"I…I want to stay here. I don't want to move. I love the ocean and the beaches." Can't we stay? With the silence broken his questions tumbled out.

"We will be come back here often, my boy. But there are new opportunities and new adventures for you on the mainland. Our space here is small. If you climb to the top of the nearest sand dune you can see how narrow this spit of land is. We will plant and raise crops on our new farm. We will also be safer if war breaks out with King George."

"But, I will miss the open sea and sailing on the *Hannah Marie.*"

"We will still sail and I will still transport goods back and forth to the Outer Banks. I will teach you how to safely sail these waters. You can grow and become a captain yourself if that is your desire."

"I would like to be a captain, Father."

"Then, a sea captain you shall be." The smile and words of his Father were suddenly reassuring. He could even see himself at the helm, feel the wind on his cheeks and see the porpoises cavorting off the bow of his own schooner.

"Tomorrow you and your brothers will be going with me to our new property. We have much work to do as I want to get crops in yet this spring. So off to bed my little captain."

They anchored the *Hannah Marie* in Wisockin Bay and took the dory up Crooked Creek to a small landing area where Papa Farrow met them with a horse and wagon.

Isaac and William returned to the ship and ferried additional supplies and tools to shore. The elder Stephen had released his crew of their duties before leaving Cape Hatteras. His crew for now would consist of his four sons.

That evening they constructed a crude lean-to shelter, struck a fire and devoured most of the meat sandwiches that Mary had sent along with them. Stephen's muscles ached from the day's activities. His father's description of the area was accurate. There were forests to explore and fish-filled creeks and sloughs to check out. It promised to be a grand adventure indeed.

The busy days of late spring blurred into the long hot days of summer and Stephen discovered there was little time to investigate the countryside. Farming was a new venture for his father, who at first had struggled to plow a straight furrow behind the horse he had purchased. They managed that year to plant a few acres of corn and other vegetables. They sailed every week or two to visit the women folk and obtain supplies. The rustic log cabin slowly took shape as they felled trees and positioned each log in place. His father and older brothers did the hard work of shaping and lifting the heavy logs. He helped as best he could for his size and strength. He would pass them needed tools, bring them the water pail for refreshment and do whatever other chores his father requested. Sunday, their only day of rest, was usually spent back on the cape.

By early fall the cabin and adjoining barn and storage sheds were completed and the entire family took up full-time residence on their Hyde County property. Mary had a hard time adjusting to the rustic nature of their new dwellings, especially the dirt floor. "This is only temporary," her husband often repeated. "Our permanent home will be finished come spring. These rough cut buildings will then be home to the slaves who will help us expand our plowing, planting and harvesting. I will also purchase a slave woman to help you with your tasks and the care of the children. It will be better then, you will see."

The move complete, Stephen now had some time on Sunday afternoons to trek about with his older brothers. Sometimes they visited Papa and Grammy Farrow, who had built their own cabin not far away. Other times they would paddle about Light Creek Marsh looking for snakes and alligators. The latter activity was generally kept secret when their mother would inquire about their outings.

One sunny afternoon Stephen and his eleven year old brother Jacob headed to their favorite fishing hole on Crooked Creek. "I am going to try around the bend. Stay here and don't get into any trouble," Jacob instructed as he grabbed his pole and headed downstream.

Stephen didn't mind being alone. He watched his bobber for a while, hoping for a bite. Then growing impatient he set his pole down and surveyed the landscape. A white egret caught his eye upstream and he shifted his attention in that direction. He thought he spotted movement at the edge of the forest beyond. He stared hard, hoping to spy some animal, perhaps a deer, red wolf or even a bear. His search came up empty and he turned back to check his bobber which was still resting undisturbed on the surface. He sat in silence, looking back at the distant forest from time to time, hoping to resolve his question. He felt as if something or someone was watching him. He felt the goose bumps on his arms and experienced the weird sensation of his neck hair standing on edge. He was scared. He thought about running to his brother or shouting out in fear. He kept quiet, almost shaking, too afraid to look again toward the trees. He would be brave and act like a man, not cry like a boy. Just when he thought he could stand it no longer, Jacob rounded the bend and broke the dark spell and awful silence. "You look like you just saw a ghost," Jacob queried. "Snake bit?"

"I'm fine…just a little cold I guess," he shivered.

"Look what I caught," Jacob hoisted a stringer of bass and perch. "There'll be fish for supper."

"Let's go home now," Stephen urged. As they started back on the trail, Stephen stopped and stared back at the forest edge. What had he seen? Was it just his imagination playing tricks on him? Suddenly the lonely piercing howl of a wolf broke the quiet of the moment. Jacob turned back in the direction of the call and joined his younger brother in scanning the horizon, hoping to spy the source of the eerie noise. They stood there for some minutes, seeing and hearing nothing.

"I think we better hurry to get back to the cabin before dark," Jacob finally spoke, turning back to the trail home. Stephen sighed with relief. So it had only been a red wolf moving in the shadows of the forest edge after all. He would hold on to that comforting conclusion, for some time.

Mary prepared the fish that Jacob had caught and the family enjoyed the fresh feast around their roughhewn table. Following supper, the elder Stephen read from the Book of Common Prayer. The blaze in the rock fireplace cast its flickering light across the cabin, barely illuminating faces. "Tomorrow Isaac, William and I will sail down the coast to Wilmington to purchase workers to help us on the farm. Jacob and Stephen, you take care of your mother and sisters while we are gone. Obey your mother or there will be severe consequences. Call on your grandparents if any problems should arise. With favorable winds we should be back in a week to ten days."

In the morning, the Brooks family gathered at the landing. "God's speed, my dear," Mary whispered as she embraced her husband.

"Pray that I find an excellent carpenter to help me build us a comfortable home, complete with a wood floor." Mary smiled at her husband's request and waved as Stephen and her two oldest sons rowed the dory toward the *Hannah Marie* anchored in the distance.

"Indeed, I will pray for that floor!"

A few days later, young Stephen was carefully splitting kindling for the cooking fire. He gathered up the pieces and turned toward the cabin. At the startling sound of the howl he dropped his load which fell like tangled pickup sticks at his feet. It was unusual to hear wolves so close to the cabin clearing. He could not pinpoint the source of the sound but as he stood there, he felt that same adrenalin rush he had experienced by the slough. Though the animal was invisible, he could almost sense the creature's steely gaze. Was this the same wolf? Was it stalking him? He quickly gathered the kindling and rushed to the safety of the cabin.

It had now been over a week since the *Hannah Marie* had

sailed south. Young Stephen, accompanied by his brother Jacob, headed toward the landing to see if they could spy the schooner on the horizon. Excited by the sight of sails in the distance they rushed home to convey the good news. Mary and the children waited with anticipation as Captain Brooks rowed the dory up Crooked Creek toward the landing. Stephen could now make out the occupants aboard. There were four black strangers together with his father, a large, strongly muscled dark man sat next to a lighter colored woman. On the floor of the dory was a boy who appeared to be about his age and a younger girl. Reaching the make-shift dock, Stephen's father secured the dory and jumped ashore. He immediately hugged Mary and the girls, then turned and beckoned to the family to step on land.

"This is Jupiter, a skilled carpenter and capable slave. Phoebe, his wife, will serve us well in field and house. These are their children, Able and Ima. Your prayers were answered Mary. We had an excellent voyage and were most fortunate to purchase such a fine family at the auction in Wilmington."

The Brooks family and the Jupiter family stayed at the landing while Stephen rowed back to fetch Isaac and William and the remaining cargo from the *Hannah Marie.* All stood in awkward silence for some minutes. Young Stephen stared at the man, his wife, and children. He broke eye contact and stared at the ground, not sure if it was correct or polite to focus on the slave family. Mary introduced the children one by one. Stephen moved toward Able unsure if he should extend a hand or bow. He did neither but simply said, "Hello, my name is Stephen; I am almost eight years old."

"I go by Able," the boy, looking down, sheepishly responded. He slightly bowed to acknowledge the white boy's status as son of his new master. Thus their friendship began.

Back at the cabin clearing the Jupiter family moved their meager supplies into one of the small log outbuildings. That would be their home until the Brooks' new house was completed.

Mary surveyed the scene from the doorway to her dirt-floored cabin. Her husband, seeing her anxious gaze moved close. "It will take some time to adjust to all this, I know, Mary. We were indeed lucky to be able to buy a family. The cost was high, but they will be much less apt to run away than single slaves." Jupiter is strong and skilled. Phoebe will ease your burdens with the care of the house and children. It will work out. You will see."

"I hope so, my love, I do hope so."

Chapter 6

FRIENDS

Stephen pushed the hoop to start it on a wobbly course and ran behind it, using his stick to keep the hoop moving. He steered the hoop around the yard multiple times, dodging obstacles until the hoop hit a rock, veered off course and fell over. "That was your best yet," Able cheered.

"Now you take a turn," Stephen gasped, exhausted from his run. The boys continued to race about pushing the hoop, enjoying the warm sunny Sunday afternoon weather. Playing was a fun respite from the normal routine of chores and manual labor.

Through the winter months the Brooks family, aided by their newly acquired slaves, had been hard at work preparing for the building of their new house. Jupiter was indeed a skilled carpenter and his trained hands churned out hewn timbers, planks, roof shakes and furniture. The supplies were stockpiled in anticipation of the spring house-raising event. Tomorrow was the big day. Relatives and neighbors would be arriving to all work together to turn the piles of materials into a fine home. Mary, Phoebe and the girls had also been busy preparing food for all the expected laborers. Taking a break from the cooking, Mary stepped outside and walked across the clearing to where her husband was going over building plans with Jupiter.

"Everything looks ready, Jupiter," Stephen turned from his slave and moved toward his wife. "In a few days you should be able to walk on that new floor."

"Thankfully," Mary replied, embracing her husband.

"How is the cooking and food preparation going?"

"Phoebe is a wonderful helper. Ima is also a hard worker and takes excellent care of the younger girls." The laughter of their son and his black playmate erupted on the far side of the clearing and both parents turned to watch as Able tripped and fell, sending the hoop crashing into the wood pile beyond. "Looks like our son is enjoying Able's company," Mary continued.

"They also work well together. We can trust Able to keep a watchful eye out when they are fishing or traveling about exploring the woods," Stephen responded, returning his wife's hug with one of his own.

The boys eventually tired of their game and paused to catch their breath. "Race you to the creek," Stephen issued his challenge and took off running before Able could respond. It didn't take long for Able to catch up and pass his competitor and he reached the goal seconds ahead. Panting the two stood silently for some time. Something on his familiar streamside stump captured Stephen's attention and he reached down to pick up the two small beautiful shells someone had left there. "Look at these shells. I wonder how they" — Before Stephen could finish his sentence a familiar sound echoed across the landscape. It was the howl of the wolf that Stephen had grown so accustomed to hearing.

"What was that?" Able asked, his voice tinged with fear.

"Just a wolf howling. I hear it often. Sometimes I think it is following me and watching me from a distance. I have never caught eye of it. It used to scare me, but not anymore."

Stephen continued to look closely at the sea shells. Suddenly he had an idea and moved to where his fishing pole was cached in the bushes. He cut the line and returned to the water's edge. Coiling the line, bobber and hook he placed them carefully on the stump. "There, a gift for a gift."

The boys headed down the path toward home. When they had gone about a hundred yards or so, Stephen ducked behind a tree. He pulled Able to his hiding place and together they watched the offering spot in the distance. Time passed slowly and finally the boys stood, ready to give up on their spying mission. Just then, Able spotted movement upstream, nudging his friend he pointed to the location. Stephen tracked the progress of the forest stranger as he dodged from one bush to the next, stopping often to survey the area to make sure he was alone. When he reached the stump he picked up the gift and examined it closely. He turned to look in their direction and as if to express his approval made the recognizable wolf sound Stephen had first heard while fishing there many months before. Stephen stepped from behind the tree and waved. The lad returned the greeting with a wave of his own and began to make his way toward them. As he drew closer, Stephen surmised he was about his age, maybe a year or two older. He was about a head taller and wore buckskin clothing which hung loosely on his thin frame. His hair was yellow in color. He was carrying a bow in one hand and had a quiver of arrows slung over his shoulder.

"Thank you for your gift," he offered as he extended his hand to Stephen.

"And thank you for yours as well," Stephen replied, taking his hand. "This is Able." Stephen tugged his black friend from behind the tree where he was still hiding and he too shook hands with the fair-haired stranger. "You have been watching me for some time haven't you?"

"Yes, ever since your family moved here and started building."

"Do you live nearby?

"My family lives near Lake Mattamuskeet on what used to be our tribal lands. All the lands have now been sold to whites. I come here to hunt the forests and trap for fur in the marshes. My name is Tom Squires. My friends call me Wolf."

"I can see why! My name is Stephen Brooks. My father is Stephen Brooks the sea captain."

"I have seen his schooner anchored in Wisockin Bay." Wolf sized up his two new acquaintances and after some moments he broke the silence with his question. "Stephen and Able, what do you say, shall we be friends?"

"I would like that, Wolf!" Stephen exclaimed.

"Me, too," Able added.

And so the trio began their adventures. Wolf showed them his hiding spot at the edge of the forest where he had first glimpsed Stephen. They checked out his trap line and watched with amazement as he skinned a muskrat he had caught. Wolf showed them how to shoot his bow."Do you think I can hit that burl on yonder tree?" Wolf asked as he pulled the bow string taut.

"No way," both Stephen and Able answered in unison.

Wolf sent the arrow toward the tree some thirty paces away and all cheered as the arrow struck the center of the burl and lodged with a solid thump. The efforts of Stephen and Able were less impressive. Stephen could hardly pull the bow back and the arrow sailed off askew. Able pulled the bow back with ease but his shot landed well beyond the burl target.

"It takes practice. You will learn," Wolf instructed. They romped about the woods for hours until the fading light of sunset signaled it was time to return home.

"Let's meet up at the stump next Sunday midday," Stephen urged.

"Next Sunday," they all agreed.

Before they parted, Wolf suggested they all adopt animal names as a seal of their friendship. Admiring the strength and dark hued skin of Able he asserted," You will be Bear."

"What about me?" Stephen asked. Just then they were startled by an alligator moving into the water on the far side of the slough.

"And you will be Gator," the blond haired Indian affirmed, prompted by the auspicious sign of the reptile.

"Good choices, Wolf," Stephen and Able nodded in approval. They clasped hands once more in celebration of their new friendships and headed off to their homes just ahead of the spreading darkness. Not long after their parting the lads heard Wolf's mimic howl in the distance and both smiled.

The community house-raising party was a tremendous success and what would have taken weeks or months was accomplished in days with the strong help of neighbors and relatives. With the structure framed in, Jupiter continued to finish the interior. In the loft area where the boys slept, he added needed furniture. He even hewed out a special niche where Stephen could store his treasure box of coins.

Mary, ever grateful for a smooth wood floor, supervised the move-in and added needed items to Jupiter's work list. With the Brooks family now occupying their new home, Jupiter and his family shifted their belongings from the outbuilding to the larger log house. While they did not have the luxury of a floor under their feet, they did have more space and a cooking hearth for which Phoebe was especially thankful.

Mary and her husband tried out the new porch swing that Jupiter had secured to the second floor joist. Mary had seen a similar swing on their visit to Bath and had requested that they add the unique feature to their outdoor décor. Jupiter had even chiseled the Brooks name into the top rail of the swing. The couple was exhausted from the hectic pace of construction, cooking for guests and moving challenges. For the first time in days they were able to rest and converse together without interruption. "The move has gone well." As Stephen spoke he placed his arm around his wife's shoulders and pulled her close. "With the work nearly completed we are right on schedule for the spring planting."

"God is good," Mary responded, sliding closer to her husband.

Wolf, Bear and Gator eagerly looked forward to their regular Sunday rendezvous at the gifting stump. Their outdoor exploits were always the high point of the week.

Stephen's parents added their approval to the triad's activities. Stephen's father knew Tom Squire's father, having been involved in some land dealings around Lake Mattamuskeet and was confident that the Indian lad would be a fine friend for his son and Able.

Stephen fetched his coin box from the cubbyhole Jupiter had chiseled in the wall. Today he would show the valued coins and share their stories with his comrades. His mother had sandwiches prepared for lunch and he grabbed these and stuffed them into his small pack. "Thank you, mother," he shouted as he rushed out the door.

"Have fun and be safe," He just barely heard her message as he closed the door and headed outside.

Bear was waiting for him at the trailhead to the creek. Together they hurried to their meeting place where they found Wolf already sitting on the stump. Gator couldn't wait to show them his collection. As he took each coin from the red pouch he relayed the details, from beach combing pirate cobs to Christmas gifts to a priest's cherished present.

"I knew Father Stewart too," Wolf broke into the steady burst of words coming from Gator. "He started the Indian school by the lake. That is where I learned to read and write. He was such a kind man. I miss him. All the students loved him too."

Wolf and Able admiringly examined each coin as Gator continued his story-telling. Hunger for the sandwiches finally got the best of them and the coins were returned to the pouch and placed back in Papa Farrow's carved box.

They ate quickly, with a sandwich in one hand they picked up rocks and tried to skip them across the surface of the water between large bites.

Tiring of the competitive activity, they laid back and rested on the soft marsh grass. "My grandfather has a coin," Wolf propped up on his elbow and continued. "He says it came from the first whites to visit this shore long ago." He now had the full attention of Gator and Bear who sat up, eager to hear more. "The coin has been passed down from one generation to the next. He can best tell the story himself. I will take you to him next week. Ask your parents if you can visit overnight. We could leave Saturday afternoon and be back by Sunday evening."

"That sounds like great fun," Gator was quick to reply to the invitation. Bear also nodded his agreement.

"Then 'tis a plan," the threesome cheered.

Chapter 7

THE LOST COLONY

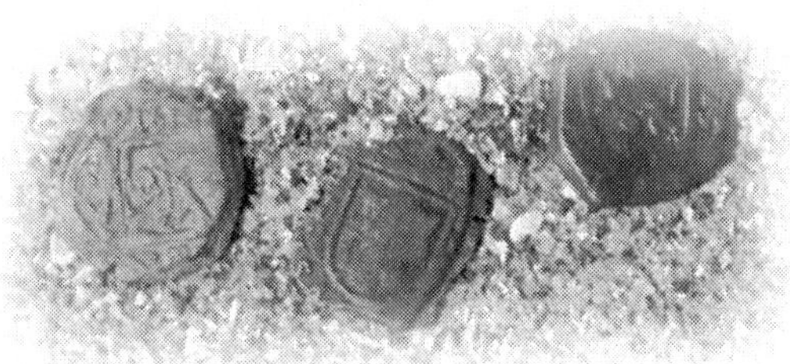

The wagon jarred hard to the right as the front wheel dipped into a deep depression on the muddy road. Papa Farrow corrected their course with a flip of the reins and Stephen regained his balance on the wagon seat. Wolf rode next to him. They were headed to the shores of Lake Mattamuskeet some five miles distant. Their plans for a solo weekend overnight adventure had changed dramatically.

Stephen's mother would not let her boy make the trip in the company of lads just slightly older than he was. She had put her foot down hard on the topic in spite of her son's pleading and the hesitant support of his father. Papa Farrow had come to the rescue. He needed to check on some of his property at the lake and had offered to take his grandson along. They had rendezvoused with Wolf at the stump meeting place. Wolf's disappointment that he was not going to be able to lead the younger boys on a grand adventure was written on his face.

Bear was not allowed to go along as he needed to work with his father in preparation for the spring planting.

Stephen was learning that the life of a slave was a hard one and even a slave boy had few privileges, cavorting about the countryside on a weekend excursion was not one of them.

"Whoa. I will pick you up here about mid-afternoon tomorrow." Jacob brought the horse and wagon to a stop at the path leading to Wolf's grandfather's cabin. "Have fun, and enjoy the old man's tales. Give my greeting to senior Squires." Jacob flipped the reins and the mare moved ahead down the road.

They found the grizzled old man rocking on his front porch. His hair was snow white and his eyes were steely gray in color. He had a faraway look and did not make eye contact with the boys as they bounced up on the porch. "Grandpapa, I have brought my friend Gator, his name is Stephen Brooks, son of the captain with the same name." Wolf pulled his friend close and brought together the wrinkled hand of his grandfather with that of the young boy. Stephen now realized that the old man was blind, his stare fixed on him but there was no emotion or recognition expressed in his sightless gaze.

"Welcome, boys! Stephen it is good to meet you. Tom has told me about some of your adventures near the bay. I know of your father. He has a fine reputation as a fair and honest man, virtues all too rare these days. Sit, we will talk and enjoy good company." For the first time since they had arrived Stephen could trace a faint smile on the tired face of his host and felt at ease.

"Grandpapa, I told Gator about the old coin you have."

"Fetch it from the house, I will tell you the coin's story." Wolf ran inside and retrieved the coin from its hiding place and returned to the side of his grandfather, placing the coin carefully in the palm of the old man. The old man rubbed his thumb across the surface of the silver coin as if to polish the tarnished surface. They all sat in silence. The old man seemed to be transfixed in another place and time. Finally he spoke.

"Where shall we start? This coin spurs many a memory. It has been in our family for many generations. When I was your age, my grandfather used to tell me how it had come into our family. Nearly two hundred years ago whites came to our shores from Britain. Over a hundred of them were left to make a home on Roanoke Island, north of here. Some of their kind had arrived a few years earlier to take claim to land here in what for them was a new world. Manteo, chief of the Croatan tribe, befriended them and traveled back with them to Britain with gifts of tobacco and maize. He returned with these colonists, determined to help them survive the challenges and risks of living among the first peoples of these islands and marshes. Alas, all did not go well for those distant visitors. Misunderstandings and hostilities arose. For fear of their lives, they fled from their village on Roanoke. Many were killed. Some lived and became a part of my people. Some of the white women married into the tribe. A few white men even married native women. Their blood is mixed with ours. My grey eyes and grandson's blond hair are marks of their place in our long ago history. They taught us their language, about words on paper and showed us their book from God. Some of their names can still be found among our peoples. Why, I believe, if my memory is accurate, that there was even a Brook or Brooks among those first colonists, a shoemaker he was. Maybe you are one of his descendants?"

The story-teller paused. Stephen was on the edge of the bench leaning forward to take in each and every word of the story. The old man reached out his hand to his young guest. "Take a look at this coin. It is well worn but if you look closely you can see the date of 1580 and make out the faint form of the English queen, Elizabeth I. This coin came across the sea, a possession of one of those first colonists. I believe it is a silver six pence. It was given as a gift to my great, great, great grandfather and has been passed down until it came to me. Like our mixed blood, it bears the touch of both your people and my people. The coin was hammered out in distant places and worn down to only faint impressions here in the swamps of Mattamuskeet. In some ways the coin mirrors the path of my people. Once we were strong and many. Our image was clear and could be seen by other tribes around us. Now we are rubbed down to next to nothing. Few of us remain. Our lands are gone, sold off to others who made their way across the big ocean. Little is left to be seen of what we once were, we are a faint reflection, like the near worthless piece of metal you hold in your hand."

Stephen examined what few details he could make out on the coin. He shifted his focus back to the Indian and thought he saw a tear flowing down his cheek. Before he could tell for sure the old man wiped his hand across his face, removing any trace. "Enough of sad old tales, I think we should have supper. Tom will you put the pot of venison stew on the fire?"

"Yes, Grandpapa, and I will return the coin to its hiding place as well." Wolf took the coin from Stephen's hand and went back inside the cabin. Stephen sat quietly on the porch until Wolf returned sometime later with pewter plates laden with the hot and tasty meal. He even enjoyed a second helping.

The boys had a hard time falling to sleep. As they lay on the straw mats they kept replaying the details of the story they had heard about the early colonists. Stephen told Wolf about how his grandfather had told him his distant relatives might have been pirates. Now he wondered if he was connected to Brooks the shoemaker who had journeyed to America centuries earlier. They watched the moon rise through the open window and searched for shooting stars until sleep finally overtook them.

Stephen was amazed by how easily the blind old man navigated around his cabin. Mixing the cornmeal he used his fingers to guide the pouring of the batter on to the griddle which he then placed above the coals with care, sensing the heat with the back of one hand while finding the edge of the fireplace with his other.

"The Johnny cakes are ready boys, eat up!"

"These are so good. Thank you for the good breakfast." Stephen took another piece of the fried cornmeal. It was the first time he had eaten cornbread made in this fashion.

"Our people have been making such cakes for hundreds of years. We taught our white visitors how to prepare and cook the meal." The senior Squires maneuvered around the furniture and reached out to take their empty plates. "Why don't you boys go and explore the woods along the lake while I clean up."

Wolf led the way down the pathway to the lake. They gazed at the far distant shore. "Though the lake is large it is very shallow, you could almost walk across it with your head still out of the water. That is if you didn't mind the occasional alligator for company." He laughed as he slapped Stephen on the shoulder.

They walked along the edge of the lake, admiring the cypress trees with their exposed roots. As they made their way into the forest, Wolf paused and listened intently. Stephen, following his lead, began to tune his senses to the surroundings. That is when he spotted the deer barely visible through the thick underbrush. "Look at the white deer," he whispered to his friend. Almost as if on cue, the doe stepped clear of the foliage and looked at them. For long minutes they stayed locked in eye contact. The boys dared not move and frighten the beautiful creature. The deer, well aware of the human presence, did not seem unnerved by their stare but turned to show her full silhouette. Then with a flick of her tail she was gone. She had seemed like a ghostly apparition, there one minute and invisible the next. While she was clearly gone the boys continued to look in her parting direction, hoping to catch another glimpse of her. Finally, convinced she was gone, they broke the eerie silence with gasps of delight.

"The white doe is a special sign to my people," Wolf spoke. He could hardly believe he had been chosen to witness the powerful omen. If not for the sharp eyes of his white friend, he might have missed the rare privilege. "We must tell my grandpapa, he will know the meaning of what we have seen."

The boys rushed back to the cabin, bursting through the door they both spoke at once trying to explain what they had encountered near the lake. The tired old man raised his hand to slow their chatter and then listened with patience as each described the white doe.

"It may be that you have seen the ghost deer. I once saw her, back when I had the gift of sight. Indeed she is beautiful and glides through the forest without leaving a hoof print trace of her presence. She is an unearthly deer. Her story is sometimes linked to the people of the coin that I told you yesterday. Come, sit, and I will tell you the legend of the white doe." The boys found a place to sit and waited with anticipation.

"We are ready Papa," Wolf pleaded.

"One of the women who came with the first whites was named Virginia Dare. When the colonists fled their protective fort on Roanoke, she, along with others, traveled west by boat across Croatan waters, now called Albemarle Bay. There she was adopted into one of the tribes. Because of her beauty, a number of warriors competed to gain her love and win her hand in marriage. One handsome Indian chief was successful in his overtures and they were to be wed. But before they could marry an ugly evil shaman, whom she had rejected, used his magic powers and in revenge turned her into a white doe. If he couldn't have her, no one else would." The old Indian paused, took a sip of hot yaupon tea and continued.

"Motivated by his undying love for Virginia, the brave warrior traveled here to the shores of Lake Mattamuskeet to secure the help of a wise and kind shaman. He hoped the shaman could help him break the wicked spell that had transformed his beautiful bride into an elusive deer. The shaman spent many hours in the sweat lodge seeking an answer for the love-sick chief. He removed one of the arrows from the warrior's quiver and dipped it into a spring known for its healing powers. Giving the arrow back to the chief he instructed him that he must shoot the white doe with this special arrow. Only such an act would break the spell and return the doe to human form." He again deftly guided the mug to his lips, sipped and placed the mug back on the table as went on with his story.

"But the white doe had attracted the attention of other hunters who believed they would achieve fame and power if they could slay the deer and possess its unique and magical hide. Many arrows were shot at the ghostly form of the deer as she moved through woods and marshes, seeking the love she had lost. She dodged each well-aimed arrow at the last second and then would vanish into the forest." The aged Indian again paused, as if letting the intensity of the story build to its climax.

"One fine day, her true love, still on his quest, spotted her feeding near the ruins of the Fort on Roanoke Island where she had once lived as a human. Using all of his skill as a hunter he closed the distance to bow range. With love and great anxiety he quietly slipped the healing arrow from his quiver and with shaking hands notched the arrow to the string. Taking aim he sped the arrow on its way toward the white doe. Virginia stood fast as the arrow moved toward her, welcoming sweet release from her sad plight. But alas, at the very same moment, another hunter also launched an arrow from the opposite side of the small clearing. Both arrows found their mark and pierced the white doe's heart. Rushing to the side of the fallen deer, the warrior witnessed her return to human form and held her tight in love. But the other arrow had also done its killing work and Virginia Dare died in his arms."The boys both sighed upon hearing of the tragic death of the beautiful maiden. Letting them feel the weight of emotion for a moment the Indian stopped talking.

"Oh how sad," Stephen finally found his words. "Is that the end of the story?"

"No, the chief did not give up. He ran many miles back to the healing spring and filled a flask with the magic water, hoping that it might restore her life. He also pleaded with the kind shaman to offer prayers for her recovery. Returning to the clearing where she had fallen he searched in vain. She was not there, nor could he find the dead deer. Many days later as he was weeping beside the magic spring, the white doe appeared just yards from him. The doe looked at him, just as you described she looked at you. He could see the love in her soft eyes, but as he reached for her she vanished into the woods. And so the tale of the white doe has been passed down over the generations. The story has been told beside Indian campfires and kept alive. Only a special few, including you, have been granted the vision of the white doe. Cherish that memory forever."

On the bumpy wagon ride back to Light Creek Marsh, Stephen relayed to his Papa Farrow both the story of the coin and their encounter with the white doe. "These sloughs and marshes hold many a secret from the first inhabitants to lost colonists and rogue pirates," Jacob laughed. "Why someday, I reckon, you will pass on your own stories to your children, grandchildren and great grandchildren about your life here."

Chapter 8

MARSH ADVENTURES

"Bear, get me a ladle of water," Stephen ordered.

"Get it, yourself," the black lad muttered in response, his voice barely audible but just loud enough for the master's son to hear.

The boys were hard at work, preparing the soil for the spring planting of 1773. Bear had been out of sorts over the past year. It had started about the time that Stephen had returned from his weekend visit with Wolf at Lake Mattamuskeet. Stephen had tried to describe to him the unique coin he had held and exuberantly retold the legend of the white doe but Able had responded with some indifference and his surly mood was now evident in their interactions. While he occasionally joined Gator and Wolf on their Sunday exploits he was frequently compelled to assist his father in some chore or activity. The inequalities of slave life were taking their toll on the lad and he had finally had enough.

"What did you say?" Stephen answered angrily.

"I said get it yourself." This time his voice resonated and was marked by clear defiance. "Are you my friend or my master too? Bear continued, staring at his onetime comrade.

Stephen took at step toward Bear, prompting the slave boy to rise from his knees. In one quick lunge he pushed Stephen backwards and the nine year old landed hard on his rump. He jumped up and tackled his rival to the ground. They rolled about, occasionally one or the other would land a punch, but most of their blows were blocked.

"What is going on here?" Stephen's father had caught sight of the scuffle from the far side of the field and now his words brought a quick end to the fight. The boys rose from the dirt to face the clearly angry adult. "Answer me," the senior Stephen grasped the shoulders of Bear. "Would you raise your fists against my son? Speak up now! You will be severely beaten for this offense. You must learn your place boy."

"We, ah…" Bear tried to find words.

"We were just playing, Father," Gator interrupted. "Just testing out our muscles and having a little fun. There is no reason to punish Bear."

"It didn't look that way to me from across the field. I better not see you fighting again or there will be harsh consequences. Able, do you understand what I am saying?"

"Yes, master." Able responded sheepishly without lifting his gaze from the ground.

"Then get back to planting seed, both of you. There is no time for this child's play. We must get the field seeded today." The upset farmer looked sternly at both boys before striding off to his own labors across the field.

"You saved my skin, Gator, thank you." Bear dusted the soil from his breeches.

"We will always be friends, Bear." Gator reached out his

hand. "I know you have been upset these past months by all the work you have to do. Wolf and I have missed you on our Sunday ventures. But let's not fight again. Friends don't try to hurt each other." Bear took Gator's extended hand and shook it firmly.

"Friends it is." Both nodded in affirmation and returned to the hard work of planting.

The bright warm days of spring were dulled by two significant losses. In May, Stephen's grandfather, the eldest of the Stephens, died at his home near Lake Mattamuskeet. While the young lad had had few interactions with his paternal Papa he often thought of his presence during that terrifying Christmas on the cape. Whenever he looked at the three pence gift he had received on that occasion he remembered the old man's kindness and his warm smile of affection. He also now had another coin to add to his growing collection. His father had returned from settling the estate of his grandpa with a small copper British Farthing dated 1749. The old coin, worth but a quarter of a pence or cent was still a valuable treasure to the boy and with gratitude he stowed it away safely with his other coins.

Wolf brought news of the other loss in early June. His grandfather had also succumbed to age and infirmity. For both boys this was their first real encounter with the fragile nature of human life and the painful loss of loved ones. They did find a measure of comfort, even laughter, in recalling memories of their papas and telling their stories aloud to each other.

Stephen had told his mother about the Johnny cake breakfast he had enjoyed that weekend at the lake. She had mastered the recipe and occasionally would serve the cakes to her family. Every time she did, Stephen would envision himself back in the cabin of the blind man, relishing his hospitality and listening intently to his tales.

"Alright, you have my permission to go on an overnight camping trip with Wolf and Bear." Mary, Stephen's mother, had finally given in to the constant badgering. "But you must let your father know where you will be and you must promise me you will be careful. Please don't play with snakes either."

"Yes, mother. Wolf knows everything about the woods. We will be safe together." Somehow her son's reassurances only brought a small measure of peace to her worried mind. To her the expanses of the mainland swamps and forests held many dangers. She missed the cape, where from a slight high point you could easily see the ocean to the east and Pamlico Sound to the west without straining your eyes. There were no snakes, alligators, bears and pumas to be found lurking in the bush or sloughs.

Stephen had also been successful in convincing his father to let Able accompany he and Wolf on the overnight outing in the woods. That news seemed to lift the spirits of the black lad and he threw himself into his labors with new energy as he passed the days until the weekend arrived.

"I have packed some food for you," Mary said, handing her son the stuffed knapsack of vittles.

"Thank you, mother, but we are going to live off the land, fishing and hunting for our meals."

"Well, just in case the fish are not biting or the game escapes your skillful efforts, you will still have something to fall back on." With a chuckle, she gave her growing boy a hug and kiss on the check. Stephen was glad that his friends weren't there to see her maternal show of affection. It didn't seem an appropriate send off for a great and mighty hunter or angler.

It would just be the three of them, alone in the forest together. The ruckus and noise of his siblings and the busy environment of the Brooks home would be left far behind. Stephen loved the wild woods almost as much as he loved the wild sea. Both held surprises, whether around a bend in the trail or over the next wave.

Wolf led the way to a special secret place he had not taken his friends to before. He boasted that the small slough close by was filled with monster perch. In preparation for the weekend he had deftly constructed a small lean-to and had gathered marsh grasses for makeshift sleeping mats. He had gathered rocks and formed a campfire pit where they would cook their quarry. The sun shone brightly and a gentle breeze helped keep the ever-present marsh mosquitoes at bay. The scene was set.

Gator and Bear were delighted with the deluxe accommodations. All three boys tossed their backpacks aside, pulled out their fishing gear and fashioned poles as quickly as they could. Stephen was the first to lob his hook and bobber into the quiet narrow waterway. Immediately the bobber went under and he yanked the foot long perch onto the bank with a squeal of delight. "I got the first one," he cheered.

"Well I guess we will have to call this Brooks Creek in your honor," Wolf applauded. They cleaned their fine catch of three jumbo perch not far from camp, tossing the heads, tails and entrails into the bushes. Wolf started a fire and they proceeded to char their meal to the desired blackness. Picking the small bits of white flesh from the burned skin and bones was a bit of a challenge but they were proud of their efforts. Having finished the fish, Stephen hauled out his mother's treasures and they supplemented their diet with some of what she had prepared. They saved some, just in case tomorrow's food quest was less successful.

Stephen woke before the other lads. He needed to relieve himself and quietly rose and traveled some distance down the trail. Coming over a slight rise he found himself face to face with a large bear and two cubs. Stephen froze. The sow rose on her hind legs as if to examine the intruder. He could clearly see the white patch on her exposed throat. He knew he must not run and trigger an attack but the knowledge offered little comfort as he curled his toes into the wet soil, standing firm. The huge sow dropped back to all fours and scurried off with her cubs in tow. The first cub continued to follow her mother, the one lagging behind however opted to climb a tree right next to the trail. The sow soon realized one cub was missing and again rose on her haunches to investigate. Now Stephen was really frightened as he was well aware of the protective measures a troubled she bear might exhibit in defense of her young. Stephen trembled. He could hear the bear calling to her youngster in the tree and fortunately the little one backed down, hurried to mother and the three turned and disappeared into the woods. It was all over in a matter of seconds, however for the lad, time had seemed to stop entirely.

Back at their camp, Stephen stirred the other lads and

shared his story. Wolf acknowledged his mistake with some embarrassment. "It was the fish heads and guts, we should have moved farther from camp and buried them. I know better. Mistakes out here can be costly. There are lots of big bears in this area. I have often seen their scat. Gator, you were lucky."

The rest of the weekend passed far too quickly for the adventurous trio. As they readied to leave their campsite, Wolf held up his hand to stop them. "Wait, we need to leave a marker of our hideaway." He went over to a nearby tree and removed something he had stashed there. He pushed the sharpened end of the stick into the soft bank. Laced across the top of the stick was a small slab of wood upon which he had carefully carved the words 'Brooks Crick.' "There, now when we pass this way or return to camp, we will remember that Gator caught the first fish." They all laughed. Then it appeared Wolf had a second thought. He pulled the sign up and knelt, scratching more on its surface. Satisfied he repositioned the stake. "And the lair of our negro friend's spirit animal too," he added. Stepping back they now could see his handiwork: 'Brooks Crick-Bear Hallo.' Homeward they trekked in fine spirits.

Chapter 9

A GOOD DEED REWARDED

Both boys were covered in sweat. The summer day was hot and humid and not a breath of wind stirred to provide some relief. As usual they were engaged in a variety of chores and farming activities. Able was the first to detect some movement in the bushes near the field's edge. "Gator, what's that?"

"Looks like O'Reilly's mule," Stephen surmised."Yep, that's his mule alright. Seems like it's always getting loose. You can see she broke her rope again. Let's see if we can catch her." The boys moved slowly toward the animal, hoping not to startle her into a run. Stephen was first to get close. With a lunge he reached for the broken tether and came up just short. The mule kicked up her heels and moved off a short ways. Able took his turn next.

"Nice muley, nice muley," he tried to calm the agitated critter. He was now within arm's reach and he dove to grab the frayed rope. He too was a tad short in his effort and again the mule kicked her heels and retreated. Their cat and mouse chase continued with each boy attempting multiple times to secure a hold on the animal's short leash.

"This isn't working," Stephen panted. "Let's rest a bit and figure out a plan." They sat down on the nearest log and contemplated their dilemma. Able was the first to propose an idea.

"Maybe we could get her to come if we fed her some grass?" Stephen thought for a second hatching his own scheme.

"Horses and mules love carrots. You keep an eye on her and I'll fetch a carrot from the garden." The lure secured, the boys moved toward the now curious beast. The trap was simple. Stephen would hold out the carrot and when the mule took the bait, Able would quickly grab the rope. The plan worked to perfection and the lads congratulated each other on their success.

"Let's take the old mule to my father and see what he wants to do with her." With mule in tow the boys crossed the field toward the house where the elder Stephen was building a chicken coop with Jupiter. "Father, we captured O'Reilly's mule. What should we do with her?"

"I am sure he would be pleased if you took her back to his cabin. Secure her with a fresh rope halter from the barn. The two of you can then take her home."

O'Reilly's cabin was about three miles away and the trip offered the boys an appreciated break from their labors in the hot sun. They took turns leading the stubborn animal. They were making fairly steady progress until they came to a small ditch filled with water. Try as they might they could not get the mule to cross the ditch. Stephen pulled, Able pushed. Able pulled, Stephen pushed. The four hoofs of the mule seemed cemented to the soil. They tried soothing words and angry rants; neither was successful in persuading the critter to move.

"I remember a story in the Bible about a talking donkey. This one doesn't talk or listen," Stephen muttered with some frustration. Tying the mule to a nearby branch they crossed the ditch, sat down and considered their plight. Almost as if on cue, the animal, now free of human touch followed them across the water. "Well would you look at that, Bear. Guess this one just likes her freedom to make her own choices."

"I think all of God's creatures want to be free," the slave boy responded.

It took them a couple of hours to reach the cabin of the Irishman. He was out hoeing in his small vegetable garden when he spotted them across the clearing. "I see you found old Nellie. I be obliged that you brought her home to me." O'Reilly rested his hoe against the garden fence as he greeted the boys. "She's a hard one to catch. How'd you do it?"

"We got her with a carrot," the boys spoke, almost in unison.

"Let me get you a drink, it's surely hot today." While the water was not cold it still offered relief to their thirst and they gulped down each pewter cupful he extended to them, drawn from the bucket on his porch. The bachelor disappeared into his cabin while the lads continued to drink. When he returned they could see he was holding something in his hand.

"Here's a reward for your kindness." He placed a small coin in each boy's hand. "These be Irish farthings from my homeland. You can even see the Celtic harp on one side of the coin. We Irish love our music. Oh, how I miss the sound of the ancient instrument. The singing, the drinking, the dancing are now but a faint memory of my birthplace."

The trip home took half the time of their outgoing trek with the hesitant mule. Both boys could not believe their good fortune in earning the quarter pence. "What are you going to do with the farthing?" Able asked his friend.

"This is the first money I earned as pay for work. It will go in my coin box. How about you?"

"I am going to save my farthing too. Maybe if I can save enough someday I can buy my freedom. Like that old stubborn mule I would like to break my bonds and run free."

"I hope you can save enough." Stephen thought about giving his own farthing to his friend but his delight in the reward was, at that moment, too strong for such an act of generosity.

By the end of the fall harvest the stifling summer heat had given way to cooler fall breezes. It was a perfect Sunday afternoon for exploring local waterways. Wolf had joined Gator and Bear and together they paddled about the interconnected sloughs that made up Light Creek Marsh. They fished for a while, catching only a few small redfish that had migrated out of the bay into the smaller slough. As Wolf lifted another one from the water, all were startled by the gaping jaws of an alligator breaking the surface, apparently in pursuit of the panicked fish on his line. Wolf dropped the fish back toward the reptile and made a large figure eight motion with the end of his pole, hoping to attract the gator back into sight. Their next glimpse of the creature was impressive. The lads gasped as the nearly ten foot alligator moved toward the splashing fish, propelled by the strong sweeping motion of its massive tail.

"That's a big one," Bear shouted as the ancient leviathan missed the wiggling fish and slipped back into the dark waters.

"Try to get it to come back," both Bear and Gator pleaded. Try as he might, Wolf was unsuccessful in his efforts. It appeared the alligator was gone for good.

The other two fishermen now re-hooked some of their catch on their poles and agitated the surface with their own offerings. Stephen moved past Able to the front of their small craft, hoping to launch his bait to a new location. He stood to cast his fish as far as he could when he suddenly lost his balance and tumbled headlong into the slough. He bobbed to the surface splashing fiercely. Both Bear and Wolf reached to grab his outstretched hands but were unsuccessful and he disappeared again.

Stephen felt the rugged armor plate of the alligator brush against his leg and felt pain as the reptile's claw tore into the flesh of his calf. He managed to get his other foot on the back of the monster and pushed back toward the surface. This time his friends were ready and they each grasped a hand and pulled him into the safety of the boat. The soaked boy shivered, but not from the cold of the water.

Wolf and Bear paddled as hard and as fast as they could. Reaching the small dock, they pulled Stephen to dry land and examined his wounds. Through the tear in his breeches they could see blood. "We need to get you to the house. Can you walk?" Wolf asked as he tore a strip of cloth from his shirt and tried to bandage the wound as best he could.

"I think so." The boys helped him to his feet and with

his arms around their shoulders they limped their way back to the house together.

Mary was returning from the newly finished chicken coop with the day's eggs when she saw the friends struggling to support her young son. With a gasp she dropped the eggs and rushed to his side. "What happened? Is it a snake bite?" The poisonous snakes of the swamp were always her first and worst fear.

"It's nothing, mother, just a scratch, I'm fine."

"A gator clawed his leg," Wolf interrupted. Removing the temporary dressing, Mary surveyed the damage. While there was a fair amount of blood the scratch was not that deep and should heal quickly.

"You could have been killed," Mary embraced her son, pulling her close to her bosom. Stephen, red with embarrassment no longer felt the twinge of pain from the wound.

That evening the entire family listened to Stephen as he embellished and retold the story of the gator attack. The gator grew a couple of feet in length and new details were added to what would become a family legend about the daring battle with the reptile and the last minute rescue attempts of his friends.

Stephen's father rewarded Wolf and Bear for their courageous act. He gave a silver shilling to both the boys. While Wolf considered possible options for purchase, Bear stowed away the treasure along with his farthing. He was planning a more substantive purchase far in the future.

The Christmas festivities that year were marked by a buzz of adult conversation. News had reached the area that the Sons of Liberty, masquerading as Indians, had raided three British Tea ships in Boston harbor. On December 16th they had dumped tons of tea into the harbor in protest of the tea tax and the monopoly held on tea sales by the British East Indies Company. Stephen, still too young to join into the adult celebration, listened in, as usual, from the loft.

"I am sure the British will respond quickly and severely to this protest action," Papa Farrow spoke loudly, between gulps of rum-laden eggnog.

"I am glad we made the move from Hatteras when we did, Stephen's father broke in. "Shipping in the area will certainly be affected by both privateers and the British navy. We can better stay out of sight and harm's way here and the farm will sustain us if supplies are cut off," he continued, drawing from his own mug and wiping his mouth with the back of his sleeve.

"I say we toast the Sons of Liberty for their bravery," Uncle Thomas chimed in, holding his mug out to the others.

"Here, Here," the adult males affirmed, crashing their mugs together.

"I would applaud their bravery more if they had not felt the need to dress up as Mohawk Indians," Farrow laughed.

"Disguised Indians or not, I hope the British get our message loud and clear. We will not be taxed without representation. I, for one, am ready to take up arms and fight for our voice to be heard, all the way to the throne of the King." All nodded in response to Uncle Thomas' strong words.

The nearly ten year old Stephen fingered the coins as he removed them from the red pouch and eavesdropped on the talk below. In his small collection he had coins from Great

Britain, Spain, Scotland, Holland and Ireland. Would these colonies, scattered along the coast of America, one day have their own money and be independent from Europe? What would a war with England mean to his family and friends? Would British troops attack and disrupt the peace of his quiet marsh home? He placed the coins back into the box and returned it to the niche made especially for its safe keeping. Stephen scratched at the scar on his calf, rolled over and fell fast asleep.

Chapter 10

CAPTAIN IN TRAINING

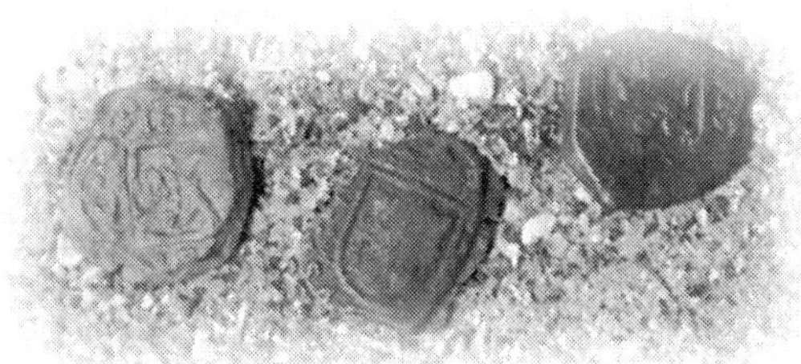

Young Stephen took the length of rope and fashioned a bowline knot at one end. He had been hard at practicing knots since his tenth birthday in February. His father had promised him a sailing trip come late spring or early summer and the prerequisite for his sea journey was mastery of the knots his father had been teaching him.

"If you want to sail, my lad, you must learn the ropes. That includes tying the best knots as well as working the ship's rigging. We will work on the knots while here on shore. You will get your lessons in rigging when we take to sea. Your older brothers are all skilled at trimming and setting the sails. They will help you. Here, tie the bowline knot again."

"Father, where will we sail?"

"We will travel north, up the coast, past Roanoke Island and west on Albemarle Sound to the city of Edenton. I have business there."

"How old do I have to get to be a captain like you and have my own ship?"

"Double your age now would be a worthy goal to set,

my would-be sailor."

"I will be a good student, Father, and learn quickly. I will have the fastest schooner on Pamlico Sound."The boy tried to tie the knot in hurried fashion and made a mistake.

"Take your time, child. A master of the sea is a patient man. Speed and brashness can lead to poor decisions and poor decisions can lead to shipwreck, even death. You must learn the rhythm of the waters, the fickle nature of the winds and how to read the weather for approaching squalls and storms. The shoals of the Outer Banks have claimed many a reckless hand on the wheel." Captain Stephen untied his son's knot and handed him the rope for another try.

"When are we leaving?" Stephen asked, taking his time with this effort and correctly forming the basic seaman's knot, he proudly handed it back to his father.

"Well done, lad. We should be ready to sail in early June, after the corn is planted."

The days seemed to crawl by, like he was trying to sail in dead calm conditions. Chores and spring planting were demanding but monotonous. Sunday afternoon treks with Wolf and occasionally Bear, helped transition from the labors of one week to the hard work of the next.

They headed out with high hopes one balmy early May forenoon. The sky was clear, the air warm and they dressed lightly. They were young lads with not a care in the world, eager to see what new adventure their marsh home might reveal.

When they passed their campsite from the previous year, Wolf stopped and straightened the leaning sign he had erected there. "That looks better," he offered, stepping back and admiring his repair effort.

They didn't stop to fish in Brooks Creek but pushed on deeper into unexplored territory. Bear was the first to notice a hint of change in the weather. "Seems to be a chilling breeze starting to blow, maybe we should turn back?" But warmed by their movement the other two lads dismissed his warning.

"Ain't nothing, let's go a bit further." Wolf answered as he brushed back the branches blocking their progress.

Kneeling next to the animal trail, Gator pointed to the fresh deer track, clear in the soft soil. "Maybe it's another white doe. Let's follow and see," he urged. On they went, losing track of time while searching for hoof prints. But when they stopped to get their bearings all agreed it was getting much colder, a north wind was gaining momentum and the sky was growing overcast. Soon it started spitting rain.

"We need to get home now," Wolf urged, sensing they might be in real danger. The rain increased in intensity and the boys started to shiver whenever they paused to plot their course.

"Look, the rain is freezing to the tree branches and the ground is getting slippery. I'm really cold," Stephen mumbled. The boys now huddled together in a state of near panic. They watched from the windbreak of an uprooted tree as in a matter of minutes the icy rain turned to sleet and the sleet turned to snow.

"Are we going to die?" Bear slurred his words, teeth chattering as he tried to speak.

As the numbing cold penetrated through their light clothing, Stephen imagined he heard his name being called above the howl of the wind. He wondered if it might be the voice of God and he tried praying. Then he saw a distant light through the swirling flakes. Was he dreaming?

"I see the light too," Wolf shivered.

"Me too," Bear added.

As the light drew closer they heard the horse's hooves and the wheels of the wagon breaking the thin crust of ice. "Stephen, Tom, Able," the shouts now broke through the awful storm swirling about them. It was Stephen's father and Papa Farrow. The boys stumbled to the side of the wagon and were hauled up into safety by strong arms. They were wrapped in warm blankets and placed next to two Dutch ovens filled with still warm stones heated on the home hearth. Papa Farrow dispensed some hot tea and warmth slowly returned to their chilled frames.

It had been an unusually late spring snowstorm, May 4th 1774. The freezing rain and snow fell from North Carolina up into Virginia and would become the stuff of fireside chats for many a generation. It was also used as a cautionary tale to remind folks of how quickly the weather could change from comfort to icy death.

The boys continued to thaw out as they now sat next to the roaring fireplace in the Brooks home. The terror that had gripped Mary, her husband and her parents had gradually been replaced by heartfelt sobs of "Praise God, and Thank you Jesus."

As Stephen sipped the warm liquid and downed another helping of hot stew he recalled the words of his wise Captain Father. "You need to be able to read the weather for approaching squalls and storms," he had been instructed. In light of their precarious escape from death's freezer, those words took on deeper meaning. Clearly there was a lot he needed to learn. In that moment, the comforting embrace of his mother seemed preferable to the deck of a schooner or a ship's wheel.

The *Hannah Marie* weighed anchor on Tuesday, June 7th. Stephen watched with amazement as his brothers negotiated the challenges of rigging the sails for their trip north to Edenton. His father called him to the wheel at the stern of the vessel and continued his lessons.

"Lad, take a look through this spy glass to our port side. Turn the brass sleeve to focus on yonder shore. That is Stumpy Point. Now look at my chart of Pamlico Sound and locate the point and you will be able to see where we are on the map. There is a narrow opening into the bay there where you can find shelter during storms. But be cautious as the waters are shallow. I hear that some of the Midgett clan are planning on buying land and building a town on the shores of the bay. Perhaps someday when you are piloting your own schooner you will turn in there to deliver supplies."

Captain Stephen stepped back and offered the wheel to the boy. "Give her a turn to starboard to catch the wind. Since we are sailing into the breeze we cannot plot a straight course but must tack from side to side, forming a Z pattern on the water." The boy proudly clung to the ship's wheel and followed his father's directions.

"I am sailing, Father?"

"Yes my boy, you are sailing. This outing you will be my junior captain." In the distance Stephen could see the bay was narrowing and there were two channels on either side of what appeared to be an island. "That is Roanoke Island, son, we will bear to the port side, through Croatan Sound, as waters are shallow and there are frequent shoals on the starboard course. You have done well at the wheel." His father kindly but firmly retook control of the schooner as they moved from the open waters toward the channel.

"Wolf's grandfather told me stories about this island and the first English who settled here." The boy thought of the silver coin the old Indian had shown him and how the colony had disappeared hundreds of years earlier.

"There are some ruins of their fort on the northeast end of the island. Perhaps we will anchor near there and go ashore and take a look on our return trip."

"I would like that," Stephen tried to focus the spy glass on the island to starboard as they passed. With the island in their wake they turned to port into the more expansive waters of Albemarle Sound. They continued to the west for a few hours before turning south into large inlet.

"Can you find Alligator River on my map, son?" The boy fumbled with the charts and finally located the spot.

"Yes, I see it."

"Good, now can you find Fort Landing on Alligator Creek?" The boy searched for some time, unable to locate the spot. With his index finger his father guided his gaze to a cove on west side of the inlet. "Son, grab the lead line, I will show you how to sound the depth so we do not run aground." The boy located the line with the heavy lead tied to the end and returned to the wheel. Captain Brooks put some fresh wax into the center of the end of the weight.

"What is the wax for?" young Stephen queried.

"The wax will tell us what is on the bottom, whether we are over sand, muck or rock. Here, let me show you." The captain dropped the line into the water, marked the depth and pulled it back to the surface. "See the sand on the wax? That tells us we are over sand. Did you see how deep the water is?" The elder Stephen dropped the lead back down and pointed to the mark on the line when it went slack, indicating it had reached bottom. "We are at mark twain. The water is two fathoms deep, or twelve feet. Each fathom is six feet. There is no more important task on the ship than sounding with the lead line. Without that information we can easily end up stranded on a sandbar or lodged on the rocks. Now you try it." The lad took his turn and could see that the line went slack before just reaching the third stripe on the line.

"Father, it is getting deeper, now we are almost to three fathoms."

"Ah that is better. We have crossed the shallow bar to the cove. The draft of our schooner is about 8-10 feet, so we do not want to go below that two fathom mark." Stephen tried to take in every detail. There was clearly much more to sailing than he had realized.

His father pointed to the far shore and clearing his throat said, "There is Fort Landing. It was built by settlers coming from Virginia almost a hundred years ago. See the wood stockade just above the high water line? They constructed that for protection during the Tuscarora War. Your Grandfather Brooks was a lad about your age when the Tuscarora tribe went to war against the farmers who were taking their lands and killing their game. The farmers would all go to the stockade when warring Indians were near."

They anchored off shore of Fort Landing for the night. The local tavern-inn owner served them a passable meal, no one was quite sure what kind of meat it was but after a long day on the water there were few complaints.

They weighed anchor early the next morning and set sail for Edenton. Near the west end of Albemarle Sound they veered north. Between the mouths of Queen Anne's Creek and Mattercommack Creek was the Chowan County seat of Edenton. Explorers from Jamestown had founded the village around 1658. It was the first such community in the province of North Carolina and had served as the capital of the colony until New Bern won that distinction. It was a shipping and marketing center for the area and its large wharves made for easy docking of the *Hannah Marie*. Stephen's older siblings took off to investigate the town as soon as the ship was securely moored.

"Lad, you stay with me, we are going shopping. Your mother gave me quite a list of things we need to obtain while here." He was glad to be in the company of his father rather than his older brothers who were constantly teasing him. So they set out on their walking tour of the town. The ten year old was impressed by the many brick buildings. He was used to smaller timber and log homes and the imposing structures quickly caught his eye.

"That is the county courthouse," his father pointed to the largest of the brick structures. Stephen stared at the two story building complete with a white tower and weather vane atop. He started counting the windows.

"Six, seven, eight, nine, that must let lots of light in."His father nodded and they continued on their way. Passing a large two story home with rusticated pine board siding he paused and looked up.

"What is that thing on the roof called?"

"That is a cupola. It has eight sides"-- Before he could finish his thought the lad interrupted.

"That's an octagon; I remember our lesson on shapes. I wish we had a cupola on our house."

Further down Water Street they entered King Mercantile. Stephen's father fished Mary's list from a pocket and they began to collect items. "Madame, where is the tea? I prefer it not be British tea."The two women who were talking together behind the counter came over and introduced themselves.

"I am Elizabeth King and this is my good friend Penelope Barker. We refuse to sell the crown's tea. We do have some fine rose hip tea mixed with local herbs. I would recommend that. I see that you have a bolt of imported flannel. Might I suggest this cloth here, made by some of our local ladies. We have had our fill of the taxes and regulations imposed by the King and as women folk we want to support our men in standing up to the British."

"I applaud your strong will and independent spirit. I will take the homemade material and two pounds of the rose hip tea. I agree with you and your distaste for tyranny," the Captain replied, startled but pleased by their pluck and outspoken gall. He liked these women. His young son also was attracted to the ladies but for a different reason. Mrs. King had fetched him a hard candy from the counter and he was enjoying the sweet lemon flavor.

"We were planning our own protest act when you entered the mercantile," Penelope said stepping forward. "A large group of area ladies will be assembling in October. We will send a formal letter to the King with our names affixed. Unlike our brethren in Boston there will be no costumes or masquerading here. We will step forward and be seen and heard loudly. Why we might dump some tea in shallow Edenton bay too."

"That should ruffle some English feathers in old Britain," Stephen laughed as he pulled his coin purse from his pocket. Elizabeth totaled up the prices of the goods and took her coin scale from the shelf. She compared the weight of each coin he gave her with an appropriate sample weight taken from her scale box. Such scales helped detect counterfeit coins and coins that had been shaved of some of their precious metal and were lighter than they should be. She completed the transaction by giving Stephen a few coins to make appropriate change. He examined the coins closely, placing all but one small silver Spanish Half Reale back in his coin bag.

"Son, here's your junior captain's wages for the trip and a belated birthday gift. I think you will want to keep this one for your collection." The boy gratefully accepted the coin and when he examined it he saw the date 1764. It was his birth date coin. He now had a coin for his own birth year as well as one for his father's birth year.

"Thank you, Father."

"Besides, son, I hope whenever you take this coin out of your box, you will recall with fondness your first lessons in sailing." They gathered up their goods from the counter, nodded a final thank you to Elizabeth and Penelope and headed out the door.

Chapter 11

CONFLICT BREWING

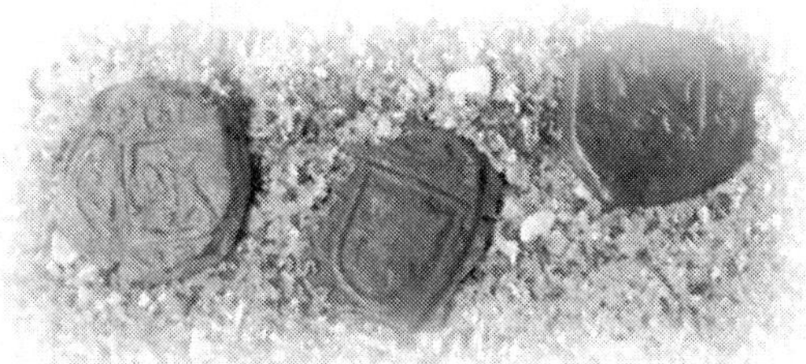

Father and son made their way back down Water Street to the dock area. "I have one more item of business here, the elder said as they came to a stop in front of a dockside building bearing the sign Hewes Shipping Company. The bell rang over the door announcing their arrival and the negro clerk seated at his desk rose quickly to greet them.

"I am here to see Joseph Hewes."

"May I tell my master who it is calling?"

"Stephen Brooks, ship's captain and citizen of Hyde County. My business is in regards to his possible appointment as a representative to the continental congress."

"Just a moment, I am sure he will want to talk with you." The clerk turned and entered an office at the back of the building. A few moments later Joseph Hewes emerged from the doorway and with his hand extended offered a greeting.

"Welcome Mr. Brooks. I have heard your name mentioned by some of my own captains. Your reputation as a gifted pilot in these waters is well known. I always have a place for men such as you if you be looking for a secure job."

"Thank you sir, but for now I prefer to be on my own. I like the freedom it gives me to sail when I wish and farm as well. Such independence gives me more time with my family too." The elder Stephen looked down and smiled at his son.

"Ah, I envy you. I once hoped for family but my beloved Isabella died before we were to marry and I have remained a bachelor all these years since. I guess you could say I am married to my business ventures. You are a much more fortunate man than me. I would guess this is one of your children." Joseph knelt to one knee and shook young Stephen's hand. "And are you going to be a captain like your Father, my boy?"

"I hope so, sir." Stephen blushed at the attention of the well-dressed company owner. His father, clearing his voice spoke.

"Sir, I have a message for you from fellow residents in my county of Hyde. We have heard that you will probably be appointed to represent North Carolina at a Continental Congress gathering this fall. We have heard of your excellent service to the community here and to the citizens of Chowan County. When you meet to discuss our serious grievances with the Crown and the intolerable acts, we hope you will speak out for independence from Britain. We are united in believing this is the best and only answer to our current woes." Joseph listened intently, nodding as Stephen voiced his concerns. He then stepped toward an open window and for some moments gazed outward as if composing his response.

"You are not alone in your views. Yet others are eager to preserve our union with King George and I hear their loud voices as well. I intend to keep an open mind in Philadelphia if I should win such a high office. But I will be honest with you, Stephen, while we must correct some of the most egregious of the offenses we are experiencing, I do not believe it is in our best interests to sever all ties and fight a war for independence. We may end up losing more than we might gain." It was now Stephen's turn to listen and he did so with respect, even though he wanted to interrupt and argue with the civic leader.

"Many of us in Hyde are ready to form a militia and I can promise you if it should eventually come to war, we will be ready to help. You can count on us."

"And I promise you, Stephen, if that be the resolved will of the people, I will not stand in the way but will give my every ship to the cause." He stepped back toward Stephen and extended his hand once more.

"Then I will sail with you for freedom and for the new union. I pledge my word. Thank you for taking time to visit with me, sir. We must be on our way." Stephen took his son's hand and started to turn toward the door.

"Please, call me Joseph, sir is much too formal. My advice to you, friend, is to cherish your wife and your children. As the Good Book says: 'Children are like arrows in a quiver, Happy is the man who has his quiver full.' Perhaps we will meet again. Trust me, Stephen, I will remember your promise and hold you to it. If we do go to battle against the British, we will need capable seamen and a navy to hold sway on the waters." Joseph made eye contact with the lad once more and leaned down toward him with a final word.

"Listen to your wise father, my boy."

"I will and I am ready to fight for freedom too." Joseph smiled at the boy's enthusiastic boast.

"Ah, the brave words of youth. Good bye Stephens, senior and junior. Be well and take care. God bless you both."

The boy strode from the Hewes office with swagger. While he didn't understand the implications of all that had been said, he had been included in the adult conversation and it left him feeling special. They were almost to the wharf when Stephen's father detoured to a tavern to secure some victuals for supper. "Wait here, son, I shouldn't be too long."

The boy found a convenient spot to sit down and surveyed the waterfront. Slaves were hard at work loading and unloading goods. Businessmen were busy about their errands and dealings. Stephen spotted three boys about his age moving in his direction. They in turn spied him continued toward him.

"You are new to our town. Where are you from?" The tallest of the three initiated the conversation as he drew close, closer than Stephen liked.

"South, from Hyde County; my father sailed here on business." Stephen wanted to push the taller boy back to a more comfortable distance but thought it best not to do so.

"And what is your business, stranger?"

"My father was pledging to fight for freedom against the British."

"So are you one of those sons of liberty, a patriot?" The bully pushed Stephen to the ground as he continued to invade his space. The other two boys laughed in response, mocking the would-be patriot. The ringleader took a British Shilling from his pocket and pointed to King George's face. He kissed the likeness on the coin. "This is your King, kiss the king you rebel." He shoved the shilling into Stephen's face, laughed along with his cohorts then put the coin back in his pocket. "Stay out of our way, boy." With his command pronounced, he turned to leave.

The three were some yards distant when Stephen found his voice, though a soft voice it was. "Bloody British." Almost as soon as the words had escaped his lips he knew he had made a serious mistake. He had first heard the curse on that traumatic Christmas day back on Cape Hatteras. He had been shocked then to hear his father swear so now he could hardly believe that he had spoken the same profanity.

All three were on him in a second; pummeling him with fists they struck him hard in the face. His nose began to bleed profusely and he hurt all over. As he curled into a protective ball on the ground he could feel their feet kicking at him too. The attack ended when a couple of adults on the street pulled the boys off of him and chased them down the street. The commotion was loud enough that Stephen's father came out of the tavern to see what was going on. His son was a sorry sight. While his father cared for his superficial wounds, the ten year old did his best to not cry. He didn't want to add embarrassment to his pained face. He briefly explained what had happened, leaving out the triggering words that had incited the brutality.

"Bullies! They ought to at least pick a fair fight, three on one is not right." His father's words provided a bit of comfort as together they attempted to stem the flow of blood from his nose. "Looks like you are going to have a black eye too, son. Guess that will have to be your badge of courage for standing up for freedom rather than the king. I think it's time we head home."

As the *Hannah Marie* sailed around the north tip of Roanoke Island, all on board could see the British ships anchored just off shore. Dories were being used to transport provisions to shore. The beach was busy with human activity as a large group of men ferried supplies up into the brush. "I had heard rumors that the British were planning to build fortifications near or on the site of old Fort Raleigh. It appears the rumors are true. I think it best that we not go ashore and explore the old fort sight on this trip, maybe on a future trip, my lad."

The youngster was disappointed as he was looking forward to poking around to see what remained from the English settlement of 1587. On the other hand he was not interested in running into any more British sympathizing bullies and he was eager to see his mother, even if his black eye was going to require some explanation.

His mother's first response was more a gasp than recognizable words. Calmed a bit, she pressed for details. "My dear, what happened to you?" Stephen had replayed this scenario over and over in his mind all the way from Edenton harbor. Still he was at a momentary loss for words. His planned script slipped from his memory as he stood before his flesh and blood mother.

"I...I...I," he stuttered, trying to speak.

"He ran into the pilot's wheel on the *Hannah*, got himself quite a shiner there. He'll be healed up shortly. Brave lad, why you should have seen him manning the wheel and turning the ship to catch the wind. You would have been proud of him."

"I am proud of him," she said. After she gave him a hug she turned to go in the house. Stephen shot a glance toward his father who shot him a wink as he followed his wife inside.

News was slow to reach the rural residents of coastal North Carolina. Stephen's father had sailed to New Bern in early November and while there had heard the latest events that had transpired. He returned home with the latest edition of the *North Carolina Gazette* and soon after gathered friends and relatives at the Brooks' home to share the contents and discuss implications. Young Stephen and all of his siblings were also present to hear the important news.

The lead article focused on the first gathering of the Continental Congress which had convened in Philadelphia in early September. Joseph Hewes had been one of North Carolina's delegates, as expected, and all present were grateful that Stephen had had the opportunity to express their position to him when in Edenton earlier that summer.

He spoke loudly so all could hear. "It says here that the Congress issued a Declaration of Rights. The Declaration affirmed we will remain loyal to the British Crown at this time but we do dispute their right to tax us. Articles of Association were passed calling on the colonies to cease importing goods from the British Isles starting December 1st if the Intolerable Acts are not repealed by that time. If our grievances are not resolved quickly the Congress has stated they will meet again May 10th, 1775. In addition, the colonies will cease to export goods starting in September of 1775 if our demands are not met. The Congress disbanded October 26th." Stephen completed his summary and laid the tabloid on the table.

"I would have wished for more backbone on their part," Papa Jacob responded, leaning forward in his chair.

"Politicians are politicians," O'Reilly chimed in. "Always hedging their bets and playing it safe," he added. Uncle Thomas, who had stepped over to the table to rescan the *Gazette,* spoke next.

"Perhaps it is the best we could have hoped for at this time. Seems to me they have taken a pretty clear and strong stand regarding issues of taxation and those awful coercive acts passed by the British Parliament after the Boston Tea Party. The next move is up to the King. Make changes or escalate the conflict."

"I agree, brother. We should know in a month or so whether the crown is willing to negotiate or whether they will take a hard line," Stephen interjected as he set his tankard down on the table.

William Gibbs, a well-respected neighbor, stood to speak. "I think the critical date is next May when the Congress reconvenes. I personally expect little to change before that deadline. Is there any other important news Stephen?"

"There is one very important local item. We have had our own tea party here in North Carolina. October 25th fifty-one ladies gathered in Edenton and added their signatures to a circular sent to the King. They will boycott British tea and other imports, and this is a quote: 'until such time that all acts which tend to enslave our Native country shall be repealed.' I heartedly admire the courage of these women.

When I was in Edenton I met their leader, Penelope Barker. She told me briefly of their plan and that they would not hide their identity but speak out loudly and openly, whatever it might cost them."

"I propose a toast to these fine women," Papa Jacob said, hoisting his tankard.

"To the brave women of Edenton!" they all affirmed as they clashed their pewter drinking vessels together.

Stephen would never forget his father's excited voice as he barged through the front door in early May of 1775. Word was traveling quickly down the postal road to the west. Shots had been fired just after dawn the morning of April 19th at a standoff between British forces and Patriot Minutemen on the Lexington Bridge in Massachusetts Bay Colony. The battle had continued later the same day in the town of Concord.

"It has begun," he exclaimed, trying to catch his breath. "It has begun!"

Chapter 12

HARD DECISIONS

The war is inevitable—and let it come! I repeat it, sir, let it come! It is in vain, sir, to extenuate the matter. Gentlemen may cry peace, peace—but there is no peace. The war is actually begun! The next gale that sweeps from the North will bring to our ears the clash of resounding arms! Our brethren are already in the field! Why stand we here idle? What is it that gentlemen wish? What would they have? Is life so dear, or peace so sweet, as to be purchased at the price of chains and slavery? Forbid it, Almighty God! I know not what course others may take; but as for me, give me liberty, or give me death!

Papa Farrow folded the paper he had been reading from and tucked it back into his breeches pocket. It was so quiet in the Brooks home, where family and friends had gathered to hear the latest news, that you could hear the proverbial pin drop. "Patrick Henry delivered those words to the Virginia Convention in March. They have been heard in public places and read in private homes up and down the colonies ever since as a call to arms. Stirring words they are and deserving of a hearty amen, I think." Before Jacob Farrow could sit down the room reverberated with the requested 'amens.'

In the months that followed the echoes of those first shots in Lexington, the residents of rural Hyde County, North Carolina, hungered for any news that might connect them to what at first was a distant conflict. They learned that patriot forces had laid siege to Boston, blocking any British access by land. The Continental Congress had reconvened in May and in early June the well-respected George Washington of Mt. Vernon, Virginia, had been appointed General of the Continental Army. He assumed leadership of the ragtag collection of fighting men following the horrific bloody battle of Breed's Hill and Bunker Hill near Boston. The British had eked out a costly victory. Even in defeat, the patriots had gained a strong sense of resolve and confidence in their abilities to stand against the better armed and trained British troops.

While the patriotic rhetoric of Henry and the progress reports of military actions had been warmly applauded in the Brooks' home, others in Hyde County and countless thousands across the colonies had differing reactions. Henry had spoken about the unconquerable will of some 3 million colonists but in reality the numbers were closer to about one million patriots eager to fight, one million loyalists pledging their lot with England and one million trying to remain neutral so they could align themselves with whoever won out in the end.

Such numbers might be the stuff of academic debate on the national stage but in a rural, usually close knit community, the percentages were often vividly and painfully evident, causing rifts between neighbors and even rending familial ties. One could accurately say that the war with Great Britain was also an American civil war.

"I hear that some of the Scottish near Woodstock are speaking out against the war and are attempting to rally others to their Loyalist views." Uncle Thomas' words pulled young Stephen back from his daydreaming ventures. But the next words spoken conjured up stronger images.

"I say we tar and feather them and drive them from the county." His older brother Isaac's strong invective drew some nods from around the room.

"I would hope we can win them to our side without such barbarism." Stephen's father tried to unsuccessfully quiet the emotional fervor all could sense. Farrow spoke next, attempting to keep the discussion going in the more positive direction that his son-in-law had introduced.

"It will be impossible to persuade some. I think we should try to concentrate our efforts on the many who are hugging tightly to the top rail of the fence of indifference and apathy, like the Squires family up by the lake." Stephen squirmed when he heard his papa mention the family name of his good pal, Wolf. Wolf, Gator and Bear had already mimicked the battle at Concord in their play but were ignorant of the larger political issues swirling about the colonies. None of them realized at that time that the travails of freedom might impact their friendship.

"I can understand why local Indians might be undecided. They have not received much positive treatment at either the hands of the British or the colonists. Perhaps Squires feels it better serves their interests to wait and see what happens. If they side with the patriots and the cause is lost they will undoubtedly suffer. But, if they align themselves with the British and we win the day, they will feel harsh repercussions. It's a no win situation." Stephen's father stroked his beard as he finished his comment.

"I suggest we issue an open invitation to all able-bodied men to join the local militia and see what choices folks make. That may give us a better sense of who are our friends and who might be our enemies." Uncle Thomas' words met with approval and they all turned from business to the supper Mary and Phoebe had prepared.

The boys met up at their usual rendezvous spot, the offering stump, on a perfect August Sunday morning. Turkey hunting was on their minds and each lad took some practice shots with their handcrafted bows and arrows. Gator and Bear were now much more proficient at shooting than they had been when Wolf first tried to teach them the skill and managed to hit their targets with some consistency.

"This here dried turkey wing bone will help us call the turkeys close." Wolf took the hollow bone from his pocket and sucked on it, making a soft yelping sound. "See, sounds just like a hen turkey. Works best in the spring when gobblers are in the mating mood and searching for hens. But we might still lure a lonely one to us, hoping to join up with the flock."

"To the hunt!" Gator said raising his bow in the air. The other two boys extended their bows as well and off they went in pursuit of the beautifully plumaged fowl. They all took their turns making wing bone yelps with great enthusiasm. But no birds answered their pleas. Growing tired of the hunt they plopped down in the shade of a cottonwood tree and munched on some venison jerky that Wolf had brought along. Their usual childlike chatter turned suddenly serious when Gator asked:

"Wolf, is your father going to fight with us against the British?" The question caught his friend a bit off guard and he continued to chew on the jerky for some minutes before answering.

"I don't know. He's talking about moving southwest to Robeson County to be closer to some of our relatives. He's not sure we will be safe here, outnumbered and disliked by both sides."

"You are not going to leave, are you?" Both Gator and Bear asked, almost in unison.

"I don't want to, but if he decides to go, I will have to. I can't live here on my own."

"You could live off the land, hunting, fishing and trapping. We could bring you food too." Bear tried to sound persuasive. Gator, on the other hand, grew quiet as he contemplated what life in the marsh would be like without his friend. Finally he broke the uncomfortable silence.

"Everything will be fine. He will choose to stay. I just know it." There was emotion in his voice and he brushed his hand at the first hint of a tear in his eye as he sought to deny the dread he was beginning to feel in the pit of his stomach.

"My father says that some slaves are siding with the British. They have been promised their freedom if they run away and take up arms against former masters and rebels." Bear thought a change of topic might be the best way to deal with Wolf's unsettling news. But he soon realized his disclosure was only adding fuel to the fire and so he quickly amended his words. "Of course, we won't run away. We like

Master Brooks, he is good to us."

At this point Gator was wishing he had never introduced the topic and that they could just go back to roaming the woods looking for lonely turkeys. "Let's get back to hunting. Wolf, can I try that wing bone call again?" All were only too eager to exchange the awkwardness of their lunch conversation with another quest in the woods.

Their search led them past the northwest corner of Papa Farrow's large garden. That's when Gator spotted his quarry. He motioned to the other two to stay put and he began crawling on his belly. He stretched out the bow and single arrow ahead of him and quietly inched his way toward a bush at the edge of the garden. The bush would provide concealment so he could draw his bow and fire in one fluid movement without being detected. His stealth proved successful and he rose to one knee and sped his arrow on its way. It hit the target dead center with a resounding thump and the boys hiding behind him cheered at his success. Together they walked to the pierced prize.

"Great shot, Gator," Wolf said, slapping him on the back.

"I hope my grandfather thinks so," Gator blushed a bit as he pulled his arrow free from the large squash. They all laughed.

It was late in the afternoon when they headed toward the Farrow place to see if Grammy had any fresh tasty pastries. Papa saw them approaching and stood from his rocker on the front porch, a serious scowl spread across his face. "Been hunting have you?" Before they could answer he hoisted the large arrow wounded squash from the table. "Lads, we generally pick the squash rather than trying to kill them."

"I am so sorry Papa. It was my idea and my arrow." Papa Farrow could maintain his composure no longer and the scowl changed to a smile and a hearty guffaw. Even Grammy joined in the cacophony.

"Well I have to say, you sure did get it in the vitals," he chuckled. Relieved by the gracious response of his dear grandparents, Stephen pledged his word that no future vegetable would ever suffer such a fate. Grammy brought out some fresh tarts and they feasted on the treats.

"Tom, would you pass on to your father that there will be a militia meeting at the Brooks' house a fortnight from this Friday. He is surely invited to attend." Jacob made eye contact with Wolf to make sure he had heard the invitation and then took another bite of strawberry tart.

"I will tell him, sir.." Gator and Bear shot sideways glances toward each other as Wolf promised to pass on the word to his father.

The cyclone hit the North Carolina coast with fury the last couple days of August and continued into early September. It would long be remembered as the great Independence Hurricane of 1775. Some saw it as a positive omen concerning the war with Great Britain and indeed many British ships were impaired or lost in the ravages of the surging seas and strong winds.

But the storm couldn't have struck at a worse time for the farmers of coastal North Carolina. The corn was almost ready to harvest and now was a total loss. The Brooks family was not spared in the disaster. Flooding caused damage to buildings and livestock and they too saw their precious corn crop destroyed. The *Hannah Marie*, by good luck or a stroke of providence survived the storm, though it would take weeks to repair rigging. Nearly two hundred residents of North Carolina lost their lives and many small rural communities wrestled not only with physical devastation but with the much heavier weight of deep grief.

Stephen moved close to the edge of the loft so he could hear the men talking below. He recognized the Gibbs brothers, members of the Harris family, and some of Grammy's Swindell relatives. Others he did not know by name. He had learned that Wolf's father had not been present at the earlier meeting and had turned down other requests to sign-up for militia service. The Hyde County Militia officially had formed on September 9th just a week after the devastating storm. This was a smaller follow-up gathering to discuss plans and organization and bring everyone up to date on current developments.

The Second Continental Congress had sent a final olive branch proposal to King George in July. He had refused to even read the petition and the British Parliament took action in August to label the rebellious colonists as traitors to the crown. The King had also secured the services of Hessian mercenaries who were now on their way to reinforce British troops. The conflict was escalating rapidly.

"Getting supplies to patriot supporters on the Outer Banks will be a critical issue." Stephen recognized the speaker as the oldest of the Gibbs brothers. Many of the men nodded in assent to his words.

"I pledge my services and commit the *Hannah Marie* to the cause. She is a fast clipper and should be able to outrun and outmaneuver British warships and other privateers sailing here. My sons can man the vessel with me." Stephen was proud of his father's willingness to risk his life and ship for the war effort. He also hoped he might be included among the crew, even if he was the youngest male in the family.

"Have any of you talked recently with Caleb Smith? I can't imagine the horrific grief he must be enduring. He and Sarah tried to have children for the longest time and then to see your wife and infant son yanked from your grasp by the cruel storm surge of a cyclone, it must be unbearable." Stephen was arrested from his thoughts of sailing in naval conflict by the sad words of his Papa. He had heard his parents talking about those who lost loved ones in the storm but until that moment had not learned the fate of the Smith's.

"I saw him on the post road headed north. Said he had closed up his cabin and was going to Philadelphia to meet up with some relatives. Just too hard to stay here after what happened. Didn't even bother trying to sell his parcel, took it as another loss." As Uncle Thomas spoke he seemed to almost bow under a heavy load like the burden of the loss was on his own shoulders. For some time all of the men sat in mournful silence.

"I hear tell the Continental Congress is going to help out each farmer who lost their corn in the Independence Storm. Forty shillings for seed for next year should keep lots of families from giving up and leaving." It was William Swindell who finally broke the dreadful stillness in the room with a shift in topic.

Stephen was heartened to hear this good news. He remembered well the look on his father's face after surveying what remained of their expected harvest. Broken and uprooted corn stalks were scattered about. Some of the corn had probably blown all the way to the next county. In response to the economic disaster he had hurried upstairs and returned with his cherished coin box. Maybe his savings could help the family. His father had only smiled and reassuringly promised all would be well. His gift, though appreciated greatly, would not be needed.

The men inventoried their weapons and ammunition in case they might be called upon to fight and organized themselves by rank, appointing leaders. Stephen's father would serve as a private. After toasts of rum, the men headed to their homes and families.

It was a damp and blustery December morn and Stephen was dashing about completing his chores and trying to dodge rain squalls when he barely heard the sound above the gusts of wind. He wasn't sure at first but during a lull in the wind he clearly detected the familiar howl of his good friend, Wolf. The sound came from the direction of the stump and was the usual signal for meeting up. His chores finished he headed that way. Wolf was nowhere in sight.

As he came close to the old stump offering place where their friendship had first been initiated through a gift exchange, he saw two items. He picked up the turkey wing bone call. It was the same one they had unsuccessfully used earlier that fall, the day of the great squash shoot. Next he fingered the well-worn silver coin bearing the 1580 date that he had seen when visiting Wolf's grandfather. The coin that bridged the years all the way back to the very first English settlers who had traveled to the New World and had disappeared into the mists of time from old Fort Raleigh on Roanoke Island.

The nearly twelve year old sat on the stump and examined the bone and the coin carefully. Each gift triggered special memories. The message was also too clear. Wolf was gone. He wondered if he would ever see him again. He focused on the turkey call and smiled. He would call in that gobbler next spring and his arrow would fly as true as the one that had skewered the big squash in Papa's garden.

Shifting his attention to the coin he sobbed. Though it was a far-fetched idea he recalled the old man's story about the mixing of Indian and white blood and for the moment wanted to believe that he and his friend could truly be blood brothers. The rain pelted the spot, washing the tears from the boy's cheeks but not removing the cherished images from his mind. Suddenly the rain and wind stopped and a shaft of sunlight broke through the dark clouds. In the surprising stillness, Stephen thought for sure he heard the cry of Wolf in the distance. "Goodbye Wolf, I will always remember you."

Chapter 13

HALIFAX OR BUST

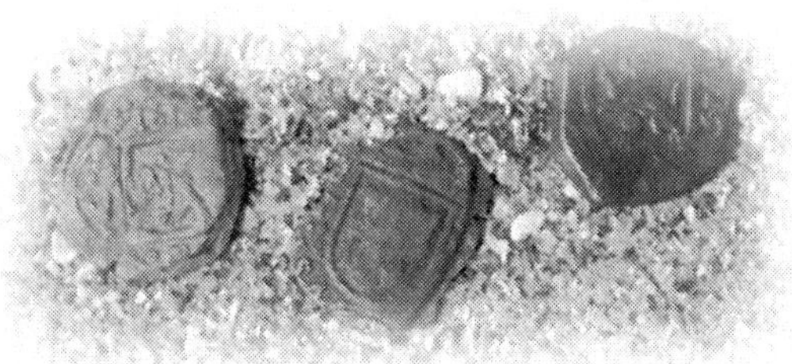

It was warm for early March and beads of sweat ran down his face as Stephen swung the axe with all the strength his twelve year old muscles could muster. He hit the piece of firewood directly in the middle splitting it in half. He placed one of the smaller pieces upright on the block and was about to deliver another blow when he heard and saw the approaching men on horseback. He stopped his kindling making chores, placed one foot up on the chopping block, leaned on the axe handle and watched as the men brought their horses to a halt near the Brooks home. His mother was out the door to greet them before the dust had even settled. He recognized three of the men immediately. The one talking to his mother was Rotheas Latham, Captain of the Hyde County Militia. Thomas Hancock and John Jordan were also county officials. Stephen didn't know who the fourth man was. From his distant observation post he was unable to hear what they were discussing.

"Stephen," his mother called, waving to gain his attention. Casting the axe aside, he sprinted to the porch. "Take these men to the dock area to meet your father. They have important business to discuss. He should be about finished with his day's work on the *Hannah Marie* and headed to shore soon."

"Yes, mother." The men tied their horses to the hitching post and looked in Stephen's direction. "Follow me." As they approached the landing, Stephen spotted his father and Jupiter rowing up the channel. Their timing was perfect. The lad helped secure the dory to the dock and then slipped back a short distance. He wanted to be close enough to make out their conversation but not so close as to arouse attention to himself. His father sent Jupiter to the house and shook hands with the men as he spoke words of greeting.

"It is good to see you Rotheas, Thomas and John. What brings you my way?" Stephen smiled and nodded as he acknowledged his friends.

"Stephen, I want you to meet Thomas Respis from Bath. He is a delegate from Beaufort County to the upcoming fourth Provincial Congress set to meet in April in Halifax." Rotheas took the lead again in speaking as he introduced the fourth man, the one young Stephen had not recognized earlier.

"We have just received word that our forces were successful in routing Loyalist insurgents at Moore's Creek Bridge near Wilmington. In addition to prisoners of war, a large quantity of guns, supplies and Spanish gold are now in patriot hands. We believe the tide has turned here in North Carolina and there is talk that resolutions will be passed in Halifax calling for all colonies to declare total independence from the crown. When our protests started in reaction to the hard hand of King George, I assumed we would achieve some measure of compromise and then things would return to normal and our allegiance to the British would be reaffirmed. But now we have passed the point of no return." Rotheas paused for a moment giving Hancock an opportunity to interrupt.

"Yes, things are escalating. Norfolk is a pile of burning rubble, following the fighting their between patriots and Dunsmore's Tory cronies. Victory may be some time in coming but it is within our grasp." As if they had prepared their script with care, Hancock paused, giving Jordan the opportunity to speak next.

"Stephen, we have come to ask your help. Can we secure your services to sail us to Edenton? And once there, can you then secure the right craft to take us up the Roanoke River to Halifax in time for our April meeting? We had planned to sail on Respis' schooner but it is not seaworthy." The lad, noticing his father's familiar gesture of stroking his beard, knew an answer was forthcoming. He leaned closer, not wanting to miss a word of his father's response to this proposed grand adventure.

"You have come at a good time. We have just finished repairs on the *Hannah.* I have contacts in Edenton and can make the needed arrangements. We will need to sail by March 15th. The upriver trek will take some time and I wouldn't want you to be late to cast your vote for independence." The boy watched as the men responded to his father's willing commitment with back-slapping, laughter and cheers. Meanwhile he began planning his own appeal to join the expedition.

The Brooks home was dark and quiet and his siblings were fast asleep. Stephen inched ever closer to the edge of the loft, hoping he could hear his parents talking. They were sitting near the fire, talking about the events of the day and the proposed trip to Halifax. "My best estimation is that we will be gone about a month. I plan to take Jupiter along. He might be tempted to run away with his family if left here with the women folk. Besides I can use his help, especially rowing up the Roanoke. William and Jacob will stay here with you and the girls. I will talk to your folks about checking in on you regularly while we are gone." Mary listened to her husband's words carefully, pondering the implications of his lengthy absence.

"I can understand your taking Isaac but what about Stephen, he is only twelve and you may encounter danger." The boy was familiar with her protectiveness and expected she would resist his going along.

"Mary, my dear, Stephen is the only one of our sons who has shown both the interest and skills necessary to one day become a captain of his own ship. I believe this trip will be very valuable training. Besides, if not for our resources, he would already be apprenticed by this age and out of our home. I will keep a close eye on him. Trust me." The lad in the loft sighed in relief and mouthed his delight with a silent 'yes!'

"I will pray for each of you daily, that is my pledge. Bring both of our boys home safely."

"I promise." Stephen reached out and embraced Mary as she cried.

Preparations for the journey began in earnest the very next day. Supplies needed to be secured and loaded on the *Hannah*. Farm business needed to be transacted and contingency plans arranged if the trip ran even longer than expected. Then, the part young Stephen liked best, learning how to load and fire the old family musket. His father started the instruction with words that only heightened his excitement for the trip.

"We may have to take up arms at some point to protect ourselves and I want you to know how to handle this weapon correctly." His father showed him how to measure and load the powder charge, and ram home the patch with lead ball. He then took the powder horn with a finer grained powder and placed some on the pan and closed the frizzen. "She's loaded and ready to fire. Aim down the barrel, take a deep breath, release it and pull the trigger. With the flash of powder expect a recoil on your shoulder as the load ignites and the ball is sent on its way." Stephen took the heavy firearm from his father and took bead on the target some 30 yards away. Boom! The boy was a rocked by the recoil but held his stance. When the smoke cleared he could see he had hit the outside edge of the target. "Good shot, boy, you appear to be a natural." Stephen continued to practice loading and shooting with continued success. The accuracy of his shots helped to alleviate the growing pain in his shoulder. "Enough for today." His father took the flintlock and together they headed back to the house. Mary had been watching from the porch. While she understood the reasons for the shooting lesson somehow each blast of the rifle only sent chills through her frame.

Hancock, Jordan and Respis arrived the evening before their scheduled departure day. Latham had family business come up and planned to travel to Halifax by overland route as soon as he was able. The farewells were tearful, for Mary and Phoebe that is. Stephen and his sons were much more stoical in their goodbyes. Jupiter was more emotional and shed some tears with his wife and daughter. Captain Brooks had decided to also take Able along. Gator and Bear had been able to spend little time together since Wolf had left, so both boys looked forward to the new adventure.

With favorable winds and no privateers sighted, the sail up Pamlico Sound was uneventful. As they turned toward the west on Albemarle Sound, Isaac spotted a sail to the east off of Roanoke Island. The ship appeared to be coming in their direction. The crew hoisted additional sails and were able to speed out of sight of the possible threat. All were relieved by the skill of their captain and the quickness of their schooner. Respis was especially impressed and commented that his schooner would never have been able to outpace the other ship.

The following morning they moored the *Hannah Marie* at the Edenton docks area and went ashore to make arrangements for the next leg of their trip. Stephen's father had been up the Roanoke River to Halifax on two previous occasions, transporting goods from Edenton upriver and then returning with a full cargo of exports from Halifax, destined for Edenton and beyond. The river carried a fairly steady flow of commerce between the towns. The bateau, a French boat first used by fur traders, was the perfect craft for hauling both heavy loads of goods and a numbers of passengers. Bateaux varied in length from 25 to 50 feet and were pointed at both ends. Their shallow draft and flat bottom design matched up well with both upstream and downstream navigation needs. If conditions were right a sail could even be hoisted, but usually strong arms and oars provided power, though in shallow water poling was the preferred method. Stephen was able to obtain the craft they needed through the Hewes Shipping Company in Edenton. He was also able to moor the *Hannah* at the Hewes dock for the duration of their trek up the Roanoke and back. Both Stephens had hoped to see Joseph Hewes again but he was away in Philadelphia, representing the province at the Continental Congress.

Jupiter, Able, Isaac and young Stephen finished transporting supplies and gear from the Hannah to their bateau that evening and early the next morning they cast off lines and rowed free of the Edenton harbor area. Fortunately they were able to take advantage of some prevailing winds and raised their single sail to speed progress across Albemarle Sound to the southwest and the mouth of the Roanoke. Paired with Able, Stephen tried his hand at the oars and it didn't take him long to fall into the rhythm and match strokes with the other rowers. "We'll find the rowing a bit more of a challenge when we encounter river currents lads." Thomas Respis, seated in front of the friends offered his advice and seemed to enjoy interacting with the two youngest crew members. He, Hancock and Jordan also took turns at the oars.

The delta area of the Roanoke offered multiple channels of navigation and some tempting dead ends. Stephen's father, familiar with the best route, was able to avoid the pitfalls and guide the craft on the most direct route. The broad expanses of flooded timber provided few options when it came to stopping sites. Finally they spotted a spit of higher ground and pulled ashore to make camp for the night. Bear and Gator were tasked with finding firewood.

"Watch out for snakes," Isaac warned as the boys headed for higher ground. A few late migrating pure white Tundra Swans made their familiar whistling sound as they flew north. The boys stopped to enjoy the melodic tune made by the bird's wings and take in the swampy scenery. The terrain was similar to their haunts back home and before long their foraging efforts produced a good supply of wood for the fire with thankfully no snakes encountered.

Jupiter broke out his fiddle later that evening as the men gathered around the fire. During a lull in the music all were startled by what sounded like a woman's high pitched scream. "Sounds like that painter doesn't care for your music, Jupiter," Respis laughed and took a draw on his pipe, blowing out a small cloud of smoke. The others joined in some good natured ribbing of the slave, whose eyes had opened wide in fear at the sound emanating from the darkness far beyond the circle of fire.

"What's a painter?" Bear nudged Gator, alarmed too by the eerie cry.

"Some call them panthers, others painters. They are big catlike creatures that prowl about in the dark looking for children to eat." Now Gator took his turn chuckling in response to Bear's obvious discomfort at his explanation. "Don't worry, they don't like the fire," Stephen replied. But another scream left both of them grateful that they were not camping alone.

As the river narrowed they began to face the more arduous challenge of rowing against the slow current. The evening campfire entertainment also varied. The night they spent near an old deserted Tuscarora Indian village was marked by vivid ghost stories. The men tried to best one another with each new tale. While the older adults seemed to enjoy the storytelling, both Gator and Bear found themselves startled by various sounds in the dark as they tried unsuccessfully to fall asleep.

But it was the events of the fifth night out that would etch the strongest memory in the minds of the two friends. It started with the now routine gathering of firewood. They were on their way back to camp when two men stepped out from behind a large tree, taking them completely by surprise. They dropped the wood in alarm and backed away.

"Stop boys, we mean you no harm." The speaker had a patch over one eye and a number of scars adorned his face. Both boys could smell the stench of his breath as he spoke and his toothless grin did not assuage their fears.

"Why look here, a nigger!" The second man seemed particularly interested in Bear, as he grabbed his shoulder and peered close into his frightened face. He was younger than the other man but no less imposing. Both carried pistols, muskets and knives. "You a runaway, boy?"

"No, no sir, my master, father, and some other men are camped nearby."

"Why I guess you all will have company for supper tonight. Show us the way." The man stepped back releasing his hold on Bear's shoulder. As they made their way to camp, the two strangers lagged behind. They were engaged in conversation but neither of the boys could make out what they were saying.

The two bizarre travelers were not exactly welcomed upon their arrival at camp, but they were offered food and they clearly planned to stay the night around the fire. Their presence created a sense of uneasiness in the group. They claimed to be trappers but most doubted everything they said.

It was still dark when Gator was awakened by a muffled groan. He opened his eyes but didn't move. The full moon provided a measure of light and as his eyes adjusted to the darkness he could see the two strangers kneeling over Bear. The one with the patch held his hand tightly over his friend's mouth. The knife in his other hand was held against Bear's throat. He could just make out their whispers.

"This boy will bring us good money," the younger one said.

"If you make a sound I'll slice your throat clear through," countered the toothless one. Let's get out of here quick," he continued. The men rose with Bear securely in their grasp. Stephen's heart was almost beating through his chest as he watched in horror. His mind raced. Should he run and try to find the musket? He thought it was leaning against a tree on the far side of the clearing. Instead he screamed as loud as he could.

"No! Stop!"

"Drop the knife and don't take another step or I will shoot." The words were those of his father. Relief swept over the traumatized youth. The others, now awake, stirred the smoldering fire back to flame as they tied up the prisoners. Jupiter, fearing what might have been, embraced his trembling son with tears of gratitude streaming down his face.

The morning sun brought better fortunes than the night. While they were trying to decide what to do with the two, they were hailed by the occupants of two bateaux headed downstream. The traders poled their craft to shore and took in the story. When Thomas Respis offered the men a monetary reward, they agreed to transport the prisoners downstream to Edenton where they could be properly tried and sentenced.

"Thank you for your help in this matter. These ruffians are certainly not worth the trouble of being rowed upstream to Halifax." Captain Brooks' words clearly captured the sentiment of the others. Later they all gathered on the beach to wave in appreciation as the trade flotilla took their dreaded prisoners out of sight around the bend.

Before they broke camp all learned the details of what had happened. Stephen was sure the strangers were up to no good and had taken up a watch position at the edge of camp, his loaded musket across his lap. He had dozed off to sleep, only to be roused by his son's cry for help at just the right moment to prevent the planned kidnapping. As the boys rowed hard that day they occasionally made eye contact and smiled. Their friendship had taken a new turn in light of the aborted abduction. They would fondly recall the event and embellish the story in the years ahead.

When they set up camp that evening, Captain Brooks announced the good news. "Tomorrow we should reach Halifax."

"With a few days to spare before the Congress commences," Hancock jokingly saluted the Captain.

"You have led us well, Stephen, we are all in your debt." Jordan's words captured the feelings of the group and all heartily agreed.

"Lad, could you fetch me a bit more coffee?" Respis

asked. Stephen lifted the pot with care from the embers and poured the brew into Thomas's cup. Coffee had become the favorite beverage of patriots ever since the Boston tea party. "Merci beaucoup," seeing the puzzled look on the lad's face he added, "That is French for 'Thank you very much'. My forbears came to America from France in search of religious freedom. I am afraid you have just learned the extent of my French, however." He chuckled as he took a sip of the hot liquid.

"Many think our French allies will play a decisive role in our conflict with Britain. What do you say Thomas?" Isaac posed his question and then took his own swig of the black brew.

"Oui, yes, now you know all my French, I think you are right Isaac. France will divide the Crown's attention in Europe which should help us here. Already we are receiving critical supplies from Paris. We will need all the help we can get abroad and at home."

Later as the men set around the campfire, young Stephen secured a spot next to the Frenchman from Bath. He had some questions on his mind. "I hope to sail to France someday in my own ship. What is it like?"

"Ah, I wish I could go with you. I have never seen the birthplace of my forebears. It was my great grandfather who traveled here many years ago and he brought little with him to remind him of the persecution and pain he had endured there."

"Why did he come here?"

"It was the same quest that brings us to Halifax, my boy, a hunger for freedom, to be able to express our ideas without government intrusion, to worship in our own way, to move about and own land and realize our dreams; it is the desire of every human heart to be free."

There was a party atmosphere around the glowing fire. Jupiter played his fiddle, the men sang tunes and Hancock and Jordan danced a jig of celebration. As things quieted down, Thomas Respis beckoned to young Stephen from across the circle.

"I want to show you something from France." He took out his coin purse and looked through it until he found what he was looking for. "This is a French Liard, hardly worth a penny, I wanted to show you this symbol on the coin. It is called a Fleur-de-lis, or Lily flower. While French royalty have used this image on their crests for centuries, I would like to believe it better represents light, life and hope. Some even see it as a representation of the trinity: God the Father, Son Jesus, and the Holy Ghost. We are now in the winter of a hard war with England. I pray that like the Lily in the spring, victory will burst forth."

"Coins tell many stories. I found an old Spanish pirate cob on the beach with my grandfather years ago. Since then I have collected a few others. I love the history stamped in metal, from Scottish thistles to Irish harps. Thank you for showing me the lily too." Stephen handed the coin back to Thomas.

"Check your change, Stephen. You never know when you might find your own fleur-de-lis."

They reached Halifax the next afternoon. Repis, Hancock and Jordan gathered their baggage and checked in for the provincial congress. Stephen's father planned to stay for a week or so, hoping that the congress would complete its work quickly and he could take his three delegate friends back down the Roanoke to Edenton and home. The congress opened on the fourth of April. In a week they transacted their most noteworthy business. On April 12th, what would become known as the Halifax Resolves, was unanimously adopted by the eighty-three delegates. Jordan rushed to find Captain Brooks and share the momentous news. He found Stephen with his two sons and two slaves loading goods they would be hauling back to Edenton.

"We have done it. North Carolina will be first in independence." He took the paper and read: "Resolved that the delegates for this Colony in the Continental Congress be empowered to concur with the other delegates of the other Colonies in declaring Independency." This should be enough to move Joseph Hewes from the fence of neutrality in Philadelphia. I only wish Rotheas could have made it here in time to cast his vote."

"Good news indeed! Will you be completing your work soon and be ready to head home?" Captain Brooks asked.

"Unfortunately it appears we will stay in session for some time. I think it best you go back without us. We can make other arrangements to secure passage to Edenton when we are finished here."

"We will leave tomorrow then. Pass on my congratulations to Respis and Hancock."

The next morning all were present at the dock to say their goodbyes. They were just about to shove off when Respis summoned Stephen to his side. "Find any coins here about?"

"No, sir."

The Frenchman reached behind the boy's ear and

pulling his hand back said "What about his one?" He placed the French Liard in Stephen's hand, closing the lad's fingers around it. "Add this to your collection. Let the lily remind you often of life, liberty and faith in God and maybe you can say a prayer or two for our French allies as well. I hope to see you again; perhaps I can one day secure a ticket to sail with you to France."

"Merci beaucoup," Stephen, trying out the French phrase, bowed and smiled.

"You are very welcome. Bonjour, my young friend."

The current pulled the bateau slowly downstream; Stephen continued to look back waving a fond farewell.

Chapter 14

INDEPENDENCE

Within a week the ragtag adventurers were back home at Light Creek Marsh. The downstream float had taken about half the time of the hard row to Halifax and without any adverse circumstances to slow their progress they had quickly sailed from Edenton, across familiar waters, to anchorage at Wisockin Bay. Mary was overjoyed at their safe arrival and both Isaac, but especially the younger Stephen, had to contend with her motherly affection. Jupiter and Able also had much to share with Phoebe and Ima about their traumatic and harrowing brush with slave kidnappers. Stephen stashed his newly obtained French Liard in the pouch with the other coins and put the prized box of memory treasures back in its niche. All now turned their efforts to spring planting chores and the daily routine of farm life.

Meanwhile, the fourth provincial congress completed their work in Halifax. They forwarded their Resolve to the North Carolina delegates in Philadelphia: Joseph Hewes, William Hooper, and John Penn. Virginia had followed the lead of North Carolina and passed a similar resolution for independence in mid-May. News of the actions taken by the Continental Congress that first week of July, 1776 did not reach Hyde County until July 7th. Stephen would always have a vivid memory of where he was and what he was doing the first moment he heard of the Declaration. He had just finished feeding the chickens and was crossing from the coop to the barn when his father raced into the yard, dismounted and rushed inside. He immediately sensed something of importance had happened and he ran to the house. Standing in the open door way he heard his father's words.

"They did it! They did it! Congress has declared independence from Britain." He watched as his father swept his mother off her feet into a warm embrace.

At supper the details of the story unfolded. In early June the resolution had first been put forward to the delegates. Voting was postponed until July 1st and a committee began drafting the words of the Declaration. July 2nd the vote was taken and the resolution adopted. July 4th, Jefferson's edited Declaration of Independence was approved by the delegates and copies began to be circulated to the colonies. Interestingly, Joseph Hewes of Edenton had been one of the last two holdouts. Only the unanimous will of his constituents, made clearly known in the Halifax Resolves, had moved him to finally vote yes. Reportedly once convinced, he sat suddenly upright and lifting both hands to heaven as if he had been in a trance, cried out, 'It is done and I will abide by it.'

Stephen's father stood at the head of the family table and read the opening words of the Declaration of Independence. He had obtained a printed copy earlier that day at the Hyde

County courthouse.

> A Declaration by the Representatives of the UNITED STATES OF AMERICA, in General Congress assembled.
>
> WHEN in the Course of human Events it becomes necessary for one People to dissolve the Political Bands which have connected them with another, and to assume among the Powers of the Earth the separate & equal Station to which the Laws of Nature and of Nature's God entitle them, a decent Respect to the Opinions of Mankind requires that they should declare the causes which impel them to the Separation.
>
> WE hold these Truths to be self-evident: that all Men are created equal; that they are endowed by their creator with certain inalienable rights; that among these are life, liberty, & the pursuit of happiness: that to secure these rights, governments are instituted among men, deriving their just powers from the consent of the governed; that whenever any form of government becomes destructive of these ends, it is the right of the people to alter or abolish it, & to institute new government, laying it's foundation on such principles, & organizing it's powers in such form, as to them shall seem most likely to affect their safety & happiness.

He placed the paper down and looked around the table at his gathered loved ones. "The United States of America," he proudly mouthed the words again for emphasis. "No longer are we colonies under the thumb of a King and at the beckoning call of his every whim. We are separate and equal states, united together. God save the United States of America."

Stephen and his brother Jacob were bundling up the corn stalks following the fall harvest when their oldest brother Isaac walked out to meet them in the field. "You two want to have a little fun? Meet me back of the barn right after dinner."

"What do you have in mind, Isaac?" Stephen asked.

"Just be there, you'll find out."

Stephen and Jacob found Isaac hitching the horse to the wagon and jumped in the back at his bidding. "I told the folks you were going with me to take care of some business by the lake. You both have to promise me you will keep our evening activities a secret. Tell no one, especially Father and Mother." The idea of a mystery combined with a secret pledge was persuasive and the young lads nodded their consent. Two of Isaac's friends, John and James, were waiting for them at the junction of the road going to the lake.

"You got the stuff?" Isaac asked.

"Yep, help us load it," James ordered.

They retrieved a small barrel, hidden in the bushes, along with a couple of sacks filled with other items and placed them in the back of the wagon. "Why'd you bring the children, Isaac? Could get us in trouble don't you think?" John looked down at Stephen and Jacob with a look of disdain.

"Thought they'd enjoy our good sport, consider it proper training for future patriots. They'll keep our little secret. Let's get going." Isaac snapped the reins and the horse responded, jerking the wagon forward.

It was dark by the time they reached their destination. Stephen wasn't exactly sure where they were but thought they might be near the Anderson cabin west of Lake Mattamuskeet. Isaac and James struck a flame and lit a couple of torches stowed in one of the sacks. John grabbed a musket he had brought along. Stephen could now see that the other sack was filled with chicken feathers. When they pried the lid loose on the barrel he could see the tar. They placed the tar in a large cooking vessel and started warming it with their torches.

"Want it just the right temperature, warm and sticky but not bubbling hot, wouldn't want to burn these Tories too badly, just put the fear of God in them," Isaac said as his friends laughed. Stephen was wishing he had said no to the evening's activities, now that he knew what was about to unfold.

"Put these hoods over your heads," John distributed the hoods around the small circle of five. When the tar was at the right consistency they gathered up their horrific tools of pain and shame and headed in the direction of the cabin. Stephen and Jacob followed reluctantly behind.

"Joseph Anderson, you bloody Tory, come out and meet your fate or we will burn down your cabin." It was Isaac who shouted the challenge. Stephen shuddered at the rage in his brother's voice. Anderson slowly opened the door to face his inquisition. His wife and young daughter huddled behind him crying.

"I am not a Tory. I just want to be left alone," he pleaded.

"That's not what others say! Step forward, man. The

good and patriotic citizens of Hyde County find you guilty. Tell your womenfolk to go back inside and lock the door. We will not harm them. It is you we want to make an example of." Again the awful words were on the lips of his brother. Stephen wanted to run.

Isaac and his friends stripped the shirt off of Anderson and slopped on the warm and sticky tar. They smeared some on his face as well and then coated him with feathers. "Looks like we have a chicken Tory here," they laughed in derision. They tied him down to the seat on the wagon. Before heading out on their shameful parade, they started the Anderson shed on fire.

"There, I think we are done here." Isaac headed the wagon down the path. In the course of the next few hours they drove by a number of cabins, rousing the inhabitants from their homes and possible slumber to witness the spectacle of the supposed enemy of freedom, decked out in his feathered finery. Finally growing tired of the sport, they untied Anderson some distance from his cabin and pushed him off the wagon. He landed with a thud, the feathers hardly breaking his fall.

Isaac and his friends continued to engage in coarse banter as they traveled back toward the Brooks home. Once he had dropped off his accomplices, the rest of the ride was marked by steely silence. Just before they reached the barn, Isaac stopped the wagon and turned to his younger brothers. "How'd you enjoy the evening?" he asked with a grin.

"I wish I hadn't come," Stephen spoke first.

"Me neither, it was awful," Jacob added.

"Being a filthy Tory is awful. They need to be smoked out like rats. Now, regardless of how you liked the night's mission, keep your mouths shut." The grin on Isaac's face was now a sullen stare. Neither boy slept much that night.

Stephen could see his father was livid. He strode across the field toward them as if on a mission. Stephen wondered if he knew. "Stephen and Jacob go to the barn, your brother Isaac is waiting for us there."

Stephen ran various scenarios through his mind. Should he confess now? Lie and hope his brothers would continue to conceal the truth too? Blame Isaac? Blame Jacob? Blame Isaac's friends? None of the options seemed quite right. As they entered the barn both Jacob and Stephen made eye contact with Isaac, slightly shaking their heads as if to say: 'we didn't tell.'

"Isaac, look at me! Did you, with the help of your friends, tar and feather Joseph Anderson and burn down his shed? With God as your witness speak the truth!"

"He had it coming, father, he's a Tory."

"No one deserves such treatment, not even a Loyalist. Anderson is our neighbor. He deserves our respect until solid evidence proves the contrary. You acted on rumors, not court facts. You should be ashamed. On top of that you took along your young and impressionable brothers to witness your cruelty. I am so angry and so disappointed at your poor judgment."

"How'd you find out?"

"That hardly matters. You used our horse and wagon. Did you think hoods would disguise your identity? Every home you went by the folks there knew who you were. If you must accuse a man, accuse him to his face. Hoods are for cowards."

"But, Father," Isaac started to protest.

"There are no excuses here and no more easy forgiveness. You have brought shame and reproach to the family by your actions. I have tried to correct you so many times and you only continue to choose wrongly. I want you out of the house by sunset. You can spend the night on the *Hannah Marie*. Tomorrow I will take you to the cape and you can stay at our property near Brigands Bay. Perhaps the solitude will do you good. At least it will put some distance between you and your rum drinking pals. See if you can make something of yourself in the new surroundings. Lord knows you haven't done well here. Be sure to bid your mother goodbye when you leave the house. At least you have one faithful soul who will be praying for yours. Now go and be ready to sail at dawn."

With Isaac gone, the father turned his attention to Jacob and Stephen. "I hold your brother responsible for most of what happened. But, I hold you two responsible for not having the courage to walk away, for not refusing to participate once you knew what was happening. There is a powerful temptation to go along with the unruly mob rather than stand alone for right. I hope you have learned that painful lesson. What's more, you will be helping me rebuild Anderson's shed when I get back from the cape. Do you understand?"

"Father, is Mr. Anderson going to be alright?" Stephen's voice wavered with emotion as he expressed his concern.

"Fortunately the tar was not hot enough to burn him. His pride is injured most and the trauma experienced by his wife and daughter left real pain that will take some time to heal. Perhaps your heartfelt confession and plea for forgiveness can start that process. It's easy to build a shed, very hard indeed to rebuild trust when it has been shattered by fear and betrayal."

Jacob and Stephen finished loading the lumber and tools into the wagon. Their father had returned from Hatteras and they were headed to the Anderson farm with two clear objectives in mind. The easy one was constructing a new shed to replace the one Isaac and his friends had destroyed. The more anxious task was confessing their part in the tar and feathering and seeking forgiveness from all members of the Anderson household. As the wagon bumped its way along the road, Stephen replayed the words he planned to speak, trying to get them just right. He could only hope the Andersons would accept his expression of contrition as being sincere. The image of the small family silhouetted in the doorway of their cabin still lodged in the boy's mind. While the father bravely and defiantly responded to the accusations hurled at him, Mrs. Anderson had clung to her husband, sobbing. Their traumatized daughter's face was just visible as she peaked out from behind her mother's skirts. He could still see her look of absolute horror, a horror he had contributed to while safely hiding behind the anonymity of a hood.

When they arrived at the Anderson home, Jacob, as the older of the two, went inside to acknowledge his transgressions. Then it was Stephen's turn. Entering the small cabin, he bowed in respect before the father, mother and daughter. "Sir, I am very sorry for the pain we caused you and your family, I was wrong to have participated." Stephen spoke the words he had rehearsed.

"Lad, we hardly hold you responsible, why you must not be much older than our daughter, Grace. It was the older youth who led the assault with whom we find fault." Stephen was shocked by the kind response but continued.

"No, sir, I am responsible too. When our brother asked us to come along, his demand of secrecy held a warning I should have heeded. I knew his intentions, whatever he had planned, were not honorable or they could be spoken aloud. I should have stayed home at the start. When his friends joined up with us, I saw what they loaded in the wagon. The tar and feathers were visible. I should have excused myself and walked home then and there. But I didn't. I chose the poor path of secretly wishing to see what would unfold. When the hood was passed to me, I could have thrown it on the ground. As we drove you past your neighbors I could have remained silent, rather than cheer and ridicule you with the others. I am guilty and ask your pardon for my offenses, not those of my brother."

"And my pardon you have, Stephen. You have been more a man than the older youth you accompanied," Joseph smiled. Mrs. Anderson crossed the room and wiped away the tears streaming down Stephen's face.

"Now there, child, God forgives and we forgive," she said as she hugged him close.

Work on the shed provided a concrete way to display true neighborliness and Stephen and Jacob, under the supervision of their father, threw themselves into the labor with energy. Early in the afternoon, Grace brought them a pitcher of water and some type of bread treat. "Let's take a rest, boys," their father ordered.

Stephen took a pewter mug of water and sat down on a

nearby stump. Grace approached him with a tray of breads. "Would you like a scone? I made them myself." she asked extending the plate toward him.

"Yes, thank you." Stephen took one of the scones and took a big bite. "I've never had a scone before."

"My grandmother taught me how to make them. It is a Scottish family recipe. Do you like it?" She smiled as she spoke.

"Very much, thank you again for your kindnesses." Stephen blushed a bit as he spoke. While he was used to being around his sisters, this somehow felt very different.

"You were very brave to come today and own up to what you did." Now Stephen sensed that maybe she was blushing too.

"It was the right thing to do." He paused, wondering what to say next. His father saved the moment by calling him and Jacob back to their shed building. "Thanks again for the water and scone."

"You are welcome, Stephen. I do hope you will stop by and visit again."

Chapter 15

WAR AND AFFECTIONS

The next time Stephen saw Grace, family and neighbors were gathered for a send-off barn dance in honor of Uncle Thomas. It was early July of 1777 and Thomas had just enlisted in the Continental Army. He would be leaving soon for his three years of service in the cause of freedom. In the months since she had served him water and scones he had thought of her often. Her friendliness and eager forgiveness, expressed both verbally and nonverbally had left a strong impression on the now teenager. He had hoped his parents would invite the Andersons to the dance and he was overjoyed when he heard they planned to attend. His mother had been working with Stephen on his dance proficiencies and he was hoping he would get the chance to dance with her. He waved a greeting when he saw her arrive with her folks. He couldn't help but notice that she seemed now to be more of a young woman than the girl he remembered from the previous fall.

Lively music filled the air, adults enjoyed a tankard or two of rum and the children and youth quenched their thirst with watered down hard cider. All enjoyed the various foods that folks had brought to the gathering. The next country dance was for youth and Stephen looked across the barn to see what Grace would do. As she moved to the dance area, he responded in kind and took his place across from her. She curtseyed and he bowed and the dance began with Uncle Thomas, Jupiter and a few other fiddlers working their bows across the strings with fervor. When the dance ended, Grace again curtseyed and Stephen reciprocated with the customary bow. "That was fun," Grace smiled as they moved to the side of the barn, away from the dance area.

"Thank you for favoring me with a dance," Stephen returned her smile with one of his own. "I think you are the best dancer of all the girls here," he added.

"It was easy, having such a fine partner to lead the way." Grace replied.

"I hope we can pair up for another dance later," Stephen answered.

"Me too," Grace quickly responded. They stood for some moments, each wondering what to say next and visibly embarrassed by the awkward silence.

"Would you like some cider?" he finally blurted out.

"No thank you, Stephen, maybe later."

"Please excuse me, Grace; Uncle Thomas is beckoning me. I need to wish him well and say goodbye."

"Wish him well for me too; he is brave to go off to war. Thank you again for the dance." Grace curtseyed as they ended their conversation.

"Looks like you were having a good time dancing with the lovely young lady, nephew." Thomas playfully gave Stephen a nudge. Stephen could feel his cheeks flush with redness at his uncle's jesting.

"She conveyed a greeting and wishes you well, uncle."

"That was kind of her. When you talk with her again, which I am sure you will be doing, tell her thank you." Thomas smiled and ended his statement with a wink.

"When are you leaving?" Stephen asked, hoping to shift the topic from himself to his uncle.

"In a couple of days, I will be traveling north with others from Hyde County."

"I hope you will write and keep us informed of your welfare. We will all be praying for your safe return."

"I am afraid my writing skills are pretty weak, but I will do my best to get word back. I am not sure what to expect or how the fighting will go. I do appreciate your prayers, Stephen." Thomas dug in his breeches pocket and pulled out something. He held out his hand toward his nephew.

"I wanted you to have this coin I got in Woodstock a few weeks ago. I thought you might like it for your collection. It is a 1775 British Half Pence. 'tis probably a counterfeit as many of these are circulating now days. The year will remind you of the start of our war for independence and the brave minutemen who fired those first shots at Lexington and Concord. Whenever you look at it, perhaps you can send a prayer on my behalf heavenward, nephew."

"That I promise, Uncle Thomas, and thank you for the keepsake." Stephen wasn't quite sure how to respond, should he bow or shake his uncle's hand. Thomas initiated the best response, opening his arms to the lad. Stephen stepped into his embrace and they hugged in an expression of warm affection.

"You will be a man when I return from my service, if

God be so willing, Stephen. Why I wouldn't be surprised if you have your own ship by then." Thomas laughed and slapped his nephew on the back.

"Godspeed, Uncle, Godspeed."

Stephen watched from a distance as Grace chatted with some other girls. While he wanted to interrupt the conversation and ask her for another dance he was too self-conscious to take any further initiative. He hoped there would be future opportunities to get to know her better.

Captain Brooks regularly ferried supplies to and from the Outer Banks that fall in support of the patriots' cause and Stephen accompanied him on each trip. He was learning the craft of sailing the dangerous waters surrounding the Banks in keen anticipation of his future career as a master of his own schooner. While they occasionally spotted other ships, they experienced no harassment from either privateers or British naval vessels.

That all changed on a late November day near Ocracoke Island. Stephen was aloft in the rigging, keeping an eye out for possible danger when he spied the ship to the south. It was headed in their direction. With his glass he could see the Union Jack waving in the breeze. "British ship to port," he yelled down to his father and crew.

They had been headed west toward home when the threat was identified. With strong steady winds from the south, the British warship would easily intercept them if they continued in that direction. Stephen's father headed north to take advantage of the prevailing breeze. The maneuver took time and the distance between the ships narrowed considerably. The lad saw the puff of smoke before he heard the sound of the cannon. The ball landed with a splash well off their bow, a clear signal to cease flight and come about to be boarded. But the *Hannah Marie* did not slow at the ominous signal. Taking advantage now of the wind, the lighter schooner pulled slowly but steadily away from the heavy warship. They were safe from cannon fire but still were in visible contact as they continued to sail north, Cape Hatteras Island to their starboard side. Just past Brooks Point they veered west. Their captain knew the narrow channel well. From his perch, Stephen could see the warship stalled by the sand bar where she had run aground in her attempt to follow. He scurried down to the deck below.

"That was close, Father."

"Yes, too close. It will take them some time to get free of that shoal. When we are well out of their sight we should be able to sail undetected to Light Creek Marsh. Don't worry your mother about the day's events. She need not know what happened, son."

While their harrowing encounter with the British ship had brought the conflict very close to home, news concerning more distant battle fronts was often slow in coming. And when they did learn of decisive battles, like the ones at Brandywine and Germantown, Pennsylvania, the reports were not favorable. The British had taken control of Philadelphia and George Washington had moved his Continental Army of some 12,000 to a winter camp at Valley Forge, twenty miles northwest of the city where the Declaration of Independence had been drafted and passed, just a year and half earlier. Brooks' family members anguished over the welfare of Uncle Thomas. They wondered if he had seen action. Was he injured, taken ill, or worse yet, had he become a fatality of the war. What news they had received in January of 1778 painted a dire picture of the condition of Washington's troops as they faced a harsh winter ill-equipped and short of supplies. They longed for some word from him, even as they daily prayed for his safety and health. In February, just before Stephen was about to turn 14, their prayers were answered.

"Is this the home of Stephen Brooks and family?" The lone rider asked as he brought his horse to a stop. The family was just about to sit down for the noon meal and everyone had rushed to the door at the sound of hoof beats.

"'tis, sir," Stephen's father answered.

"I bring a letter for you from Thomas Brooks, private, now quartered at Valley Forge under the command of General George Washington."

"Come, please join us for dinner, you must be hungry," Mary urged.

"I right am, madam. I'd be much obliged."

"Welcome to our home, Mr.?" The elder Stephen realized he did not yet know the man's name.

"I'm George Hansen from Woodstock." The men exchanged handshakes and all headed inside.

Before Phoebe served the meal they learned the full story. Hansen had been delivering supplies to the Valley Forge camp when Thomas had recognized him. A friend of Thomas had helped him pen a letter home, but there was no way to post it. When he saw Hansen he inquired if he was planning to return to Hyde County and if he was, would he carry the letter to his brother there.

"How is my brother? We have heard awful stories of Valley Forge, that hundreds have died of starvation and disease."

"He is thin, but of strong health. The numbers dead are closer to 2,000. Your brother is one of the fortunate ones indeed. In recent days the situation has gotten better. Shelters have been constructed. Supplies are now arriving almost daily and morale has improved greatly. There has been some harsh criticism of Washington's leadership, but I can tell you, from what I saw, he would do anything to help his troops."

While all were relieved to hear that Thomas was well, dinner was quickly consumed in anticipation of the letter being opened and read aloud. Phoebe and Ima had hardly cleared the pewter plates when Stephen broke the wax seal and pulled the folded parchment from the envelope. Young Stephen, along with all of his siblings were leaning forward, fully attentive as their father began to speak.

My dearest Stephen, Mary, nephews and nieces, I hope to relieve your worries, I am doing well. I trust the Almighty that you are also in good health. God has spared me the pain that many of my brothers in arms have experienced here. I never thought I would give thanks for a pair of shoes, but such is the case now. When we marched here in December, some were barefoot and the snow was colored red from their bleeding feet. Washington had us inoculated for small pox, but still some died of the dreadful disease. We were hungry for want of food; some days our only nourishment came from thin firecakes made from flour and water. On a good day we had pepper pot soup or tripe broth. General Washington interceded on our behalf and needed supplies have come.

The best news we have received is that France is now our ally in the war. Also, we have a Prussian drill master, Baron Von Steuben, who is teaching us military techniques and I believe come spring, we will be better prepared for battle. The General had a good plan for the Germantown fight last fall. It just did not fall our way and the loss was severe. I saw men fall to my right and left. I know not how I survived, God knows.

My friend Wilson has helped me write. I am in debt for his kindness. I am not sure if I will have the good fortune to get another letter to you or not. Be assured, all of you, of my deep affections and love.

Yours, Thomas

As the war drug on, Stephen continued to accompany his father on supply missions to the villages of the Outer Banks. When he was not on the water, he was kept busy in the fields. He and Bear often worked side by side, but they missed those forays they had once taken with their friend Wolf.

"Bear, did you hear that turkey gobble?" Stephen leaned on his spade, listening to the distance call of the regal bird, strutting somewhere in the woods.

"Sure did, reminds me of Wolf. I bet he could lure in that big tom with his old wing bone call." Bear paused from his hoeing and took in the springtime antics of the birds engaged in mating rituals.

"We need to go hunting, Bear, for old time's sake."

"Maybe, if you were lucky, you could get a turkey with your arrow, like you pierced that old squash on your papa's place." Bear laughed as he recalled their last hunting trip.

A few weeks later, in late May, they got their chance. The boys took advantage of a Sunday rest day and Stephen secured permission from his father to borrow the horse for a hunting venture near Lake Mattamuskeet. "So, son, you think the turkeys are more plentiful over by the lake? Or might you just be looking for a chance to stop by the Anderson's for a visit with Grace." Stephen's father winked as he finished his sentence. "Either way lad, good hunting."

"Thank you, Father." Stephen couldn't resist adding his own wink as they parted.

The boys moved quietly through the brush, looking for their quarry in fields near the edge of timber. Bear stopped and imitated the call of a crow. In the distance, they heard the faint gobble response. They closed the distance and found a convenient bush to camouflage themselves. Stephen fished the wing bone call from his pocket. He had removed it from the coin box that morning. He had placed it there the day Wolf had left, leaving him both the old silver coin and the call as parting gifts at their old meeting stump. He softly sucked on the hollow bone, attempting to make the sound of a hen turkey looking for love.

"He heard you, Gator, I think he's coming," Bear whispered softly. Stephen put an arrow on the string and called again. The tom gobbled, this time, he was closer and the boys strained to spot his location. The big bird stepped into an opening, not 20 yards away. When the turkey turned sideways and stretched his neck to listen, Stephen released the arrow. Flying true the arrow hit and the tom jumped in the air, then fell to the ground thrashing.

"You got it, Gator," Bear yelled. As they approached the downed critter, the turkey righted itself and took off running with Bear and Gator in hot pursuit. The speed of Bear prevailed and he launched himself, landing atop the struggling bird. He stood, wringing the neck of the bird as both whooped and hollered their delight.

"Wolf would be proud of our team effort, Bear," Stephen guffawed. They dressed out the turkey beside a nearby stream, cutting the carcass into pieces.

"They'll be some good eating for your family," Stephen said as he handed a portion of the prize to his friend.

"And yours as well," Bear replied.

"I was just thinking that maybe the Andersons could use the fresh meat more than we need it."

"Yeah, I bet Grace really likes turkey," Bear said through a wide grin. Fortunately the Anderson farm was but a half mile distant.

Chapter 16

QUESTIONS

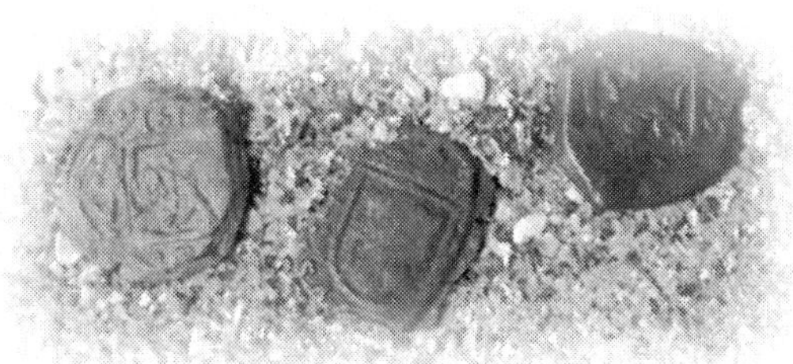

The *Hannah Marie* was adrift in Albemarle Sound when the light of morning turned to the darkness of night. The dead calm was accompanied by a wispy fog that filtered the dimming rays of sunlight. Stephen, along with the members of the crew, stood at the railing transfixed by the celestial event taking place in the eastern sky. The darkness was not a surprise. Captain Brooks had read them the June 24th predictions in the 1778 Boston Almanac the night before. Now they were observing the fulfillment of those words as the moon moved across the yellow orange orb blocking more and more of the light.

"'tis getting colder, you can feel it," Stephen said to his brother William, who nodded in agreement. It seemed almost sacrilegious to break the stillness with words and Stephen regretted his decision to speak. All would remain quiet over the next several minutes. Suddenly as if by some stroke of fate or perhaps heavenly cue, the fog and clouds parted revealing the scene in fullness. The moon now covered the sun in completeness and a bright circle of light danced around the edges. The eclipse's corona, Latin for wreath or crown, was breathtaking and it seemed all aboard collectively gasped, awestruck by the rare scene before them. Stars shone in the darkness and even old seasoned sailors wept, overcome by the Creator's splendid handiwork. Then, as the moon moved off of center the sun's bright rays burst bright again, like a sparkling diamond on a ring.

"Best look away now men," Captain Brooks shouted, "lest the piercing light damage your eyesight." Stephen obeyed his father's instructions. He looked down on the deck where the sun's growing light was focused through a small hole in the sail above. There he watched in amazement over the next hour as the thin crescent of light cast through the hole became steadily larger. With half the sun uncovered the day became brighter and the air much warmer. Finally the moon finished its trek across the sun's surface and normalcy returned.

"Mother, the eclipse, did you see it?" Stephen had rushed from the dock and was hardly through the front door when he burst out with his question.

"Yes, son, indeed I did! 'twas a marvelous, mystical and eerie sight to behold. Why Able even told me the chickens went to roost sensing the day was over and night was upon them. In the darkness the words of the Psalmist came to my mind: 'O Lord, our Lord, how excellent is thy name in all the earth! Who hast set thy glory above the heavens…when I consider thy heavens, the work of thy fingers, the moon and the stars, which thou hast ordained; what is man that thou art mindful of him?"

"I felt very small and insignificant in that moment, Mother. Does the Almighty really care about us when He has a universe to keep in order?"

"I believe He does dear one, I believe He does."

Fall harvest had been especially bountiful and folks were looking for a way to celebrate as well as tell their own stories of the eclipse event. The need to help a new family in the community raise a barn before winter set in provided the perfect solution. Families would gather for a communal meal while the men and older boys put up the building.

The Brooks family had an additional reason to be grateful. They had received another brief letter from Thomas. In late June he had fought at the Battle of Monmouth in New Jersey and had survived both the stifling heat and the flying lead. According to his uncle, more men had died of heat stroke than from battle injuries as the temperature soared to over 100 degrees. The Continental Army and British forces, bolstered by Hessian mercenaries, had battled to a draw, but Thomas said that the patriot troops had fought in a much more disciplined and effective way in light of their training exercises at Valley Forge. If a tie could be a victory then this was surely one for Washington and his soldiers. The eclipse had also had an impact on the troops. Washington had prepared his soldiers so they weren't taken by surprise by the darkness. Thomas relayed how many had seen the spectacular heavenly display as a positive omen, renewing confidence for the impending battle.

Grammy had made her famous squash soup. Phoebe, Ima and Stephen's mother had been cooking for days in preparation for the feast. Baskets of food filled the back of the wagon, leaving hardly enough room for family members. Stephen and his older brothers, William and Jacob tagged along on foot. Their destination, the Watson farm, was only a couple of miles away.

The Watson family had recently moved from Eastern Maryland. William and his wife Sophia had five children. Their oldest was Israel, followed by Easter, James, Jenny and Comfort. Israel was a strong and handsome eighteen year old who had already made quite an impact on the community. His wit, humor and story-telling skills seemed to attract a crowd wherever he went.

"What do you think of Israel Watson, brothers?" Stephen asked as they drifted further behind the wagon to avoid the dust kicked up by horse and wagon.

"I reckon he'll win the heart of some fine maiden in not too many years, what with his good looks and charm," William answered, swatting at a mosquito that was buzzing about his face.

"Seems like a nice enough fellow, might serious about God, I hear tell," Jacob added, taking a swipe at his own annoying insect pest.

This was Stephen's second community building venture. He had been too young to offer much help when the Brooks house was raised. This time he would be able to assist, like any man in the community. His familiarity with heights on the masts of the *Hannah Marie* made him the natural choice to help with the highest rafters. He was high astride the ridge pole when he saw Grace arriving with her mother. She spotted him too and waved her greeting. He waved back enthusiastically.

At noon the women folk set out a table fit for kings. The quantity and variety of the potluck menu was truly something to behold. There was beef, pork, lamb, turkey, chicken, venison, fish and seafood of all kinds, potatoes, squash, and vegetables a plenty, combined with breads, pastries and pies. There was hard cider in abundance. As all gathered about the table, William Watson quieted the crowd.

"Dear friends, we are so grateful for all your labors on our behalf. We feel truly loved and welcomed into your community here. Thank you so very much. Before we partake, I have asked my eldest son Israel to pray God's blessing on our meal together." The good-looking older teen rose and spoke.

"Come, Lord Jesus, our guest to be and bless these gifts bestowed by Thee. We thank you Lord for these dear folk, now our friends. We also pray for those who today are in want as well as those in harm's way fighting for our freedom. Keep them, and we gathered here, safe in the hollow of your strong hand. I thank you for the assurance of your forgiveness, your marvelous grace and your eternal faithfulness. Help us to love and trust you with all our strength, soul and heart. For Jesus' sake we pray, Amen."

While Stephen was use to recited table grace, he was not accustomed to the way Israel prayed, earnestly from the heart and like you might talk with a close friend. He wondered if this is what his brother Jacob had meant when he said Israel was 'serious about God.' He remembered back to his childhood, his mother and father reading from the Book of Common Prayer as well as the Bible. He thought about the old priest in Bath who had befriended him and Sundays when the family would gather for worship. The move to Light Creek Marsh and the busyness of farm and sailing had crowded their lives, leaving little time for talk about or with God. Now that the colonies were at war with Britain the British flavor of the Anglican Church was not only stiff and staid but seemed unpatriotic as well. The Brooks family had not attended a service for some years. Stephen realized he had not given much thought to God either except for the occasional prayer for the welfare of his Uncle Thomas. Somehow the words of the eighteen year old had stirred something deep within him.

It was early evening when the men finished their work for the day. There was still food to be eaten and some music to be enjoyed. Stephen looked around to see where Grace might be and located her, together with his sisters and a small group of other youth, seated on the grass listening to Israel talk. He walked over to join them and listened.

"See those sparrows yonder? We can learn much from them. Our Savior talks about them in the Bible. In Matthew 6 he tells us to 'look at the birds of the air, how they neither sow nor reap nor gather into barns, yet their Heavenly Father feeds them. We children are of far more value to him than they.' Or in another place in Matthew 10 he says, 'are not two sparrows sold for a farthing, yet not one of them falls to the ground without your Father knowing. Fear not, you are of much more value than many sparrows.' Remember those words this week."

As the children scattered to find their parents, Stephen saw that Grace stayed for a moment, talking with Israel. Their conversation concluded, she made her way in his direction. "Did you hear him? Wasn't he just wonderful, Stephen? He has such wisdom and faith for a young man."

"I only heard the very end, Grace. I liked the story about the farthing and sparrows."

"He said his family may have Sunday worship gatherings in their home, for all who are interested. Maybe we can go sometime?"

"Maybe," Stephen replied, finding himself wrestling with a new emotion. He was jealous of Grace's interest in Israel and wondered how he might compete with the confident and personable young man, four years his senior.

"My parents are ready to go. Goodbye Stephen."

"Goodbye, Grace."

Stephen's mind was clearly somewhere else as he took a shortcut through the woods on his way to see his grandparents. Usually he would have exercised a bit more caution as he stepped over decaying timber and pushed through the brush. He didn't see the canebrake rattlesnake coiled up in the shade of the log and the brief rattle before the snake struck was hardly warning enough to change his course. He felt a stabbing pain in his leg as he moved to put some distance between himself and the riled serpent. He chastised himself for his carelessness and knew he was in real danger. His heart raced as he considered his plight. He was much closer to the Farrow farm than he was to home so it only made sense to make his way there as quickly as he could. He pulled his pant leg up to reveal the fang marks on the back of his right calf. He could already see redness and swelling around the bite. He was scared and in desperation offered up a quick prayer. 'O God, help me.'

He saw his Papa weeding his vegetable garden as he broke into the clearing. "Papa," then he cried louder, PAPA! Help, snakebite!"

Jacob Farrow rushed to meet his grandson. Stephen

collapsed into his grandfather's arms. "Do you know what kind of snake?" he asked with concern.

"Rattler, a pretty big one," he showed him the two puncture wounds.

"We need to get you inside. Here, lean on me." Jacob helped the lad up the steps and through the door. He had him lie down on their bed. Stephen could hear his Grammy's worried pleas.

"Jacob, what will we do?"

"Amey, get me that bottle of ammonia and also fetch some hard cider, the boy needs to drink." Then in hushed tones he whispered. "Send Ezekiel immediately to get Stephen and Mary, and pray. There isn't much else we can do. It all depends on how much venom he got. I've seen such bites before and watched the agony set in. It could take his leg or worse."

Amey let out a soft shriek and sped to her tasks. She returned with the ammonia and cider, then left to give instructions to their slave. Jacob swabbed the bite with the ammonia and offered his grandson some cider. Now it would be a waiting game to see how the poison might affect his limb and the rest of his body. The boy was still conscious and seemed alert. The irritation of the ammonia had brought tears to his eyes and a cry on his lips. Jacob placed his hand on Stephen's heart and could feel the rapid pulse. He gently wiped beads of sweat from the boy's brow. Amey entered the room.

"Ezekiel is on his way," she said as she gently placed a poultice on the wound.

"Good. Hopefully they'll be here within an hour or so." Jacob set back in the chair and sighed deeply, the concern was clearly etched on his face. Stephen had closed his eyes and seemed to be, for the moment at least, free of any pain.

"Jacob, do you believe in miracles?" Amey came close and rested her hand on his shoulder. Stephen did not open his eyes, but he clearly heard her say 'miracles.'

"As surely as God is in His heaven, dear, I have seen things I can't explain with my human reasoning." The snake bit boy on the bed just caught his papa's hopeful words before he dozed off to sleep.

When Stephen's anxious parents arrived, their son was still asleep. "It's a positive sign, Mary," Stephen sought to reassure his wife as he held her tight.

"There doesn't appear to be much swelling and his heart is beating normally now too." Jacob said as he lifted the poultice to let them see the bite.

"Thanks be to God, it must have been a dry bite with little or no venom. By this time there would be very different symptoms if the snake had injected a full dose of poison." Perceiving his father's voice the teen stirred and opened his eyes.

"Am I going to die?" he asked hesitantly.

"Not today, my boy. Appears that old rattler forgot to fill his fangs, or maybe your leg was just too tough for his liking." The elder Stephen smiled and patted his boy on the shoulder.

"I'm sorry Mama, you always warn me to watch out for snakes. I was careless."

"I forgive you. Praise Jesus you are alright. Now go back to sleep and get some rest."

Stephen and his parents spent the night at the Farrow's. By the next morning his leg was still a bit tender and sore but close inspection by parents and grandparents revealed no damage other than the two puncture marks. As his Grammy prepared breakfast, he slipped out of the house to relieve himself, just in time to see the sunrise glowing orange and red on the eastern horizon. It was breathtaking. Birds were also adding to the beauty with their wakeup songs. He spied a small flock of sparrows joining in the chorus and remembered what Israel had said, 'fear not, you are of much more value than many sparrows.' For the first time in his young life, Stephen felt the powerful, mysterious and reassuring presence of a caring Heavenly Father. Still looking to the dawn he offered up his own heartfelt, 'thank you.'

Stephen pulled the coin box from its special niche, opened the pouch and carefully spilled out the coins onto this straw bed mat. Looking through his small hoard he found the coins he was looking for. One was the British Farthing, his inheritance coin from his Grandpa Brooks. The other was the Irish Farthing O'Reilly had given him for returning his lost mule. The small copper coins were the lowest of value, worth but a quarter of a cent. As he fingered the pieces of metal he again thought about the message of the sparrows. Insignificant birds sold for a mere Farthing yet known and loved by God; what was that verse that Israel had quoted?

He put the coins away and headed down from the loft. Taking the family Bible from the stand by the fireplace he headed outdoors and trekked to his favorite place, the old stump by the creek. He had not read the Bible since his reading lessons years earlier. Thumbing through the pages he found the Gospel of Matthew. He couldn't remember the chapter he was looking for, but he found a bookmark at chapter five and began to read.

> Blessed are the poor in spirit: for theirs is the kingdom of heaven. Blessed are they that mourn: for they shall be comforted. Blessed are the meek: for they shall inherit the earth. Blessed are they which do hunger and thirst after righteousness: for they shall be filled. Blessed are the merciful: for they shall obtain mercy. Blessed are the pure in heart: for they shall see God. Blessed are the peacemakers: for they shall be called the children of God.

He closed the Bible and looked out across the winter landscape. Trees stood naked of leaves against the wind. In just a few days he would turn fifteen, Feb. 18th, 1779. He had so many questions and he wasn't sure who to seek out for answers. There were questions about love, or at least he thought it might be love, as he thought of his feelings for Grace. There were questions about God. His close encounter with the rattlesnake had been a sobering experience. Life was fragile. War, accidents, illness, all could cut short one's hopes and dreams. What would endure? Was there more beyond what one could see and touch? Was God distant and unmoved by human emotions and fears? Or was He as near as the sparrows? What did it mean that the poor in spirit would find the kingdom of God? Or how could those that mourned find lasting comfort? What did it mean to hunger and thirst for righteousness? How could one be pure in heart?

Stephen stood and closed the top of his outer coat against the chill of the wind. With the Bible safely tucked under his arm he turned toward home. At least he had found one answer that cold morning. Come next Sunday, he would visit the meeting at the Watson home.

Chapter 17

BIBLE AND BATTLE 1779

Stephen ladled the cornmeal mush into his bowl and joined his sisters Charity and Sara at the table. As he ate his breakfast he planned out his day. Chores and spring farm activities would consume most of the hours ahead. If he worked hard and fast, he might be able to finish by mid-afternoon, giving him time to be at the Watson home for the evening religious meeting. It was Easter week and it seemed a good time to check out the gathering. Maybe Grace would even be present.

"I'm planning to go over to Watson's tonight for the Bible class. Anybody want to go with me?" he asked, taking a swig of cider.

"I'd like to go," William answered as he entered the room.

"Me too," Charity chimed in.

"Me three," added Sara with a giggle.

"Son, I'd like to find out more about these Methodists, I'll go if you don't mind the company." Stephen's mother wiped her hands on her apron, smiling.

"I'll have the wagon ready right after supper then,"

Stephen said as he put down his spoon.

"Stephen, you have some corn mush on your face," his younger sister Sara pointed at her chin as she spoke.

"Did that get it?" Stephen rubbed the back of his hand across his mouth.

"No, you only smeared it worse," Charity now joined in the fun. Both girls were laughing as Stephen tried to locate the offending food.

"Where's a mirror?" he jumped to his feet in frustration.

"April Fool's Day!" the girls shouted in unison.

"You girls got me good," Stephen replied as joined in the laughter around the table.

"April 1st and Maundy Thursday, a strange coincidence indeed," Mary pondered. "Now children, you best be off to your chores." She looked around and signaled their slave, Ima, to start clearing the table.

Stephen reined the horses to a stop in front of the Watson house. He was glad to see the Anderson's wagon there too. Chances were good that Grace was inside. His brother, William, had decided to stay at home but his mother and two sisters had come as planned. The teen was having some second thoughts about his decision to attend. If Grace really was sweet on Israel it would be a hard evening. And then there was his anxiety about being at a Methodist meeting. The Watson's were the first Methodists to move into the area and he knew little about what to expect.

There were about twenty folks crammed into the small Watson home. If any more arrived, they would have to stand out on the porch and listen through the doorway. Stephen saw Grace sitting with her parents on the far side of the room. They briefly made eye contact, smiled and nodded a greeting. William Watson welcomed everyone to their home and briefly prayed asking the Lord's blessing on the gathering. He then introduced his son.

"Israel has a real call from the Lord to be a minister of the gospel so he will lead our service." William sat down and Israel rose to speak.

"As you all know, this is holy week. Tonight we remember how our Lord graciously washed the feet of his disciples the night before he was crucified and a few days before he rose from the grave. It is also April 1st, Fools Day. I have no practical jokes planned for tonight, but rather would remind you of the psalmist's words, 'The fool hath said in his heart, there is no God.' Let none of us be so foolish as to reject the invitation to life that Jesus Christ extends to us all."

Israel then led the small group in a few hymns. Anglicans did not sing like this in their services so this was a new experience for Stephen. Fortunately, Israel lined out each phrase of the song, giving the listeners an opportunity to then repeat what he had voiced.

O for a thousand tongues to sing
My great Redeemer's praise,
The glories of my God and King,
The triumphs of His grace!

My gracious Master and my God,
Assist me to proclaim,
To spread through all the earth abroad
The honors of Thy name.

Jesus! the name that charms our fears,
That bids our sorrows cease;
'tis music in the sinner's ears,
'tis life, and health, and peace.

He breaks the power of canceled sin,
He sets the prisoner free;
His blood can make the foulest clean,
His blood availed for me.

He speaks, and, listening to His voice,
New life the dead receive,
The mournful, broken hearts rejoice,
The humble poor believe.

Hear Him, ye deaf; His praise, ye dumb,
Your loosened tongues employ;
Ye blind, behold your Savior come,
And leap, ye lame, for joy.

Glory to God, and praise and love
Be ever, ever given,
By saints below and saints above,
The church in earth and heaven.

Stephen was impressed by the sincere enthusiasm Israel demonstrated as he led the tiny congregation through each verse of the song. The high liturgy that he was more familiar with lacked this spontaneity and energy.

"I think seven verses is enough; Charles Wesley actually wrote nineteen," Israel said as the group finished singing, 'earth and heaven.' "My scripture text for tonight is found in John 13:34 and 35. This is the chapter where Jesus washes his disciples' feet and urges us to follow his example by washing each other's feet. Hear His words: 'A new commandment I give unto you, that ye love one another; as I have loved you, that ye also love one another. By this shall all men know that ye are my disciples, if ye have love one to another.' "

While Israel's sermon on Christian love was sincere and passionate, it did drag on for some time and Stephen began to struggle to stay awake, the hard day's work taking its toll. He was beginning to feel that the preacher was trying to match the nineteen stanzas of the hymn writer as he repeatedly exhorted his listeners to love and good works. Stephen was greatly relieved when Israel concluded his appeals with 'Amen', an 'Amen' that was quickly echoed by a tired audience. While the teen would retain little from the lengthy message, he was deeply moved by the concluding hymn by Isaac Watts, a hymn that seemed to capture the full meaning of Passion Week in a few powerful sentences.

When I survey the wondrous cross
On which the Prince of glory died,
My richest gain I count but loss,
And pour contempt on all my pride.

Forbid it, Lord, that I should boast,
Save in the death of Christ my God!
All the vain things that charm me most,
I sacrifice them to His blood.
See from His head, His hands, His feet,

Sorrow and love flow mingled down!
Did e'er such love and sorrow meet,
Or thorns compose so rich a crown?

Were the whole realm of nature mine,
That were a present far too small;
Love so amazing, so divine,
Demands my soul, my life, my all.

Israel intercepted Stephen before he could make it to the door. "Thank you for coming lad. I hope you enjoyed our gathering and will come again. If you would like to know a little more about our Methods, I would be glad to meet with you and try to answer your questions." Israel grasped Stephen's hand as he spoke and pumped a handshake or two.

"I might take you up on that some time, Mr. Watson." Stephen chaffed at the word Israel had used to greet him, "lad".

"Please, call me Israel. Like the tribes in the Old Testament."

"Good night then, Israel, and a fine Easter to you." Stephen knew he had been a bit short with his host, but he was in a hurry to try and catch Grace.

"He is Risen, Stephen, He is Risen indeed, forget it not," Israel added.

The Anderson wagon was barely visible in the distance when Stephen finally got free of formalities and made it outside. Stephen took some comfort in the fact that Israel had visited with him after the meeting rather than Grace. The ride home to the Brooks farm was a quiet one. Charity and Sara quickly fell asleep in the back of the wagon and Mary seemed preoccupied with her own thoughts. Stephen didn't mind the silence. It gave him an opportunity to replay the evening's tunes once more in his mind.

June proved to be a troublesome month on the waters of Pamlico Sound. A small fleet of privateers, supportive of the British cause, had been harassing ships in the area. On June 26th one of the vessels pursued a schooner from Edenton as it made its way across the Ocracoke bar. Fortunately darkness impeded the pursuit and the schooner was able to make its way on to port at Bath. Word spread quickly about the threat and the Beaufort County Militia, under Colonel Thomas Bonner, worried about a possible land raid by the intruders. He and his forces headed northeast to link up with the Hyde County Militia located in the Lake Mattamuskeet area and plan a response. However, before Bonner arrived, word of the danger had already reached the area. A number of the militia convened early the next morning at the Brooks landing, ready for a fight.

"Son, I want you to go along; I may need you to sail the *Hannah* to safety if we engage those filthy Tories on Cape Hatteras banks."

Stephen was thrilled to be included and eagerly helped ferry men and equipment to the waiting schooner, anchored in its usual protective mooring behind the island in Wisockin Bay. On his last trip he made sure that his father's musket was included among the supplies. "Father, here is your musket, powder and shot. Sounds like you may need it today." Stephen handed the old weapon, the one he had learned to shoot before their trip to Halifax, to Captain

Brooks.

Stephen was high in the rigging as the *Hannah* sailed out into the open sound. Every eye below as well as his atop the mast were peeled on the horizon. No one knew for sure where the privateer ships had sailed after breaking off their chase of the previous evening. They sailed cautiously north, past Stumpy Point and Roanoke Island. At Chickahawk a boat was sent ashore to see if the ships might be on the seaward side of the Outer Banks. The spy party returned with good news. They had located four ships, two brigs, a schooner and a sloop sailing north from Nags Head.

"I think we might be able to lure a landing party to shore if we set out the right bait." Henry Gibbs, one of the spy party, proposed as the men considered their options.

"I bet they would be interested in some fresh beef," Rotheas Latham said, pointing to a small herd of cattle on the sound side of the dunes, not too far in the distance. "All we need to do is move the cattle to where they can see them and set ourselves up an ambush. What do you think?"

"It's a sound plan," Captain Brooks was the first to speak, but all the men soon agreed.

"Son, I am going ashore with the ambush party. I want you to stay here, ready to weigh anchor if you see any enemy vessels. Also, and hear me well, son, if we do not return after a possible battle, you must sail home immediately. Do not come ashore hoping to rescue us." Save yourself and the rest of the crew. I promised your mother I would keep you from harm." His father embraced him for a moment, looked him again straight in the eyes and repeated. "Promise me you will obey my words."

"I promise, Father." The young teen, now fully realizing

the severity of the moment, silently sent a prayer heavenward for a successful mission.

The small force of twelve, split evenly between two boats, rowed speedily to shore. They rounded up a few head of cattle and drove them across the high sand dunes to where they were clearly visible to the ships, still some distance to the south. They then hid themselves behind the dunes closest to the beach and waited.

"The trap is set," one of the Gibbs brothers winked as he spoke to the three men who were huddled closest to him, including Captain Brooks. All double checked to make sure their muskets were loaded and primed.

"If they should take the bait, be sure to wait until they are up the beach some distance from their small boats before you rush them and fire." Rotheas spoke final instructions.

"They're coming," Brooks whispered.

They could clearly see the ships haul sail and slow their progress. Three row boats were lowered over the side and the landing party began to oar their way to shore. The surf was light and the boats all arrived together. The men poured out of their small crafts and pulled them high above the waterline. While they did have weapons, they seemed confident that they were alone on the shore. The militia in hiding could even hear them joking about their good fortune in finding fresh meat so ripe for the taking. The odds were even. The landing party included the same number of twelve souls as those ready to spring their trap. They were about fifty yards up the beach when Rotheas shouted and led the charge.

"For freedom and for North Carolina," the other eleven also sprung up from behind the dunes and rushed toward the unwary cattle rustlers. Brooks aimed and fired. As the smoke cleared he could see his target lying face down in the wet sand. Four other lifeless bodies were strewn about near the debris left by the outgoing tide. The remaining raiders hurried to their boats. Some returned fire as they scrambled aboard, giving them enough time to push free of the shore and row to deeper water and safety.

"Hooray," the men shouted, tossing their hats into the air in celebration. A couple of men who had reloaded ran toward the water and took unsuccessful parting shots at the fleeing targets.

Stephen could hear the distant shots fired and wondered as to the outcome of the skirmish. Again he tried praying for his father and the men with him. He scampered up the rigging to see if he could spot any movement on shore or detect any approaching ships from north or south. The crew prepared to raise anchor and sail at a moment's notice if danger was imminent. It was with a sigh of relief that about an hour later he observed the ragtag army making its way over the high dunes. With his spy glass he watched and quietly counted to himself, 'six, seven, eight, nine, ten, eleven, twelve.' All were safely in view. They loaded their spoils of war into the boats and rowed back to the *Hannah Marie*. Stephen learned the full details of the battle once the men were all back aboard the schooner.

Later that evening, as they sailed back toward Light Creek Marsh, Captain Brooks pulled his son aside. "You did well today, my boy. I knew I could trust you to follow orders. I brought you something from the pocket of one of the fallen, perhaps it will serve as a memento of our victory in years to come." His father held out to him a copper coin.

Stephen could tell it was a German coin, a One Heller, from the European state of Hesse-Kassel. "The British tyrant, George III, has hired many German mercenaries from Hesse to do his dirty work here in America. Perhaps the dead sailor was such a one or perhaps he did business with a German here. If you look close, it appears there is even a drop of blood on the coin, probably only rust. I know a bloody coin is a rather gruesome prize, but it is a mark of the cost of war, a war one can only hope will end soon."

Chapter 18

LOSS

Uncle Thomas returned home from the battlefield that fall. It didn't take long for family members to recognize that the war had taken a heavy toll on their normally good-natured and happy-go-lucky loved one. Even his walk had lost its spring and his posture mirrored that of one carrying a heavy weight on his shoulders. There were steady complaints about physical pain, ranging from headaches to vague muscle fatigue. Nightmares disturbed his sleep and often all were awakened by his terrifying screams. There were days he would withdraw and hardly talk to anyone, preferring to be alone or to wander the woods as if searching for something lost. His unpredictable responses put everyone on edge. If you asked him about his memories of the war or specific conflicts, he would sometimes talk for hours, revealing lurid details of maiming injuries and ugly deaths. The next time the topic was broached he would retreat into a silent world or storm out the door. Stephen could see the pain, confusion and concern etched on the face of his father who didn't know how to break through the wall of anxiety, guilt and shame erected by his brooding brother. Over time, family members found ways to give him the space he seemed to need, trying as best they could to reassure him of their love.

"Uncle, I'm going fishing down at the creek. You want to come along?" Stephen tried to read the nonverbal cues to discern whether he should push his request or back off. For what seemed like minutes there was no answer from Thomas, just a blank stare. Finally, as if jerked back into the present he responded.

"I could use some fresh air."

Stephen gathered up some gear and they walked the relative short distance to the family fishing hole. He offered a pole to his uncle who declined the invitation, preferring to sit on a nearby log and watch his nephew. After an hour or so of fishing without any catching, the teenager joined his uncle on the log. There they spent another hour in virtual silence.

"I brought you a coin," Thomas broke the spell. "It's a Spanish 1 Reale with the date of Independence, 1776. Got it as change in a tavern somewhere in Pennsylvania. Want it?"

"I'd love to have it! That's a pretty special date to remember, thank you so much, Thomas."

"'tis nothing, I've got it back at the house in my stuff, I'll fetch it for you later." The hollow sound of his voice disturbed Stephen and he took a risk.

"The war's been really hard on you, hasn't it?" There was a lengthy pause as Thomas seemed to be searching for the right words.

"Don't seem right that I should be alive when so many good men have died. Fate seems to deal a pretty stacked deck of tragedy to some, second chances to others, a bed of roses to a few. I can't stay here safe. I will be leaving soon. I plan to head south and rejoin the action somewhere around Charles Town. I am worthless here. 'tis time to see what I will be dealt in the next hand." Stephen watched as his uncle slowly rose from the log. He looked much older than his years. "I have made up my mind. Let's go back to the house. I need to pack and say some farewells."

Early the next morning the family gathered on the porch to see their uncle and brother set off once again to war. They braced themselves against the December chill and their own fears. Eyes were moist with emotion. Sentences were filled with promises of goodwill and fervent prayers. Stephen wondered if he would see his uncle again, or if the man who might return would ever resemble the man he remembered so fondly. Just before Thomas hoisted himself up in the saddle, he handed his nephew the tiny silver token.

"If I don't see you again on this side of eternity, remember me with love," Nephew. And then he was gone, galloping to some unknown rendezvous with questions, pain and suffering. While Thomas might not be listed as a casualty on some government ledger he was none-the-less a real victim of war's terror and loss.

For some time Stephen had been dodging Israel Watson. He had not been back to the weekly Methodist meetings, nor had he found time to sit down with the young preacher to learn more about their beliefs. But the troubling days spent with his war-shattered uncle had soften his heart and he decided it was time to ask Israel some tough questions about life and faith.

A new year, 1780, had dawned laden with many

uncertainties and little optimism. The soon to be sixteen year old found Israel chopping wood out behind the Watson house. "I know it's been awhile. Is that offer still open to talk?"

"Certainly, Stephen," Israel buried the head of the axe on the splitting block and moved toward his guest with an outstretched hand.

"We've missed you at our Thursday night gatherings. You know you're welcome anytime."

"Been a might busy, what with sailing duties, farm chores and the like."

"I'm glad you came by. Let's take a rest on the porch, no one will disturb us there. Like some cider?"

"No thank you, Israel. Wondered if you might tell me more about those methods you mentioned."

"I'll do my best. First maybe a bit of history will help. The Methodist movement began with two brothers, John and Charles Wesley. Have you heard anything about them?" Israel leaned forward closing the distance between himself and Stephen as he spoke.

"Just that Charles wrote lots of verses to his hymns," Stephen smiled and Israel, remembering his comment about 19 refrains, reciprocated with laughter.

"Well nearly fifty years ago, I believe it was around 1735, both brothers came to the colony of Georgia to propagate their Anglican faith among the Indians. They returned home feeling like total failures and lacking any assurance of their own salvation. John wrote something like- 'I went to America to convert the Indians, but who shall convert me?' Both despaired of the ministry and were ready to quit. Charles was the first to experience conversion and full forgiveness. A few days later, John too came to experience Christ's grace and new life. The story goes that he had reluctantly gone to a meeting out of a sense of duty. There, someone was reading about the change which God works in the heart through faith in Christ. He felt his heart strangely warmed. In that moment he did trust Christ, Christ alone for salvation and received an assurance that his sins had been taken away, that he was saved from the law of sin and death." Israel stopped, realizing that his penchant for over-talking was probably numbing his young listener. But Stephen had been paying attention and jumped into the conversation.

"I don't really understand all those words about conversion, salvation, or the law of sin and death. Guess I just thought that religion was belief in God, going to church, and praying when you find yourself in a pinch, like when I was snake bit." Stephen leaned back in his chair, as if he needed more space between himself and this zealous promoter of the faith.

"Stephen, God wants to have a relationship with you, like the closest of all friends. He wants you to trust Him, love Him, enjoy Him and follow his path as revealed in the Bible. That's where Wesley's methods come in. There are three levels of commitment. First, a believer needs to be committed to the society meetings, like our Thursday evening worship time. That is where we learn more about what it means to know God. We do that through singing hymns, praying together and studying scripture. Second, we have what are called class meetings. This is a smaller group, up to twelve people, who regularly gather to encourage one another to grow in holiness and obedience to God. Third, we have bands of three or four. In this intimate group we share our deepest struggles, questions and sins. We hold each other to account, confessing our failures to love and serve God faithfully." Israel could sense the teen was struggling to comprehend what he was saying. He noted how Stephen was looking around, like he had had enough and wanted out of the discussion.

"Thanks for explaining it to me, Israel. Sounds like a lot of fuss and hard work. Maybe I'll try to get to another society meeting, but I just don't have the time to do all that other stuff. You know, I am going to be a captain of my own ship in a few years. I plan to sail the high seas, visit Europe and seek my fortune. Maybe someday, I'll...," Stephen's voice trailed off and before he could complete his thoughts Israel held up his hand to stop him so he could speak.

"Stephen, It's great to have dreams, but don't leave God out of your hopes and pursuits. Let me leave you with just one verse, spoken by our Lord Jesus. He said, 'what shall it profit a man if he gains the whole world but loses his own soul? Or what shall a man give in exchange for his soul?' Promise me that you will think about those questions. I hope we can talk again soon."

Stephen was glad to be back on the water. Storms and spring planting had interfered with scheduled trips to deliver supplies to villages along the outer cape. There was a certain renewal he always experienced as he felt the wind catch in the sails, as he balanced his movement on the heaving deck of the ship or climbed to his perch aloft where he felt like a seabird, free and alive. This trip would take them to Ocracoke which meant traversing the narrow bar that separated Pamlico Sound from the sea beyond. These waters were always dangerous and required knowledge and a steady hand at the wheel. Stephen was lost in his daydreams. He imagined himself at the helm of his own vessel, sailing into port somewhere in South America, Europe, Africa, or beyond.

The enemy schooner lay just off the coastline to their port side. It may have been visible for some time but Stephen was far away and had missed it in his mental haze.

"Privateers to northeast, coming fast," Stephen heard the warning shouted by one of the men below. He knew he had failed to be alert, a mistake that could cost them valuable time.

"Yes, enemy vessel in sight," he yelled, inwardly chastising himself.

The chase was on in earnest. Captain Brooks took advantage of the wind to maintain his speed before taking evasive actions. Off Portsmouth he turned south, then back to the west. His planned route took them past Cedar Island where he steered north toward the Pamlico River. He hoped his speed would keep distance between himself and the pursuing schooner, although the similarities between the two vessels might make it a closer match than he preferred. If he could reach Rose Bay, near Swan Quarter, he thought his chances good of alluding capture.

His other option would be to follow the river to Bath where safe harbor might be found. In spite of his knowledge of the waters and the disciplined action of his crew, he was not able to pull away. The schooner was slowly closing the gap between them. Just off the mouth of Rose Bay disaster struck. The *Hannah Marie* hit a sandbar. Their quick response and efforts to free themselves proved futile. Lacking any means of defense other than a few muskets, they had no choice.

"Let down the dory, we must abandon ship." A chill ran through his body as Stephen heard his father's order. Soon, he and his father along with the crew of four were rowing hard away from the *Hannah*. The privateers had little interest in taking prisoners; their focus was the loot aboard their prize and the value of the ship itself. Reaching the mainland near the mouth of the bay, the men pulled the boat into the bushes above the high water mark. From there they looked on as events unfolded.

"They will try to float her free and tow her away; that would secure them the greatest profit," Captain Brooks said as he watched the scene before him.

"Father, I am sorry. 'tis my fault. I failed to spy the ship in time, costing us dearly." Stephen tried hard not to break into tears as he spoke.

"What has happened has happened, lad. I place no blame. At least we are all free of harm."

The crew aboard the privateer vessel worked feverishly. They transported booty from the *Hannah* back to their ship by means of rowboats, hoping to lighten the vessel and free her from the sand. When that failed they attached a hawser from the stranded craft back to their vessel and waited.

"They will see if high tide drifts her loose," Captain Brooks interpreted their actions. Stephen kept his eye on the beach. He could see that the tide was beginning to recede. The *Hannah* had not moved. They all watched in horror as the captors executed their final plan. Returning to the stranded vessel they scuttled her with axes, emptied barrels of tar down the hold and across the deck, ignited the tar with a strike of flint and rowed away. The intensity of the flames increased, consuming deck planks and timbers. Tongues of fire moved up the masts, engulfing the sails.

They were all alone. The privateers, content with their limited victory, had set sail and were now out of sight. The setting sun and increasing darkness only served to outline the destruction before them. Masts fell, flames turned to red coals, embers hissed as they met the water. It was well after dark when the final flame was extinguished. No one spoke. There was really nothing that could be said.

Following a restless night they rowed across the bay. They walked until they met up with a rider who took word of their plight back home. Late in the day, William arrived with the wagon. The loss wore heavy on each one, especially young Stephen.

Chapter 19

LICENSE

Each member of the Brooks family responded differently to the loss of the *Hannah Marie*. The Stephens in the family, father and son, grieved deeply. They both loved the salt air, the rush of wind, and the new adventure of each sailing opportunity. They were men of the sea and now their ease of access to the water had been destroyed suddenly and sadly.

Mary, on the other hand, could see good coming from the disaster. It meant that her husband would not be absent for long days of uncertainty. Her anxieties about the welfare of both her Stephens, facing the dangers of the sea as well as potential enemies, were eased.

Easter was especially relieved because it meant no more heaving decks and unpleasant seasickness. Charity and Sara likewise enjoyed the stability of a home on soil rather than one shifting with current and breeze. The older boys, Isaac, William and Jacob, had endured their stints as crew members but had never entertained thoughts of a career aboard ship. They preferred the land and farming.

In early June the family learned that Charlestown had

fallen to British forces on May 12th. While the event was significant in the ongoing conflict for freedom, it had more personal meaning for the Brooks'. They had received no word from Uncle Thomas who they believed had joined troops in that very area. The silence could simply mean he was unable to get them a letter. Or it could mean he had been taken prisoner, the fate of many continental soldiers there. Worse, he might have been a fatality of the fighting.

Stephen's father had traveled to Edenton on what he described as family business. No longer able to sail there on his own ship, he had gone to Bath to secure passage on the next ship headed north. He had been gone nearly two weeks and the teen eagerly awaited his return. He thought maybe the 'family business' might have something to do with his own future and dreams of the high seas. When the elder Stephen rode into the yard, his son was the first to greet him. "Did you have a good trip, father?" he asked excitedly.

"That I did, and I have news I think you may be glad to hear." He slid from the saddle and handed the reins to Able who had heard his master coming and was dutifully present to care for the horse. "Boy, could you fetch me some rum, I am a might thirsty," Stephen said as he gestured to the black teen. Able felt the familiar pain of being called 'boy.' He knew he was a man and deserved to be addressed so.

"Yes, master, soon as I put your horse in the barn." Able bowed in respect to his owner.

"Son, let's talk." Both moved to the front porch and took seats in the shade, out of the bright and hot June sun. A few minutes later, Able returned with a tankard of rum for the senior Brooks and a tankard of hard cider meant for his teenage friend. He again bowed in respect and left them.

"I visited with Robert Smith in Edenton, business partner of Joseph Hewes, who sadly passed away last fall in Philadelphia. He is carrying on their shipping company alone." Stephen sat his cider down and leaned forward, anxious to hear what his father would say next. "He is looking for capable men, especially those already with sailing skills, who might become prospective captains in his fleet. He is willing to offer you an apprenticeship, which if you successfully complete, will provide you the captain's license I believe you are so eager to possess." This was exactly the news that Stephen had hoped he would receive. "I had expected that you would obtain that license under my direction, son, but alas, minus the *Hannah,* this seems our best plan. What do you say?"

"Yes....certainly....yes!" Stephen hoisted his tankard and extended it toward his father for a toast. The pewter mugs clinked together as he said, "to the *Hannah* and to the sea."

"I thought you would agree, so before I left Bath I made arrangements for your passage to Edenton. The sloop, *Cary,* should be at anchorage in Wisockin Bay on or about July 1st. You will need to be ready to sail then. That gives you less than a week to settle affairs here and say your goodbyes. Let's go tell to mama and the rest of the family."

Stephen could now see the Anderson farm in the distance. He wasn't exactly sure what he was going to say to Grace, but he had to see her before he left. He slowed the horse to a walk and mulled different lines over in his mind. Nothing he came up with seemed to capture his emotions. 'Guess I will just have to see how it goes and hope for the best,' he finally said to himself. He knew he had strong feelings for the young lady but so far their interactions had been brief and shallow in content. He wondered if she had any special affection for him. Not knowing how long he would be gone on his apprenticeship also clouded the horizon. Perhaps she would be attached to another, maybe even Israel, before he returned. Since their relationship was in no way serious at this point, he could not ask her to wait so they could formally court each other at some unknown future date. He glimpsed Grace, picking pole beans in the garden with her mother, as he brought his horse to a halt and dismounted.

"Good morning, Mrs. Anderson, morning Grace," Stephen slightly bowed to acknowledge the ladies in a gentlemanly fashion. "I am going to Edenton to apprentice and earn my captain's license. I just wanted to stop and…" he paused not sure what to say next. Mrs. Anderson, sensing his intentions picked up the conversation, saving him further embarrassment.

"I am sure you would like to speak to Grace for a moment. I'll be in the kitchen, working on these beans." She dismissed herself and went across the yard and into the house.

"I was sorry to hear about your ship being burned, but glad to hear you were not hurt," Grace resumed the conversation, smiling as she spoke, "thought maybe I would see you again at the Watson's church meetings."

"Been a might busy; sure have missed seeing you though," he answered, immediately wondering if he had been too forward with his comment.

"How long will you be away?" As she spoke, Grace took

a couple of steps toward the nervous teenager.

"Not sure, maybe a year, maybe two, maybe more."

"I will pray for your safety and that it will be one or two years, not more." Grace had closed the distance and was standing inside what was a casual space for conversation. She leaned forward and kissed him gently on the cheek. "I hope you will write me from Edenton, or wherever you go."

"I promise," he reached out and for a moment took her hand then released his touch. "Good bye, Grace."

"Good bye, Stephen." Their words spoken, he turned, crossed the yard, swung himself up in the saddle, waved and rode off.

His other farewells were easier to negotiate. He loaned his bow, arrows and turkey call to Able, hoping his slave friend might get a chance to shoot one of the big birds in his absence. Stephen thought about visiting with Israel before he left, but his hesitation led to inaction and time ran out without any contact. He joked with his brothers and sisters, urging them to behave themselves while he was gone, gave his mother the reassuring hugs she needed and promised his father he would make him proud by his dedication and hard work. Jupiter constructed a false bottom in a sea chest with a clever and intricate mechanism that opened a hidden compartment. It was there that Stephen placed the coin box and a small wad of shilling notes his father had given him for unexpected expenses. His clothing and other miscellaneous items were then packed atop.

The *Cary* arrived on the expected day. His father rowed him to the waiting sloop, affording him a final opportunity to prepare his son for what might lie ahead."Son, it will be different being on your own, whether at sea or on shore leave. There will be new temptations and hard choices that you will have to make without the counsel of family. You will now be the master of your own life. Enjoy your freedom, but also be careful. Trust only those who prove themselves trustworthy. Be a man of your word and try to write a word or two to your anxious mother and father when you can." They shook hands like men, loaded the small sea chest aboard, then his father was gone and the excited youth was on his way to Edenton.

On the main wharf in Edenton harbor Stephen secured a hand cart to carry his chest. He walked up Broad Street to its intersection with Water Street. A crowd was gathered in front of the Market House and as he drew closer he could hear the sound of bidding. A young black woman, probably close to his own age, was on the slave auction block and a number of loud men were clearly competing to be her new owner. She was scantily clothed to reveal her womanhood; he looked away in shock and embarrassment and continued up Water Street to the east. He picked up his pace to put some distance between himself and the shameful spectacle he had just witnessed. With a sigh of relief he spotted the sign above the door and entered the office of Hewes-Smith Shipping Company.

"Ah, you must be young Stephen Brooks; you are the spitting image of your father, minus the gray hairs of course. Welcome to Edenton. I trust you had a good sail here. I am Robert Smith."

"Sir, it is good to meet you," Stephen bowed in greeting, showing deference to both an elder and business owner.

"You will be staying at Horniblow's Tavern, a block north of here on King Street. You can also take your meals there until you ship out. Your vessel, the *Intrepid*, will be leaving port day after tomorrow. Be here tomorrow mid-morning and I will introduce you to Captain Peters. Do you have any questions?"

"No, sir, thank you, sir, I will be here tomorrow morning." Again Stephen bowed in respect.

"Sleep well, lad, and a word of warning- I would avoid the stew if I were you, sometimes it goes bad." Smith waved and chuckled as the teen made his way out the door.

As Stephen entered the Tavern he noticed two older men playing backgammon and another man tossing coins at some type of target. His curiosity got the best of him and he went over to see what the coin game was all about. The game board was made up of five lines with various sized rectangles marked off in each line. There were numbers written in each shape ranging from a high of 20 down to just 1. The goal of the game was pretty obvious, try to earn as many points possible in a given number of tosses. He also noticed that the man throwing coins was quite inaccurate, bouncing coins off the back and sides or missing the board all together. He seemed to have had perhaps a bit too much rum and was in good spirits in spite of his inaccuracies.

Aye, mate, want to try your hand at a game of Brother Jonathan? The man held out a penny. "Best score for five flips wins the penny."

"I'll give it a try, sir," Stephen said as he accepted the coin and the challenge.

"You go first my boy. The rule is the coin has to be inside the lines, no liners score," he slurred.

Stephen tossed the coin, which landed squarely in the middle of the third line, scoring 7. His second throw scored a 1 as it came to rest in the middle of the second line. The teen took careful aim at the upper left corner of the board and successfully brought the coin to rest inside the 20 point box. He scored 3 more points on his final two turns.

"31 be a mighty fine start! Now just watch and see how it's really done." The man wobbled some as he took his spot behind the line and let fly. His five throws only managed to garner 10 points. "Guess you won that one. Will you give me another go?"

"Sure, sir," Stephen was beginning to think this might play out quite well and as luck would have it, plus a slightly inebriated competitor, the young man quickly had a winning streak going at seven wins. The two older gents playing backgammon as well as the tavern's proprietor had now become spectators too and joked about putting their own money on the next winner.

"Well, I be down a host of pennies. What do you say we play one more, this time for a five shilling note?" He finished his proposal with a large gulp of rum, followed by a loud belch. "You go first; are you in?"

"Five shillings it is, plus I'll add the pennies, winner takes all." Stephen was feeling pretty cocky at this point and grabbed the penny for his first throw. He finished with a respectable 28 points, well beyond anything the old man had yet achieved, and began considering what he might do with his small windfall.

The first flip of his rival sailed a good two feet beyond the board. He missed as well with the next two throws. His fourth landed softly and squarely in the 20 point frame on the far right side of the second line of numbers. Stephen watched intently as the final throw arched toward the waiting target and stopped squarely centered in the box right behind his 20 pointer. It was a 9 point tally; he had lost by just 1 point. The man took one more swig of rum, wiped his lips with the back of his coat sleeve, gathered up the wagers and stuffed the notes and pennies in his breeches.

"Got lucky on those last ones, I did. Do hope we can play again sometime, lad." The spectators laughed while the winner grinned and strode out of the tavern.

Stephen took his bruised ego and empty pockets to bed. Luck was a fickle master indeed. He made sure he arrived early the next morning at the shipping company ready for a more positive outcome to his labors. Smith beckoned him to enter the main office. As he walked through the door, Captain Peters rose to meet him. Stephen was stunned; it was the coin thrower himself. His bow of respect was tinged by some shame as well.

"Why if it isn't last night's Brother Jonathan near winner," Peters broke out in a deep belly laugh as Stephen felt himself blush in response. "Good to meet you, Mr. Brooks. I can't get over how much you look like your father." He came over, extended his hand and placed the notes and pennies into the hand of the shocked teenager. "When I saw you come into the tavern, I just had to have me some fun at your expense. But, lad, there are some important truths here that I hope you don't miss; things are not always what they seem. What matters usually doesn't come easy and skill wins out over luck every time."

"You humbled me good, Captain; I shall not forget the

lessons you taught me at the Brother Jonathan board." Stephen again bowed again, this time feeling a measure of gratitude.

"Well, the lessons will now be about sailing, Stephen. I know your father well and I am confident he has taught you skills that will make you a fine captain. We sail at high tide in the morn. Stow your gear and plan to sleep aboard the *Intrepid* tonight. I wouldn't want you to lose your shirt spending another night gambling at Horniblow's.

Chapter 20

LETTERS

Stephen was pleased to learn that the *Intrepid* was headed to port in Bath. Shore leave there would provide him a chance to pen a letter to Grace and he was pretty certain that he could find someone traveling from there to Hyde County who would deliver his message to the Anderson farm. As the ship passed familiar landmarks, he considered what he might say. He began with the address, 'Dearest Grace,' but crossed that off in his mind as too intimate a salutation in light of their fledgling relationship. 'Dear Grace,' sounded better but 'dear' still seemed too forward. 'My good friend Grace,' was quickly rejected as lacking the warmth he hoped to project.

The strong westerly wind pushed the *Intrepid* across the swells of Pamlico Sound with some speed. The slicing bow of the ship sent droplets of salt spray skyward and the daydreaming teen was taken by surprise as the mist caught him full in the face. He shook his head to clear his senses and remove the offending water. As he ran his hand down his cheeks to dry his face, he thought back to the sweet kiss she had planted there at their last meeting. Stephen had his answer; he would begin with just her name, 'Grace.'

August 15, 1780

Grace,

I do hope that you and your parents are doing well. Please express my warm greetings to your mother and father. My ship is docked for a few days here in Bath, giving me an opportunity to write. I am safe and well. I have a fine captain who treats me kindly and the crew members are generally a solid lot.

I think of you often. When we sailed past home I waved in your direction, so wishing that I could have rowed ashore to visit. I imagine you are busy with farm chores as fall harvest time approaches. Are you still attending meetings at the Watson's? If so, let Israel know I welcome his prayers on my behalf.

I do long to hear some word or receive a letter from you. When at harbor in Edenton, I stay at the Horniblow's Tavern; you could send any correspondence there and I should get it.

Stephen

Captain Peters entrusted the ship's wheel to Stephen for

the final leg of the trip back across Albemarle Sound to Edenton. The trip had been uneventful in terms of weather or privateers with the only excitement coming from the youth's new hobby, playing cards with crew members. Gambling provided quick and easy entertainment, whether the *Intrepid* was docked or at an evening anchorage. So far he had about broken even in winnings and losses, but he was clearly hooked on the excitement and rush that came with a good hand. As they drew close to the wharf his mind was not on games; however, he was eager to return to lodging at Horniblow's hoping that he might have a letter awaiting his arrival.

September 1, 1780

Dearest Stephen,

Your mother and I send our love and warm greetings even as we pray for your welfare daily. You are much missed by all your family. All here are in good health. Your brothers and sisters pass on their greetings as do Papa and Grammy Farrow. I heard from Robert Smith that Captain Peters has taken you under his wing. He is a fine man and a skilled sailor; you are in the ablest of hands.

We recently received word from your Uncle Thomas. He was, as we feared, taken prisoner in Charlestown. The good news is that the majority of captives were freed if they would but sign a pledge not to lift up arms in the future against the King. Thomas said 'twas an easy pledge to sign and even easier one to betray. He is back with patriot forces and ready to fight again for the cause of freedom.

Your mother and I have taken up attending Methodist meetings at the Watson's. Your brother, William, is now friends with Israel and seems to have a keen interest in matters of the soul. Perhaps we will be having home meetings here when you return to us.

The corn crop looks to be excellent this fall if we can but escape any threatening weather before harvest. Able wanted you to know he shot a turkey with your bow and call. We all enjoyed the fine fowl cooked up for us by Phoebe.

Do write, son, to ease our minds and lessen our anxieties for you.

Always in our love and prayers,

Mother and Father

Stephen looked at the date of the letter; over three weeks had passed since his parents had somehow sent it north to him. He found his quill and ink, took a page of parchment and began to reply.

September 25, 1780

Dearest Mother and Father,

I cannot express my great joy at arriving back here at Edenton and opening your wonderful letter. Hug each of my sisters for me and convey my best to my dear brothers. We had a safe and easy voyage delivering goods. Father, your words about Captain Peters are indeed true. It is a privilege to sail under him. I am learning, albeit little new that I had not already been taught by you.

What grand news to learn that Uncle Thomas is hale and hearty and at odds again with all the king's men. I do hope his dour mood has improved too. May this hard season of war soon end in our favor so that a time of healing can commence.

If all goes as planned, the Intrepid *will sail north to Virginia soon. I am not sure how long we will be at sea or when I will be able to write again. I trust it will be by Christmas time.*

Your adoring son,

Stephen

Fortunately for Stephen, their departure was delayed by some needed repairs on the *Intrepid*. The extra week at Edenton meant he was still there when Grace's letter arrived.

September, 1780

My Stephen,

Your letter of August arrived here by courier three weeks to the day after you wrote it. What a most wonderful gift to receive. Your words brightened my day and eased my concerns for you. Oh how I wish I had been on the beach to wave back as you sailed by.

My mama and papa send their regards and prayers. I have seen your parents at the meetings at Watson's and they have been kind toward me, promising they would pass on any word they might get from you. When I told Israel of your letter he told me to tell you to read Psalm 91 as a good word from the Lord for your heart and soul. I have been trying to memorize the words: 'He that dwelleth in the secret place of the most High shall abide under the shadow of the Almighty. I will say of the Lord, He is my refuge and my fortress: my God; in him will I trust.' Perhaps we can both commit the words to memory?

Each day I will rise with expectation that perhaps it will be the day another letter comes.

Your Grace

Stephen studied the letter closely, perusing the content multiple times. Two words in particular stuck in his mind, her address of 'My Stephen,' and her closing phrase, 'Your Grace.' Her terms of endearment indicated a possible escalation in the seriousness of their relationship, or was he reading too much into her words? Dipping his quill into the ink well, he began.

October 1, 1780

Dear Grace,

I thank God that we were delayed in sailing this week as it meant I was still in Edenton to receive your heartwarming letter. To have been at sea and unable to read your words, for who knows how long, would have been painful beyond measure. Please thank your parents for their thoughts and prayers. Each kind expression of concern helps to close the distance between here and home and loved ones. I know not how long I will be away, but when I think of you, one day more is too many.

Thank you, Grace, for the greeting and words from Israel. I hope to save enough to buy a Bible soon so I can read the whole psalm. I trust when we next meet, we can recite the entire chapter together.

We sail in the morning up the coast toward Virginia. Maybe we will even reach Maryland, your colony of birth. Thoughts of you will make for a pleasant voyage, especially the hope that upon my return here another letter by your hand will have arrived.

I will write as soon as I can, certainly by Christmas. Till then, I hold you affectionately in my mind and heart.

Stephen

The plan was to sail the *Intrepid* north to Yorktown, Virginia, and if favorable weather and a scarcity of British presence was encountered to continue to port in Baltimore, Maryland. Both conditions prevailed. The trip took Stephen to new waters and Captain Peters took advantage of the opportunity to add to the teen's expanding knowledge of reading charts and setting course. The ship's first mate, apparently lost in the fog of a drunken stupor, had failed to be aboard when they left Edenton and the Captain had elevated the youth to that important position. Peters was keenly interested in how the lad might lead, especially with older seasoned sailors. Would he be inflated by the power, creating animosity, or would he continue to maintain the respect and loyal devotion of the crew? Stephen passed the test with flying colors. The Captain was a man of few words and his praise was unspoken. Still, Brooks could sense his mentor's admiration. His fondness for the Captain was only outdistanced by his love of gambling and his enjoyment of rum.

He removed the coins from his breeches and examined them more closely by candlelight as he lay in his hammock below deck. These were the rewards of his latest efforts, won while docked in Baltimore. One coin caught his attention, one he had not seen before. It was a half-penny dated 1773 and bore the colony of Virginia's name. He would keep this one. When he was alone, he placed it in his coin box securing it away in the secret compartment at the bottom of his chest. The coin had circulated near the birthplace of Grace on the eastern shores of Maryland. Oh, how he hoped a letter might await him at Horniblow's.

"Madame Horniblow, did any mail arrive while I was at sea?" Stephen bowed in respect to the wife of the Tavern's owner, longing for an affirmative response.

"No, I am afraid not, Mr. Brooks. You know how fickle postal deliveries can be," she replied, trying to offer some hopeful explanation for the empty box.

December 7, 1780

Dearest Mother and Father,

Christmas Joy to my beloved family. Oh, how I trust all is well with you both, with dear Papa and Grammy and my brothers and sisters. I returned yesterday to Edenton after a most exciting trip to Yorktown and Baltimore. I have never seen such as city as Baltimore with many people and so much noise and commerce. Father you would be impressed by the shipbuilding activity at the docks and dear Mother the stores and fineries would provide you endless shopping opportunities.

I was blessed by a stroke of good fortune. Our

first mate missed cast off and Captain Peters entrusted me with that responsibility. I hope he was pleased by my efforts and hard work. The crew was cooperative and we had a successful voyage.

Have you heard from Uncle Thomas? Talk here is filled with news of the King's Mountain triumph in South Carolina in October. I understand a bunch of backwoods patriots from the west, in a place called Tennessee, showed those British and Tory traitors a thing or two. Some are saying that the victory has settled matters in the south and that now the outcome rests on battles further north.

Are you still going to meetings at Watson's? Grace said she had seen you there and she much appreciated your kindness. I will be writing her soon to wish her a Merry Christmas. I will so miss the holiday feast, music and dancing. Toast a rum and eggnog for me, knowing my thoughts and love are for you all.

I hope to receive a letter from you soon.

Your loving son, Stephen

Stephen rested his quill, folded the parchment and

sealed the letter with wax. He had opted to write the easier of his two letters first. He dearly loved his family, but Grace stirred a much different emotion in his chest.

December 7, 1780

My dear Grace,

I hope I can be the first to wish you and your family a most Merry Christmas. The gift I long for most this season is to see you face to face. Since that is impossible the next best present would be a letter from your hand. And yet, letters seem such an inadequate way to express thought and matters of the heart. Then there is the long delay between penning one's own words and the cherished moment of opening the seal and reading your loved one's reply. I have read your letter of September so many times the parchment is nearly torn from the constant folding.

We did reach Baltimore, Maryland, on our last sail. It would have been such fun to go from store to store with you, showing you all the delights of a big city. I hope that someday I can take you there on my ship or maybe further beyond our shores to Europe.

My training is going well and I now have the

position of first mate on the Intrepid. I am indeed fortunate to have that rank at my age. The faster I can obtain my captain's license the sooner I shall see you again.

I imagine there will be a Christmas party, perhaps at my parent's home or elsewhere. I fondly recall our first dance together and wish I could be your partner for a Christmas jig this winter season.

We should be in port until the first of the year so I do hope I will hear from you that all is well.

Much love, Stephen

Writing the letter had proven much more difficult than he had anticipated. He struggled over each line, wondering how much to say or if maybe he had already over-stepped his bounds with the last letter. Not hearing back from her was torture, raising all kinds of anxieties in his young mind. While absence might make the heart grow fonder, it also left unanswered so many questions and intensified so many fears. Sadly Christmas passed without word from Grace or his parents. Sensing his bout with home-sickness Captain Peters invited Stephen for dinner on Christmas day. While he was grateful for the kindnesses of Peters and his wife, it hardly took the edge of his melancholy. Soon the *Intrepid* would be under sail again. The days were numbered and the mail totally unpredictable.

November 15, 1780

Dear Stephen,

Your warm letter of October 1st arrived this afternoon and ended many weeks of concern for your welfare. I envisioned shipwrecks and renegade privateers preventing you from being able to write or that you might have contracted some awful disease. Our neighbor just happened to be in Woodstock on business and was asked, by chance, if he knew the Andersons. He was kind enough to deliver the letter this afternoon on his return to this side of the county.

I have the most wonderful news to tell you. It happened two weeks ago at the Watson weekly meeting. Stephen, God met me in prayer as I confessed my need for His forgiveness. Israel says it is a 'new birth.' I claim by faith II Corinthians 5:17. 'Therefore if any man is in Christ he is a new creature, old things are passed away: behold, all things are become new.' God has blessed me with a new hunger to know more about His love and truth. This will truly be my best Christmas ever since I now know the one who was born in Bethlehem so long ago. He is my Savior and Lord. I can't wait to see you and tell you more. My prayer is that you will come to know Him also and that together we can follow Him.

I can't imagine what it must be like to be far from your family at Christmas time. You must be very lonely. Please remember that I love you in the Lord and that God so loved the world he gave us his Son, Jesus. Mama and papa send their greetings.

Wishing you Christ's joy this Christmas,

Grace

Stephen looked again at the date of the letter. Grace had sent it his way over six weeks earlier. He probably would have received it sooner if he had been in Europe rather than only a hundred or so nautical miles away. But her message perplexed him more than the postal details. It appeared his girl had gone and gotten religion. What did it mean that she 'loved him in the Lord?' Was that different from 'she loved him?'

The Methodists were a curious lot but he was only interested in a superficial level of involvement that might improve his odds with the girl of his dreams. He wasn't ready to commit to all those different types of groups and meetings Israel had told him about. Now that Grace was a member, she would most certainly be more attracted to a Godly preacher like Israel than to a rowdy sailor like him, prone to too much gambling and addicted to strong drink.

Chapter 21

YOUNG CAPTAIN BROOKS

"Captain is in his cabin. He's asking for you. He's taken sick." The crew member relayed the message to Stephen; his facial cues communicated the seriousness of the situation. The *Intrepid* had been at sea for weeks running supplies to various ports up and down the coast of North Carolina and Virginia. Except for a few rather close encounters with some privateers and a distant spotting of a British warship the trip had gone smoothly. Now it appeared things had taken a turn for the worse.

"Captain, you don't look well," Stephen was shocked by how pale Peters looked. His eyes were closed and for a moment he wondered if his leader was even breathing. The painful moan answered that fear as the Captain briefly stirred on his bed and with a grimace opened his eyes. He tried to speak but Stephen could not hear clearly. Moving closer he put his ear to the Captain's lips. He strained to make out the words.

"Too sick, you in charge, home." Exhausted by his efforts to communicate the Captain closed his eyes again and was unresponsive to Stephen's hand on his shoulder. The youth called one of the crew members and told him to stay at Peters' side. He then returned to the deck, gathered the crew about him and told them they were making for Edenton immediately. Stephen figured they were at least two days away from port provided the winds were favorable. If the conditions changed, it might be even longer.

The course was set and one of the crew was put in charge of the wheel while Stephen climbed up near the top of the mast to look for any dangers on the horizon. The dizzying height and constant swaying motion of the ship made the perch a punishing position. Somehow Stephen had always been immune to the seasickness that usually resulted and so under the present uncertain circumstances he took the responsibility on himself. He was not there long when he located the threat. His spy glass revealed the hated British flag. Feeling his pulse quicken, he descended to the deck below and took control of the wheel.

"She be a faster vessel than us, mate, what do you plan to do?" Job, clearly the crew's designated pessimist voiced the concern that all felt as the distance between ships was clearly shrinking. They were just south of Brooks Point on the sound side of the cape. Stephen recalled the narrow escape his father had executed in these same waters and made his plan.

"Boy, you'll run us aground," Job shuddered with a shrug of his shoulders as their course was taking them ever closer to shallow water. The newly designated Captain shockingly ordered for some sails to be taken in, slowing their craft even more and allowing the chase ship to draw closer. Then he executed the change of direction that would take him through the channel only he knew was there. Gaining deeper water he called for full sails and turned toward the northwest. The crewmembers, their gaze fixed behind them, saw the brig hit the sandbar. Cheers erupted on the *Intrepid's* deck. Job was the first to give a congratulatory slap on Stephen's back.

"That was some of the finest sailing I've seen in my many years on the water. How did you know we'd clear?" he said.

"My father took us this way on the *Hannah Marie* a few years back when we were being chased. Figured it might work again and luck was with us."

"I wouldn't call it luck, son, but a steady human hand directed by a stronger hand of providence." Micah, second mate, added with a broad and nearly toothless grin.

Blessed by prevailing winds they reached harbor at Edenton the next day. Captain Peters was sitting up in his bunk, better but still too weak to walk. Stephen had been quiet about their harrowing escape; however, Micah had filled him in on the details in the lad's absence. Crew members fetched a stretcher and toted the sick man to his home and the care of his dear wife. When Stephen checked on his progress a few days later he was much better.

A week later Stephen got word that Robert Smith wanted him to report to the office. When he arrived he saw that Captain Peters was already there. "Come in Mr. Brooks," Smith opened the conversation. Stephen bowed to both Smith and Peters.

"Good day, sirs, 'tis good to see you up and about Captain."

"I wouldn't be here or maybe even alive were it not for you," Peters extended his hand to the seventeen year old. "Micah told me how you evaded that brig and brought the *Intrepid* safely home. 'twas quick thinking and fine sailing! You'd make your father proud."

"And I have good news for you," Smith broke in. "Your apprenticeship is completed and your license secured. Your act of heroism under distress is to be admired. Captain Peters has vouched for both your mastery of sailing and your fine leadership of men. There will be a ship awaiting your command, once this awful war has been settled and the waters safe again for commerce." Smith now extended his hand to Stephen, shaking it firmly.

"Thank you sir, Thank you Captain," Stephen again bowed in respect.

"I imagine you might like to let the folks back home know of your success. As soon as I am ready to sail, we will take you back to Light Creek Marsh for a well-deserved furlough." Peters rested his arm on the lad's shoulder as he continued, "well done Captain Brooks, well done!"

Stephen penned two letters that evening, one to his parents and the other to Grace. Depending on the health of Captain Peters, he figured he would be back to Hyde County late spring or early summer. Their belated Christmas greetings had not gotten to his hands until his return from his recent harrowing adventures at sea as a fill-in captain. The news was old but it still brought relief to know that his loved ones, family and Grace, were well and thinking of him every day. He was already counting the days and hours until he could be reunited with them.

Captain Peters' health concerns and slow recovery postponed sailing dates on two different occasions. During the delay, Stephen acted as temporary captain of the *Intrepid* and was assigned short sailing runs around Albemarle Sound, including multiple jaunts to Mackey's Creek and north from Edenton up the Chowan River arm. They were not always alone on the water. In early June, the British row galley, *General Arnold*, began to attack and burn vessels on the Chowan River. Stephen had never seen such a craft before. Instead of relying on fickle winds, a row galley was propelled by oarsmen. The Arnold had 50 men who could keep the war ship moving, a real threat when winds abated leaving sail-reliant schooners adrift like sitting ducks.

Conversations on the Edenton docks were centered on the *General Arnold* raids and Stephen soon learned the story regarding its loyalist commander, Michael Quinn. Quinn had begun his military career as a member of the 10th North Carolina Regiment, but he had turned traitor to the patriot cause and joined the Tories in 1779. In June of 1781 he had taken charge of the *Arnold*. Having achieved a measure of success creating turmoil on the Chowan River, Quinn moved ever closer to the Edenton harbor. Residents were anxious, even fearful of his crew rowing right into the harbor and setting ships and wharves ablaze.

Stephen was on the dock when the alarm was sounded. The row galley was rounding the point and coming at full speed toward the harbor area. Sailors were scrambling in all directions, unsure what course of action to take. Arms were limited to muskets; no cannon bearing vessels were at port that could be moved into defensive positions.

"He'll run aground on that course, they're too close to shore," one of the sailors standing next to Stephen offered.

"By Jove, I think you're right," Stephen replied. At that moment the *Arnold* grounded hard and folks on the wharf could see the crew working hard to free her. In response to this stroke of good fortune, local militia members took to various small boats and successfully captured Quinn, his oarsmen and the galley. The naval victory was accompanied by a roar of cheers of those back on the shore.

Stephen was still on the pier when Quinn, bound fast, was roughly manhandled from boat to shore. Various epithets were hurled his way from bystanders. 'Bloody traitor!' 'Judas!' 'Benedict Arnold!' 'Tory dog!' 'Loyalist pig!"- these were some of the printable ones Stephen heard and would remember.

As Quinn was shoved past him, the youth flashed back to the night the *Hannah Marie* was ransacked and burned. From their shore-side hiding spot he had watched the horror through the lens of his spy glass. Was this Quinn the same man he had seen giving orders and torching his father's beloved ship? He looked again and then stared at the beaten man. The internal dialogue went from 'Could be,' to 'I think so,' to 'yes he's the one.' Stephen spit at him in disgust and when Quinn tripped to the ground, the captain-to-be planted his right foot hard into his side. Sadly the violent act gave him only a slight measure of satisfaction and revenge.

The final week he was in Edenton he received letters from both his parents and Grace. There was good news regarding Uncle Thomas. Earlier in the year he had fought at two pivotal engagements in the Carolinas. In January, patriots, including his uncle had defeated the British commander, Tarleton, at the battle of Cowpens. Coupled with the victory at King's mountain the previous fall, the fate of South Carolina had been secured in favor of the Americans.

The next decisive conflict was at Guilford's Court House in central North Carolina around mid-March. While the British under General Cornwallis, could claim victory, it was a costly one in terms of loss of life for their ranks with casualty estimates running above 25%. Thomas said it was, in essence, a strategic victory for the patriots.

Stephen had heard considerable talk about town regarding the Guilford outcome. The Tory David Fanning had been working hard to recruit North Carolinians to the British cause and his accomplices had been doing their dirty work locally, creating a general sense of insecurity. With the outcomes at Cowpens and Guilford Court House swaying public sentiment, they had withdrawn from the area, leaving folks much more confident of an eventual American victory. While Stephen was encouraged by the updates regarding his Uncle and patriot forces, he was even more excited to hear from Grace.

May 1781

Dear Stephen,

God be praised. I cannot tell you how happy I was to receive your news that you are coming home soon and that you have reached your goal of becoming a ship captain. My parents send their best too, happy to learn of your success. I will be looking daily down our road hoping to see you coming.

Have you finished memorizing Psalm 91? I pray daily for your safety from fowler's snare, the terror of the night and the arrows of the day and that you will put your trust in the Most High as the psalm calls us to do. I am now a part of a small band of four women who are meeting weekly to spur one another on to love and good works as we follow the Savior. I have so much to share with you. God is so good.

I have heard that your family will start having meetings at their home sometime soon. They are faithful in their attendance at the Watson's. Till I see you again, all my prayers and best thoughts.

Grace

Her religious words put Stephen again in some discomfort. He had not, as of yet, secured a Bible but made a mental note to make sure he copied down the psalm and began working on committing it to memory so he would not disappoint Grace. He figured a little religion couldn't hurt if it left a positive impression on the one for whom he had such strong feelings. It was early August before Captain Peters finally felt up to taking the helm of his ship again and transporting the impatient youth back to Hyde County, to his family and his Grace.

Chapter 22

RECONNECTING

Stephen couldn't help but notice the change in Grace. His eyes had quickly noticed the physical nuisances of her transformation into womanhood, a development he had to admit pleased him greatly. While her smile still flashed an engaging winsomeness, she seemed to him much more serious in her outlook on life. Clearly her spiritual "conversion," as she called it, had altered her interests and shifted her values.

He had managed to memorize the words to Psalm 91 aboard the *Intrepid* on the sail home from Edenton. Grace seemed genuinely pleased at his recitation of the verses while he had only felt the pressure of passing some test regarding his godly sensitivities.

As he rode toward the Anderson farm he hoped his new proposal might move their relationship forward on a more romantic level. Their brief meetings since his return had been awkward compared to their more expressive and affectionate correspondence. Stephen was finding face-to-face conversation much more difficult than penning words on paper. Grace waved a greeting from the open front door as he rode into the yard.

"Good morning, Miss Anderson, 'tis a fine October day, is it not?" Stephen bowed respectively as he stepped up on porch.

"Yes, Mr. Brooks, 'tis a fine day indeed." Grace smiled and chuckled at their formal exchange and added, "It is good to see you Stephen." Stephen reciprocated with a smile of his own.

"And it is good to see you, Grace, I trust all is well with your parents?"

"Father is off for supplies in Woodstock and mother is putting down pickles inside. We can sit and visit here on the porch if you wish." Grace opted for a single chair, avoiding the porch swing which would put them side by side.

"So I take it you had a good crop of cucumbers this season?" Stephen sat alone on the swing as it was the only other available choice and struggled to make conversation.

"A splendid harvest indeed. We will enjoy pickles from the old crock well into winter. Perhaps mother will bring some to the Methodist meeting at your house Thursday night," Grace answered.

"I will look forward to a crisp sample then." Stephen paused and leaning forward turned to his real intent for the visit. "I was wondering if you might like to go to the barn party Saturday night at the Gibbs'. There should be some fine fiddling and lively dancing." Stephen tried to read the nonverbal cues as Grace reflected on his words, apparently searching for the right response. She broke eye contact with him and looked away before replying.

"Stephen, I thank you for your invitation, but I must decline. I believe I should abstain from dancing as such behavior does not advance our sanctification or the Kingdom of God. I do hope you will find it in your heart to understand my reasons for saying no to your request, but I must seek to put God first in my decisions." Stephen was taken aback by her obvious religious devotion. On the one hand he wanted to argue for the virtues of dancing as a harmless and enjoyable social activity. On the other hand he held his tongue, realizing that it was impossible to convince Grace otherwise. Her mind was clearly made up on the subject. This was more of that seriousness of soul that he had come to expect from her.

"Of course, Grace, I would not want you to violate your conscience," he stopped speaking and focused his gaze on her before continuing, "I do so enjoy your company." Grace sighed and shifted her position in the chair, creating a bit more physical distance between the two of them. Stephen was not prepared for what came next.

"I fear, Stephen, that I may have been too forward in my past behavior and too intimate in my letters. I am sorry, but we are young and must guard our affections with great care. I want to be your friend, but I think it best, at least for now, that we only see each other at social gatherings such as church meetings." Grace stood and turned toward the front door. "I need to help my mother with the pickles. Goodbye Stephen." With that she was through the door and out of his sight before he could even mutter his own parting words. Embarrassed, perplexed and deeply hurt he turned his horse toward home.

Stephen pulled his coin box from the niche and emptied the contents onto his straw sleeping mat. He found the

Virginia Half Pence, his 'Grace' coin, and examined it closely. The cold metal offered no solace for the pain he was feeling. His real wish was that he might hold Grace in his arms rather than a worn copper token of her birthplace. For days he had been replaying her words over and over in his mind. One phrase offered a glimmer of hope, 'at least for now.' Friends, at least for now; social settings only, at least for now; guard our affections, at least for now; goodbye, at least for now. The candle near his bed flickered in response to some fickle air current. Stephen eyed the candle as it burned bright again and found a measure of comfort in the small omen. At least for now their love was not totally extinguished; perhaps, with care and patience, it would flame again. He gathered the coins, put the box back in its place and blew out the candle.

"Good morning, son," Mary greeted Stephen as entered the cooking area. His sullenness and apparent bruised ego had not escaped her parental gaze and she had rightly interpreted the source of his grumpiness. "Coming to the meeting tonight?" she continued, "the Anderson's will no doubt be here."

"Reckon I will come, mother," Stephen replied. He had initially planned to avoid the gathering and a potentially uncomfortable encounter with Grace, but the coin-candle moment of the previous evening had altered his strategy. Nothing but misunderstanding would result from his absence. He would not nurse a grudge by running from Grace; rather he would make every effort to win her heart. He was pretty sure that her new faith was both the source of their conflict and the key to its resolution.

Isaac Watson opened the gathering by leading the worshippers in an exuberant rendering of a familiar hymn by Isaac Watts.

Our God, our help in ages past,
our hope for years to come,
our shelter from the stormy blast,
and our eternal home.

The reason for the added enthusiasm in praise was the news that had spread rapidly that day around Hyde County and beyond. The British commander, General Cornwallis, had surrendered at Yorktown, Virginia on October 19th. American and French troops had secured the victory and taken some 8,000 prisoners. Rumors were circulating that this might mark the end of armed conflict and that the patriots had finally prevailed in their pursuit of independence.

"For my text tonight I am reading from Psalm 32, verses 12-22. Now hear the word of the Lord!"

> Blessed is the nation whose God is the LORD; and the people whom he hath chosen for his own inheritance. The LORD looketh from heaven; he beholdeth all the sons of men. From the place of his habitation he looketh upon all the inhabitants of the earth. He fashioneth their hearts alike; he considereth all their works. There is no king saved by the multitude of an host: a mighty man is not delivered by much strength. An horse is a vain thing for safety: neither shall he deliver any by his great strength. Behold, the eye of the LORD is upon them that fear him, upon them that hope in his mercy; To deliver their soul from death, and to keep them alive in

> famine. Our soul waiteth for the LORD: he is our help and our shield. For our heart shall rejoice in him, because we have trusted in his holy name. Let thy mercy, O LORD, be upon us, according as we hope in thee.

The small audience listened intently as Isaac expounded on the verses. Stephen had to admit that the young preacher seemed especially inspired as he contrasted a lasting and steadfast hope in God with the weak and inadequate sources of human strength and wisdom offered by a king. He could see Grace nodding in agreement as Isaac's words crescendoed to his concluding appeal to personally trust in the mercy of God alone for salvation, that only in Christ could one find a lasting peace in the heart.

The message touched Stephen deeply and he found himself struggling to maintain his composure. He quickly brushed away the tears and glanced about hoping no one had seen his emotional display. But Grace was fixed on him; her face smiling as she silently mouthed words that Stephen struggled to interpret. She repeated the phrase again and this time he understood what she was saying, 'I am praying for you.' Her petition on his behalf was more than he could handle and not wanting to make a spectacle of himself he rose and fled the room. Once outside and away from the swirling emotions of the moment he dismissed the experience as just an expression of relief that the war might be truly ending. It would be some time before such yearnings of the soul would stir him again.

"Bear, I wonder if the fish are biting down at Brooks

Creek." Stephen hadn't addressed Able by his boyhood name for years but the warming spring weather had the eighteen year-old recalling memories of creekside fun.

"You mean Bear hollow, Gator?" Able laughed.

"What do you say we get away for a couple days of camping and fishing? I'll talk with father and see if we can take some time away before planting starts."

"I just wish Wolf were here to join us," Bear was now reminiscing too and both shrugged, acknowledging they still keenly missed their childhood friend.

They were surprised when they spotted the sign Wolf had carved and placed by their campsite years earlier. Amazed that it was still standing, they examined it more closely and discovered that someone had recently affixed the old sign to a new post with care, clearing the surrounding brush away so that it was visible again. As they stood looking at the strange omen they heard the howl of their favorite Wolf. A few moments later he emerged from the woods, grinning from ear to ear and leading a fine black horse. The threesome exchanged warm hugs and hardy pats on the back.

"How'd you know we would be here?" Able finally asked.

Wolf chuckled and revealed the truth. "I stopped by your house not long after you had left and William told me where you were headed. I just had to speed ahead and do my magic before you arrived."

"We could have had no better surprise, my friend. It is so good to see you again. You were on our minds as we planned our trip and as we trekked our away here along familiar paths. Whenever I hold your farewell coin it also prompts many fine memories of our adventures together in the marsh. Tell us you have you come back to stay."

"I am on my way west to a place called Tennessee or maybe even beyond to Kentuck. I hear there is abundant game and lots of space to get lost in. I have no more family to hold me to this land and, as you well know, us Indians are not always welcomed here abouts." Wolf loosened the strap and pulled the saddle from his horse. "But before I go, I sure would like the taste of one more bass from your creek."

The campfire blazed hot, shooting sparks up into the clear night sky. The fresh fish, coupled with fried potatoes and hard cider made for a splendid meal. But the food was bland compared to the re-telling of their favorite stories and ever-so-slightly embellished exploits. Their boyhood banter, now transformed into the mature laughter of young men, hung in the air and echoed across the silent marsh, a tribute to lasting friendship.

Stephen woke at the sound of the whinny and propping himself up saw Wolf was almost finished saddling his horse. Able was also awake and the two stood and joined Wolf for farewells. "If you ever get to Tennessee or Kentuck, keep an eye out for me and listen for the howl." Wolf extended his hand, first to Stephen, then to Able. "You will both always be welcome in my camp." He swung himself into the saddle and gently spurred his horse forward. Before reaching the timber he stopped, wheeled about and waved a final goodbye and then he was gone.

When they arrived back at the house there was a letter waiting for Stephen. He broke the seal, carefully pulled the parchment from the envelope, unfolded the note and read.

April 10, 1782

Dear Mr. Brooks,

I hope you and your family are well and that your time home has been refreshing. Please convey my greetings to your father and mother. Captain and Mrs. Peters also send their best. As I write this, news that peace talks will soon begin in Europe is encouraging and a signed treaty with Britain and King George III can't be too far in the future. Work is currently underway on a clipper ship at the Washington ship building facilities. That ship will be yours to command when it is ready to sail. Perhaps you would like to travel there to observe the construction? The last word I received projected the ship should be finished by late summer or early fall, in time to make some supply runs before winter weather sets in.

If you do travel to Washington and have time, might you ride the King's Highway to Edenton so we can discuss further the details of your commission? Do exercise caution as reports still swirl about of hostilities with small raiding bands of Tories. Seems they cannot accept the certainty of their defeat but continue to fight the inevitable.

Most affectionately,

Robert Smith

Smith's letter couldn't have come at a better time for Stephen. His relationship with Grace was going nowhere and seeing her at social gatherings was painful. While he had continued to attend weekly prayer meetings he remained fearful that another disturbing emotional display might catch him by surprise, a thought he clearly did not relish. He also had to admit that a trip to Washington and on to Edenton was much more exciting than the boredom of spring planting. His father, however, did not share his excitement for such a speedy exit. He would not be free to go until the corn was planted. His last task, before leaving, was to pen a note to Grace.

May 20, 1782

Grace,

I will be gone for some time. My parents can give you details about my trip. I do thank you for your prayers on my behalf. I accept that at this time our relationship is one of friendship and, while I might long for more, I will respect your wishes.

Affectionate thoughts until we meet again,

Stephen

His parents were up early to see him on his way. He gave his Grace note to his mother, asking her to pass it on at the next prayer meeting. As usual, tears accompanied her pleas and warnings about safety. His stoical father was more practical in his farewell.

"Take this and keep it close at hand for protection, son." The elder Stephen handed him a satchel, inside was a fine smooth bore flintlock pistol, along with lead balls and a powder horn. "Be sure to give my greetings to both Mr.

Smith and Captain Peters and may God speed your return home." Stephen nodded to his father, gave his mother another quick embrace and was on his way.

Chapter 23

BEAUTY AND UGLINESS

The sights, sounds and fragrances of spring were intoxicating. The wild olive bushes were alive with small white flowers, their sweet aroma wafted over Stephen as he gently nudged his horse along the road. How ironic, he thought to himself, that the beautiful shrub should be dubbed Devilwood, just because it was difficult to split into firewood. He detected the next scent even before he spotted the twining vine growing nearby.

The sweetness of the Yellow Jessamine flowers filled his nostrils like an overpowering perfume. Blanket flowers carpeted both sides of the wagon path. Sun-yellow and red-flame petals danced in time with the breeze. Their color and unique undulations had earned them the more common name: fire wheels.

Stephen reined Pilgrim to a stop next to a Honeysuckle vine. Hummingbirds were working the trumpet shaped scarlet flowers like a swarm of honey bees. Stephen sat bewitched by their purposeful movements as they took in the nectar, darting from one blossom to another and then flying off to a distant perch to enjoy their prize.

"This looks like a good spot for a bite to eat. What do you think Pilgrim?" The horse, named by Stephen's mother after the lead character in Bunyan's 'Progress', cocked his head toward him, made eye contact and seemed to say, 'is there a carrot for me?' Slipping from the saddle, the young man picked up on the request and pulled a stubby carrot from his saddle bag. Tying Pilgrim to a convenient branch he sat down on a log and quickly devoured the sandwiches his mother had prepared for his day's journey.

Then, as if on cue, the after lunch entertainment began. First he watched a Great Egret perform his courtship ritual in a marshy area a stone's throw away. The lovely bird would preen itself then stretch its neck high in the air; snapping his head down he would then preen himself all over. The plume of feathers on his back shimmered with each sharp movement.

A bright red cardinal hopped back and forth on a low hanging branch singing his heart out. Cheer, Cheer, Cheer, Birdie, Birdie, Birdie, Birdie, he repeated his song again and again; apparently hoping to woo his own lover.

The sharp caw of a crow triggered an immediate gobble from an old tom turkey. It wasn't long before this new character strutted onto the stage; his gaudy plumage opened into a huge radiant fan of color as he drew his wing tips along the dusty roadway. His lusty gobble was also an appeal for female companionship.

"Well Pilgrim, seems all of nature is looking for love and some are a might more successful than me."

Stephen ruminated about his actions earlier that morning. As they had approached the turnoff to the Anderson farm he had given serious thought about a brief visit with Grace. In his hesitancy he had slowed Pilgrim's pace. The horse had taken this as a cue they were about to turn and veered, on his own, toward the familiar lane. Stephen had quickly corrected Pilgrim's direction with a rein to the left, decision made.

Stephen rose and stretched his legs with a short walk along the forest edge. He spied the Maypops or Passion Flower in the shade. What a fascinating and remarkable creation; large white petals below, a ring of blue, white and black quills radiating out from a green center, topped off by another sprout of light green petals. Arrays of butterflies were passionately enjoying their own interactions with the flowers.

Stephen offered Pilgrim another bite of carrot before he saddled up. The warm sun, cacophony of bird songs, and dazzling bouquet of May blossoms had worked their magic. He wished he had the talent of a poet to capture the moment in eloquent words. It was as if God had pulled back a curtain onto His splendid and magnificent handiwork. He offered a prayer of thanks for the glimpse and then softly spurred Pilgrim into motion.

Stephen made camp along a tributary flowing into the Pungo River. He figured he had traveled about 30 miles. At this rate he reckoned he would reach Washington day after tomorrow. Detours around sloughs and marshy areas slowed his progress and added miles to the journey. He managed to fish a few perch from the stream which he prepared over the fire. He enjoyed the company of Pilgrim. The horse's occasional neighs seemed to dull the loneliness as darkness set in. The sliver of moon provided little light.

Stephen stoked the fire and readied himself for sleep.

Unfortunately a Mockingbird decided it was time for a nightly serenade. For what seemed like hours the bird ran through his repertory of songs. The mimic began with a rendition of lilting warbler tunes. Stephen had just about been wooed to sleep when the bird shifted to crow chatter, a mix of caws and clicks that clearly did not make for a restful lullaby. The disgruntled teen rose and threw a rock in the direction of the noise. The bird seemed to heed the warning and for a few minutes the night was still. Then, to Stephen's dismay the little bird decided he wanted to play robin. The last song of the night he remembered before finally drifting off to sleep imitated the sweet cadence of a thrush.

Pilgrim's wet nose was not an especially welcomed introduction to the new day. At the end of his tether he was just barely able to nuzzle his sleeping rider by stretching his neck as far as he could. "Morning Pilgrim, you must have slept better than I. Ready for another day's ride are you?"

The two fell into a steady rhythm marked by long stretches of dry ground interrupted by the occasional need to ford a stream. About mid-afternoon Stephen saw smoke in the distance. Not sure of what he might discover he pulled the pistol from his saddlebag, checked to make sure it was loaded, and secured it in a small scabbard attached to the saddle.

He was still some distance away when he saw the source of the smoke. It was not coming from a chimney but from the charred remains of a small cabin still smoldering in the afternoon heat. Puffs of gray billowed skyward. Not far from the rubble sat the distraught family. The woman appeared to be treating her husband's wounds. Both looked dazed by the disaster and hardly responded to Stephen's approach. A young teenage girl was holding a baby; a lad, perhaps six years of age or so stood next to his crying sister. Stephen grabbed his flask of hard cider and drew near to the small circle of pain.

"What happened? Would you like a drink?" He extended the libation to the trembling hands of the mother. All were in shock and sobbing.

"We were attacked about sunrise by three men on horseback. Tried to hold them off with my musket but ran out of lead. They set fire to our roof and when I came out to fight they knocked me unconscious with the butts of their weapons. They done violated the womenfolk and we couldn't save our youngest from the flames. He is dead there in his sister's arms. Can you help me bury our boy?" Stephen had never witnessed such ugly terror nor felt such utter despair.

"Certainly, I will do whatever I can," he answered feebly. Stephen ransacked his supplies for anything that might help. He returned with some meager food stuffs and bandaging strips and assisted the grief stricken parents in binding up the head injury. Little was said. There was so little that could be said. Stephen did learn that the attack seemed to have been politically motivated. The riders had shouted 'long live the king' and 'death to patriots' during the assault. Defeated in the battles of war, the Tories had apparently turned their anger against the defenseless couple and their children.

The family name was Goode. The parents were Jonathan and Elizabeth; their children were Charity and Luke. The dead infant, only a few months old, was William.

Elizabeth pointed to the spot among the wildflowers and Stephen began to dig the tiny grave. He fashioned the small coffin from some scraps of lumber he had located in an outbuilding. He watched, tears streaming down his face, as the couple and siblings said their final goodbyes, kissed the baby, and gently placed their son and brother in the makeshift casket and lowered it into the cavity in the ground. Stephen recalled the words he had memorized and in that awful moment found his voice.

"He that dwelleth in the secret place of the most High shall abide under the shadow of the Almighty. I will say of the LORD, He is my refuge and my fortress: my God; in him will I trust. Surely he shall deliver thee from the snare of the fowler, and from the noisome pestilence. He shall cover thee with his feathers, and under his wings shalt thou trust: his truth shall be thy shield and buckler. Almighty God, we commit to you little William, confident in the hope of the resurrection and life everlasting. Jesus as you blessed the little children, now take William close to your side and cover him in your love. Amen."

Stephen's moment of divine inspiration seemed to bring some needed comfort to the heart-stricken family. In future years, whenever he stood graveside, he would flashback to this scene of tranquil beauty and terrible loss.

Stephen stayed on with the Goode family for the next three weeks and helped out as they tried to rebuild from the ashes. He and Pilgrim rode many miles around the surrounding area, rallying neighbors to come to their assistance. Many strong arms made quick work of felling trees and erecting another cabin. Supportive friends brought needed supplies, an abundance of food, and most importantly open hearts and listening ears to aid in the healing process.

Stephen, confident that the Goodes were not alone, knew it was time to continue his journey. He marveled at what could only be the hand of providence in all that had transpired. He embraced the children first, then the parents. "If all goes as planned, I should be back this way in a few weeks, maybe a month. You will be always in my thoughts until then."

"You were clearly a God-send in our darkest hour, Stephen," Jonathan said as he gave him another firm bear hug.

"God's touch is on you, Stephen. I wouldn't be surprised if you turn out to be a minister one day," Elizabeth added, smiling through her tears.

"See you soon," he waved back and headed west to Washington.

The Washington shipyards were just south of town on the east banks of the Pamlico River. The town had been established in 1776 by Colonel James Bonner and was the first village in the colonies to be named after General George Washington. The community had played a critical role in supplying goods during the war as the area had never come under British occupation. With close proximity to an almost endless supply of timber it was a natural setting for the burgeoning shipping industry. To date the yards had been primarily building sloops and smaller two-masted schooners. The clipper that Stephen was to captain would be their first three-masted creation.

Stephen hitched Pilgrim to a railing and began a walking tour of the yards, looking for the foreman in charge. Most of the work was being done by skilled slave labor. The wood artistry reminded him of the fine work Jupiter had done on the Brooks home. He watched as a group of slaves stoked the fire used to steam heat the hull planks so that they could be bent into the desired shape. The partially finished hull of his ship loomed on the scaffolding before him. The shallow draft and lines of the craft would be perfect for the waters of the local estuaries, open sounds and beyond.

"She'll be fast and nimble, she will. Can I be of some help?" The burly foreman had spied the young man prowling about his yard and wondered what his business might be. Stephen acknowledged him with a respectful bow and introduced himself.

"Good day sir, my name is Stephen Brooks, soon to be captain under commission to Robert Smith of Edenton." Upon learning his name the man moved quickly to welcome him with a handshake.

"Been expecting you, we have. Mr. Smith wrote us that you would be coming to inspect our work and progress on your ship. My name is Hezekiah Chambers and I am in charge here. What do you think of her?

Stephen ran his hand along the hull near the bow of the vessel and was impressed with how finely fitted the heavy planks were and how carefully they had been planed smooth. "She is a beauty; your workers are excellent craftsmen indeed. When do you anticipate she will be ready to sail? Stephen leaned forward eager to hear the answer to his question.

"I would guess mid to late September if we do not encounter any problems with ordered rigging and other hardware. I know Mr. Smith is eager to get you on the water yet this season and I am confident we should meet his expectations. Will you be staying in Washington until she is seaworthy?" Finishing his statement the foreman shot a wad of tobacco juice that landed on a nearby pile of lumber with a brown splash.

"Oh, no, in a few days I plan to be on my way to Edenton to meet with Mr. Smith. On my return trip I will decide whether to remain here in Washington or travel back home to Hyde County. Could you suggest a good tavern where I might find lodging and a passable meal?"

Hezekiah stroked his beard in thought and then sent off another tobacco projectile. "*The Three Sails* has the best food by far. But if you are looking for a good time, if you know what I mean, I would suggest *The Rusty Anchor.* Just ask for the wench named Rose and tell her I sent you. She will gladly satisfy your needs for a few shillings. We wouldn't want you to spend a cold night alone in bed."

Stephen was not used to such crass language and he felt himself flush red with embarrassment at the foreman's words. Hezekiah just laughed when he saw his crude comments had achieved their desired impact on the young man. "Guess we'll see you tomorrow morning unless you sleep in." The grizzled foreman was clearly making sport of Stephen and couldn't resist more needling. "Tell Rosie I'll be by for my kiss soon."

Stephen couldn't make his way back to Pilgrim fast enough. Swinging into the saddle he spurred the horse toward the small town. He sped up as he passed *The Rusty*

Anchor and was finally relieved to eye a sign with three sails.

The next morning Stephen made sure to rise early and was at the shipyard before Hezekiah and his crew arrived. He leisurely strolled about, enjoying the various smells from sawdust and woodchips to turpentine and pitch resin before turning his attention to carefully inspecting every inch of his future ship. She was just over 112 feet in length with a beam width of about 25 feet. He estimated the draft would be near 8 feet. Content that she was free of imperfections he climbed the ladder to deck level. Slaves were now hurrying about, engaging in their various work assignments.

"What are you going to name her?" Hezekiah startled him, appearing from around the corner of a building.

"I didn't think that would be my decision," Stephen responded with surprise.

"Smith told me to heed your instructions and have your choice carved and painted on her bow."

"She will bear the name *Grace*," Stephen responded without a moment's hesitation.

"Then *Grace* it shall be," Hezekiah accented his words with his usual spit of tobacco juice.

Chapter 24

JUSTICE

Confident that the construction work on *Grace* was in good hands, Stephen headed to the northeast the next morning. It was good to be away from the noise and temptations of the town and alone again with Pilgrim. Stephen could have opted for a stagecoach ride to Edenton, but he much preferred the solitude and controls over his own schedule that traveling by himself provided. He was on the Virginia Path section of the King's Highway, a continuous thirteen hundred mile ribbon of road, ruts and mud that ran from Boston all the way to Charlestown, South Carolina. Charles the II had ordered its construction back in the mid 1600's and it had taken nearly a hundred years to complete. The route would take him directly to the town of Edenton and his appointment with Robert Smith. It was a two day trip if he averaged about 30 miles each day. Making ferry connections might cost him another day.

"I think they are going to need to change the name of this road, Pilgrim. The King's Highway just doesn't seem appropriate now that we have won our independence from the crown. Got any good suggestions, my friend?" Stephen found conversations with his travel companion helped pass the time. At times he even thought the horse might be participating in the dialogue. Pilgrim snorted and whinnied. "Was that Oats lane, or Carrot Avenue?" Stephen chuckled back. "I think Freedom Highway would be the best choice. Are you good with that?" Again Pilgrim's neigh seemed an affirmative response.

They forded the Roanoke River just past the cutoff to Williamston. The spot brought back memories of the trip to Halifax some six years earlier; that was indeed an adventure not to be forgotten. The 1656 French Liard coin he had received from Thomas Respis was a tangible reminder of the dangers and successes of their journey.

The wagon coming his way interrupted his daydreams. The driver reined his team to a stop and signaled as if he wanted to talk. "Good afternoon, sir, how far to Windsor?" Stephen asked. The wagon held a small family and a load of possessions.

"You won't make it by nightfall. Would you like to camp with us? We are ready to stop for the day, 'tis safety in numbers." Stephen's first impulse was to go a bit further and camp by himself but something about the man's reference to possible threats caught his attention.

"Well, thank you, I think I will accept your invitation. My name is Stephen Brooks. I am on my way to conduct business in Edenton." Stephen dismounted and approached the wagon his hand extended in greeting.

"We're the Smiths, I'm Charles and this is my wife Sarah, our son Jacob and daughter Temperance. We are on our way to South Carolina to start a new life. It's good to meet you."

Later, while setting up camp, Charles pulled Stephen aside. "I didn't want to speak fully in the presence of the children and cause them worry. About an hour or so back we passed three men who were watering their horses near the road. They were a suspicious looking lot and we kept right on going. Their glances in our direction stirred a real sense of alarm in my spirit. I was relieved to find you, thinking that if they followed us, I would not be able to resist them alone."

"Could you describe them?" Stephen asked. As Charles recounted what he had observed, Stephen's worst fears were realized. The picture Charles painted matched the sketchy details the Goodes had provided concerning their assailants. One of the men walked with a noticeable limp. Two were average height and build while the third was short and stocky. Two rode on Bays; one was astride a black and white horse. There were too many similarities to be coincidental. Charles, a look of horror on his face, listened as Stephen related how these same men were responsible for crimes of arson, rape and murder.

"What will we do? We're too far from any towns of refuge; oh God, my wife and children. What if they come tonight?" There was real panic in the man's voice and Stephen tried as best he could to calm him so they could plan some course of action. They were taking stock of their weapons when they heard riders coming. Charles nervously grabbed for his musket and tried to load it, in the process he dropped it on the ground. The man had turned white as a sheet, his eyes darted about. Stephen managed to grab him before he took off running.

"Calm down Charles, that can't be them. The sound is

coming from the south, not to the north where you last saw the scoundrels." The young father was still trembling violently but let out a sigh of relief. The group of five horsemen, seeing their camp, came on at full speed, the dust swirled as they reined their mounts to a stop. The apparent leader of the group removed his hat and wiped the perspiration from his brow as he spoke.

"We are militiamen from Williamston, a posse in pursuit of three renegade Tories, guilty of treason and worse crimes. Have you seen them, two are on bays, the third rides a black and white?"

"I, I, I saw them…I saw them just an hour or so ago north of here." Charles struggled to speak as his body and mind tried to adjust to the switch from total dread to the assurance of rescue.

"The same three committed unspeakable acts northwest of the Pungo River nearly a month ago." Stephen quickly filled them in on what had happened at the Goode cabin.

"They have left a trail of murder and mayhem behind them. They will pay with their lives." The bitter anger in his voice suggested to Stephen that this man had experienced his own loss at the hands of the three. "You best stay alert, keep your guns a ready." With that final comment hardly off his lips the five spurred their horses hard and sped off north in hot pursuit.

Charles answered the inquiring looks of his wife and children with partial answers of what had happened, sparing them the anxiety that a full revelation would arouse. The men took turns on watch through the night. Stephen thought he heard distant gun fire soon after the inky darkness had enveloped them but he couldn't be sure whether it was such or just his imagination playing tricks.

The night passed without any cause for alarm. The stressed travelers eagerly welcomed the dawn, taking in the warmth of the rays as they spread light across the campsite. Sarah prepared breakfast; before they ate Charles said a word of grace.

"Lord, you have spared us the terror of the night. We are grateful for your protection and for bringing Stephen to us to steady our hands and calm our hearts. Strengthen us with this food and give us and Stephen success on our travels. In the strong name of Jesus we pray, Amen."

After the shared meal they broke camp. Stephen saddled Pilgrim and headed north. Charles and his family loaded the wagon and rumbled southward.

It was close to noon when the duet reached the community of Windsor. Riding down King Street Stephen saw a crowd gathered in front of the courthouse and turned aside to see what the ruckus was all about. Two men were fastened tight in pillories, exposed to the taunts and abuse of the local citizens. Their injuries oozed blood but no one was attending to them with care. In front of the wooden frames lay the body of a third man. Stephen recognized the man who stood over the corpse, his foot planted on the body as if he was posing with a trophy. It was the leader of the posse. They had captured their quarry and it appeared justice was being served.

The jeering assembly and vivid scene of guilt and punishment left a strong imprint on him. On the one hand he had no sympathy for the criminals as they were getting the proper reward for their acts. Apart from any political loyalties, the three were guilty of vile evil. But he also realized that the righteous vengeance of the crowd could in no way fill the emptiness that now resided in the hearts of Jonathan, Elizabeth, Charity and Luke any more than his angry kick into the ribs of Quinn had been able to raise the burned hull of the *Hannah Marie*.

While the leaders of nations might secure a peace in Europe that would officially end this war, how would trust and community be restored between neighbors who had for years battled, lived in suspicion, holding fast to bitterness and hatred? Would the masses round up known and imagined Tories and parade them about in ridicule, bruising their bodies and seizing their property or find it in their hearts to extend forgiveness and create a new unity? Would a true United States arise from the ashes of conflict, betrayal and evil intent?

Stephen reached Edenton in late June. The trip had taken him much longer than he had expected, due largely to the important, but lengthy time he had stayed with the Goode family following their tragedy. He headed straight to familiar haunts, Horniblow's Tavern, to assuage his thirst and greet the owners who had befriended him during his earlier stay in Edenton. With rum in hand he took a seat and surveyed the room. It was here he had first met Captain Peters and been snookered by him in a game of Brother Jonathan. Fond memories and important lessons hung in the air of the old inn.

He noticed two men having a rather heated debate at the bar and cocked his ear to see if he could make out what they were arguing about. "How can you question the choice of the eagle as our national symbol, 'tis the grandest of birds and is unique to our shores. It soars on wings of strength and is the image of regal majesty as it sits on its perch." Having made his point the man slammed his tankard hard on the counter top as an exclamation point.

"Listen to reason, my good friend and consider the wisdom of Benjamin Franklin, signer of the Declaration. I agree with him, it should be the splendid turkey." He lifted the newsprint and began to read:

> I wish that the bald eagle had not been chosen as the representative of our country, he is a bird of bad moral character, he does not get his living honestly, you may have seen him perched on some dead tree, where, too lazy to fish for himself, he watches the labor of the fishing-hawk, and when that diligent bird has at length taken a fish, and is bearing it to its nest for the support of his mate and young ones, the bald eagle pursues him and takes it from him.... Besides he is a rank coward; the little kingbird, not bigger than a sparrow attacks him boldly and drives him out of the district. He is therefore by no means a proper emblem for the brave and honest. . . of America.. . . For a truth, the turkey is in comparison a much more respectable bird, and withal a true original native of America . . . a bird of courage, who would not hesitate to attack a grenadier of the British guards, who should presume to invade his farmyard with a red coat on.

He then mockingly mimicked his friend's tankard slam with one of his own, as if to say, 'take that and smoke it in your pipe.'

And so the jabs went back in forth, a verbal boxing match, with blows landed by each side, one for the turkey, the other for the eagle. Stephen couldn't resist joining the fray and moved to the arena to add his voice. He learned that the Continental Congress had just selected the eagle as the national symbol and, like Franklin, not all were pleased with their decision. While his experience with the eagle had been limited to an occasional glimpse of the soaring creature, he was intimately acquainted with the wily behavior of tom turkey. Stephen had to side with iridescent fowl with the glowing head colored red, white and blue, hues that matched the flag design adopted in 1777. The good-natured fun lasted for some time, only ending when the eagle lover ordered another round of rum for all. His generosity finally quieted the opposition.

The next morning the future Captain Stephen Brooks Jr. was at the office of Robert Smith. He brought Smith up to date on the progress of construction and they signed papers regarding his captain's commission and the ship to be called *Grace*.

" 'tis a fine choice of name, Stephen. 'twill remind crew, captain and all who see her of our desperate need for divine grace. I recently received a letter from a dear relative in Britain who penned words about such marvelous grace. Let me see, where did I put that letter?" Smith shuffled items on his desk top until he found what he was looking for. "Here it is, the words are by the Anglican Priest, John Newton, who pastors the parish in Olney where my relative attends. She says he wrote the hymn some ten years ago.

Amazing Grace how sweet the sound
That saved a wretch like me
I once was lost but now am found
Was blind, but now I see
'twas Grace that taught my heart to sing
And Grace my fears relieved
How precious did that grace appear
The hour I first believed."

Any commentary that Robert Smith might have added at that moment was interrupted by a knock at the office door. It was Captain Peters. "I had to stop by and add my word of congratulations, Stephen." He firmly shook his hand, then let go and embraced him. "It is so good to see you. Mrs. Peters sends her love as well. I brought you a small token to celebrate the occasion." Reaching into his pocket he pulled out a silver coin. "Someone told me you had a small hoard of coins and I thought this would be a perfect addition to your collection. I picked it up years ago in Antwerp, Holland, on one of my cross Atlantic sails. It's called a Ship Shilling. Look here and you can see the fine imprint of a sailing ship. While it won't make you rich, by any means, it should serve as a fine keepsake to remind you of this day of achievement." Peters handed Stephen the coin along with another affectionate pat on the shoulder.

"I will always treasure it, Captain. Thank you so much." Stephen inspected the Six Stuiver coin, admiring the likeness of the three-masted ship.

The return trip home took only a week with a short visit to the shipyards to see if things were still on schedule and an overnight stay with the Goode family. Stephen could see that trauma and grief were not easily left behind in trying to move forward. The presence of friends was helpful in lightening the load but there was still a heavy burden that only they alone could understand and would have to bear.

He told them about the Smith family and briefly described how their attackers had met justice in Windsor. They ate together, laughed together and cried together. Touched afresh by their pain and reflecting on the powerful words of "Amazing Grace," he headed on to Light Creek Marsh and his own precious ones.

Chapter 25

THE STING OF DEATH

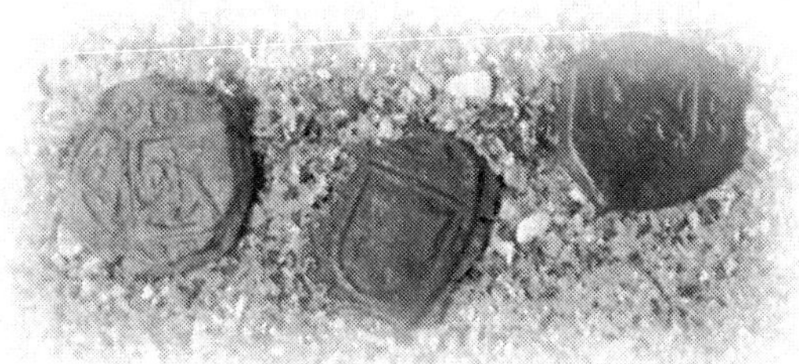

Stephen wrung out the cloth and placed it again on the forehead of his grandmother. Grammy Farrow's health had been declining for some time but had taken a serious turn for the worse in late October. Family members were taking turns staying at her bedside to give Papa Farrow some respite. She would not die alone; her daughter Mary had stressed that point loud and strong. 'No one should pass from this veil of tears into eternity without feeling the comforting touch of a loved one.' She had repeated the phrase multiple times during her mother's prolonged illness. Stephen had expected to be at sea by this time, captaining his new vessel, *Grace*. He was grateful that delays had postponed his departure so that he would be at home when she died.

"I will be back by early afternoon, son," Mary said as she wrapped a cloak about her to provide protection against the chilly fall wind. "I don't believe it will be long now. She may be gone before I return." She was out the door before he could respond. The momentary silence was soon shattered by the wheeze and snort of Papa's snoring in the adjoining room.

Stephen sat and reminisced. Grammy had cared for him, with her miracle poultice, when he lay on this very same bed, stricken by a rattlesnake bite. His mind flashed back to childhood days and the countless times she had provided him with some treat as he ran in from play. Her warm smile, her laughter, her physical presence had lit up the Farrow house with cheery brightness. What a contrast to the cold dark dampness that seemed to now fill the room.

The Angel of death was becoming a too frequent intruder in Stephen's life; from infant grave to pillory post to an elderly bedside. He realized that unwelcomed death could visit at any age and any place. It was a sobering reality. What was it that Israel had said at a recent home meeting, 'teach us to number our days that we might apply our hearts unto wisdom.' What needed wisdom was he to draw from these deaths? Maybe he needed to have another talk with the young Methodist preacher.

"Any change?" The voice startled him. Papa was awake and standing at the doorway. The strong grandfather who had tossed him playfully into the air as a lad now looked drawn, tired and feeble.

"No, the same," he answered. Together they sat for what seemed like hours. Jacob held her hand. They listened to her shallow and raspy breathing. Suddenly Amey opened her eyes and looked at both of them intently, a faint but certain smile appeared and then she was gone. It was her final gift to both of them and one they would hold fast to in their grief.

Stephen immediately sent Ezekiel to relay the sad news. Mary, along with two close friends from the community, arrived to care for the body. They would lay out Grammy for a coming time of visitation. Family, close friends, and even relatively unknown community members, would be coming to pay their respects. Preparations also needed to be made for the coffin, home funeral and procession to the grave and burial. Mary steeled herself to the task, going through her mental checklist.

"Son, please go toll the bell so all will know she has died. Seven long peals, one for each decade of her life here on earth. Then ride home and have Jupiter start on the coffin. Tell Phoebe to begin preparing food for the visitors, and, and…" Mary stopped talking when she drew near to the bed. "Oh, dear mother," she gasped. Her father and Stephen drew alongside and together they wept and held each other as the reality of grief and deep loss took hold of them.

The bell provided a simple answer to their need for community communication. Danger, fires, deaths, call to arms, and announcements of gatherings could all be signaled across the country side by a variety of different rings. Stephen spurred on Pilgrim and they soon reached their destination. Stephen took the rope and pulled. After the loud ring had resonated he counted to ten and then pulled again. Seven long sad tolls. The solemn message would be heard and understood by many. Others would soon learn by word of mouth that Amey Elizabeth Swindell Farrow had passed.

Mary draped black crepe across her mother's mirror and also affixed the material to windows and porch railings. Bands of the material were cut into strips to be worn on the left arm by male family members at the funeral. Black knots would adorn the left side of the women folk. Mourning gloves were sent out to extended family and close friends, inviting them to attend the services. Jupiter carefully crafted the nine sided coffin. Israel Watson was asked to conduct the funeral.

Over the next day and a half a steady stream of family and community members passed through the room where Grammy's body lay. It was a unique and cherished time to share special memories, comforting hugs and words of encouragement. There were also many toasts offered in honor of a life well-lived. Grace offered her condolences as well, along with reassurances to Stephen that he was always in her prayers.

Israel's loud clear voice called the mourners to attention as he read from the Anglican Prayer Book familiar words from John, Job and Timothy.

> I am the resurrection and the life, saith the Lord: he that believeth in me, though he were dead, yet shall he live: and whosoever liveth and believeth in me shall never die. I know that my Redeemer liveth, and that he shalt stand at the latter day upon the earth. And though after my skin worms destroy this body, yet in my flesh shall I see God: whom I shall see for myself, and mine eyes shall behold, and not another. We brought nothing into this world, and it is certain we can carry nothing out. The Lord gave, and the Lord hath taken away; blessed be the Name of the Lord."

The words of Psalms 39, 90 and the lesson from I

Corinthians 15:20 left little impact on Stephen as he glanced about the cramped room and shifted his weight on the hard pine bench seat. He did catch the phrase about 'numbering our days,' and the reference to our years being three score and ten, a perfect match to the lifespan of his grandmother. Israel's concluding words cut through the dullness of his mental daze leaving him with a strange mix of hope tinged by doubt. "Death is swallowed up in victory. O death, where is thy sting? O grave, where is thy victory?"

Stephen, his brothers, and cousins took turns as pallbearers during the long procession to the far side of the Farrow property and the grave site by Cypress Creek. Together six young men hoisted the weight of the coffin to their shoulders and slowly walked for a distance until the next team assumed their place beneath the load. The transfer was carefully made without coming to a complete stop. The men had all been instructed about the superstition that a halt to the procession might soon be cause of another death.

Stephen couldn't help but observe the contrast between this late fall grave scene and William Goode's spring burial. There were no flowers to brighten the setting and no songbirds added a positive note of cheer. Only noisy waterfowl, etched against the leaden skies, beat their wings against a steady cold wind. Dried leaves, their former trees dormant for the impending winter, swirled about on the ground. He hoped that the threat of rain would hold off, at least until the grave was closed. Reaching the site they laid their burden down on ropes beside the open wound in the earth. Israel again read, his voice raised to conquer the sounds about and the noises within.

"Man that is born of a woman hath but a short time to

live, and is full of misery. He cometh up, and is cut down, like a flower; he fleeth as it were a shadow...In the midst of life we are in death: of whom may we seek for succor, but of thee, O Lord...O Lord most mighty, O holy and most merciful Saviour...Thou knowest, Lord, the secrets of our hearts; shut not thy merciful ears to our prayer; but spare us...merciful Saviour."

Grasping the ropes in unison they lifted and slowly lowered the coffin into the ground. First Jacob, then Mary the eldest daughter followed by her siblings, and finally each of the grandchildren dropped handfuls of soil into the grave as Israel recited words of promise.

"For as much as it hath pleased Almighty God of his great mercy to take unto himself the soul of our dear sister here departed, we therefore commit her body to the ground; earth to earth, ashes to ashes, dust to dust; in sure and certain hope of the Resurrection to eternal life, through our Lord Jesus Christ..."

Closing the prayer book Israel looked skyward and began to sing with deep conviction. "Lord, have mercy upon us. Christ, have mercy upon us. Lord, have mercy upon us." He repeated the words and the mourners began to sing along in unison.

The crowd, following the lead of the young pastor, recited the Lord's Prayer. "Our Father, which art in heaven, Hallowed be thy Name. Thy kingdom come. Thy will be done in earth, as it is in heaven. Give us this day our daily bread. And forgive us our trespasses, as we forgive them that trespass against us. And lead us not into temptation; but deliver us from evil. Amen."

Bowing in prayer, he paused once more, giving all a

moment to collect their thoughts before the closing benediction. "Oh Merciful God, the Father of our Lord Jesus Christ, who is the resurrection and the life…who also hath taught us…not to be as men without hope…We meekly beseech thee, O Father, to raise us from the death of sin unto the life of righteousness; that, when we shall depart this life, we may rest in him, as our sister Amey did, that, at the general Resurrection in the last day, we may be found acceptable in thy sight; and receive that blessing, which thy well-beloved Son shall then pronounce to all that love and fear thee, saying, Come, ye blessed children of my Father, receive the kingdom prepared for you from the beginning of the world: Grant this, we beseech thee, O merciful Father, through Jesus Christ, our Mediator and Redeemer. The grace of our Lord Jesus Christ, and the love of God and the fellowship of the Holy Ghost, be with us all evermore." Departing from the script, Israel added, "and all God's People said Amen." And so they did.

Just as the final shovel load of dirt landed on the tomb a soft rain began to fall. A faint peal of thunder echoed in the distance. The funeral guests quietly retreated from the scene, leaving close family some privacy for their final goodbyes.

"The thunder and rain are reassuring omens that mother is home with Jesus," Mary said as she leaned hard into the embrace of her father.

"Yes dear, she lived, she loved well. She loved all of you children so much."

The bow of the *Grace* deftly sliced her way through the early December chop on Pamlico Sound. She was all that Stephen could have hoped for in a sailing craft, quick and nimble yet steady to the course. The sea was again performing its special magic on the youth. The rush of the wind cleared his head from troubling thoughts about his shore-bound Grace. While the ship was responsive to his touch its namesake continued to hold herself at a distance.

Sailing was also a therapeutic break from the gloom that had settled like a fog over the Brooks home following the death of Grammy. Mary was having a hard time adjusting to her mother's passing. There were sudden bursts of tears, followed by days of dark despondency. Each member of the family was handling this season of bereavement differently. His father threw himself into activity, apparently unsure how to respond to the swinging moods of his wife.

Stephen's siblings charted their own paths through the unfamiliar waters of loss. While William wanted to recount memories of his grandmother, Esther preferred silence and would try to hush her brother when he would start reminiscing.

The death for Stephen had taken on a spiritual dimension as he struggled with the surging tides of his soul. One phrase had lodged itself firmly in his mind, 'Death is swallowed up in victory, O death where is your sting?" Israel seemed so certain of the promise of eternal life, and though the idea was appealing to Stephen, he knew deep down that he lacked such a heartfelt assurance of his own future destiny. Grace too radiated hope of God's victory over the last enemy death. Oh how he envied her simple faith. For now, the demands of sailing provided a welcome diversion for the young captain. He would deal with these heavy questions later.

They had not been long at dockside in Portsmouth when they heard the word; a preliminary draft of Articles for Peace had been signed the last day of November in Paris by both British and American representatives. The town was buzzing at the good news and Stephen soon found his spiritual questions displaced by tankards of celebratory rum and busy activity at the gambling tables.

His head swirling from too much drink he found himself relying on the steady arm of the barmaid as they negotiated the steps toward his room. Her low cut dress pushed her bosom high and close to his face, flooding his mind with thoughts of temptation. She opened the door and helped him to his bed. She turned, closed the door and then came back and sat down next to him.

"My company is yours for the night, sailor." She moved close and kissed him with a passion he had only dreamed about. "A few shillings will bring you much pleasure," she said, leaning back to read his eyes and see if her proposal would be accepted.

"I never…I haven't," his voice slurred as he struggled for words.

"Ah, your first time, is it? I will be gentle with you," she laughed. "twill be a night you won't soon forget." She held out her hand, awaiting the promise of some tangible reward for her allure.

Stephen reached into his pocket to fish out the required coins. His mind and pulse raced. He was far from home, no one would know, no one would see. He had needs she seemed eager to satisfy. Grace had rebuffed him. This wench was eager to hold him. The battle raged as he pulled his hand from his pocket. His eyes fell on the tokens he held in his palm. It was the Virginia Half Pence 'Grace' coin, the one he had secured on his trip to Baltimore, a keepsake reminder of his sweetheart's birthplace. An overwhelming sense of guilt and shame came over him. God saw, God knew. It was as if the stench of death was wafting about the inn room, as if the devil himself had entered the place. He could not betray Grace, he could not sin so.

"No, I can't…no, go, leave now!" Stephen rose, struggled to open the door and directed her out with a swing of his head and a final word of "go." In tears he fell on his knees beside the bed. "God forgive me. Grace forgive me." The prayer was repeated multiple times before he finally collapsed on the bed, totally exhausted from his conflict with evil, but grateful that he had avoided one of death's sharp stings.

Chapter 26

EMBRACED BY GRACE

The next evening Stephen opted for the solitude and safety of his cabin aboard the *Grace*. Lighting the candle beside his bed he picked up the well-worn book and turned to where he had left off reading. His mother had given him Bunyan's "*The Pilgrim's Progress,*" to provide some reading entertainment while he was at sea. He fondly remembered the old Anglican Priest in Bath who had passed on Bunyan's fanciful allegory the same day he had put the Scottish Bawbee coin into his young hand.

Stephen had enjoyed following the exploits of Christian as he traversed the arduous path from the City of Destruction to the distant Celestial City. The intent of the writer was clearly revealed through the colorful characters encountered along the way, from Obstinate and Pliable to Help, Faithful and Hopeful. Stephen found himself intrigued by other players in the drama, like Mr. Worldly Wiseman, Evangelist and the Giant Despair.

A few days earlier he had been caught off guard by another surprisingly emotional moment. He was grateful that this time he was alone, not surrounded by inquisitive family, friends or Grace. It happened as he trekked up the hill with Christian at the place of the cross. He could almost feel the heavy burden on Pilgrim's back as he tried to run up the steep slope where stood the awful instrument of death. Then the miracle of release happened and Stephen wept. The burden fell from Christian's back, rolled down the hill and disappeared into the empty sepulcher, never to be seen or felt again. Tears continued to fall as Bunyan pictured the indescribable joy experienced by the weary pilgrim at that moment of load-lifting.

> Then was Christian glad and lightsome, and said with a merry heart, He hath given me rest by his sorrow, and life by his death. Then he stood still awhile to look and wonder; for it was very surprising to him, that the sight of the Cross should thus ease him of his Burden. He looked therefore, and looked again, even till the springs that were in his head sent the waters down his cheeks.

Their tears seemed to mix as the drops from Stephen's eyes splattered on the page before him. What was leading to these spontaneous outbursts? Was it the result of bottled up grief at the deaths of William Goode and Grammy Farrow? Had it something to do with his recent hour of temptation in the Portsmouth tavern? Might it be the stress of assuming leadership of the *Grace*? Or was it the quiet whisper of the Spirit, the gentle but persistent wooing voice of God? Stephen weighed the various theories and wondered if maybe it was the combination of all these factors.

This night he picked up the story in Beulah Land. He envisioned Bunyan's landscape alive with beautiful flowers and nourishing fruits which Christian and his companion, Hopeful, enjoyed to their full. He read on as the path brought them to a river with no bridge to cross. In his weak attempt to pass over Christian struggled helplessly against the deep water and raging current. Caught up in the suspense, Stephen continued on, relieved to learn that the strong presence and encouragement of Hopeful led to Christian's rescue from the overwhelming flood. Reassured of Christ's love he stepped from near drowning to the solid rock of the eternal shore.

Stephen took the helm of *Grace* and turned her toward deep waters. The strong wind pushed them swiftly along toward an unknown destination. He relinquished the wheel to the first mate and strode with pride along the deck. It was his ship. Well, technically it belonged to the Smith Shipping Company, but it was his to captain, and he only eighteen years of age. Bright promise, future years marked by successful endeavors, and images of abundant prosperity flashed through mind. He would sail away with his Grace, he was certain his achievements would finally win her heart.

Near the rear of the ship he jumped up to the railing to take in the view. It was a costly misstep as he slipped on the wet board and disappeared over the side. The plunge took him far into the waters and before he bobbed to the surface the speedy vessel was moving away at a fast clip. He struggled to clear the salt water from his nose and throat and tried to yell. Again and again he pled, hoping that someone on board would see him astern and turn the craft back. He fought the raging fears within; no one seemed moved by his screams for attention. Soon the *Grace* disappeared on the horizon. He was desperately alone with no lifeboat or rope to cling too. He fought to stay on the surface but the pull of the depths seemed stronger and he slipped below the waves.

"Captain, Captain," he vaguely heard the words from his watery grave. "It's just a dream, Captain, wake up!" Startled he opened his eyes. It was his mate. "You were thrashing about and yelling like you were drowning, Captain." Stephen sat up, drenched with sweat, as if he had been awash in deep waters. It had all been a nightmare of the soul. He was indeed safe and within the strong hull of *Grace*.

Stephen was overjoyed that he would be home for Christmas. The *Grace* was secure at moorage in Bath, his crew released for holiday shore leave and he was free. While the tired old horse he had purchased was considerably slower than Pilgrim he would still be at the Brooks house soon. He had been sorely tempted to turn up the path to the Anderson home as he neared Lake Mattamuskeet but he would abide by Grace's wishes and keep their contact strictly on a social level at group gatherings. Perhaps he would see her at the weekly Methodist meeting at his folk's place.

His dreamt brush with death had triggered a number of questions so he decided to first stop and visit with the young pastor, Israel Watson. He found him in the barn, feeding the livestock.

"Why if it isn't young Captain Brooks, home for Christmas I would guess?" Israel set the pitchfork aside and moved quickly to greet him. "And how is it with your soul these days?" Stephen was taken aback by the abrupt turn to spiritual matters but then again that had been the reason for his detour. At Israel's invitation he poured out the details of his recent struggles, fears, doubts and unresolved questions. The minister listened actively without interruption. He nodded to affirm his understanding and even endured some rather long pauses in the rambling narrative to provide his young guest with the opportunity to find his own words.

"So what do you make of make if it all, Israel?" Stephen had reached the end of his story and the perceptive man of God had the opening he had been waiting patiently for.

"I believe 'tis the Almighty's hand of conviction upon you, Stephen. The inner turmoil you are experiencing reveals His gracious touch upon your spirit as He calls you to trust him fully. He can speak through nature, through the words of others, even through dreams to make Himself known. He is pursuing you with love. He wants to roll your sins into the empty tomb of our Savior that you might find forgiveness and release from your burdens." Israel paused and knelt to one knee and gently embracing a young lamb into his arms, stood and continued.

"You might remember the story of the lost sheep in the gospel and how the Shepherd left the ninety and nine, safe in the fold, to pursue and rescue the one who had by his own stubborn will wandered far away. Stephen, recognize you are that helpless astray lamb. He wants to embrace you with His saving grace. Turn toward Him, not away, as His voice often grows weaker when we repeatedly reject His kind invitation. There is a powerful picture of this in John's Revelation, the last book of the Bible. He describes Jesus standing outside our heart's door, gently knocking. The Christ will not force his way in. The latch to open the door is on our side only. He speaks, 'Behold I stand at the door and knock: if any man will hear my voice, and open the door, I will come in to him, and sup with him, and he with me.'" Israel stopped speaking and placed the lamb on the floor. He could see that Stephen had heard enough for the present moment as he glanced about, looking for a way to escape.

"Thank you for your counsel, Israel, I will give thought to your words, but the sun is setting and I want to reach home before dark. I suppose I will see you next Thursday at the meeting?"

"Lord willing, I will be there. Have a joyous Christmas with your family. Please excuse my persistence but hear the author of Hebrews warning as you go; 'today when you hear his voice, do not harden your heart.' God bless you Stephen and goodnight."

"Merry Christmas, Israel," he answered as he turned the weary nag toward home.

The holiday festivities at the Brooks home were dulled by the recent loss of Grammy. Mary had left the black crepe draped across the mirror, but no visible symbol was really needed to remind the family that she was gone. All felt the pain of her absence, illustrated by the empty chair next to Papa Farrow at dinner. There would be no fiddle playing, singing or gift giving, just a quiet meal, shared stories of past Christmases, and the traditional scripture readings from the Book of Common Prayer. Only one phrase lodged in the mind of Stephen as his father read the familiar passages and prayers for the day celebrating Christ's birth.

> He came unto his own, and his own received him not. But as many as received him, to them gave he power to become the sons of God, even to them that believe on his name: which were born, not of blood, nor of the will of the flesh, nor of the will of man, but of God. And the Word was made flesh, and dwelt among us, and we beheld his glory, the glory as of the only begotten of the Father, full of grace and truth.

Stephen pulled the coin box from the niche and removed the red pouch. Grammy had made it for him; a Christmas gift when he was just a little boy of five or six. The bright crimson triggered a vivid image in his mind drawn from the pages of *The Pilgrim's Progress*." Suddenly, in his mind's eye, he was back at the foot of the cross, where Christian's burden had been lifted. The place of shed blood, of death had become for Pilgrim a place of new life. Familiar emotions stirred within; leaving the pouch on the bed he descended the ladder and slipped quietly out the door.

The air was crisp. He trembled, but not from the cold. The three quarter moon provided more than adequate light for him to navigate the familiar path to creek side. He sat on the giving stump where he and Wolf had exchanged childhood trinkets and sobbed until that place of dead wood became a sacred sanctuary, a meeting site with God. He would always cherish memories of that moment, the assurance of sins forgiven, of his own burden rolling into an empty sepulcher, of welcoming the warm embrace of divine grace as he opened the door of his life to the Christmas Savior.

Stephen sat quietly through the Methodist meeting the following night. He was processing the marvelous transaction that had taken place at the stump. In time he would tell all, to family, to Israel, and to Grace. He followed the lead of Israel in singing the hymns and a smile crossed his face as he sang with deep meaning the words of Charles Wesley's salvation song.

And can it be that I should gain
An interest in the Savior's blood?
Died he for me, who caused his pain?
For me, who him to death pursued?
Amazing love! how can it be,
That thou, my God, should'st die for me?

He left his Father's throne above;
So free so infinite his grace!
Emptied himself of all but love,
And bled for Adam's helpless race:
'tis mercy all, immense and free,
For, O my God, it found out me!

Long my imprisoned spirit lay
Fast bound in sin and nature's night;
Thine eye diffused a quick'ning ray;
I awake: the dungeon flamed with light;
My chains fell off, my heart was free;
I rose, went forth, and followed thee.

No condemnation now I dread;
Jesus, and all in him, is mine!

Alive in him, my living Head,
And clothed in righteousness divine,
Bold I approach the eternal throne,
And claim the crown, through Christ, my own.

Over the next week he rose early each morning and made his pilgrimage to the stump for prayer and Bible reading. For the first time in his life, he found the pages of scripture appealing. While his study did not answer all of his questions or relieve all of his doubts; still there was a sense of serenity and deep joy he could not adequately explain and he knew God was at the center of it all.

He bowed and smiled at Grace as he welcomed the Anderson family to the Thursday night gathering. It was January 1, 1783 and exchanges were marked by many 'Happy New Year's Day' greetings. During the opening hymn Stephen began to tremble with fervent enthusiasm, overcome by the presence of his Redeemer and Great Friend. Seeing this unexpected display of religious excitement, Israel called on Stephen to pray. This time there was no embarrassment or shame as he cried out in prayer, tears streaming down his face.

"Precious, merciful Lord, you love us so. We come tonight, always in need of you. Meet us here by your Spirit. Stir in us a deeper love for you and grant us courage and insight to follow you all our days. Make your face to shine upon us and be gracious to us, lift up your countenance upon us and give us your heavenly peace, we pray in the name of Jesus, Amen."

Stephen poured out his conversion story as family and friends gathered around him eager to learn more about

God's transforming touch on his life. As the details spilled out, his parents and siblings all came under conviction and found sweet release in personal expressions of new found pardon and faith. Israel, sensing that no sermon was needed, guided the worship with selected scriptures punctuated by spontaneous prayer and occasional shouts of 'Hallelujah' and 'Amen.' Grace gave Stephen a hug and a smile of warm understanding and acceptance. Hours later Israel finally dismissed the meeting with a benediction taken from II Corinthians."Therefore if any man be in Christ, he is a new creature: old things are passed away; behold all things are become new." All added hearty 'Amens!' It was truly a New Year evening of divine encounter that the Brooks family would often recall with joyful thanksgiving and praise.

Three short days later Stephen was headed back to Bath and his Captain's duties. But his first stop was for dinner at the Anderson home. Grace's parents had invited him following the remarkable events of Thursday night and while he was excited to see Grace he was also anxious about what his new faith might mean for their relationship. As he nudged his pokey mare along the road, he also replayed other conversations that had taken place the last couple of days. The most disturbing interaction had taken place with his father's slave, his friend Able.

"I hear you found God, Master Stephen," Able said as he gave his childhood buddy a playful shove.

"I think it might be more accurate to say God found me, my friend," Stephen gently pushed back.

"Either way you put it, I have a question. My parents have heard stories that the Methodists don't look kindly on slavery. I was wondering, are you thinking about giving us our freedom?" The tone of the conversation had obviously taken a sudden serious turn that Stephen had not anticipated and he wrestled with how to respond.

"Able, this is all pretty new to me right now and I am afraid I don't know much about what the Methodists believe regarding owning slaves or a lot of other things for that matter. I will talk to Israel and see what he has to say." This was Stephen's first but certainly not his last question as to how his encounter with God and decision to follow might impact his values, social understanding and day-to-day practices.

There had not been enough time, or at least that was his excuse, to pursue the matter with Israel. But the young minister had loaned him Wesley's *Doctrines and Disciplines* and Stephen hoped that might address the issue.

He turned the reluctant beast up the Anderson pathway. Joseph, his wife and Grace were waiting for him on the front porch of their small home and he waved as they came into his view. The delightful meal was accompanied by friendly chit-chat, nothing more. Stephen needed to be on his way having some distance to cover before nightfall, but he hated to leave with unresolved tension in the air between Grace and himself. He slid his chair back from the table, preparing to rise.

"Mrs. Anderson, what a wonderful dinner. Thanks again for the invitation and chance to visit. However, I do need to be on my way." He stood, his gaze focused on Grace.

"Stephen, could we talk for a moment before you leave?" Grace acknowledged his eye contact and clearly interpreted what he wasn't saying in his words. Together they walked outside and strolled to the garden area behind the house. Having found a bit of privacy, Grace turned, took hold of his hands and looked directly at him. "I know I was cruel when you first returned from the sea and invited me to the dance. I so wanted to continue our relationship but knew I had to wait, wait so that God could do his own work in your life. I felt that you would have only continued to be interested in faith as a means to know me and that would have been wrong for both of us. I praise God that in His timing you have found new life. Stephen, I do hope you understand." Tears were welling up in her eyes as she spoke.

"I do understand, my focus was on you, not on His grace. You rightly interpreted my heart and my intent. Now God has changed, is changing, my heart and mind. I am not sure where He will lead but I am determined to follow."

"I do so love you, Stephen," Grace wrapped her arms around him and kissed him and for precious moments they embraced. Gently breaking her hold, he tenderly placed his hand under her chin and lifted her face till their eyes met and answered.

"And I love you, Grace."

Chapter 27

SHIP AND SHORE

The *Grace* was headed south, her ultimate destination the Caribbean. Below deck were naval stores of pitch and turpentine, destined for Dutch held ports. It would be by far the longest sea adventure of Stephen's life and take him to unfamiliar waters. He was grateful that his first mate, Jonah, had made frequent trips there prior to the Revolution.

"So tell me Jonah, how did you get your Biblical name?" Stephen asked as together they plotted their course on the navigational charts spread out on the desk.

"I was christened Jonas and that was the name I went by until my days aboard a whaling vessel out of New Bedford. I managed to get myself caught up in some ropes and pulled overboard while we was chasing a harpooned bowhead. The crew fished me out and laughingly dubbed me Jonah and the name just stuck." Jonah drew another hard pull on his pipe and blew out the smoke.

"Guess there is a bit of Jonah in all of us, friend," the young Brooks winked as he stored the weathered chart.

"What do you mean, Captain?" The mate looked puzzled as he scratched his scalp.

"Well I was reading Jonah's story in the Bible, remember how he ran from God? Seems to me we are all running so, yet He keeps chasing us in love, even putting whales and things as such, in our path to get us to stop and turn to Him."

"Maybe so, sir," Jonah turned to resume his duties on deck. The crew had become accustomed to their captain prodding them with God comments and questions since his last shore leave. It seemed he had gotten religion or something. Jonah wondered if it had something to do with the nightmare he had awakened Stephen from a few months earlier.

They passed Charlestown, South Carolina, the next day. His Uncle Thomas had been briefly held there as a prisoner of war. The hated British had finally been ousted from the city in December. Stephen wondered if the townsfolk might want to change the name now they were free of old King George; maybe something with less of a ring of royalty to it.

Leaving the mainland of Florida in their wake, they headed past the larger islands of Spanish Cuba, French Saint-Dominque and another isle first named San Juan Bautista, by Christopher Columbus. The latter was now called Puerto Rico or Rich Port, after the discovery of gold there. Back a century or more this had been prime pirate territory. Stephen thought of his first coins, pirate cobs that might once have jingled in the pockets of buccaneers sailing these very waters.

"Saint Eustasius to starboard," one of the crew shouted. So this was the tiny island of great fame and fortune Jonah had been boasting much about, the so-called Golden Rock. The first mate came alongside Stephen and recounted bits and pieces of local lore and history.

"See Quill there, 'tis the volcano out from which the small island spreads. You'd never guess this nearly barren hunk of stone was once a most prosperous Dutch port. Why wealth flowed through here like a mighty river. Enterprising merchants took full advantage of the fine harbor and key location to fill their pockets. There were no British, French or Spanish trade problems here, only great economic opportunity." Jonah paused, took a draw on his ever present pipe and continued his narration. "'tis the first place we was saluted as an independent country too." Jonah was enjoying his edge in expertise and waited for the young Captain to ask his question before revealing too much.

"How did that happen to be?" Stephen inquired, taking Jonah's bait.

"Back in November of 1776, the American Brig, *Andrew Doria,* sailed into this harbor, flying our new colors. Her Captain fired off a thirteen gun tribute to the colonies. The local governor fired back an eleven gun cannon salute from Fort Oranje. The two less shots, as you know, is a clear signal of welcome to a free and sovereign nation. It was the first time our independence was honored by another international power. But there is even more to the story." Jonah again fell silent. Timing was everything in a good story. Finally he went on. "If they hadn't sold us munitions the war would have been over before it hardly started. We relied on those needed military supplies time and time again and they were more than willing to provide. Some say though, that our final victory is also tied to this place." Jonah strained at the distant island again delaying the conclusion to his saga.

"Jonah, would you finish your tale?" Stephen could not stand the suspense any longer.

"Well, the British didn't take kindly to folks helping us out so or saluting us as free. A goodly number of their battle ships sailed here from our shores to make them pay. They burned, looted, imprisoned and virtually destroyed everything. If those same ships had stayed off Virginia, instead of coming here, they might have prevented the triumph of French and American forces at Yorktown and we would not have hope of a treaty in our favor." Confident he had successfully reached the climax to his history lesson; Jonah smiled and gestured with pride toward the United States flag waving high on *Grace's* mast.

It was hard to leave the inviting warm, clear and bright blue waters of the Caribbean Sea. *Grace*, her hold now filled with a cargo of molasses, salt and sugar, sailed north toward the roily waters of Pamlico Sound. They had obtained the goods at the port city of Willemstad on the island of Curacao, just off the north coast of South America.

In addition to such commodities, the city was better known for its trade in human flesh, slavery. Crew members had even joked about smuggling some slaves and rum on board to increase their profits on the return trip. "A half dozen of them would fetch us a nice sum on Saint Dominque where the demand for slaves is high. No one would be the wiser, Captain," Jonah had said with a wink. At least

Stephen thought he was only jesting.

Stephen's initial reading of Wesley's words on the topic of slavery had left him uneasy. Clearly human bondage was not held in favor by the founder of Methodism. He wasn't sure how he would answer Able's question when he returned home. His grandfather owned slaves, his father owned slaves, his uncles and countless neighbors and friends owned slaves. Surely freeing a large number of slaves would create economic hardships for both the owners and the owned. It would upset the social structure. Didn't the Bible also speak in support of the institution, encouraging proper behavior on the part of both master and slave? Stephen was confused and not a little conflicted on the subject.

On a much brighter note he was excited to get home. They had been at sea for months and the uncertainty of their schedule had made correspondence impossible. He wondered about and worried some for the welfare of his family and his dear Grace. They had covenanted before their last parting to pray daily for each other and to memorize the words of Psalm 139. That had been a wise and sustaining decision. He could sense her prayers and they had brought comfort and strength.

He had tried hard to honor God among the rough and calloused hearts aboard ship. The men seemed to have no hunger for God, no interest in discussing His goodness or His ways. They were a hard and disinterested audience for his weak efforts. Their ports of call were dens of iniquity and he had frequently barricaded himself in his cabin rather than go ashore and face constant temptation. It would be good to join voice with like-minded believers in song, prayer and study. He even looked forward to the usually long and sometimes dry messages of Israel. He would have never guessed that in a few short days he would be doing the sermonizing.

The Goode family was as happy to see him as he was to see them. Hugs abounded, complimented with joyful laughter and mixed with a fair share of tears. Stephen found it a bit difficult to embrace Elizabeth as she was clearly heavy with child.

"If it be a boy, he will be named for you, Stephen," Jonathan said proudly.

Over supper Stephen shared the news of his conversion experience at Christmas and his New Year proclamation of faith at the Methodist meeting. It was Elizabeth who came up with an idea.

"What if we invited some neighbors, would you tell your story, show us how to start our own prayer meetings?" Before he could answer one way or another she answered herself. "Good, we will get out the word tomorrow for Thursday night."

Frankly Stephen was amazed when nearly twenty folks, adults and kids, crowded the small home two nights later. There were even a few out on the porch listening through the open doorway. He could only remember one hymn and his memory there was limited to a single verse. But he taught it to them as he had learned it. He sang a line and they repeated it, trying their best to raise the roof in heartfelt worship.

O for a thousand tongues to sing
My dear Redeemer's Praise
The glories of my God and King
The Triumphs of His Grace.

It seemed only right to him to talk about grace, not his sweetheart but the unmerited favor of God. He knew not how to organize a sermon, but he spoke from the heart and God was in it. He knew it; he could feel it and soon his audience gave evidence that they felt it too. People cried with joy as they came to faith. First Jonathan, Elizabeth and their children Charity and Luke; then others believed and found assurance of divine forgiveness. Amazing supernatural grace flooded every nook and cranny of the place. Stephen slept little that night, as he tossed and turned he kept repeating the words he and Grace had been memorizing from Psalm 139.

> O lord, thou hast searched me, and known me. Thou knowest my downsitting and mine uprising, thou understandest my thought afar off. Thou compassest my path and my lying down, and art acquainted with all my ways. For there is not a word on my tongue, but, lo, O LORD, thou knowest it altogether… Whither shall I go from thy spirit? or whither shall I flee from thy presence?... How precious also are thy thoughts unto me, O God! How great is the sum of them! If I should count them, they are more in number than the sand: when I awake, I am still with thee.

As he left the next morning, Elizabeth again got in the

final word. "I told you God had his hand on you and that you'd be a minister someday. I think I was a might prophetic, Stephen."

He couldn't wait to tell Grace what had happened, how he had been able to serve God in a small but meaningful way with the Goodes and their neighbors. He had to admit that he had found the experience even more exhilarating than his first love, sailing.

There was no detour around the Anderson farm now. He even spurred the old horse to try and gain a bit more speed as he turned down the long path. She saw him first and sprinted toward him, lifting her skirts a tad so she could run faster without tripping. He jumped from the horse and swung her feet free of the ground as he hugged her tightly. Then realizing he had perhaps been a bit too forward, he backed away and bowed in customary respect.

Grace radiated a special kind of beauty. Her physical attributes were clearly stunning to Stephen, but her character bore the winsome mark of a sure and steady faith, an attractiveness that was revealed through her words and manner. They walked and talked, laughed, prayed and caught up on recent events. She listened with keen interest and obvious delight as Stephen recounted the details of the prayer meeting at the Goode home.

"God is good and as He says, 'we shall reap in due season if we do not lose heart.' Guess I will have to call you the preaching captain, my love." With that she gave him a soft kiss on the cheek. Stephen went on and tried to describe the rare wonder of the Caribbean, promising to take her there someday so she could behold the breathtaking scenery.

Then Grace took her a turn in the conversation.

"Oh, your Uncle Thomas is home. Now that peace seems certain, General Washington has started dismissing the troops. Hasn't taken him long to find love either. He and Angelica Riordame are right sweet on each other. I think there will be a wedding soon." Stephen was sure he spotted a twinkle in her eye at the reference to a possible wedding.

"Good for him," Stephen whooped. "Thomas deserves some marital bliss after what he has endured on the battleground. It will be a great joy to see them tie the knot." Now Grace perceived a similar gleam in her young suitor's eyes.

The Andersons kindly made it their practice to come early and stay late each Thursday prayer meeting night of Stephen's short furlough. The added hours gave Stephen and Grace needed time to talk and dream about their possible future together.

His nearly month-long visit home went by far too quickly. There was time for ribbing his uncle about robbing the cradle, as his bride to be was much younger than he. His reply was brief but full of eyebrow raising passion. "I am a lucky man indeed." Their wedding date was set for early December, some six months in the future. Stephen would make sure to be back to Light Creek Marsh for the joyous occasion. He had missed his brother William's wedding in February and wasn't about to let that happen again.

There were also long talks with Israel Watson about a wide range of topics. The slightly older minister quickly assumed the role of mentor and friend. A deep bond was forged between them as they wrestled with matters of faith and conscience. Stephen's brother William joined the two forming a trio of spiritual accountability. His sibling's involvement, especially his struggle and adjustments to married life, gave Stephen much to ponder as he thought about his own future and relationship with Grace. Together they confessed their struggles, sins and doubts and sought to 'spur one another on to love and good works.'

Israel gave Stephen opportunities to speak at each of the prayer meetings during his stay. He soon recognized that the young convert was uniquely gifted with the ability to communicate insight and encouragement to the fledgling congregation and began to earnestly pray that his peer might sense God's call to ministry.

Stephen relished the tranquility of the Brooks home. Now the family was united on a deeper spiritual level and times of prayer and Bible reading were marked by devotion not duty. His mother still struggled with some dark hours and days of sadness but for the most part she had regained her bright and hopeful demeanor. Her new faith had also eased the burden of her dear mother's passing.

Able patiently waited for his friend's undivided attention, a gift he unfortunately was not to receive during this visit. There was only a brief exchange just prior to Stephen's departure in which he reminded the expectant black that ultimately it wasn't his decision regarding any release of slaves. That would be up to his father. Able perceived it for what it was, a deft shift by his so-called friend to get off the hook of responsibility, for the time being at least.

The *Grace* anchored the next morning in Wisockin Bay. Jonah and crew had sailed the short distance from Bath to pick up their young captain. Stephen walked with his father toward the waiting dory, seizing the final moment to seek his advice.

"Father, you know how I love the sea. I feel so blessed to have this commission," he paused not exactly sure how to phrase his next words.

"But something is disturbing you, is it not?" The elder Brooks rightly interpreted his son's silence, making it easier for him to continue.

"I can't quite explain it, since Christmas so much has changed. I am torn between ship and shore, between a life on the water and serving God here on land. It's so hard to…to…to..."

"To be away from those you love, I know the feeling son. You will have to follow your heart and what you sense to be God's plan for you. While I am proud of your accomplishments at sea, you do not need to be a captain for me. Your mother and I will pray that you see your way clearly. Godspeed, Stephen."

"Thank you father," Stephen had rehearsed this part. There would be no tears or shown emotion. He extended his hand to his father. The elder retired captain took the offered hand and placed his other on his son's shoulder. It was as close to an embrace as he could expect from his rather non-demonstrative parent. It was all he needed.

Chapter 28

WEDDED BLISS

Stephen gasped for air as he ran down the forested pathway. He wasn't sure he could keep up the pace much longer and he feared those chasing him would overtake him. He dodged from side to side, trying to avoid bushes and low hanging branches. At the same time he tried to keep an eye out for rocks and roots that could send him tumbling. He could hear them coming, they were clearly gaining ground with each stride. His side ached, his legs were leaden; he felt as if each step was sinking into an ankle deep quagmire. If he could just stay ahead a little longer, his opponents had to be tiring too. But their jeering shouts were louder, their footfalls closer. He spied the clearing and for a few brief moments victory seemed certain.

Just yards from his goal, his brother Jacob passed him and swooped up the winner's jug of fine rum. Stephen and the other runners collapsed on the ground, panting and laughing at the same time. The crowd of guests cheered hurrahs for victor and losers alike. Finally catching his breath, Jacob pulled the cork and took a deep refreshing swig from the stoneware jug. Satisfied with his prize he handed the jug to Stephen who in turn passed it down the line of racers. It was a joyous start to the day's wedding festivities.

Stephen reclined on the grass, enjoying the mildly warm late December sunshine and drinking in the scene. Family and friends had gathered to witness the union of his favorite Uncle Thomas to Angelica Riordame. The independence war veteran had come home to find true love, the greatest prize of all. The community was ready to celebrate. First and foremost they were eager to toast the lucky couple. The news that the long awaited peace treaty had finally been signed earlier that fall in Paris only added intensity to their already exuberant spirits. This would be a fine party indeed.

Brother William and his wife Martha had also shared that they were in a family way, bringing even more joy to the Brooks household. He could see the couple receiving the appropriate congratulatory greetings, a hug for Martha and a slap on the back for William. Martha seemed to glow with her expectancy. He had heard folks talk about how a child in the womb would light up the countenance of the mother-to-be, but this was the first time he had actually witnessed such. He envied his brother's state, the intimacy he enjoyed with his beloved and the blossoming of a lifelong relationship of love. It was a mystery to behold, a picture of Christ and His church.

His gaze came to rest on his love, Grace. A good friend of Angelica, she was attending the bride and busily engaged in her duties. He wondered what they were saying as they laughed and occasionally whispered asides to each other. Angelica was dressed in her best, a lovely blue dress that accented her features nicely. Stephen could only agree with his uncle's assessment, he was truly a very lucky man. As he continued to watch, Grace caught sight of him and smiled back. He too was a most fortunate, blessed man. The wedding atmosphere breathed love into the air, triggering a rush of romantic thoughts through his mind.

"Dearly beloved, we are gathered together here in the sight of God and these witnesses to join together this man and this woman in holy matrimony; which is an honorable state and instituted by God." Israel Watson began with the familiar words of welcome for the wedding ceremony found in the Book of Common Prayer and went on to talk about how Jesus, by his presence, blessed the wedding feast at Cana in Galilee. Then it was time to exchange vows.

"Thomas wilt thou have Angelica to thy wedded wife, to live together after God's ordinance in the holy estate of Matrimony? Wilt thou love her, comfort her, honor, and keep her, in sickness and in health; and, forsaking all other, keep thee only unto her, so long as ye both shall live?"

"I will." Stephen subtly winked at Grace as Thomas pronounced his promise.

"Angelica, wilt thou have Thomas to thy wedded husband, to live together after God's ordinance in the holy estate of Matrimony? Wilt thou obey him, and serve him, love, honor and keep him, in sickness and in health; and, forsaking all other, keep thee only unto him, so long as ye both shall live?"

"I will." Grace, in turn, slyly winked back at Stephen the instant that Angelica pledged her love.

Israel led the couple through repeated vows of devotion and commitment until, at last, the ring was securely on

Angelica's left hand with Thomas's strong affirmation. "With this ring I thee wed, with my body I thee worship, and with all my worldly goods I thee endow: In the Name of the Father, and of the Son and of the Holy Ghost. Amen."

Following prayer the couple was introduced, accompanied by raucous cheers from all in attendance and not a few flintlock blasts. The couple sealed their moment together with a kiss and applause erupted along with more gun fire. Family gifts were exchanged and the feasting began.

The long table was laden with delicacies from the sea and land. Chowders, baked fish, oysters and clams were followed by wild turkey, duck, venison, roasted pig and assorted potatoes baked squash, vegetables, and breads. Candies and nutmeats were placed next to the heavy rich rum slathered wedding cake containing even more nuts and dried fruit. There was plenty of hard cider punch and rum available to help wash everything down. The eating, drinking, music and dancing would go on long into the night.

Each young woman of marriageable age carefully ate their slice of fruited cake, hoping to find the baked nutmeg inside, an omen that they would be the next to wed. Stephen's older sister Easter was the lucky one and her shriek of delight rose above the din of noise and conversation enveloping the Riordame front yard and house. While Stephen had been secretly pulling for Grace to find the nutmeg he warmly congratulated his sibling with first a bow and then a hug.

Stephen was enjoying his second helping of his mother's seafood muddle, his favorite dish from childhood days, when Grace, now free of her bridal attendant responsibilities, found him. "'twas a beautiful wedding. They make a wonderful couple. I do wish them much happiness and many lovely children." Grace paused then went on. "Sorry you came in second in the race, Stephen."

"And I am sorry you didn't find the nutmeg," Stephen replied. Together they chuckled about their mutual losses.

"I am so glad you could be home for the joyful event. Will you be headed back to your ship soon?" Her tone of voice and mannerisms quietly shouted the answer she hoped to hear.

"Grace," he took hold of her hands and continued. "I will be leaving in a few days to sail to Edenton to meet with Robert Smith to discuss my commission; pray he will release me for this next year. I am uncertain as to what God's will is for my life but I believe I must find the answer here ashore. Israel has encouraged me to preach and to assist him in ministry while I seek direction. That is my plan. The year will also give us time together to consider His possible will for our relationship." Stephen drew her close as she answered.

"'tis a good plan, my love and I will pray faithfully, daily for His blessing on it."

Thomas and Angelica climbed up to the seat of their wedding carriage as they prepared to leave her parent's home to start their new life together. Stephen's older brothers had successfully secured an old boot by string to the back of the carriage as a hopeful omen of a long and happy marriage. They might be alone in the carriage but they would not be traveling unaccompanied to Thomas's home. Their unmarried friends including Stephen and Grace followed on foot to participate in the throwing of the socks.

The newlyweds reached their destination ahead of the gang and took to their marriage bed, safe and secure beneath the blankets. Each of the young women took their turns. Standing at the foot of the bed, back to the couple, each launched a balled up sock hoping to hit the bride on the head. Socks flew in all directions; one hit Thomas, another the wall behind the bed, and two landed short of the mark on the bed. One sailed true to the target and softly struck Angelica's barely exposed night bonnet. It was Grace's effort. All cheered her success; she would most assuredly be next to wed.

Then the socks were handed over to the young men to see if they could conk the groom on the noggin. Their over the shoulder tosses were launched with considerably more muscle but the results were similar. Two bounced off the bed post closest to the wide eyed Thomas. Another ricocheted off of poor Angelica who pulled the covers completely over her head in response. Stephen's toss caught his uncle squarely between the eyes. The lucky sock went to Grace. It was destined for her hope chest. The doubly successful efforts seemed a fortuitous sign of future wedded bliss.

There was one more important item on Stephen's to do list before he set sail for Edenton. Grace had never been aboard his ship; in fact, she had not been at sea on any vessel. Today that would change. He reined Pilgrim to a stop and helped Grace down from the wagon near the small dock on Light Creek. Safely seated in the dory she placed the lunch basket on her lap as her beau rowed slowly toward the waiting Clipper. He remembered how seasick his sister used to get on family voyages and sent a small prayer heavenward that Grace would not be so inclined. He also hoped his crew would abide by his instructions to focus on their tasks, respect the couple's privacy and withhold any ogling glances in the direction of his sweetheart. They passed alongside the bow and the clearly etched and painted letters *Grace*. She looked up and asked. "*Grace*?"

"Yes, *Grace;* named for you and for God's amazing eternal kindness to us in Jesus."

It was an idyllic day for sailing. The breeze was steady but gentle, creating only a comfortable chop on the surface. Grace quickly gained her sea legs and moved about the deck freely. The love starved crew couldn't help but follow her movements but they were respectful and thankfully avoided lengthy stares in her direction. As they moved across Pamlico Sound toward the ocean beyond, she found a favorite spot up front on the bow. Together they enjoyed their picnic while watching a small school of dolphins cavort along the waves sent out as the hull sliced through the water.

"I can see why you love sailing so," she said, facing the distant horizon, her hair flying free in the wind. "Everything is so, so beautiful, quiet and peaceful. It is almost like you can hear the voice of God whispering sweetly in the air."

"Yes and sometimes God shouts through the strong gale and terrifying storm." The young captain continued the nautical image, "reminding us that we are frail humans adrift on dangerous waters. At peace or amidst raging tempest, we are not alone. I know that now."

"Those are wise words, Stephen. Our world is at peace for the moment, but I am sure we will face strong currents, buffeting winds and overpowering seas in the future. We must trust Him to still the turbulent waters as only the Savior, who quieted Galilee's sea so long ago, is able to do." Grace turned back to gaze out on the vast Atlantic Ocean. She held out her arms as if to embrace it all in grateful wonder and praise.

It was after dark when they reached the Anderson farm. As Grace opened the front door, she turned back to say goodnight. "Stephen, I will never forget sailing on the *Grace,* I will cherish the memory of this day to my final breath."

Chapter 29

VISIONS

As they neared the cutoff, Stephen slowed Pilgrim to a stop and turned to his mentor and friend, Israel Watson. "I think I'll stop in and visit a bit with the Anderson's. Do you want me to say a word about our successful trip this week at meeting?" He took off his hat and wiped the sweat from his brow. "Sure is hot for April."

"Kind of figured you had Grace on your mind, but not Biblical grace mind you," Israel laughed. "I am sure the folks would love to hear about God's blessings at the Goode home so yes, plan on a report. Just be sure to leave me a little time for preaching. Give my best to the Andersons." Israel spurred his mount and rode out of sight.

"Stephen, you are an uncle!" Grace announced as she greeted her minister in training. "She was born on the 4th, your sister-in-law Martha and baby Margaret are both doing well. I am not sure if the same is true for your brother, William. Last Thursday he seemed to still be suffering from a puffed up chest of pride." Grace smiled and took his hand as they walked to the porch.

"This has been a year of wonderful news," Stephen said

as he sipped the hard cider Grace had fetched for them. "First, congress ratified the treaty of peace in January. Then Robert Smith kindly gave me leave of my ship's duties for a year so that I might serve God and seek His will. Uncle Thomas and Angelica are expecting a child and now I find myself an uncle too. Then my love, there is the truth that you grow more beautiful every day." Grace blushed at Stephen's last sentence. Both felt so alive and blessed. They basked in both the warm April sun and their perceptions of the splendid goodness of God.

"I had the most vivid dream last night, dare say, perhaps a vision, and it was about you." Grace leaned forward as she spoke. "You were on your horse, with just a few possessions, a Bible and Wesley's hymnbook in your saddlebags. You were off to serve God in far off places. I was so proud of you."

Stephen pulled a small pouch from his pocket and found the tiny coin. "Did I look like this?" He showed her the image on one side of a boy or man on horseback. "When I was in Edenton, I stopped in at the King Mercantile and in the course of my shopping, the owner, Elizabeth King engaged me in conversation. I remember meeting her as a boy and how she would weigh out my father's coppers and silver on her scale to verify they were genuine. So I asked her if she ever came across any unusual coins in her trade. She dug into her drawer and came out with this one."

Grace sat her cider aside and took the small piece of metal from Stephen's hand. She studied it closely. "I've never seen anything like this. Where did it come from?"

"She got it from a Greek sailor who had carried it with him from his homeland in the Mediterranean Sea. He said it was over 2,000 years old. Imagine, Grace, this coin was circulating before Jesus was born. Think of the countless hands it has passed through on its way to our shores. Why old Paul, the Apostle, might even have held this coin when he was in Philippi, Athens or Corinth." Stephen took another drink and placed his tankard on the railing.

"Maybe our Lord has given both of us a glimpse of the future, for me a dream, for you a coin." Grace handed the coin back to Stephen and then rested her hand atop his as he closed his fingers around it.

"Why that brings to mind the prophet Joel and the very verse that Israel preached about last night at the Goode home. He talked about God pouring out his Spirit; sons and daughters prophesying, old and young dreaming and seeing visions. It seems God gave to you both a vision and a word of prophesy." He placed his other hand gently atop hers as a quiet exclamation point to his comments.

Stephen leaned back in the porch rocker and watched with delight as Margaret and Thomas squirmed about on the blanket before him. The mild late fall breeze made for a most pleasant day and he was thoroughly enjoying his opportunity to watch over his little niece and cousin. He did the math in his mind; Margaret was 6 months old, her personality already coming through her frequent smiles and coos punctuated by cries for attention, especially now that she was beginning to teethe. She sat on the blanket sucking her thumb, content for the moment which was a welcome relief to her somewhat anxious babysitter.

Tiny Thomas, not yet a month old, wiggled about on his back, kicking his feet in the air. Angelica was inside the house with his twin, David, who had been sickly since birth. The wee one's poor health weighed heavy on his parents. Stephen could see the pain and questions etched on their tired faces. He could only imagine what it must be like to be in their shoes. He envisioned himself and Grace standing beside a crib praying for their child to thrive while fearing death might be near.

While love brought tremendous promise it also carried great risk and uncertainty. He flashed back to the graveside of the infant William Goode. His folks, Jonathan and Elizabeth, distraught with the pain of unbearable loss had lived and loved on with unbelievable hope. He had seen their tears of sadness and unbounded joy mix that summer as Israel baptized their newborn son, christened Stephen William Goode, his namesake.

Stephen's daydreaming was interrupted by the squeak of the opening front door. It was the beaming grandmother out to check on the welfare of the babes and her neophyte care-giver son. Thomas whimpered and she knelt down and lifted her nephew, cuddling him in her arms. As if on cue, Margret started to fuss and Mary gently transferred Thomas to the arms of Stephen so she could attend to her granddaughter. Soothed by human contact the two little ones quieted.

"When are you leaving?" Mary asked.

"Day after tomorrow. Israel wants to get an early start so we can reach the Goode home by midday." Stephen answered while he played with the tiny hand of his cousin. The baby closed his chubby little fingers around his cousin's pointer finger in a grasping response. "I am sure going to miss these tots, 'tis amazing to watch them grow by the day."

"The Andersons will be at meeting tonight so at least you'll have a chance to say goodbye to Grace before you leave. My, how you two are taken with each other like birds of a feather you are and I couldn't be happier for you." Mary smiled with parental approval as she spoke. "Why your courting is the talk of the community."

"In a year or two maybe that talk will be about an upcoming wedding," Stephen said as he returned his mother's smile with a wink before shifting his focus back to the infant in his arms.

Stephen felt a bit guilty that his mind really wasn't on Israel's sermon that evening. He tried to focus on the Bible in his hands but he kept thinking of Grace and how much he would miss her over the coming weeks. Israel thought they might be gone three or four weeks. They would be headed west, revisiting some new believers and seeking to share the gospel wherever they had opportunity in homes, cabins, barns or out in the open air. They had to be back by early December so that Israel could travel to Baltimore for the Methodist Episcopal Conference set to start on Christmas Eve.

His seafaring days were now becoming a dim memory as he threw himself with full energy into the work of preaching and teaching the good news. It had been a glorious summer of satisfying work. While he had to admit he sometimes missed the sound of the wind in the sails and the incredible sense of freedom that open waters stirred within him, those rewards were nothing compared to being a part of something truly eternal in significance.

But there was one troubling uncertainty in his path. Israel had shared with him the Methodist way of circuit riding ministers. Frances Asbury, bishop of the American Methodists, discouraged his preachers from marrying. He wanted them to be free of family ties, able to move from circuit to circuit; traveling most months of the year, a difficult challenge if one had a wife and children back home. As much as he relished the excitement and meaning of ministry, he wasn't sure he could make that kind of commitment. Leaving Grace for even a few weeks now was agonizingly difficult. If they should marry and God blessed them with dear babies, how could he ride out on his love and offspring for months at a time?

Israel's sermon seemed longer than usual, perhaps he was making up for the weeks they would be gone. Finally, he concluded with a hymn and benediction and Stephen was free to talk with Grace. They took a short walk to secure a bit of privacy.

"I will pray for you every day Stephen, that the Almighty will give you great success in your journey." Grace snuggled close to him as she promised her support.

"The days will pass quickly and we will soon be together again." Stephen tried to sound confident and strong, but he was afraid his emotions were betraying his words. "I love you Grace. I will hold you in my heart until I can again hold you in my arms." Together they embraced. As he held her tight he could feel her shivering in his hold. "Are you all right?" he asked.

"'tis just the cold night air, we should head back. My folks will want to be going home soon." Grace kissed him softly and passionately and then added, "remember always my love for you my dear brave circuit rider."

Ten days later Stephen and Israel were about ten miles north of the town of Washington where they had conducted a rather dull prayer meeting with a handful of curious but clearly uncommitted folks. They hoped more fruitful days of labor were ahead. The apathetic had also turned out to be inhospitable as well so the two made their own camp by a creek near the main road. Stephen managed to get a fire going and was stoking the flames when he heard hoof beats, a rider was approaching fast.

"Stephen, Israel, Oh thank God I have found you." Stephen recognized the voice of his brother Jacob as the horseman sprang from the saddle and ran to the campfire. "'tis Grace, brother, she is terribly sick. I have been searching for you for days. You must get home at once."

It took Stephen scant minutes to ready his horse. Jacob and Israel planned to follow at daybreak but he would not delay till then. The clear night and full moon seemed a Godsend. He hoped and prayed it was an omen that Grace was already better. The three huddled in a moment of earnest prayer as they cried out to God both figuratively and literally.

"We will continue to pray for Grace and for your safe travel, brother," Israel said as he hugged him. "She is in the strong arms of Jesus, take heart." Almost before the sentence was finished Stephen was in the saddle. He wheeled Pilgrim about and headed into the night.

Through the night and into the next day he rode, taking only short breaks to rest and water Pilgrim, who also seemed to sense the urgency of their mission. He alternated between moments of hope and longer periods of brooding melancholy. He took some solace in the words of Psalm 91; the psalm Grace had urged him to memorize when he first went to sea. He tried to pray but his efforts turned quickly into bargaining pleas promising lifelong devotion in exchange for a divine miraculous cure.

The sun was setting as the weary horse and rider approached the Anderson home. As the front door opened, Stephen thought he caught sight of Grace, coming to greet him. She was so beautiful. But the vision soon turned to reality. It was her father instead. His eyes were red with grief and Stephen knew, without a word being spoken, what the dreadful truth was. "She is gone son, gone; safe for eternity with Jesus." They wept.

Chapter 30

LOST

Stephen sat dejectedly on the old stump. Here he had met his friend Wolf. Here he had committed his life to Jesus. Now it was the site of his solitary grieving. The chilly February north wind only served to intensify the coldness he felt in heart. It had been two empty, lonely and soul-wrenching months since Grace's death and the numbness of loss that had first taken hold of him on the Anderson porch had in no way abated. It seemed more real and paralyzing day by day. The dream had become a nightmare; laughter and hopefulness had been transformed into dark sullenness.

Family and friends had tried unsuccessfully to comfort him but following the funeral he had pulled away and drawn within, ignoring their words and gestures of caring. His faith offered no answers to the resounding why questions echoing in his mind. The heavens were also brazenly silent in response to his raging emotions of denial, anger and depression. He had stopped attending prayer meetings and had repeatedly rejected the invitations of Israel and William to join them for study and support. They had patiently endured his initial refusals, respecting his need to mourn, but as of late they had become more insistent that he join them. He wasn't ready for that; he wasn't sure if he would ever be ready for that again.

There had been no Christmas celebration at the Brooks home as cruel misery upon cruel misery visited them. Only weeks after Grace's unexpected death, baby David, Thomas' twin, succumbed to the maladies that had marked his few months of frail life. It was like rubbing salt into Stephen's fresh wound, bringing forth a fresh round of heaven sent rants. The declining health of Grandfather Farrow also had the family deeply troubled.

He stood and pulled the coat tight at the neck trying to keep out the penetrating wind. Too cold to sit, he plodded along, following the creek toward the bay and continued along at the water's edge. The tide was out, leaving an assortment of debris in its trail. He had come here with a purpose.

He stopped, pulled the silver coin from his pocket and sobbed. The love token was to have been a gift to Grace when they announced wedding plans. The silversmith in Edenton had fashioned it for him a year earlier. The jeweler had smoothed one side of the shilling creating a backdrop for his artistry then carefully he had followed Stephen's instructions, carving a heart in the center and vining flowers around the edge of the coin. Next to the heart were their initials SB and GA and below the year 1785. Wiping away his tears he took one last look at what was now a meaningless and painful piece of jewelry and hurled it with all his strength beyond the breaking waves.

He collapsed on a log bench and stared out at the gray waters of Wisockin Bay. Unfolding the note he again looked at the terse final message of his Grace, 'Isaiah 55: 8 and 9'. Mrs. Anderson had copied the Biblical reference down at her daughter's bedside before the Yellow Fever had rendered her child delirious and incoherent. It was one of many verses Grace had committed to memory and Stephen had heard her recite it often. "For my thoughts are not your thoughts, neither are your ways my ways, saith the LORD. For as the heavens are higher than the earth, so are my ways higher than your ways, and my thoughts than your thoughts."

Clearly their thoughts and ways, their anticipated life together was not to be as they had hoped. God had written a very different ending to their love story. He wondered again what she might be trying to say from beyond the grave but the words offered no light in his self-made abyss of pity tinged by guilt; the guilt that he should be able to accept his loss with resolute faith. Of one thing he was certain, he could not continue in ministry. He was broken and lost and had no gospel, no good news, to share with others.

Lifting his gaze from the cluttered contaminated shoreline he caught sight of sails far out beyond the confines of the bay. Though he wasn't looking for signs or omens the distant ship did answer his immediate question of what to do next. The sea was familiar. The sea was an available escape. He could not remain here haunted by memories of what might have been. He was tired of trying to meet the expectations of family and friends, tired of trying to respond to their efforts of encouragement. The sea was safe. The decision was made.

Stephen dipped his quill in the ink well and penned his closing words then added his signature. When the ink was dry he folded the note and tucked it in the envelope with care and placed it on his bed. It was easier this way. He preferred to slip away unannounced, avoiding the emotional displays of his mother and siblings and the probing questions of his father. He had communicated his love and intentions on paper and that was enough for now. He quietly finished packing and lifted the candle. The eerie flickering light cast its faint glow about his sleeping area revealing the coin box stored in the wall niche. He pulled it lose and removed the lid, exposing the red pouch inside. For some moments he stared at the open box as if lost in thought. Putting the lid back on, he stowed the cherished Christmas gift of his grandfather at the bottom of his satchel. He gathered up his bag, slipped down the ladder, and was out the door undetected.

"Was you just going to ride away without a word?" Able questioned from the dark shadows of the barn. Stephen, startled by the unexpected voice, turned from the task of saddling Pilgrim to face his slave friend. "I take it you are headed back to sea?" Able continued.

"Yes, I have to get away from here," Stephen replied as he looked away, tightening the cinch strap.

"I know you been hurting much and it probably isn't my place to speak, but I will. You can't outrun the pain. You will only take it with you wherever you go. Here you have people who love you and want to help carry the load." Able moved toward Stephen as he spoke.

"You are right Able, it isn't your place to speak." Stephen swung up into the saddle and spurred Pilgrim into motion.

"God go with you," Able shouted out to his boyhood companion. Stephen didn't bother to slow or even turn to acknowledge the farewell.

There was one visit he had to make; no letter could adequately express his fondness for his papa, this goodbye had to be personal. Stephen was rightly worried that by the time he returned his wise and loving grandfather would be buried alongside his Amey at Cypress Creek.

He waited patiently for daylight to arrive and when he saw the old man open his door to welcome the day he made his approach. Stephen brewed coffee and they sat and visited long into the morning. They reminisced about Captain Farrow's days as head of the local militia, back before the revolution. They laughed about the arrow-pierced squash. They remembered the miraculous snake bite cure Grammy had prepared. They mourned their losses together with a measure of tears, gratitude and reverence.

Stephen thought to himself how easily his grandfather now displayed his emotions, something that had been quite rare years earlier. Was it the death of a spouse, a softening of his soul with the passing of years, his physical weakness, or some combination thereof, which prompted this vulnerable expression of humanness so? Whatever the reason, he admired and, in some ways, envied the genuine healing and sense of hope his weeping conveyed. There seemed to be no bitterness in his recollections, only thanksgiving, something Stephen longed for in his current state.

He fished out the box Jacob had carved from an old scrap piece of driftwood. Papa had found it the same morning that he, as a rambunctious lad of five, had discovered his first pirate coin. Together they examined the collection which triggered more fond memories.

"I'm sure you'd like to put some miles on old Pilgrim before nightfall, son," Jacob offered, providing them with an appropriate way to bring the conversation to a close.

"Yes, I should be going," Stephen responded. There was so much more he wanted to say. He paused, determined that he would not leave unsaid the most important words. "Papa, I love you, I will always remember you, if…if…," Stephen struggled to go on.

"No regrets, what if and if only are life's greatest killjoys. I love you my Grandson! Life and love only come laden with risk and hard choices. Change, expected and unexpected, is our lot here, only God's love is certain, constant and changeless. I know you will live and love again. Godspeed, Stephen." Jacob rose from his rocker and toddled forward, embracing him with surprising strength, he held on to him for precious minutes.

"And Godspeed to you, Papa," Stephen finally got the words out amid his own tears.

"In heaven we shall know and be known fully, my boy. I will see you yonder."

"In heaven, Papa, in heaven."

A week later Stephen was aboard a sloop headed to New Bern; his fare financed by the sad sale of his faithful mount, Pilgrim. He had tried to dull the ache by consuming way too much rum at the Bath tavern and he was still reeling a bit as he tried to navigate the heaving deck of the small ship. Upon reaching the port town he hired on as crewman aboard a tired looking old schooner bearing the name *Jezebel.* He tried to recall the Biblical story about the wicked wife of King Ahab who had earned such infamy that her name had become synonymous with wickedness and betrayal but the details eluded him. Somehow there seemed to him a strange and fitting irony in his choice of ships. He was glad to be free of the responsibilities of captain or even first mate, here he could blend in, do what was asked of him and hopefully find some solace on the open sea.

If he had been more careful in his job selection, he might have asked questions about the specific nature of the *Jezebel's* business dealings and sought out a different vessel for the sake of his safety and moral conscience. As it was, the nefarious nature of the ship's enterprises only became fully revealed when they were anchored in a small cove along the coast of Dominique in the West Indies.

Under the cover of darkness the crew rowed two dories to the beach where they were met by a motley bunch of buccaneers overseeing a collection of black men, women and youth. Each group of ten was linked together by a common chain with shackles restricting the movement of both hands and legs. By the pale light of the quarter moon, Stephen realized he had signed on with a group of slave smugglers, transporting valuable human cargo from the Indies up the coast to the Carolinas.

In yet another cove they took on kegs of rum, destined to be sold on the illicit "black" market, skirting normal channels of shipment. He had made a terrible mistake, one that could certainly cost him his reputation, maybe even his life. Getting free of the predicament was also not going to be easy as he had already gone into considerable debt with the first mate and captain as a result of his penchant for gambling. They were not about to let him slip out of their clutches until he had paid them in full. He was trapped.

Stephen was appalled and guilt stricken by the inhumane treatment of the slaves as the responsibility fell on him to give them meager rations of food stuffs that were not even fit for livestock. He recalled, with shame, how he had treated Able upon his departure from home. His friend had meant him only well and he had rebuffed his genuine concern with scorn and rude indifference.

Able had also been right, Stephen had not been able to flee the deep pain that was crippling his spirit. The salty breeze and gentle waves could not cleanse his soul of the root of bitterness growing there. And so the days passed into weeks, the weeks into months until more than a year had passed.

The routine continued unabated-- slaves, rum and ebbs and flows of luck at the gambling table, leaving him always short of his longed for ticket to freedom. Stephen's only medication for the awful horror about and the lingering heartache within was to try and drink it away with his own share of rum.

The distant melody of a familiar hymn took Stephen by surprise as he stumbled along with some fellow crew members on shore leave in New Bern. The others heard the sound too and before long Zed proposed a plan. "What do you say we make sport with yonder religious folks and disrupt their prayer meeting?" he slurred.

"God knows you need to find the straight and narrow," George chimed in with laughter. His senses numb from alcohol, Stephen still recoiled at the thought of such blasphemy but his inner discomfort did not lead to spoken words of protest and he continued with them to the entrance leading to the gathering. A tall, clear eyed believer met them there and blocked their entry.

"We be needy seamen, seeking God," Zed pleaded with him. "We mean you no ill, please let us go in." Reluctantly the man complied and opened the door. Stephen felt like he was being transported back in time and space to his parent's house, the man up front lining the song even resembled Israel.

Torn between joining the chorus and running from room, he stood paralyzed at the back wall. His companions now began their horrid charade, mocking the fervor of true repentant sinners; they raised their voices and disrupted the joyful assembly. In seconds the tall man, together with a handful of other devout followers, rounded them all up and ushered them out the door with a shove and a reprimand.

"For shame, I pray the Almighty have mercy on your degenerate souls. You are not welcome here!" Having spoken his peace he returned to the meeting, locking the bolt as he went back inside.

Soon the sound of singing reached Stephen as he stood outside. He knew the words well, it was Charles Wesley's powerful hymn, 'And can it be that I should gain an interest in the Savior's blood.' One phrase stirred suppressed memories and brought forth a surge of guilt, 'died he for me, who caused his pain.' His spiritual indifference and resentment over Grace's sudden death had now grown into an overt act of betrayal, inflicting fresh pain on the crucified Lord.

With guffaws the amused men made their way on down the street. Stephen split off from the group and wandered aimlessly for some time around town. His regret and shame seemed like a huge burden on his shoulders and he trod on slumping as if pressed down by an invisible weight. His unplanned path eventually took him to the waterfront where he took a seat on a discarded empty crate. The docks were alive with workers loading and unloading various cargoes.

The *Jezebel* was moored at the end of the nearest pier and as he focused on the detestable craft he couldn't believe what he saw. There in the slip directly opposite of his floating prison was the *Grace*. The sleek and beautiful clipper ship he had once captained must have just come into port. He spied Captain Peters, his mentor and friend, making his way down the gang plank. Stephen stood in panic. He could not stay and be seen in his sorry state by the finest seaman he had ever known next to his father; there were no adequate explanations for his plight.

He quickly fled the scene zigzagging down back allies and streets until he felt safe and alone. Reaching into his pocket he searched for a coin with which he might purchase a tankard of ale to drown his sorrows but he withdrew only an empty hand. Then he remembered his collected stash of coins hidden in his gear back at his tavern lodging. They could provide him with more than a few drinks of mind dulling elixir.

Chapter 31

FOUND

Stephen dumped the odd assortment of coins onto the dirty quilt covering his bed. Their monetary value didn't amount to much but he was thirsty for relief and they could be exchanged for what he thought he needed, a stiff drink. He fingered the various pieces of copper and silver, selecting out those of most value and the ones most likely to be accepted by the bartender.

An inner dialogue matched his examination of each item ranging in tone from a cautious yes to a strong never. How could inanimate trinkets be so laden with such meaning and memory? He resisted the voice that begged for keeping all and steeled himself to the task. Last to catch his eye were two dark brown well-worn farthings, one British the other Irish. They were the least valuable of all, worth but a quarter cent each. But he could not put them down in either his keep or discard pile and for long minutes he looked at them intently. There was something about these two that triggered thoughts and emotions he had not considered for some time.

He stroked his beard and closed his eyes trying to identify the specific source of his quandary. Birds flooded his memory, sparrows flying in all directions. There was a tree full of them looking straight at him, chirping and singing while cocking their little heads from side to side as they focused on the human standing before them. What was the meaning of this strange sight he pondered, thinking that perhaps he needed a drink more than ever. Then he recalled the verse of scripture, one of the first that had spoken deeply to his heart years earlier. 'Are not five sparrows sold for two farthings, and not one of them is forgotten before God? But even the very hairs of your head are all numbered. Fear not therefore: ye are of more value than many sparrows.'

It was not the ale or rum that he needed or really wanted but the assurance that he was loved and not abandoned by God, that he had value, an eternal value infinitely beyond a multitude of sparrows. He gathered up the coins, returned them to the pouch and secured them safely in the box. Rather than a lonely bar stool and the momentary allure of alcohol he was headed back to that Methodist meeting house.

There was a spring in his step that had been missing for some time and he even managed to whistle a hymn tune as he walked above the wharf area on his way to worship. So focused was he on the path ahead that he was oblivious to the three men hiding off to one side at the mouth of an alley. Seeing and hearing him come they had hid there, planning to ambush him as he passed. They were on him before he could offer any resistance. They bound his hands behind his back and shoved him on before them as they made their way to the dock. Stephen instantly recognized them even though dazed by the blow he had received on the head. It was Saul, captain of the *Jezebel*, accompanied by crew members, Zed and George, the very ones to whom he was indebted.

"We want what you owe us, now!" Saul was in Stephen's face, his breath reeking of rum.

"You got money hid somewhere and we want it," Zed said as he landed a fist in Stephen's stomach.

"Let's dunk him. Maybe that will loosen his lips," George slurred. The men fastened a rope about his feet and suspended him down toward the water from the edge of the dock. He struggled against the rope but couldn't keep his head out of the water. They dropped him lower, submerging his head. He tried to gulp air before he went under. They held him there for what seemed like minutes and then pulled him free of the surface; a dead man could offer them no money.

"You ready to talk?" they queried as Stephen gasped for air. His silence was followed by another dousing and yet a third time they repeated the torture. He was under when another voice was heard on the dock.

"Pull him up or we'll fire and you can find out how hot lead feels in your belly." The men obeyed and drug him onto the dock gagging and coughing all the way. He struggled to catch his breath. The man holding the pistol knelt beside him while the two others with him continued to level their pistols at the perpetrators.

"My God, Stephen Brooks, is it you?" Captain Peters helped him to his feet, staring in bewilderment at the sight before him. Stephen was still too weak to speak and nodded in agreement. "What is the meaning of this?" Peters asked the guilty trio while including his nearly drowned friend in his gaze.

"He owes us money, gambling losses. We was settling the matter when you showed up and interrupted our inquiry," Saul sneeringly replied, stepping forward.

Captain Peters reached inside his coat and retrieved a heavy pouch; opening the draw string he poured the contents into Saul's outstretched hands. "Does this cover his debt?" Zed and George crowded around their captain and inspected the hoard of large Spanish 8 Reales, silver dollar coins. They smiled and wagged their heads in satisfaction.

"Yes, 'tis more than enough," Saul smirked.

"Good, then be gone, you no longer have any claim on this man. If I find you anywhere near him again you will answer to me." Peters turned and embraced Stephen and slapping him on the back added, "Why I do believe you were about the last person I expected to see here in New Bern. Come on board *Grace*; we have some catching-up to do."

One of the crew fetched a cloth to dry his hair while another came up with a shirt to replace his soaked garment. His breathing rate gradually returned to normal and he was able to speak.

"You saved my life Captain. How can I ever repay you for rescuing me? If you hadn't shown up when you did I think they would have killed me for sure once they realized I had no money."

"Consider us even, my good friend, remember you saved my skin off the Cape with your daring maneuvers. Suffice to say, I had a good night too at the Brother Jonathan table, so the cost for me was little," Peters winked as he finished his sentence. The gesture took Stephen back to the scene of their first meeting, the coin toss table at Horniblows Tavern in Edenton. If he had followed the wise advice the Captain had offered him, after soundly thrashing him at the gambling game, he surely wouldn't have ended up in this current mess.

The men enjoyed a round of refreshment together in the Captain's quarters as Stephen recounted the events of the last couple of years from ministry joys to the sudden death of his beloved Grace to his poor decision to sign on with the *Jezebel.* The rough and seasoned salts responded with surprising support as he opened his heart to them, acknowledging the pain of loss and the stupidity of his choices. The vulnerable disclosures were also remarkably cathartic and strengthened his resolve to seek out fellow believers with whom to share his confessions and hopefully secure a measure of forgiveness.

"You would be a welcome addition to our crew if you should wish to sail with us," Peters offered as Stephen concluded his story. The crew members nodded their heads in agreement.

"That would be more than generous, Captain, but I have some important business yet here in New Bern before I return home to Light Creek Marsh. My family must wonder if I am still alive and I need to relieve their anxieties." As he verbalized the word anxieties he thought immediately of his mother. His lengthy absence and lack of any communication would be weighing especially heavy on her mind.

"We sail to Edenton in less than a week if you should change your mind, or if your business is concluded, we would gladly provide you transportation home." Captain

Peters firmly grasped Stephen's hand and shook it hard to affirm his invitation.

"I just might take you up on the offer, thank you all again. Your intervention was providential and I am most grateful. I will see you again in a few days if the Lord kindly blesses my plans." Stephen moved around the circle of men and thanked each one personally before leaving.

"What is your business at this late hour?" the gruff voiced muttered from the darkness. Stephen could barely see the speaker in the light of the candle she was holding as she cracked the door and peaked out through the narrow slit. He could see that she was quite short and plump and the dim light revealed her hair to be silver white.

"I am looking for the band of worshippers who were gathered here for Sunday service earlier today," Stephen offered sheepishly, embarrassed as he realized how late it was.

"They're long gone and fast asleep by now, as should you be," she replied harshly as she shut the door in his face. Stephen turned to go, then stopped and knocked once more.

"Please, can you tell me when they next will meet?" He rapped again in desperation, hoping his persistence would pay off.

"Bishop Asbury is in town and will speak tomorrow night at elder Brown's home on Fifth Street. You should be able to find them by the sound of singing." This time there was more warmth in her voice and she opened the door a tad bit farther as she peered out. "I do hope you find what you are looking for young man," she faintly smiled.

Stephen tossed and turned on the smelly mattress as he conjured up visions of Francis Asbury. Israel had talked with reverence about his encounter with the leader at the Christmas Conference at Lovely Lane Chapel, Baltimore in 1784. It was there that the Methodists had formally organized themselves as the Methodist Episcopal Church of America and Asbury had been ordained as Superintendent. Israel had boasted that Asbury seemed an astute judge of character. Would he consider him worthy of his time? Would he stoop to converse with a backslidden young preacher who had lost his way or would he dismiss him as an object of scorn? Would he hear words of forgiveness and encouragement or be blistered by sharp reprimands. He tried praying and reciting a few familiar verses but there was no mystical or magical calming of his nerves. Memories of Grace and her optimistic spirit buoyed him up for the uncertainty of the coming day. He might not know how Asbury would respond but he sensed that his departed love would be proud of his course of action.

Oh no, even from a distance Stephen recognized the sentry posted at the elder's front door. It was the tall young man who had tossed him and his wicked crew members out of the Sunday service. He cupped his hands and exhaled a breath to see if there was any hint of alcohol. Relieved to find none he stepped off the street and examined his likeness in a store windowpane. He had spruced himself up the best he could for the meeting but he wanted to make sure he looked as presentable as possible. He smoothed his beard and hair before replacing his hat. He then dusted off his outer coat, thinking that he little resembled the disheveled sailor he had been a day earlier. Convinced he would pass the test and gain admittance he strode forward with prideful step.

"Back again are you? Was not one day of shame enough for your sad humor? A little spit and polish does not cover the sinner. Leave, you are not welcome here. Leave quietly or I will call for assistance and show you the way." As he spoke the tall man moved toward him with aggressive stride.

"But I must see the Bishop; I come with no disrespect but only as a seeker of forgiveness," Stephen protested.

"A likely story, but can a slave smuggling rum running leopard really change his spots? Seeking forgiveness, ha? If that be true then I am the archangel Gabriel. Be gone with you."

Stephen backed off and wandered some distance up the street where he finally found a place to sit down and bemoan his predicament. The posted guard was just doing his duty. Uninvited rowdies often sought to sneak in and make fun of the pious. Order could only be maintained by trying to weed them out before they wreaked havoc as the devil's servants.

Music signaled the start of worship and he cocked his ear to listen to the words of praise. Methodist saints sure did love 'O for a Thousand Tongues to sing.' He chuckled to himself wondering if they would sing all twenty-six verses of Wesley's hymn. He mouthed the words that he remembered and then, as if by divine impulse, slumped forward to his knees in adoration. Warm tears coursed down his cheeks as if a dam, deep within his soul, had burst. He closed his eyes in prayer, shutting out the occasional passerby who stopped to survey the strange scene. The soft touch on his shoulder pulled him back into the present place and time. Kneeling next to him was the tall man.

"My name is Matthew, Matthew Roberts. Come sit on the porch with me; the window is open and you can hear the Bishop speak. It is too crowded to get inside. Can I ask your name sir?"

"Brooks, Stephen Brooks. Thank you Matthew for your kindness and understanding." They sat on the porch and sang and listened together. The gentle fall breeze off the water cooled the evening air. Stephen detected movement out of the corner of his eye and looked on as a little flock of sparrows landed in a nearby plum tree, heavy with fruit. They lined up on the branch as if perched in their own pew, yet another divine touch that encouraged the young penitent.

"My text tonight is I John 1:9, 'If we confess our sins, He is faithful and just and will forgive our sins and cleanse us from all unrighteousness.' " The voice of Asbury wasn't exactly what Stephen expected. He thought the leader would command the pulpit with energy and a strong voice. Instead there was what could best be described as a genuine sense of deep conviction, coupled with quiet humility. His passion was not displayed in volume but in heartfelt concern for his audience and the state of their souls. Stephen recalled Israel's evaluation following the Christmas Conference: 'a sincere lover of God and people, though not the greatest of preachers.' The assessment seemed accurate as the message unfolded through the slightly ajar window frame. What touched Stephen most was not the persuasiveness of a man but the power of God, whispering in loud and certain tones through a frail human channel. It was the exact message he needed to hear. It was as if Asbury was speaking only to him and specifically addressing his ache for forgiveness and cleansing.

"Matthew, is it possible to speak to the Bishop?" The service was over and people were making their way home. Maybe now was his chance to go inside, meet Francis Asbury, and seek his counsel.

"He was in ill health when he arrived and he must be exhausted after preaching for well over an hour. I wouldn't get your hopes up, but I will see?" Matthew slipped through the visiting folks still gathered by the door and disappeared inside. He soon returned with Stephen's answer.

"I talked with one of his associates who recommended you make an appointment for later this week, say Thursday or Friday. The Bishop should be feeling better by then." Matthew could see that Stephen was crestfallen at the news.

"That will be too late. I need to sail home to Hyde County by the end of the week. Thank you for your welcoming friendship in spite of my behavior yesterday. I will always remember your kindness in kneeling beside me and inviting me to sit with you at the window. God willing I will meet Francis Asbury at some future date. Goodnight."

Stephen walked for some time, headed in no particular direction. The sun was beginning to set in the western sky with various hues of yellow, orange and purple mixing together creating a breathtaking scene. He thought of the Psalmist's proclamation, 'The heavens declare the glory of God,' and paused to take it all in as he weighed his options. Should he stay and forego the opportunity to sail on the

Grace, waiting until Asbury was well enough to see him? Should he head home and make things right with his family, the Andersons, Israel and Able? He chastised himself again for the wasted year and a half of physical and spiritual wandering, for his selfish cowardly flight from responsibility and faith. Finally he hit on a third choice. He would go back and try once more to see Asbury. What did he have to lose; at least he could try to gain an audience with the devoted man of God. If he failed, he was resolved to sail to Wisockin Bay with Captain Peters and his crew.

The soft glow of hearth and candlelight was visible through the window, a positive sign that maybe Asbury had not yet retired for the night. Stephen approached and knocked softly. He could hear the sound of chair legs sliding on the wood floor as someone pushed back from the table and moved toward the door.

"Good evening sir, my name is Stephen Brooks and I must see Francis Asbury."

"I am sorry but Superintendent Asbury is resting and asked not to be disturbed." The man whispered his response, clearly not wanting to wake the weary preacher. However his efforts were unsuccessful and Stephen heard another voice from inside.

"Who is it, Andrew?"

"A Mr. Brooks, Stephen Brooks."

"Brooks of Hyde County, North Carolina?" the voice responded.

"Yes, I am from Hyde County but how…" before he could finish his question Asbury was at the door shaking his hand and welcoming him inside.

"But how do you know my name, sir?" Stephen asked in bewilderment, stunned by the sudden turn of events. Asbury furrowed his brow in thought and replied.

"Well by divine revelation, think you not that God passes on such details to bishops?" Seeing he had successfully mystified his guest he broke into laughter and continued. "Israel Watson shared your name with me at our Baltimore Conference. I have been praying for you ever since. He said you had been a ready servant of the Almighty but that grief and disappointment had darkened your heart and you had lost your way. So, my son, you're coming tonight is an answer to prayer. Come, sit and tell me how it is with your soul."

Chapter 32

HEALING

The southerly breeze moved the *Grace* effortlessly north across Pamlico Sound. Stephen leaned against the railing, taking in the familiar scenery as the ship rounded Green Point toward the back channel that would take him to Light Creek Marsh and home. He had left bitter and angry. He was returning hoping to find renewal and healing. The three days he had spent behind closed doors with the wise Bishop Francis Asbury, had been truly transformational and would, in many ways, shape the rest of his life's journey.

The vivid symbolism of the three days had at first escaped his notice but now in retrospect became crystal clear. Jonah had been three days in the belly of the great fish. Jesus had been three days in the grave. It was like Francis had guided him through his own death and resurrection experience, gently moving him from the pain of Good Friday to the glorious dawn of Easter. Each day they had risen at five, beginning the day with prayer, Psalms and hymns of praise. This was followed by reading sermons of John and Charles Wesley that Asbury carefully selected for their relevance to his struggle and questions. They would break bread and spend the afternoons and evenings in discussion. The Bishop was an excellent listener and he had kindly let him vent, analyze and reach conclusions at his own pace, without resorting to judgmental pronouncements or trite platitudes to fill in moments of silence. In response to his heartfelt confessions, the pastor to pastors, offered reassurance of divine forgiveness. While he knew in his head that God forgave, there was a blessed release in hearing Asbury pronounce the words aloud, 'son, your sins are forgiven in the powerful name of the Savior.'

As they neared anchorage, Stephen replayed the words that Francis had repeated on more than one occasion during their three day encounter. 'Sometimes you have to step backwards before you can stride ahead.' His first impulse had been to run far from this place as if distancing himself from familiar sights, sounds and memories would also distance him from his troubling emotions and deep melancholy. Going home would certainly reconnect him with grief, but most importantly going home would unite him with those who knew him best and loved him most. Again Asbury's words resonated, 'accept and learn from their comfort, 'tis the comfort God gives so that we might be a source of support, encouragement and comfort to others in their time of need. God is fashioning your heart, Stephen, God is fashioning your heart.'

The homecoming party was a joyous and festive event and the welcoming embraces ministered healing. At the same time the vacant rocker, where Papa Farrow used to sit, was a stark reminder of what he had missed by his lengthy absence. Uncle Thomas uniquely interpreted the occasion and mood when he verbally jabbed at Stephen.

"Well if it isn't the prodigal returned from his wanderings." The intent of the comment had been playful but Stephen couldn't help but see his connection to the Biblical story. He had squandered time and resources in far off places and instead of condemnation and accusatory glances he had been received back with gifts and a feast. The lost truly felt found and the rejoicing was real on earth and maybe, he mused, even in heaven.

The refreshingly cool autumn air drew him outside to the porch. Extended family and guests had left and the noisy celebration had been replaced by a restful silence. His father found him there, lost in thought and missing his papa.

"Able has something to show you son, yonder." His father smiled and pointed toward the outbuildings, only heightening Stephen's curiosity. He then went back indoors without any further explanation of what might be in the barn.

The black was putting away harnesses and didn't see him approach. He had thought about this moment and what he would say to Able countless times in the past week. The planned conversation, as he played it over in his mind, had varied in content and tone from a sincere apology to a cold justification for his rudeness to saying nothing at all. After all, he had mused, what did he owe a slave? The answer had come back loud and strong: he owed him what he owed any man, the truth.

"Able," he paused; hearing his name the black rose from his work and turned toward Stephen. "I was wrong. I treated you shamefully. I pray you will find it in your heart to forgive me for what I said and how I acted." Able closed the distance between them and bowed in acknowledgement of his status.

"Master Stephen, 'tis so good to see you alive and well, I feared something awful for you. No need to ask my pardon, I forgave you the day you left."

The two young men, equal only in age, stood facing each other for a few awkward moments. Stephen's first impulse was to embrace Able and thank him for his gracious response but he hesitated and then offered his hand which the slave took hold of firmly. They shook in silent testimony to a restored relationship.

"Come, see your Grandpa's last gift to you." Able tugged him toward the stall in the corner of the barn. The coal black horse whinnied and put his head over the railing to investigate the newcomer. The white star on his forehead was a perfect match to Stephen's first horse, Pilgrim.

"He was born a few months after you left, foal of Papa Farrow's mare, Jane, and good ole Pilgrim." The horse nuzzled up to Stephen as he slowly stroked the star between his eyes.

"Pilgrim always liked me to rub his forehead too," Stephen's voice broke, wavering with emotion as he thought about the quick sale of his faithful friend in order to finance his escape to the sea. "I had forgotten the horses were together and might have mated. But then I wasn't thinking about much but feeling sorry for myself."

"Mr. Farrow, he surely did love you. He talked about your last visit every time I saw him to care for Jane and her colt here. It was a sad day when he died, but he made it clear, both in spoken word and in his will that Barnabas was to be yours when you returned. He never gave up hope that you was coming back." Misty eyes and choking emotions seemed to be contagious in that corner of the barn and Able dapped at his face with an old handkerchief.

"When did you say he was born?" Stephen asked as he fastened a rope to the halter and opened the stall door, leading the colt out for a closer look.

"Early last June, so that would make Barnabas about 16 months old. He's a fine one, be fast too." Stephen could see the fondness Able had for the young horse as the black jostled his mane and ran his hand down across the withers, back and quarters. "Growing strong and should be ready for the saddle in a few months." He continued to gently pat the horse with affection as he spoke.

"So you named him Barnabas?" Stephen questioned as he walked around the beautiful animal.

"No, that was the name your papa gave him at birth. He insisted that be his name, said it was from the Bible, seemed almost like God had told him the name somehow. Sometimes, though, I call him Barney for short." At the sound of his name the yearling bobbed his head and neighed loudly as if echoing his agreement with Papa's name choice. "Mr. Farrow told me the meaning of the name, Barnabas, 'son of encouragement.' I know he hoped the horse would be an encouragement to you; I think that's why he chose that name."

"Well, Barney, Barnabas, Son of Encouragement, you and I are going to share many a mile and many a memory." As Stephen spoke, he and Able gently petted away in unison as they stood on opposite sides of the contented young stallion that was clearly enjoying the attention.

Purple Spreading Aster were usually easy to find, blooming late into the fall, their bluish purple petals dotted by sunshine yellow centers made for bright autumn bouquets. Stephen was conducting a serious search to find enough to take to Grace's gravesite but he was not having much luck in places where they were usually abundant. Most of the blossoms were past their prime or the plants had lost their flowers all together. They were Grace's favorite, as was the color blue. Finally he managed to put together a handful for a small tribute.

Her grave was near the Anderson cabin and he briefly visited with her parents before walking alone to the spot. Their faith was an anchor, providing hope beyond the earthly 'veil of tears,' as Mrs. Anderson had put it. They still regularly attended the weekly Methodist meeting at the Brooks' home. Even after nearly two years, they had dark days, like he did, when a cloud of sadness would take them by surprise, raising questions and doubts. Together they shared and received words of comfort, cherished sacred memories and shed a tear or two.

As Stephen stepped into view of the stone that marked her final resting place, he stopped and smiled. A blossom laden Aster bloomed just a few feet from the rock, alive with vitality, the flowers at their peak of autumn perfection. He looked at the slightly withered collection he was holding and cast them off to the side. God was able to provide a much better floral tribute than he. Grace would have chuckled too, he thought, and then she would have quoted some Biblical phrase to celebrate the serendipitous moment.

Hovering near the petals was the largest Buckeye Butterfly he had ever seen. It fluttered and flitted from one flower center to the next. What beautiful, abundant symbols of life in a setting of death, he pondered. Asbury had counseled him with words from I Corinthians 13 and they flooded back into his mind even as the sun bathed the death scene with penetrating light. 'For now we see through a glass, darkly; but then face to face: now I know in part; but then shall I know even as also I am known. And now abideth faith, hope, charity, these three; but the greatest of these is charity.' The verses made perfect sense in light of Grace's final reference about divine ways being profoundly different than human thought. It was the 'dark glass' that blurred the present, giving frail humans only imperfect glimpses of the heavenly and the eternal. Grace, praise God, now knew her Lord face to face. She knew, even as she was perfectly known. It was now his challenge to walk by faith, until hope became reality, knowing that love would remain forever.

"Israel, I owe you both a confession and a thank you, which would you like first?" Stephen spoke as the two men sauntered along the trail to the creek back beyond the Brooks' barn. Israel had come for the Thursday evening prayer meeting and this was their first real opportunity to talk since Stephen's return.

"I would think the confession might be the hardest, why don't you start there," Israel stopped and made direct eye contact with Stephen, waiting for him to speak.

"Agreed brother. I betrayed my covenant with you and William by failing to hold myself accountable to you in our weekly sessions and by leaving the way I did. I also was unfaithful to the work of ministry we were engaged in together. I would like to start again if you would have me back." Israel reached out and embraced him with all his might and responded.

"Welcome back, Stephen. Confession noted and accepted. God is good, our prayers are answered and new beginnings are something our Heavenly Father delights in. Did you say there was a word of gratitude too?"

"Yes, thank you for sharing my plight with Bishop Asbury at the Baltimore Christmas Conference. He remembered my name and invited me to spend some days with him in New Bern. Thus your intercession on my behalf brought me back to faith and home again." This time Stephen initiated a second embrace.

"I trust you will tell the group your story when the time is right, my brother, so all can benefit from your account of God's grace?" The vocal inflection at the end of the sentence let Stephen know the statement was meant as a question.

"Maybe not tonight, but soon Israel, soon I will give testimony." Together they walked back to the house.

A certain routine developed over the weeks that followed. Stephen engaged in hard physical labor with his father and brothers as the seasons transitioned from fall to winter. There were long family chats around the dinner table, punctuated by good humor and more serious times of prayer. There were hours spent in the corral training, exercising and bonding with Barnabas. Weekly times with Israel and William along with worship gatherings and Methodist meetings rekindled his passion for preaching and shepherding God's people. Playing with his two and half year old cousin, Thomas, brought laughter and respite from some of the more taxing work. It was all he could have hoped for and more, healing his heart and soul.

Chapter 33

PARADOX

"Yankee Doodle went to town a riding on a pony, stuck a feather in his hat and called it macaroni." The children danced and sang the familiar tune, once used in jest by the British but adopted by the Americans in celebration of their triumph. Now it had become a favorite for Independence Day festivities. Stephen watched as the youngsters rode their stick horses about, reenacting the battle of Yorktown with their pretend weapons. It was July 4th 1787 and in gatherings from northern Maine to southern Georgia, citizens of the fledgling nation were honoring the eleventh anniversary of freedom with picnics, games and fireworks. Red, white and blue bunting decorated the tables and neighbors, like the children, were getting in the mood for a grand time beside Mattamuskeet Lake. His three year old cousin, Thomas, ran by and pointing his play pistol in his direction shouted, "Bang," before continuing to hunt for would-be soldiers hiding behind some Cypress trees at the water's edge. The animated conversation of a number of men nearby caught his attention and he moved closer to hear what they were saying.

"July 3rd was the day they signed the Declaration, we should set that day aside for remembrance," Bernard German's strong voice, marked as well by his heavy accent, could be heard above the others.

"Adams has argued it should be the 3rd," Stephen's Uncle Thomas added his two bits to the debate. Some nodded, while others shook their heads in disagreement.

"The real question may not be which day we choose, but whether this nation will endure the birth pangs of dissent and revolt raging from north to south. Daniel Shay's rebellion in Maine may have been quelled by armed forces but his objections to the abuses suffered by many a poor and debt-ridden farmer is echoing throughout all of the states and even has local advocates calling for change." The side conversations came to halt as all now listened to Samuel Swan take charge of the debate by raising a much more serious concern.

"Then there are those of us who risked our lives as members of militias and the Continental Army. We have received little or no pay or remuneration for our services and are hard pressed to hold on to our lands. It is a grievous wrong that must be rectified."Veteran Uncle Thomas' voice was tinged with anger as he spoke. Swan waited for Thomas to finish and then continued.

"'tis a good thing that Congress has convened in response to these critical issues, hopefully they can amend our Articles of Confederation and remedy the situation before we erupt in a civil war."

"Here, here, Swan, I will drink to that," Michael Gibbs concurred as he raised his tankard in a symbolic toast. The other men joined their mugs together with his in consent. "Such needed changes cannot come too soon," he said as the tankards clinked. Wiping his mouth with his sleeve after a large gulp of ale, Gibbs again spoke. "Rumor has it they are meeting behind closed doors drafting a new constitutional structure. Wish I was a mouse in the corner of their chambers and could listen in to their lively debate," Thomas, still seething over the failure of the government to recognize his plight, got in the last word.

"It will be the rich and powerful who determine our lot. Sadly we are but silent mice in the argument. I for one wish we had more poor farmers in that room to state our case." He punctuated his government critique by slamming his tankard onto the table in disgust.

Stephen moved along observing the preparations underway. Slaves were doing the bulk of the work, setting out various foods on the tables. He spotted Phoebe, Able's mother, among the women and reflected on the scene. Here they were celebrating freedom and yet a significant number in attendance were not free.

He recalled the strong words of Francis Asbury who had vehemently decried the institution of slavery as a 'sin against highest heaven.' Many blacks had testified to faith and joined the Methodist movement but sadly in some communities separate churches were being created for those of color. Does not the Bible shout out, 'In Christ there is neither Jew nor Gentile, slave nor free, but all are one in Him, 'tis not right that we should be so separated,' he had responded when Stephen had pushed him on the subject during their three days together. The tension was beginning to surface in local Methodist gatherings around Hyde County. He had heard the whispers among some white believers who felt uncomfortable worshipping with slave converts. While some were more outspoken in their protests others extended at best a cold shoulder when it came to welcoming into fellowship those who for the other six days of the week were treated as possessions, not brothers. 'No good will come from fretting over what is,' his father had said when Stephen had brought up the topic. 'Why the good book speaks of slavery as if it is just a part of God's plan, as long as we treat them kindly.'

"Brooks, are you racing today?" Stephen was jerked back into the present moment by the interruption of Frank Bridges. "I hear you have a two-year old stallion; does he have a mind and legs to run?" Bridges was the resident horse racing braggart of the community and had an impressive win streak going back some years. In fact, Stephen couldn't remember the last time someone else had beaten him. "Why my old Admiral would enjoy a little exercise, not that you would likely be much competition for him," he boastfully continued. Stephen had never cared much for the crusty horse breeder. Word had it he was cruel in his training methods which seemed likely as he was often seen whipping his horse while speeding to another victory.

"Barnabas is young, not sure he's ready to battle with a veteran like your Admiral. But give us a few years and maybe we will be up to the challenge," Stephen countered.

"Ah, if you had ten years to prepare, the likes of your mixed breed pony would always come out second best," Bridges jeered as he move off to search for other would-be jockeys and their mounts. Stephen sighed, glad to see him go. He had been sorely tempted to say something he knew he would probably soon regret.

Someone had set up a Brother Jonathan game board and a small crowd had gathered to watch folks try their hand at racking up the most points tossing their coins. Stephen was drawn to the action having experienced his fair share of both success and humbling failure there many times before. He also was intrigued to see what unusual pieces of copper and silver might find their way onto the table. He remained a silent spectator, as a young man he did not recognize, won round after round with a copper token.

"Anyone else eager to lose their money?" the man said as he searched the faces of the few still standing nearby, hoping to recruit a potential challenger.

"Could I see your coin, friend?" Stephen asked, stepping forward.

"Surely," the man said as he handed him the large copper cent. Stephen examined it closely. It was a coin he had never seen before. The words Nova Caesarea curved around the top edge framing a horse head. Beneath the head was a plow and at the bottom the year 1786. He turned the coin over and found a shield with the phrase 'e pluribus Unum' encircling it.

"Where do you call home, sir?" Stephen requested as he continued to look at the images.

"New Jersey, but I am headed west. I hope to settle in Kentucky. Maybe you can help finance my trip. Care to wager?"

"Could you tell me more about your coin; I have never seen one like it."

"It is a New Jersey cent, the horse head is...well it's a horse head. I don't know what the words mean, never learnt much letters."

Stephen reached into his trousers and pulled out the 1773 Virginia cent that he had carried for years as a reminder of his sweetheart Grace. Its presence had saved him from more than one indiscretion. He looked at the two coins and made his proposition.

"Tell you what, how about one throw best score wins. Your New Jersey cent, my Virginia cent, do we have a deal? You can go first." Stephen extended the Nova Caesarea in his left hand and held out his right to shake.

"A cent is a cent," the stranger replied taking the coin and his hand. With careful aim he tossed the New Jersey penny toward the numbers, landing squarely in the small 15 spot. Stephen, in turn cast his copper, which came to rest aside the first coin.

"Looks like a tie, go again," he said, handing the horse token back to his opponent. This time the result was a 12 which Stephen immediately duplicated. Then it was two 10's, followed by two 14's. The Kentucky traveler was getting a bit flustered as he launched his next throw which barely stayed on the board in the 7 square. Stephen had had his fun and put the poor man out of his misery with a finely crafted flip that hit the board and never moved from its landing spot, a perfect 20.

"I know when I'm beaten, here's your cent." The dejected gambler reached out to Stephen who took the coin and smiled.

"Beginner's luck I guess. I thank you kindly. By the way, what's your name?"

"Roark, John Roark." Stephen grasped his hand once more and introduced himself.

"I'm Stephen Brooks. Welcome, John, to our county and our 4th of July party and may God speed you on your trip west.

The races began mid-afternoon, after folks had rested up a bit following the abundances of the picnic dinner. Preliminary to the main event there were foot races for the children and youth and three-legged races for young couples. Winners held their blue ribbons high in festive triumph and in response to the hardy applause of the spectators. Then the announcement everyone was waiting for: "Riders have your horses ready and at the starting line at four o'clock sharp."

The course was out about a quarter of a mile to a fence post, around the post and back to the start-finish line. Stephen had not planned to run Barnabas but the words of Frank Bridges had stuck in his craw and he wasn't about to give the man the satisfaction of saying after the race, 'so you was afraid to run was you?'

Eight teams lined up at four. Barnabas was jumpy and eager for the adventure. Other riders also tried to calm their agitated mounts in anticipation of the starter's pistol. Bridges' horse stood poised and at the ready, as if well aware of what was about to transpire. The discharge of the gun startled Barnabas who reared up as if to shake Stephen free of the saddle before starting off after the other horses. Bridges made the turn with a good three horse length lead. Gibbs was in second on a filly named Jane. Stephen was coming on hard in third, another length back. He leaned low over Barney's neck and whispered the magic word, "carrots." The black stallion got the message and surged ahead, past Jane and alongside of Admiral. They galloped hard, matching stride with stride, Barnabas nosed slightly ahead. They were almost to the finish line when Stephen gently reined back the young horse and Bridges, whipping his horse for all he was worth, edged across the line in first to the cheers and applause of the crowd.

Stephen brushed Barnabas; massaging his fingers into the horse's withers he ran the brush down the sweaty sides of the strong two year old. As he rewarded Barney with a carrot he whispered.

"You ran well, boy, you are the best!"

"That is some horse you have there," Bridges said. Stephen had been so focused on Barney he hadn't seen the victor approaching. "Why did you pull back?" he asked, with a puzzled look.

"Barnabas is a young horse, I didn't want to see him over-stressed or injured," he continued to gently pat the horse as he spoke.

"You had me beat, the race was yours." Stephen turned and faced his competitor who now looked and sounded more beaten than a winner.

"Guess we'll never know how it might have come out. Congratulations on a fine race. I do hope you will lessen the whip with that fine steed of yours. Admiral will father many future winners I am sure." Stephen smiled and reached out to shake Frank's hand.

"But, but, I still don't understand, why?" Clearly the troubled horse breeder was struggling to find his words.

"You needed the win more than I; besides, you had that long winning streak to keep intact." Stephen paused in thought and went on. "Would you mind, Mr. Bridges, if I give you a verse of scripture on the matter to mull over? No offense meant." Seeing his agreeable nod, the horse racing preacher quoted part of Psalm 147: "God delighteth not in the strength of the horse…the Lord taketh pleasure in them that fear him, in those that hope in his mercy. Do remember Frank, there are some things far more important than winning." At that the grizzled old race veteran walked off slowly. He stopped and looked back, tilting his head to one side he pursed his lips as if to say something and then shaking his head from side to side he turned and left.

Israel Watson held the small group of children spellbound as he related another Bible story with his usual zeal and creativity. Stephen watched with admiration, and a bit of envy, as it took a special gift to connect so effectively with a lively audience of little ones. When Israel finally sent the energetic tykes scampering on their way, Stephen approached.

"I remember well the first Bible story I heard you tell, Israel. It was Jesus and his lesson about the two sparrows sold for a farthing. You will never know how much that bit of scripture has meant to me. Are we still heading north this fall to preach and seek new believers?"

"'tis the plan, Stephen, I would like to journey as far as Murfreesboro if God should so bless our travels. By the way, that was quite the race you had with old man Bridges. I have never seen him so humble in accepting his prize. I think maybe you won, even though you lost." Israel winked as he finished his sentence.

"The real win would be if we could see him come to faith wouldn't you say?" Stephen slapped him on the shoulder to complement his wink. "Here, I have something to show you, won it from a gentleman headed west to Kentuck." He removed the New Jersey cent from his pocket and showed first one side, then the other to his good friend as he handed it to him. "What do you think? The words Nova Caesarea stood out to me. If I recall correctly, Jesus went to Caesarea with his disciples? Not sure how this New Caesarea came to be New Jersey. Do you know?"

"I have no idea, Stephen. But I do recognize the Latin phrase 'E Pluribus Unum.' 'tis the motto of our grand country, adopted after the Declaration was signed in 1776. Out of the many, we are one. I understand the first United States seal design had this motto on a banner beneath a collection of shields. There were five shields in the center with symbols representing our European roots. There was a rose for England, thistle for Scotland, harp for Ireland, fleur-de-lis for France, lion for Holland and eagle for Germany. Surrounding these were thirteen shields for our thirteen founding states. Perhaps too many shields for the would-be engraver as the approved seal some years later just had the eagle with the banner bearing our motto firmly in its beak." Finished with his inspection and commentary, Israel extended the copper coin "Oh the horse head is, well it is a horse head."

"I surmised that much," Stephen laughed as he stuffed the coin back in his trousers. "I'm keeping this one in honor of Barnabas and the race I lost but he won."

Bernard German lit the wick and ran for cover as the rocket zoomed into the night sky. The children and adults alike oohed and aahed in delightful response as the projectile splintered into bright glowing fragments. The storeowner had obtained the fireworks on a trip north to Philadelphia where they were becoming a regular feature of 4th of July celebrations. Many in the crowd had never seen the likes before and applauded with each colorful explosion. Uncle Thomas had a less favorable reaction as each blast reminded him of the horrors of battle and the tragic deaths of comrades, victims of enemy cannon fire. With the last of the rockets, folks drifted back to chat by campfires or made their way to tents for a night's rest after a long day. Children were still squealing for want of more fireworks and some overtired tots were fussing and crying along the way.

Stephen remained alone on the grassy knoll. The mosquitoes were especially annoying but he lay back in the grass, still warm from the heat of the day, and took in the night sights and sounds. The noise and flashing had been interesting but he preferred the stillness. An owl hooted at the edge of the trees, probably on the hunt for unsuspecting mice or voles. Off toward the lake the real show of the evening was underway. Thousands of fire flies were doing their usual summer evening dance, their tiny rears emitting little sparks of light that splattered the darkness with bursts of brilliance. He found their display infinitely more beautiful than the manmade fireworks, even poetic in grandeur. They seemed, at least to him, to offer a night song of praise to the Creator.

Chapter 34

ETHICS

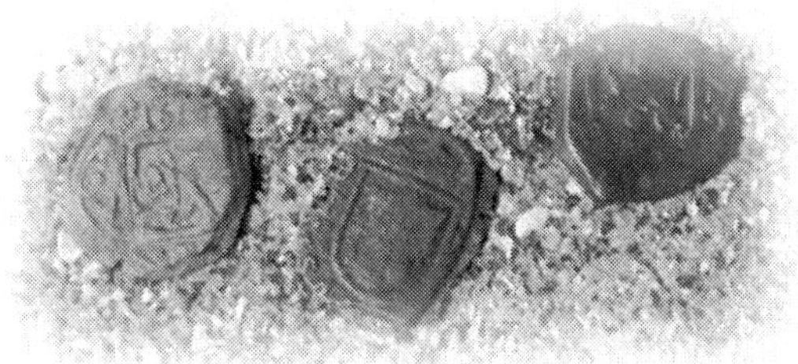

"Stephen this looks like a good spot, even has a nice stream. What do you think? They were traveling north of Bath along the Post Road and Israel had endured enough miles in the saddle to want to call it a day and make camp. "Brother, where are you anyway?" Stephen had failed to respond and had that faraway look that Israel had often seen on the countenance of his companion. "Stephen," he increased his volume and finally got his attention.

"Sorry Israel, what were you saying? My mind was a wandering, back to the Goode home. I can't get over how fast that little lad of theirs is growing. What a precocious four-year old, he never stopped asking questions and I don't think he stood still for longer than a few seconds. It warmed my heart when he climbed onto my lap and said, 'I love Jesus, do you?' Then before I could answer he was off again running across the yard." Stephen leaned forward and softly stroked Barnabas behind the ears as he spoke. Barnabas, enjoying the massage, turned his head back and whinnied.

"Your wee namesake is already following in your preaching path I do believe. Childlike faith is always a good check on what really matters in this lost world. Sadly, we often grow out of that sense of trust and wonder and turn into hard hearts, like those folks we pled with last night. Lovers of darkness rather than light they were; oh that they might have received God's grace like a child." As Israel completed his point he swung out of the saddle, sighed deeply as his feet gladly hit the ground, and tied his horse to a branch.

"We must be pretty close to Ahotskey by my reckoning," he continued, "Hopefully we will find a more receptive audience there. Then I propose we split up to cover more territory. I'll go on further north to Murfreesboro while you turn east to the area around the Gates County courthouse." Israel pulled the saddle free of his mare and placed it on the ground. He groaned with some discomfort as he returned to a standing position. "I don't think my backside was made to fit in a saddle."

"Ah, you're just getting old my friend," Stephen laughed. "So you are sending me toward the Great Dismal Swamp are you? Guess there are lost sheep no matter what direction we take. Your plan is fine with me. Now, let's see if we can rustle up something to eat, I'm starved."

The homestead was just off of the main road. The small house and outbuildings were in immaculate condition and especially inviting to the weary lonely traveler. Stephen thought to himself as he drew near that a straw bed sure would be a welcome change from the hard ground and open air. He hoped the family might be hospitable as well as open to the gospel. The man chopping wood near the barn saw him approaching and paused from his labors to wave him over. Stephen secured Barnabas to the railing and firmly grasped the extended hand of his host.

"Welcome, stranger, my name is Adam, Adam Pease. What brings you to Gates County?"

"The work of the Lord, sir, I'm Stephen Brooks a traveling Methodist preacher."

"You must be exhausted and thirsty. I invite you to spend the night under our roof; we have victuals enough and fodder for your fine horse too. I have been eager to learn more about you Methodists for some time. My wife and I are Quakers." Adam placed his arm on Stephen's shoulder and directed him toward the house before he could even blurt out a grateful yes to the invitation. Before they reached the front porch, Adam's wife was outside to meet them. "Stephen Brooks, this is my dear wife, Eve." Sensing the usual response to their unique names he went on. "No, you haven't landed in Eden, as you can see we are dressed in far more than fig leaves." He followed up his comment with a hearty and friendly laugh.

"Adam and Eve, 'tis a pleasure indeed to meet you and I thank you for your kind hospitality!" Stephen politely bowed to Eve, who seemed to blush at his form of greeting and nodded again toward Adam.

After supper the two men sat on the porch and visited. Adam lit his pipe and took a deep draw from the burning tobacco. Pungent but pleasing wisps of smoke swirled about as he set forward his proposal.

"Tomorrow is Sunday, our 'first day' of the week. In the morning we gather for worship at our meeting house not far down the road. What do you say to visiting our group and learning more about what we believe and practice? In turn, we will invite some of our neighbors over and give you an opportunity to preach come evening." Adam leaned forward in anticipation of a favorable response.

"'tis a fine and fair offer, Adam, I accept." He answered while mirroring the body posture of the young Quaker as he spoke.

"Wonderful. One word about our meeting, we value silence as we listen for God's inner voice. Any and all are free to speak as God reveals His truth; we have no ministers or priests in our ranks but all are teachers, all are learners." Adam seemed to look beyond Stephen as if he had spotted something or someone near the side of the house. He rose.

"Excuse me for a brief moment as I have some business to attend to." He went inside the house and returned with a book in hand. He disappeared around the far corner of the house and when he came back a few minutes later the book was gone.

"I'm trying to help a local lad learn to read. He was a might embarrassed to show his self. Please forgive my rudeness. Eve and I have not been blessed with children, but rather than constantly grieve our loss we have tried to aid others when we can."

"I understand and there is certainly no need to apologize for such an act of love." Stephen said nothing about the black face he had seen reflected in the window pane just before Adam had excused himself. The book was obviously meant for him, a slave? Stephen wondered.

It had been a delightfully full Sunday of activity but the two men were still not ready to retire to bed. The room illuminated by only the weak light of a flickering candle, Adam and Stephen talked long into the night, exploring the similarities and differences in their understanding of God and Christian practices. They tried to keep their voices low so Eve could hopefully sleep; they were only partially successful as their comments and questions often triggered an increase in the tone and tempo of the conversation. The final sentences spoken before extinguishing the candle flame captured their best insights gleaned from the day.

"I was strangely and powerfully moved by the quiet spirit and reverent silence in your meeting, Adam. It is good to be still in God's presence and to listen for His word. Our noise and glib words often drown out his soft whisper. Today you folks also warmly and clearly lived out your name as a Society of Friends. I will not soon forget our rich time of fellowship together."

"Thank you for your kind words. You are a passionate preacher, Stephen. God's light truly shines bright in your heart. You are an effective messenger of His grace and I know He will use you mightily. Remember you are always welcome here."

It was midmorning before Stephen left the Pease home. He and Adam had continued their discussion about slavery from the previous evening over breakfast and multiple cups of coffee. Adam continued to press his guest for answers regarding what he perceived to be inconsistencies between Methodist doctrine and practice. If Methodists believed, as their leader John Wesley taught, that slavery was wrong, why did some church members continue to own slaves? Should they not join hands with the Quakers and other groups to seek the abolition of the abhorrent practice of slavery? Now alone with this thoughts on a backcountry road, Stephen mulled over his weak, inadequate response to Adam's probing inquiry.

"What's bothering you, Barn?" The horse stepped from side to side and then stopped in the middle of the road as if he sensed some hidden danger. Stephen's first thought was of a robber's ambush and he reached to pull the pistol from his saddlebag for protection. He urged a reluctant Barnabas forward. As they came around a turn in the trail they both caught sight of the threat. A large panther crouched low, its steely eyes riveted on them. What happened next was a blur. Barnabas reared back and bucked him out of the saddle. The last thing he remembered before everything went black was the discharge of the pistol as it hit the ground.

He opened his eyes slowly; the searing pain in his head and shoulder was overwhelming. How long had he been out? He had no idea, perhaps seconds, maybe minutes. He tried to sit up but was still too dazed to see clearly. He could not move his right arm to prop himself up as his shoulder appeared to be out of joint. "Barney," he tried to yell but could muster only a whisper.

When he was finally able to focus the horse was nowhere to be seen. Using his left arm he inched across the dusty ground trying to reach the protective shade of the roadside. There, hurting, exhausted and parched he closed his eyes to rest.

He woke to what he thought was the sound of humming. Before he could discern if it was a dream or reality he felt a wet cloth on his forehead. He slowly tracked up the dark arm holding the cloth until his gaze came into focus on the black face peering back at him. Tattoos were deeply etched into each cheek, tribal marks from another continent. The sound he was making was comforting but haunting in tone like a mournful song coming from the deep recesses of his soul. Stephen stirred, trying to move sent stabs of pain through his body. Dizziness in the head was accompanied by throbs of agony in his shoulder.

"Barnabas," he finally spoke, "Barnabas." The black looked back puzzled at his strange word. Then pointing to his own chest, he said,

"Charlie," patting himself he repeated, "Charlie."

"Stephen, I am Stephen Brooks," he answered, understanding the black man's communication effort he tapped himself with his good left hand as he spoke. "My horse is Barnabas. Have you seen my horse?" He raised his voice, as if that might somehow help Charlie understand what he was saying.

"Yonder, he come back. Look for you, I tie him." Charlie pointed and Stephen could see Barney was safely tethered to a branch.

"Thank you. I am grateful for your help."

"You hurt, right thing to help." Charlie rose from his knees and moved to a pack he had stowed back in the bushes. Stephen could see a shackle still fixed around the slave's right ankle as he returned and offered him a drink. The taste was unfamiliar but a welcome relief to his burning thirst.

"Charlie, do you live near here?" he finally broke the awkward silence. The dark man seemed to understand his request but hesitated and did not answer as he re-soaked the cloth, wrung it out and placed it back again on Stephen's head. A few minutes later he found his words.

"Runaway, go north, be free." Stephen said nothing in reply. His dislocated shoulder was throbbing and he tried to massage it carefully with his left hand. "Me fix?" Charlie asked seeing Stephen's discomfort.

"Can you, do you know how?" His look pleaded for relief. "Yes, please."

"Trust," was all he said as he moved next to Stephen and gestured for him to lay on his back. He gently moved the injured limb carefully until the right elbow was tight against Stephen's side and his forearm angled ninety degrees upward toward the sky. With one hand he kept the elbow in place and with the other he ever so slowly began to pull the raised arm outward away from his body. There was no jerking or sudden movement and Charlie stopped whenever he sensed tenseness in his patient's muscles. Suddenly with a clunk, the joint slipped back into place. The slave doctor tenderly placed Stephen's arm back across his chest. "Keep there," he instructed. Next he fashioned a crude sling to keep the shoulder immobile. "Better?" he inquired when finished.

"Much better, the worst of the pain is gone," he nodded with gratitude.

"I find us food, you rest now." The black was out of sight before Stephen could say more.

Charlie continued to care for Stephen over the next few days as he mended. He would check in on him, bring him food and drink and disappear into the forest for the better part of the day. Near sunset he would return to see how he was doing and then leave again for the safety of the woods. Stephen supposed he was fearful about being spotted and captured again. He was surprised and challenged by the runaway's actions on his behalf. The slave's successful flight to freedom was obviously jeopardized by remaining in the area. Wasn't he at least a bit concerned that the white man he had aided might turn on him and take him prisoner in compliance with the law?

Friday dawned bright and Stephen rose feeling well enough to travel. He needed to get going soon if he was to rendezvous with Israel at the Ahotskey junction in a few days. Being late would only cause his good friend added worry. He removed the sling and tested his shoulder. It was still sore and he was not about to over test it. Saddling Barnabas would be a difficult chore one-handed, he thought. Apparently Charlie had sensed his plan and was well on his way north. Good. If he was indeed gone, it took care of any lingering moral dilemmas the young Methodist minister would have to face.

He extinguished the small fire and turned to attend to his horse. There was Charlie. He was cinching down the saddle strap. He held out the reins to greet him and cupped his hand to provide an added boost onto the horse. Words of thank you were barely out of his mouth when he heard the sound of riders coming."Quick, Charlie run and hide."

The three horsemen galloped into view and reined to a stop. "Have you seen a runaway by any chance? We've been hunting for him for days. He escaped from a plantation south of here near Edenton." The rider spit as he finished his inquiry and repositioned himself in the saddle.

"Has some god awful marks on his face and goes by the name of Charlie," a second rider added as he ran his sleeve across his brow and cleared his throat of the road dust.

"'tis money in it for you if you can point us in his direction," the third rider entered the conversation.

"Men, I wish I could help you. But the only critter I've seen lately was a scrawny old panther that got me bucked off my horse. I have been laid up here recovering from my bruises, headed now on to Ahotskey. If I come across him, I'll do my best to arrest him and deliver him to the authorities." Stephen hoped his lie sounded persuasive and that he had masked any cues that might contradict his words and give him away.

"Keep an eye out; if he makes it to the great swamp he's good as free." The first rider again spoke as the three wheeled their mounts about. They were soon out of sight far down the road.

That night, by the light of a half moon, the white and the black rode double to the Pease home. Adam and Eve listened with understanding attentiveness as Stephen poured out the story of their remarkable meeting. With Charlie safely hid away in the barn, the two men walked together back to the porch. Adam reached out and put his hand on the shoulder of the conflicted young preacher.

"You did the right thing coming here, Stephen. We have contacts and can make sure Charlie reaches the Great Dismal. He will be safe there with fellow maroons. The slave hunters do not have the means or the will to follow deep into that snake and gator infested jungle."

"I hope so, Adam. I broke the law and lied. A part of me feels I did right, but a part of me also believes I did wrong." Stephen sighed, wrestling with a mix of emotion ranging from relief to guilt. Adam stopped and turned toward him so they were face to face and gently placing his hands on Stephen's shoulders he responded.

"Listen to me, my friend. Which is the greater good-- a man shackled like an animal, beaten and scarred with the whip, or a liberated soul, free to love and live, even if in a dangerous swamp? God will forgive and God will guide you.

Israel got a much condensed version of the story on the trip home. He learned about the hospitality of the Pease's and the fall from Barnabas, nothing more. Stephen wondered if not telling the whole truth was any different than a boldly spoken lie.

Chapter 35

A FUTURE AND A HOPE

"I don't trust those aristocrat politicians in Philadelphia, why what do they know about our lives as struggling farmers anyway?" Stephen eavesdropped as a small group of local men voiced their opinions about the proposed new Constitution.

"Aye, patriot Patrick Henry of Virginia refused to even attend the convention, said he 'smelt a rat." If he was suspicious of their intentions, so ought we to be," the Scot, William Campbell, added.

"If ratified, I hear rumors that George Washington will be the first president. What's to say he won't turn out to be just as much a king as old George was?" Johnson took a swig of hard cider as he asserted his view. Stephen's Uncle Thomas heard the comment and taking offense stepped into the fray.

"I served with Washington at Valley Forge and would follow his lead wherever. If he says this is the right decision, I for one will stand with him, to the death." Thomas was in Johnson's face as he spoke. For a moment Stephen was afraid blows might be struck as the men tensed their muscles.

"I think we can all agree that something had to change, the Articles of Confederation were just not working, people were suffering and we were too loosely connected, too independent of one another. I say let's give this new government structure a chance." Stephen's father said trying to ease the brewing conflict by shifting the focus from General Washington.

"But we must preserve the rights of the states and not be swallowed up by a federal bureaucracy," John Smith urged. "Next thing you know they will force us to free our slaves," he pressed his point further.

"Or take away our right to bear arms and protect ourselves against abuses of power," Campbell enjoined. "I say we wait to ratify until our rights have been clearly stated and added to this constitution. We need not assurances there will be a Bill of Rights, but actual measures in place," he continued.

"I can agree with that," Johnson replied nearly spilling his cider as he gestured with both hands. "Our freedoms are precious, some of us nearly died fighting to obtain them. We must guarantee people will be able to speak out without fear of reprisal or government seizures of property and wealth." He sat his tankard on the table as he finished his sentence and glared back at Thomas who still stood too close for his comfort. Stephen, energized by the reference to rights took advantage of a moment of silence to interject his thoughts.

"Yes, we must preserve our right to gather and worship as we choose. We cannot have a state or federal church to which we must pledge allegiance but must be able to seek and serve God with unfettered hearts, minds and words." Some of the men nodded in agreement as he spoke.

"Aye, the young preacher speaks well," Campbell chimed in, "'tis essential too that we have a free press to hold the feet of our leaders to the fire of scrutiny and criticism. Despots always move first to quiet dissenters."

"Add to that our right to assemble like this and raise our questions and express our grievances," Thomas rejoined the conversation. "I may not agree with you but I will defend your right to speak freely," he looked directly at Johnson as he concluded.

The gavel hit the desk with a resounding thud and the noisy throng of men finally quieted their side conversations and gave their attention to the chair. It was a hot and humid day in late May and the crowd gathered for the town hall meeting in Woodstock was clearly worked up and hankering for a raucous debate. At issue was the design of government put forward by the Philadelphia Convention the previous September after months of deliberations behind closed doors. For the document to become the law of the land nine states needed to ratify it and those in attendance were well aware that their neighbor to the south had become the eighth state to do so just days earlier.

The national and local battle lines had formed quickly. Federalists, supporters of the new structure, wanted to see a stronger central government. Those who feared such governance would lead to a new form of monarchy and a loss of power to the states took a contrary stance, earning them the title of Anti-Federalists. Hyde County males had recently elected their delegates to attend the important and potentially decisive North Carolina Convention scheduled in July at Hillsborough. Those representatives now sat before their peers to hear their concerns and answer their questions. The five were all respected community leaders: Abraham Jones, John Eborne, James Jasper, Caleb Foreman and Seth Hovey.

"Gentlemen, Gentlemen," Caleb rose from behind the desk and made eye contact around the room as he spoke. Foreman was a revolutionary war veteran, Hyde County clerk, and brother of Martha Foreman Brooks, spouse of Stephen's older sibling, William. He had easily garnered the necessary votes to secure him a seat at the state's upcoming convention. "Before we begin our deliberations I believe it would be fitting to ask divine guidance. Brother Brooks would you be so kind as to offer a prayer on our behalf?" Stephen stood, cleared his voice and began.

"O God, You have been our help in ages past and You are our only hope, now and for the future. We pray for wisdom and discernment in the affairs of state that cause us to gather here. Forgive us for trusting too much in men and not enough in You, for believing that manmade legislation can cure the ills of the soul and usher in peace and tranquility. These are Your gifts alone. We do pray for those entrusted with the reins of government. May they be as our Lord taught us all to be, wise as serpents and as harmless as doves. In Your mighty name we pray, Amen."

The lively town hall meeting went on for hours. The personal views that had been expressed earlier were articulated and examined again and again before the larger audience until all felt they had been heard. The straw poll taken at the end of the meeting was far from unanimous but the majority instructed the Hyde County delegates to cast their votes in favor of ratification. Before bringing the gavel down in adjournment, Caleb affirmed that the delegates would also speak clearly and strongly in support of needed amendments, a so-called Bill of Rights, that would insure the liberties local residents felt were so essential.

"Mr. Brooks, might you have a minute?" Stephen was almost out the door when he heard his name. He turned and saw it was Frank Bridges, the winner of last year's Fourth of July horse race. "Your words today got me thinking again about what you said to me the last time we talked. I am getting old and probably don't have too many races left in me. You was right, my hope and faith have rested on the speed of my mount. I haven't given much thought to God or what's beyond. Was wondering if you could tell me more about that peace and tranquility of the soul you mentioned in your prayer."

Stephen rode home in the company of his father, brothers and uncle but as they continued to replay the day's political dialogue he remained silent, his mind in another place. Frank Bridges had been under the conviction of God's gracious Spirit and was ready and willing to accept the Savior's invitation to new life. He chuckled to himself when he thought of the strange twist the day had taken. Men might argue about the best form of government but the real eternal question was whether or not they would bow the knee to Jesus as Lord. Surprisingly the focus had shifted from earthly kingdoms to divine matters. Praise God, Frank Bridges was now a citizen of heaven, a child of the ultimate King. Stephen leaned forward and patting Barnabas on the neck whispered low, "See, Barney, told you, we won the race after all."

The summer of 1788 brought triumph to the cause of the Federalists. New Hampshire became the crucial ninth state to approve the Constitution making it the law of the land. Virginia followed days later and before July was over, New York too had answered in the affirmative.

The national news, though, was a distant issue in light of the tragedy that struck local residents with a vengeance. The late July hurricane, later to be dubbed the George Washington Cyclone because of Washington's journal descriptions of the storm, raged across the northeast corner of North Carolina and Virginia causing widespread damage and havoc. The winds and torrential rains took their toll on the Brooks' farm, destroying the corn crop. But that was a small price compared to those who lost much more. Uprooted trees fell, just missing the Goode cabin but crushing several outbuildings. The Andersons were less fortunate. The large Cottonwood nearly leveled their small home. Almost as if by supernatural prompting, the couple had rushed from their shelter just seconds before the mammoth tree had crashed to the ground. They would have been killed for sure if they had remained inside.

But prayers of gratitude were mixed with tears of grief and mourning for those who lost loved ones in the tempest. The deluge past, folks did what they always did best, they came together and provided solace and strong hands to rebuild what was gone. Israel and Stephen ministered to believers and unbelievers alike. The young preacher discovered that hard summer that at times it was best to keep silent. Words were no cure for deep pain and attempts to explain away God's apparent abandonment seemed so shallow and terribly inadequate. It was far better to offer a hand, a shoulder to lean on and a quiet presence amid the devastation.

The small store, owned by Bernard German, was abuzz with activity. Copies of the latest edition of the *Edenton Intelligencer*, the region's first tabloid, were stacked on the counter and folks were eager for a look at the headlines. The lead article announced what all were now fully aware of, the North Carolina Convention, by a significant margin, had voted to not ratify the Constitution. So was North Carolina in or out of the union? For now at least, it appeared they were on the outside looking in. The Constitution was set to take affect the next March and nobody knew for sure how the Hillsborough decision would impact their future as a state.

Stephen took some coins from his pocket and purchased a newspaper. Bernard handed him his change and drew attention to one cent in particular. "First to come in the store, hear it's called a Fugio or Ben Franklin cent, been keeping it for you, hoping you might stop in." Stephen had heard of the coin, the first attempt to mint United States currency. Franklin was supposedly behind the symbolic design, thus the attribution to his name. He turned the coin back and forth, carefully inspecting both sides. On one side were displayed thirteen rings surrounding an inner circle bearing the words United States, We are one. The other side had a sundial in the center, with a sunny face and shining rays streaming from above. Fugio, Latin for 'flee or fly' was circled on the left, 1787 on the right. The words 'Mind your Business' boldly finished the design below the dial. Satisfied he had deciphered the meaning of the symbols, Stephen offered his interpretation.

"Guess Mr. Franklin is telling us that time flies and we should focus on our own affairs and keep our nose out of other people's concerns, huh Bernard? Thanks for thinking of me and putting the copper aside. In the days ahead we can only hope that North Carolina will remain as one of those thirteen circles and that we will not so mind our own business as to be left apart from the union."

"Mother has a letter for you," Stephen's father took the *Intelligencer* his son extended to him and pointed to the kitchen, "Oh, and thanks for the paper."

Alone on the porch he opened the envelope. It was from Bishop Francis Asbury. He carefully unfolded the parchment and read.

Brother Brooks

Stephen, I thank my God for you and remember you often in my prayers as I recall our precious hours and days together seeking His face. I have heard of your excellent service for the Kingdom and that you remain faithful to your calling. Thus I invite you to our meetings next January in New Bern, to present yourself to be set apart for ministry. We will meet to question you in regards to your testimony and your doctrine. If all goes as I would expect, you will be admitted on trial and under supervision commence your work as a circuit riding preacher of the good news. I look forward to hearing an affirmative word from you about your presence at our conference.

Respectfully In His Service,
Francis Asbury

Stephen set the letter aside and closed his eyes. He thought of the vision Grace had shared with him years earlier. She had glimpsed him in the future, traveling about on horseback, a Bible and hymnbook in his saddlebags and a gospel word upon his lips. Oh how he wished she might have lived to see this moment.

"Admitted on trial, Brother Stephen Brooks," Stephen rose as Asbury pronounced his name and walked to the front of the small sanctuary. There he knelt as Asbury and other elders, including his good friend, Israel, laid hands on him and prayed. The Bishop's sermon that followed was based on the text of Jeremiah 29:11, 'For I know the thoughts I think toward you, saith the Lord, thoughts of peace and not of evil, to give you an expected end.' He spoke about the promise of that expected end, a future and a hope grounded in the timeless promises of God. Most of what was said would blur in the ecstasy of the moment but Stephen would never forget the closing hymn, penned by Charles Wesley.

A charge to keep I have,
a God to glorify,

a never-dying soul to save,
and fit it for the sky.

To serve the present age,
my calling to fulfill;
O may it all my powers engage
to do my Master's will!

Arm me with jealous care,
as in thy sight to live,
and oh, thy servant, Lord,
prepare a strict account to give!

Help me to watch and pray,
and on thyself rely,
assured, if I my trust betray,
I shall forever die.

After the crowd had dispersed, Asbury sought him out and taking him aside handed him two things. The first was a note with the simple message: 'Stephen Brooks ordained to gospel ministry, January 17, 1789. Bishop Francis Asbury.' The second item was a British Shilling.

"My dear Stephen, this shilling is roughly equivalent to what your daily salary will be as a circuit rider, if you receive any pay at all. You may be poor by human standards but remember that 'He who owns the cattle on a thousand hills' is your Father. In Him you are rich indeed; He will supply your needs according to his wealth in glory. Welcome to the work." Asbury embraced him warmly.

"Thank you sir, I will give my all for Him." Stephen was a bit hesitant, not knowing for sure if it was his place to raise his concern. Finally he spoke, "I do have one question, sir, if I may be so bold to ask." Asbury smiled and replied.

"Certainly, what is it?"

"When the circuits were announced I did not hear my name? Where am I to serve?"

"You will be going with me, Stephen, through the Cumberland Gap to Kentucky. You will receive your specific charge there." Seeing the startled look on Stephen's face he continued. "We may encounter hostile Indians on our way. Are you afraid?" The newly ordained preacher thought for a moment and answered.

"Bishop Asbury, they can only kill the body, not the soul. I am ready. 'For me to live is Christ, to die is gain.' "

"Well said my son. Well said."

Epilogue

Stephen spilled the contents of the small red pouch onto his bed quilt and slowly sorted his way through the collection of some twenty coins. Each one had a story to tell of special people who had shaped his life, of places never to be forgotten and of events that had changed him and the larger world around him.

The Pirate cobs took him back to his childhood jaunts on the beach with his dear papa Farrow. What fun they had had searching for treasure on the beach and finding it. Tales of swashbuckling Pirates had accompanied each amazing discovery. Those were simple days marked by the innocent pleasures of a young lad playing in the sand, running into the edge of the surf, throwing rocks as far as his tiny arms would allow. Each time he opened that carved driftwood box and fingered the velvet pouch he could see the faces of his loving grandparents. The vivid memories of their caring sacrifices and words of wisdom were exceedingly more valuable than any and all tokens of silver or gold. He would take them with him in his heart and mind wherever his Lord and journeys might lead him.

It was the first Christmas he could really remember, marked by snowflakes, threatening British sailors and most importantly the first meeting with his grandpa Brooks. The little silver three pence was his gift that day. He sadly wondered what stories he might have heard had he had more years to crawl up on his namesake's lap and listen. The British Farthing he held marked his grandpa's untimely death, Stephen's first encounter with the last enemy. Ironically the nearly worthless piece of copper had saved his life. On the brink of self-destruction it had been used of God to bring him, like the wandering prodigal, to his senses. It had started him back on the pathway of mercy, grace and forgiveness.

The tiny silver half Reale was a present from his father, or was it his first pay as a sailor in training; Stephen smiled. He recalled all the lessons of the sea and of life his father had taught him. He picked up the Dutch Stuiver marked 1728, a beach find that remarkably matched the birth date of his pa. Next, he looked carefully at the German Heller until he located the apparent blood stain on its surface. Retrieved after a successful militia ambush on Hatteras, his father had given it to him to mark the victory. It spoke volumes of his father's courage and commitment to freedom.

His parents were now in their sixties, a rich and full life for the times. As he held the three coins a flood of sacred glimpses from the past washed over him. Amid all the recent farewells he had tried not to think of one likely outcome of his circuit riding commitment, that being he would probably not see his parents again this side of heaven. He paused and thought of the scriptures that emphasized the goodness of God from generation to generation. In that moment he offered his own prayer of gratitude for their faithfulness, their example, their tutelage. He didn't bother to brush away the steady stream of tears flowing down his cheeks. He only hoped one day he would be able to parent his own offspring with the same enduring patience and compassionate love.

A collage of mental images came sharply into focus as he moved from coin to coin. One moment he was a small boy standing before an old Scottish priest learning a lesson about the thistle. Next he was prizing his reward for returning a stubborn old mule to an Irish neighbor as his finger traced the outline of a harp etched on one side. Then he was transported to Paris, beholding the city's delights as he focused on the fleur-de-lis pattern of his French Liard. What a river adventure the coin brought to mind along with its meaning of faith, hope and love.

As he held the gifts of his uncle Thomas he could hear the musket fire at Concord and smell the burning powder in the air. He saw himself gathered with the fathers of the new republic as they penned their signatures to the Declaration of Independence.

Familiar salt water scents filled his senses; he was sailing *Grace*, the wind was at his back, filling the sails and speeding the craft across the waves. Stephen held the Ship Shilling given him by his dear mentor, Captain Peters and was moved yet again by the ransom Peters had paid to free him from the *Jezebel's* ruffians. He set the Dutch coin aside and picked up the three that evoked the strongest memories.

The old hammered British coin was over two hundred years old and the faint images were hard to decipher. What wasn't difficult to make out was the impact of one who had left the thin piece of silver on their hallowed spot, the giving stump. He closed his eyes and heard the distant howl of his friend, Wolf. What adventures they had shared along with Bear. Together they had moved from childhood to adolescence to adulthood. A white doe, old Indian legends, fanciful tales of colonists long dead, it mattered not what was true and what was the stuff of myth, what lasted, what marked the soul was the power of love that transcended race, culture and time. Supposedly Wolf was off somewhere west, maybe in Kentucky. Would their paths cross again? He wondered as he placed the coin back on the quilt with the others.

Lastly there were Grace's coins, the Virginia Half Penny marked her birth and the ancient Greek coin matched her vision of him on horseback spreading the gospel to faraway places. He had kept the penny in his pocket during his seafaring days, from the dawning of his love for her through the dark days of grief. More than once it had kept him from sacrificing honor and purity for momentary pleasure. Dearest Grace, he could see her face, hear her laughter. Her example of Christ-following faith and her persistent prayers on his behalf had moved him from unbelief to curiosity to heartfelt commitment. He would never forget her.

Overcome with emotion he backed down the loft ladder and slipped quietly out of the house. He needed to visit the old stump one last time before his departure. He watched in awe as the sun painted another glorious sunset picture on the distant horizon. The sun was not only setting on the Brooks family home on the North Carolina coast, the sun was also setting on a chapter in his life.

The next morning before a final embrace for his beloved mother and father, he entrusted his coin box to his older brother, William. He would keep it safe until his return, whenever that might be.

Able extended the reins to his childhood friend, now grown to manhood, and offered a goodbye and a promise. "I am still saving my farthings Stephen. Don't be surprised if you see me, a free man, someday out west."

Stephen gently spurred Barnabas away from the homestead. Some distance down the road he stopped and turned back, waving to his family and to Able who were still gathered on the porch. Then, nudging Barnabas, he leaned forward and spoke to his equine companion. "Barn, great adventures lay ahead. Why I wager you are going to take a liking to Bishop Asbury's horse, Little Jane, too. 'tis on to Kentuck and the future the Almighty has in store for us."

CONTENTS OF STEPHEN'S COIN BOX

1625 Spanish Cob
Stephen's first
Beachcombing
Pirate Treasure

1624 Spanish Cob
More Pirate
Treasure

161? Spanish Cob
Another Beach find

1763 British
"Maundy" 3 Pence
Grandpa Brooks'
Christmas Gift

1728 Dutch Stuiver
His Father's birth
date keepsake

1679 Scottish
Bawbee Thistle
A Priest's Present

1749 British Farthing
An "inheritance" from
Grandpa Brooks

1744 Irish Farthing
Reward for returning
A lost mule

1764 Spanish Half
Reale Stephen's birth
Coin and first sailor's pay

1580 British 6 Pence
Lost Colony artifact?
Wolf's farewell gift

1656 French Liard
Memento of a River
Adventure

1775 British Half Penny
Uncle Thomas' souvenir
of the "Shot heard round
the world"

1727 German States Hesse Cassel Heller Booty from Hatteras Ambush

1776 Spanish Half Reale Thomas' Independence Coin

1773 Virginia Half Penny Stephen's "Grace" reminder

1764 Dutch 6 Stuiver Ship Shilling Captain Peter's gift for a young Captain

359-336 BC Macedon Philip II Youth on Horse A Circuit Riding Vision

1787 U.S. Franklin Fugio Cent A Store Keeper's saved change

1786 Nova Caesarea
New Jersey
"E Pluribus Unum"
Brother Jonathan
gaming win

1787 British Shilling
Bishop Asbury's
illustration of a
circuit rider's daily
salary

ABOUT THE AUTHOR

Doug's professional career has had two major focal points. He served over fifteen years in Christian ministry as a pastor. Following a graduate program in Communication he shifted to the education arena, teaching Speech and related courses at the community college level. Both pathways have intensified his fascination with and passion for history, transformative relationships, the power of storytelling and the challenges of social justice; themes that are woven together in this novel.

Retirement has provided the time and opportunity to put fingers to the keyboard and unite together figments of imagination, events of the American Revolution and a curiosity for numismatics with the compelling story of his ancestor, Stephen Brooks (1764-1855). This work is the first in a trilogy. The *Coin Box* series will continue with *On the Circuit* and *Legacy of a Circuit Rider.*

Doug and Betty Rae live in Castle Rock, Washington, where they enjoy clear days that provide for awesome views of Mt. Rainier. He enjoys whistling familiar old hymn tunes he learned years ago from his grandmother, mother and Aunt Mildred.

Made in the USA
San Bernardino, CA
02 February 2018